THE
BLOOD WHISPERER

Also by Zoë Sharp

KILLER INSTINCT: Charlie Fox book one
RIOT ACT: Charlie Fox book two
HARD KNOCKS: Charlie Fox book three

the first three Charlie Fox books are also available as an
e-boxed set:
A TRIPLE SHOT OF CHARLIE FOX

FIRST DROP: Charlie Fox book four
ROAD KILL: Charlie Fox book five
SECOND SHOT: Charlie Fox book six

the second three Charlie Fox books are also available as an
e-boxed set:
ANOTHER ROUND OF CHARLIE FOX

THIRD STRIKE: Charlie Fox book seven
FOURTH DAY: Charlie Fox book eight
FIFTH VICTIM: Charlie Fox book nine
DIE EASY: Charlie Fox book ten

FOX FIVE: a Charlie Fox short story collection

ABSENCE OF LIGHT: a Charlie Fox novella

For more information on Zoë Sharp's writing,
see her website: www.ZoeSharp.com

THE
BLOOD WHISPERER

Zoë Sharp

Murderati Ink [ZACE Ltd]

Murderati Ink [ZACE Ltd]
Registered UK Office:
Kent Cottage, Bridge Lane, Kendal, Cumbria LA9 7DD

First published in Great Britain 2013
Murderati Ink [ZACE Ltd]

ISBN-13: 978-1-909344-32-7

ISBN-10: 1-909344-32-X

Typeset in 12pt Cambria / 11/14pt Arial

For Derek and Jill
Who've helped keep it all together
and
Sarah and Tim
Who've been there since the beginning

—Prologue—

SHE WAKES TO the smell of blood.

It saturates the air to lie metallic across her tongue—so fresh-spilt it has not had time to spoil.

She knows the scent well enough to be calm and yet also terrified. It is not that she is squeamish but the implications are clear to her.

What the hell is happening here? And where is here?

She gradually returns to herself, realises she is lying face down on a hard surface. Her whole body feels gripped by the aftermath of a fever. Her head is turned slightly to the side, legs splayed as if to mimic running and arms twisted behind her. The position is awkward, like she dropped in mid-stride or was flung there. She flexes her wrists half expecting to find them bound but she is not restrained.

She takes a moment to examine if this makes things better or worse.

The answer doesn't come readily.

In fact nothing comes readily, neither awareness nor memory.

Mentally she fumbles backwards for her last clean recollection. It remains blurrily beyond reach.

That alone is enough to start the panic forming a bubble in her chest. It compresses her heart, squeezing her lungs against her ribcage so she can hardly breathe.

She forces her eyes open.

From this perspective the room has tipped sideways. It seems familiar but she doesn't recognise it. Maybe the bloody pool seeping across the boards towards her has something to do with that.

The encroaching tide jolts her out of lethargy. Her adrenal gland fires a staccato burst into her system and she flinches from the shock of it, tries to roll away. Instead she flops raggedly onto her back, gasping. It's a start but not much of one.

Her eyes slide closed again and she discovers her limbs are not yet her own. They refuse to know her, fighting every attempt to control them. She growls in frustration-laced fury.

And all the time the smell of the room overloads her senses. She has the educated palate of a connoisseur. Underneath the sharp tang of blood she detects the lingering slurry of fear.

The kind of fear humans embrace when there is nothing else left to them.

Her own fear motivates her eyes to reopen. They do so with reluctance akin to peeling a limpet from a tidal rock.

The room is still there. She'd been hoping to blame some kind of waking nightmare but this is real.

Far too real.

A crowd of images jostle her, elbowing for supremacy. She grasps the analytical part of her brain by its scruff and shakes it into concentration. Sluggishly she notes the blood pool leads away from her.

She lies still for a moment and monitors her own body as the extremities slowly come back online. She aches right down to the roots of her hair as if from a beating but as far as she can tell there's no specific damage.

So the blood isn't mine.

Of course it isn't hers, she reasons. She can recite the facts as well as anyone—that the human body holds between three-point-five and five-point-five litres. A loss in excess of forty per cent is almost invariably fatal and experience has shown her exactly what that kind of exsanguination looks like.

To have this amount of blood let must surely mean ...

Her heart leaps into her throat and bounces there.

With a grunt of outright effort she makes it up onto one elbow. The room sways and distorts alarmingly before it steadies.

Progress, of a sort.

What she sees next is not progress of any sort.

The body is no more than two metres away. Blood haloes around it and edges ever closer as if seeking a living host. It leaches from a dozen ragged slits in clothing and skin.

The face is turned towards her, features bisected by a diagonal slash from cheekbone to chin. The lips are peeled back in the parody of a sneer.

Even in death the eyes are flatly accusing.

In the past she has seen the aftermath of violence too many times to count, but this? This finally overbalances her. She scuttles backwards instinctively from the sight of it, a moan of horror and despair escaping her.

Pure visceral emotion rises along with bile. She feels her stomach give a lurching heave and she reaches to cover her mouth—an instant reflex to avoid contaminating the scene.

It is only then she realises she is clutching something in her right hand so tightly her fingers are locked around it.

She pulls back, staring dumbly. It takes a long time for her to register she is holding a knife.

The blade catches the light and gleams darkly wicked.

It is blooded to the depths.

And so is she.

—1—

TYRONE WASN'T FAZED by death. But as he shouldered open the door the only thing on his mind was getting the job done and getting out of there fast.

It wasn't as though he couldn't hack it—he could wade through gore as well as anybody. It was just something about *this* job was freaking him out.

He bent to put down the plastic gallon-drum of chemical enzyme cleaner onto the bathroom floor. As he did so he felt the back seams of his disposable Tyvek oversuit start to rip like they always did.

They were supposed to be one-size-fits-all but that didn't take account of the fact he was six-foot-plus and well into his sports. He'd shot up while he was still at school and now at nineteen he'd finally grown into his shoulders. It looked good but didn't help him find an oversuit that fit.

Still, at least they didn't have to wear masks for this one.

Tyrone inhaled cautiously just to be sure. The only smell was a kind of sticky sweetness with only a hint of sour at the back of it, like emptying the kitchen bin in the flat for his mum *only just* before what was in it went bad.

That was the upside of gunshot suicides. They made so much noise they were found quick and there wasn't time for decomp to set in. The quiet ones—where nana died in her bed and was left to seep into the mattress for weeks before her loving family even *began* to wonder—now they *were* bad news.

He straightened and took in the bathroom.

Man, this place is huge.

He glanced to where Kelly Jacks stood across the other side of the room. She was far enough away that if he stretched out his arms all the way he still wouldn't be able to touch her.

Kelly's suit didn't fit any better than his. She always had to roll up the cuffs and the ends of the legs and the crinkly material ballooned round her narrow waist. On just about anyone else it would have looked like some kind of clown. Funny thing was, he thought Kelly looked great whatever she wore.

Tyrone opened his mouth ready to make a snappy remark, a joke. But something about the way she stood there, staring at the place where it all went down, had the words dying on him.

"I know that look. What's up Kel?"

He moved across, careful not to slip on the Italian tile. The boss made them wear plastic booties for work. Tyrone thought it made him look a right prat but he'd soon found that trying to scrub God-knows-what out of the treads of his boots at the end of the day was far worse.

Small hard lumps crunched under his feet. He didn't have to look to know they were fragments of bone and teeth. When he'd first started this job he'd been surprised at the distance stuff travelled from this kind of head wound. *Man, how those suckers could* bounce *on a hard surface like this.*

But at least the tile meant not too much was wedged into the walls. Brain sludge set like cement and scraping it off fancy wallpaper was a right pain.

Kelly raised her head but she didn't really see him. A frown carved twin dents between her eyebrows.

She only just came up to Tyrone's chin and he'd felt like a big brother since they'd been teamed up, even though at forty she was old enough to be his mum. *Hell, the way some of the girls round home get themselves knocked up soon as they hit puberty, she could have been a grandma by now.*

Not that you'd know how old Kelly was, not really, with that short choppy haircut, clear skin and the little diamond stud through the left-hand side of her nose. Amazing she looked so fit what with all she'd been through.

"What's up?" he asked again.

Kelly shook her head, murmured, "There's something not right here."

Tyrone peered over her shoulder down into the blood-swilled bathtub with the exploded hole in the tiles at one end and the cast-off spray across the snazzy window blinds. There was something so *careful* about it made him shiver.

"Well she puts on her best gear, climbs into the empty bath with one of her old man's rifles and blows her brains out, yeah?" he said trying to nudge Kelly out of introspection. "'Course there's something 'not right' about that."

Kelly shook her head and for once didn't lighten up. Every now and again she could be like that—all quiet. Like she folded in on herself.

It bothered him at first. He'd worried it might be something he'd done or said, but in the end he'd accepted that prison made people go that way. He'd seen enough of it to know.

Tyrone wasn't sure what Kelly had been inside for and it wasn't something he would ask. But she knew stuff about the scenes they were sent to that she shouldn't—*couldn't*—know unless she'd worked right there up alongside death all close and personal.

Tyrone didn't think he had an overactive imagination but sometimes Kelly freaked him out just a little too.

"It's the blood," she said now, almost to herself. "There's something not right with the position of the blood."

Tyrone bit back the comment about how maybe that was because blood was supposed to be worn on the *insides* of a body. Besides, he always tried to look beyond the mess to what was underneath it. Their job was to put things back the way they were before—to wipe out not just the mess but the memory.

He and Kelly had done jobs where they'd had to rip out skirting boards because of what had leaked behind them, scrub textured ceilings, take down light fittings. And they bantered while they worked. It was the only way to deal. But this was the first time he'd heard her so *unsure* about anything.

It worried him.

He looked at the bath trying to see it through those cool brandy coloured eyes. Like the bathroom the tub itself was huge—big enough for a family to stretch out in easily—with fancy whirlpool fittings and real gold taps. The tub was sunk into a raised platform by the pair of tall plain glass windows where you could just lie back and enjoy the view. No need for coy frosting when the nearest neighbour was a mile away.

So much luxury and yet this Veronica Lytton chick had still wanted to end it all in a way that was all drama and *real* messy, he thought. A way guaranteed to cause maximum grief to her family.

Man, that was cold.

Tyrone shook his head. This woman had the kind of up-there lifestyle he knew a black kid from Tower Hamlets was never going to live this side of legal. Maybe that's what was making him so uneasy—the feeling that the likes of him didn't ought to be here.

The bathroom in the housing association flat he shared with his mum and younger brother and sister was about the same size as the walk-in shower in this place. At home the pedestal sink overhung the loo cistern on one side and the half-length bath on the other. Getting fixed to go out in the mornings was a battle of wits and wills and elbows between the four of them. He couldn't imagine what it must be like to have so much *space,* all to yourself.

6

Bloody miserable, if Mrs Lytton was anything to go by.

"Look, if Plod wasn't satisfied it was suicide they would never have let this Lytton guy call us in, yeah?" he tried, aware that time was getting on and they were not.

"Hmm," Kelly said, distracted. "Still, I'm going to give the boss a call—maybe even send him the 'before' pix and see what he makes of them."

She stepped back, stripping off the blue nitrile gloves and making for the door with that loose-limbed yet compact stride. The one he always thought made her seem like a long distance runner.

"Kel—" Tyrone protested. She stopped, glanced over her shoulder as she pulled off her booties. Tyrone spread his hands helplessly. "I don't get it. We done gunshot suicides before. What's so different about this one?"

"I'll be back in a couple of minutes," she said flashing a rare smile. "Until then … see if you can work it out."

—2—

BY THE TIME she'd got hold of Ray McCarron, sent over the pictures and waited for his opinion, twenty-five minutes had gone past. It was quite a trek back to the bathroom on the upper floor from the van parked in the courtyard to the rear of the house—the tradesman's entrance. Nobody wanted a big white Mercedes Sprinter bearing the name McCarron Specialist Cleaning Services parked smack outside the front door.

May as well issue open invitations to gawp.

Kelly was halfway up the sweeping staircase when she heard raised voices from above. She increased her pace, jogging the last flight and hurrying along the plush corridor to the master suite. The house was cool inside but the van was parked in the sun and she'd stripped her oversuit halfway off while she talked to Ray, tying the arms around her waist. She was aware that she didn't exactly present a picture of authority but it would have to do.

Just before the final corner she paused, took a steadying breath. Relatives and friends of the violently deceased were often emotionally erratic. Suicides had the worst effect on them. They needed to lash out at somebody and the cleaners were the people eradicating that last link with the dead.

By definition McCarron's team moved fast and the messier the tragedy the more he charged for making all visible signs of it go away, which in itself could cause bitter resentment. What it was to offer a service that was wanted least when it was needed most.

Usually Kelly was good at spotting confrontations early enough to divert or avoid them but sometimes she was glad of Tyrone's bulky presence on the job.

This time Tyrone was the one taking flak. He hovered awkwardly in the doorway to the suite, head ducked as if to protect his ears against the verbal blows.

Not that the man with him looked set to get physical. Kelly read anger in the tight lines of his body, yes but not that dangerous boiling rage. She willed herself to relax knowing calm reason was the best form of attack.

"Can I help you?" she called aiming her voice low and pleasant.

Both men twisted in her direction. Kelly kept her body language neutral as she closed the distance between them.

The quick relief in Tyrone's expression would have been comical in other circumstances but Kelly's eyes were on the newcomer.

She'd initially thought he must be a member of staff. The comfortably middle-aged housekeeper had let them in. She showed them as far as the right corridor before she fled but a property this size needed more than one domestic to keep it in shape. It would be no surprise if the Lyttons employed a major-domo—the kind who'd get shirty on his employer's behalf for a job running behind.

The man turned. She caught the way his suit moulded across his back, the fabric draping casually back into place and she didn't need to spot the exclusive watch and handmade shoes to know she was dealing with serious money.

Uh-oh.

He stood with feet braced apart but arms folded in an unconscious contradiction of gestures that piqued Kelly's interest.

"You must be Mr Lytton." She held out her hand so that good manners compelled him to uncoil long enough to respond, turning his upper body away from Tyrone as he did so. The man nodded as he treated her to a fleeting handshake. She said, "We apologise for any distress caused by the delay."

He studied her for a moment without speaking. There was a compressed energy to him that was not simply anger but also contained more than a trace of shock. It made her suddenly very wary.

"I was just explaining 'bout the blood Kel," Tyrone put in nervously over Lytton's shoulder. "I didn't see it right off but then I spotted it, yeah? The bit you said—"

"It's all right Tyrone," Kelly said softly, her eyes still on the client. Lytton had dark hair a little on the long side, styled but not too fancy, a strong nose and eyes the colour of old Welsh slate—dark grey with a hint of green. "I've just spoken to the boss. Wait in the van would you?"

Tyrone hesitated. "You sure?"

A brief smile flickered across Kelly's face. "I'm sure."

Reassured, he loped off along the corridor with his oversuit rustling as he went. The man watched his hasty exit with an expression that was now hard to discern. Kelly wondered about her earlier conclusions. Had she been wrong about the shock?

"Bit young for this kind of job isn't he?" he demanded as if Kelly had a say in it. His accent was not the cut-glass she'd expected. So he probably made his money rather than inherited it. She stifled an inward groan. Sometimes with self-made men it was nice of them to take the blame for what they'd made of themselves.

"Tyrone's a good worker," she said. "Very competent."

"I've no doubt but is this—" he jerked his head towards the doorway, "—the sort of thing a kid his age ought to see on a regular basis?"

Kelly put her head on one side. *Hmm is that a social conscience I detect?*

"He makes good wages. They help support his family. And some of us don't have the luxury of being shielded from the harsh realities of life Mr Lytton," she murmured. "Tyrone saw his first OD while he was still in primary school."

A muscle clenched in the side of his jaw. "And that makes either of you experts at distinguishing suicide from ... something else does it?"

Kelly felt the jolt of his words go through her but she'd taught herself not to let her emotions show outside her skin. Learned it in a hard place where any sign of weakness got you beaten or killed.

So she merely raised an eyebrow at the hesitation and didn't pursue it. "It wasn't our call to make," she said instead which was the truth—as far as it went. "My boss has told us to hold fire until he's double-checked certain disparities in the scene with the investigating officer. Until then everything needs to stay as it is. I'm sorry."

He sighed, a thin hiss of pure exasperation. "The police told me as far as they're concerned the case is closed. She killed herself. End of story," he threw out. "And believe me, they looked hard."

Not hard enough. Kelly shrugged and dug a business card out of her back pocket, held it out. The cards held the firm's name and contact details but no personal information. "You're welcome to speak to Mr McCarron directly if you like."

He took the proffered card and fingered it for a moment but made no moves towards a phone. His next words surprised her. If the look on his face was anything to go by they surprised him too.

"Show me."

She arched an eyebrow.

He gave a shrug of frustration. "You must have seen it first," he said. "The kid—Tyrone? He mentioned something about the blood."

Kelly hesitated. Ray insisted that they were efficient, professional, neat and respectful at all times but she'd never encountered this kind of morbid curiosity from the deceased's nearest and dearest before.

"The blood spatter is inconsistent," Kelly said at last, keeping her tone neutral.

"Inconsistent," Lytton repeated flatly. "What does *that* mean?"

All Kelly's instincts warned her not to get into details. She'd said too much already. If there was the slightest chance the case might be reopened she needed to stay as far away from it as possible. To say anything else was self-destructive madness.

Kelly shifted her stance. "I'm sorry but I can't say more," she said. "It's not my call. Until I've had absolute confirmation we can't disturb the scene."

"Can't or won't?" His eyes narrowed on her face, the scrutiny uncomfortable. She'd met people before with eyes like these. Mostly the wrong sort of people in the wrong sort of places. It had rarely ended well.

"I'm sorry," she repeated, "but I'm afraid you need to speak with—"

His step forwards was enough to cut her off in mid-sentence.

"No," he said quietly, "I believe the person I *need* to speak with is you." His head tilted a little as he looked down into her face. "You suspect I had something to do with it? I wasn't even in the country when Veronica died."

Kelly felt the angry intensity, the urgency behind his words. It mattered to him that she believe him but she didn't know why. She suppressed a shiver and hated it. Not the shiver itself but the reason behind it.

"We're not accusing you of anything Mr Lytton," she said carefully. She was suddenly aware that she was alone with the guy in part of a house big enough so that a scream from one wing could hardly be heard in another. And she'd stupidly sent her back-up well out of earshot in a misguided attempt to protect him.

He stepped back abruptly and Kelly tensed in automatic response but he swung away from her, staring down into a pit of his own making.

"I did not kill my wife," he said quietly. "I had no desire to do so and no need."

He glanced back at Kelly's expressionless face but she gave him nothing in return. He gave a brief nod as if he'd expected that and turned away.

She let him make it almost to the doorway then said, "How much do you know about high-velocity gunshot wounds?"

He turned back, stuffed his hands casually into the pockets of those well cut trousers.

"I hunt," he said shortly. "Mate of mine has to cull the local deer population every now and again or they strip his plantation. He doesn't always choose his marksmen ... wisely. So yes, I've seen what the odd wild shot can do."

Kelly recalled, perhaps too late, that it was one of the man's own hunting rifles his wife had apparently chosen for her demise. *Or someone else had chosen for her.*

Damn. Ah well too late now.

"Then you'll know there's always blowback spatter from the entry wound and forward spatter—projected spray and debris—from the exit." Her voice matched his own, cool and dispassionate.

"But?"

She hesitated again. *Ah well, in for a penny.*

"You'd better see for yourself," she said and moved over to the bathtub.

He joined her with only fractional reluctance. Kelly wondered if she thought more or less of him for that.

Side by side they stared down into the carnage left by violent death, smeared by the paramedics and the forensics teams that followed. What remained was somehow damaged, dirty and sad.

"How can you see anything *inconsistent* through all that?"

"Because I know what to look for." She crouched careful not to touch anything and used a pen as a pointer. "Void patterns in the spatter confirm the position of the ... of your wife at the time of the shooting," she said choosing her words with great care.

"You can refer to Veronica as 'the victim'. The police certainly did damn well often enough," he said tightly. "I won't bite."

Kelly gave a faint smile, recognising the grim humour for what it was. "You can see here the back spatter from the entry wound. It's very fine, almost a mist, travelling in the opposite direction to the bullet."

"And you can tell that how, exactly?"

Kelly rose, reached for her camera and flicked through the stored images. "Look at this one," she said. "You can see it's teardrop-shaped—rounded at one end and with a streak at the other. The streak always points in the direction of travel. See?"

She zoomed in and tilted the camera screen towards him without thinking. He stepped in close to look and Kelly suddenly felt crowded, hot, trapped. Her fight or flight response tried to kick in. She had to stamp on it firmly before she either belted him or ran. Or both.

"So, the opposite of something like a comet tail?"

"Exactly. As the droplet hits a hard surface the back edge holds its form while the front edge breaks into what looks like a tail. It's how we can fix the directionality of the spatter."

Lytton straightened without apparently realising how near he'd been to serious injury. He was frowning.

"And you think there's some problem with that directionality?"

"It's possible."

"Look just spit it out will you?"

Kelly took a breath and said in her best evidence-giving voice, "I observed an additional void pattern on the side of the bathtub in this area here."

Lytton leaned over the bath holding his tie flat to his chest with one hand to prevent it dangling.

"I don't see this void you're talking about."

"You won't," Kelly said. "It would appear to have been filled in."

"Filled in." Again that dead flat sceptical delivery. Again the command: "Show me."

Kelly indicated with the pen. His face stayed expressionless.

"I can't see any difference."

"It *appears* correct at first glance but when you look closer you can see the directionality is actually totally opposite," she allowed. "My guess would be someone dipped into the spilt blood and flicked it across the void to cover it. If it wasn't for the difficulty of flicking it upwards instead of down I might not have spotted it."

For maybe ten long seconds he said nothing. Then he stepped back as if to distance himself from her.

"That's it?" he demanded. "That's the reason you've put this whole job on hold? A tiny patch of blood sprayed so fine you can hardly make it out with the naked eye, when I've had half of Thames Valley and the Met crawling all over this place for days? And *that's* all you have?"

His hands twitched in a gesture of frustration or despair. Kelly refused to cringe in the face of his anger. She kept her head up, aware she came barely to his chin.

"Once this is gone it's gone," she said indicating the bloodied bathtub. "I just need to be absolutely sure I'm doing the right thing."

Lytton snorted. "Yeah of course you do." He passed a tired hand across his face. "I ... apologise. I'm sure you can appreciate that I'm anxious to get this over with—try to put it behind me."

"Of course. Just as I'm sure *you* can appreciate that we have to work strictly by the book."

He tensed, mouth flattening. For a moment she saw the swim of mixed emotions in his face, his eyes. Instead of the sorrow she'd been expecting there was only anger and confusion and a fleeting trace of something Kelly recognised as guilt.

Whatever else had been part of Veronica Lytton's life she considered, that didn't include a happy marriage.

She forced a smile to soften the blow and put a placating hand on his arm. "I'm very sorry for your loss Mr Lytton but I can't ignore what the evidence is telling me."

Lytton withdrew his arm fast, almost jerky as if he felt tainted by her touch. He was at the doorway before he delivered his Parthian shot with unknowing but deadly accuracy:

"This evidence you set such store by—suppose what it's telling you is wrong?"

MATTHEW LYTTON STOOD in the shadows by his open study window and stared down into the rear courtyard where the crime-scene cleaners' van stood parked.

He could see the pair of them lounging in the front seats— doors open, waiting—and was aware of a ticking resentment at their idleness, however involuntary.

Lytton had made his considerable fortune in construction, demolition and renovation. Casual labour was a necessary evil that all too often lived up to its name. He'd become adept at turning up on site when his guys least expected. If he'd found any of them sitting on their backsides reading like this pair he'd have fired them so fast they would've left scorch marks.

Now, from his vantage point on the upper floor, he could see the big black kid was engrossed in a sports magazine. The woman was reading a book. Not a cheap paperback but a hardcover. When the distant trill of her cellphone drifted up to him she held her place with a bookmark rather than dog-ear the page before answering it.

As a man who'd grown up without books Lytton had come to treat them with respect. Grudgingly he found himself thinking better of her for doing the same.

When he first saw the woman striding along the corridor towards him with her choppy black hair and her pierced nose he'd thought she was just a girl. Something about the petite frame, the easy way she moved despite the unflattering garb, spoke of youthful vitality.

But where he'd expected truculence she'd responded only with reason. And when he looked deeper he saw she was nearer his own age than that of her young apprentice. That had thrown him as much as her stubborn refusal to be riled. Even if his overriding impression remained one of suppressed energy behind the calm facade.

His late unlamented wife had been the epitome of calm, cool and collected. He once swore that it was unnecessary to put ice in Veronica's afternoon Pimm's. One touch to her lips and the glass would be laced with it. But what you saw was what you got.

The only fire that burned inside that perfectly stage-managed body was ambition. First for him and—when that was achieved without apparent satisfaction—for herself.

He glanced down and realised he was holding their wedding photograph. Slowly, he smoothed his thumbs across the ornate silver frame. He'd come across the picture while he was sorting through his wife's things and been almost surprised she'd kept it. Mind you she kept everything else. There seemed to be endless notes, shorthand reminders of conversations, social engagements, names and dates. Deciding what was rubbish and what was important had begun to give him a headache. And that was before he'd had his run-in with the cleaners.

Finding the photo gave him an excuse to pause a moment and reflect. It hadn't been a big wedding but Veronica had still insisted on something overly lavish for their finances at the time. Looking at their frozen expressions with the benefit of twenty years' hindsight he reflected that neither of them looked particularly ecstatic at the union.

He'd had no illusions he was the love of her life of course, just as she had not been his. They'd discussed their proposed marriage in coolly practical terms before the announcement was drafted for *The Times.*

Veronica came from a grand family of rapidly declining fortune and though her parents had sniffed and muttered that Lytton "wasn't quite of *our type* my dear," they hadn't needed tarot cards to see his star was firmly on the rise.

Lytton had come from nothing equipped with no more than an instinct for a deal, a nose for run-down property and the vision to see what it might become. He'd started at the bottom of the building trade and sweated his way up through almost every discipline. Now he had the hands-on expertise to turn that vision into profitable reality.

Veronica supplied class and she did it in spades.

Still their marriage had been more a business partnership than anything else—more so over the last decade. She played lady of the manor here while he spent more time at the London apartment. They'd even talked vaguely of divorce although just as there was nothing holding them together equally there was nothing in particular driving them apart.

He never asked if she'd taken lovers but assumed she had. She'd certainly been discreet. And the two of them still rubbed along all right—still talked, discussed and debated. Perhaps their separate lives had helped give them plenty to say to one another.

But even now he couldn't find it in him to grieve openly for her as anything other than a vague acquaintance. The knowledge unsettled him.

He wondered if there was anyone else out there, beyond her parents, for whom she meant more.

Lytton had allowed his in-laws to take charge of the funeral arrangements with relief, but also knowing they probably needed the comfort of ritual. Nobody expects to outlive their only child.

He looked again at the wedding portrait as if it showed a pair of strangers. Viewed with a dispassionate eye it had some artistic merit he supposed. A black and white image lightly tinted by the photographic studio. And the frame was heavy and hallmarked if not to his taste.

He hesitated a moment then turned the picture over and removed the back. The frame could be sent to some charity organisation—the inimitable Mrs P would see to it—but the photo inside? He found himself undecided whether to keep it as a memento or throw it away.

Behind him on the far side of the room the door opened after a perfunctory knock. Annoyed, Lytton swung away from the window in time to see Steve Warwick stroll into the room.

If his business partner was not exactly the last person he wanted to see right now he was pretty high up on the list.

"It's quite all right Mrs P," Warwick was saying breezily over his shoulder. "He's expecting me."

"No I'm not, Steve," Lytton said. "Go away."

But Warwick had already closed the door firmly behind him, leaving the flustered housekeeper on the outside. Now he paused and was regarding him with a half-smile playing at the corners of his mouth.

Warwick was a few inches shorter than Lytton. He had a fulsome stockiness that belied his flair and determination on the squash court. Left to his own devices Warwick made business decisions with the same reckless abandon. Maybe that explained why he'd been weeks from bankruptcy when Lytton had bought out the major share of his property development company more than a decade ago. Lytton had mistakenly assumed gratitude would temper his partner's impulsive nature.

"You want me to leave you to wallow in your grief? Oh, please, this is me you're talking to. Spare me the theatrics at least," Warwick taunted, once again damning that hope. He shook his head. "My friend you look like shit."

"Were you expecting to find me in celebratory mood?"

Warwick laughed. He laughed easily—sometimes too easily at the expense of others. His were classic English blond, bland, blue-eyed good looks coupled to a public school drawl. Warwick often made Lytton feel like a rough-arsed gypsy by comparison—albeit scrubbed up and on his way to the dock.

Warwick came forwards pursing his lips as he gave the quiet book-lined study a cursory inspection. "I can never understand why with all this space you choose to hide yourself away back here," he said. Another flashing grin. At least Warwick didn't have typically English teeth. "Unless you let the lady Veronica beat you to the decent rooms of course."

"You know as well as I do that I'm hardly ever here." Lytton turned back to the window. The woman was still talking on her cellphone. She seemed somehow familiar.

Kel, the black kid had called her. Kel short for Kelly? Hmm, Kelly ... He could swear he knew the face but couldn't place it. Why hadn't he asked her full name? "I like to see the comings and goings."

It had been Veronica who'd favoured the pomp and grandeur of a central room at the front of the house above the imposing entrance hall. There she could survey her domain oblivious to what was going on behind her.

Lytton wanted his finger on the pulse. Otherwise you found yourself robbed blind by people who blamed you for not catching them sooner when the company went to the wall.

He prided himself that he'd never lost his grip even if he'd come close to it today—with a cleaner of all people. A moment's sympathy, empathy—like she knew what it was to lose someone—and he'd almost let her see the truth.

That he didn't give a damn.

Lytton wasn't sure how he would have explained if she'd chosen to call him on it, that he'd stopped loving his wife a long time ago. The feeling had been entirely mutual.

"*Specialist* cleaners? My God that's a little on the vulgar side isn't it?" Warwick spoke at his elbow, peering down at the white van below. "I'd no idea such people existed. How very American."

Lytton's jaw tightened. "You'd rather I'd asked Mrs P to sweep up the pieces of my wife's skull, wrap them in newspaper like broken glass and put them in the dustbin with the potato peelings and the remains of last night's supper?"

Even Warwick flushed at that. "Hardly. But we can't afford for this to get out Matt, can we? Now especially—when the Big One is so close."

He didn't need to be more specific. The *Big One* in question was the Lytton-Warwick Cup—although Lytton wanted to change this to the Lytton-Warwick *Memorial* Cup since Veronica had put so much work into the arrangements. It was a horse race on the flat over a mile and four furlongs with a purse to rival the classics. The company's first foray into corporate sponsorship, designed to give them maximum kudos with the type of people Veronica's parents really *would* consider social equals.

"I'm assured they're very discreet." Lytton said now, nodding to the cleaners' van.

"Hmm, were you assured they were very industrious too?" Warwick asked still looking downwards. "If so, I might ask for a discount if I were you."

"There's some kind of procedural hold-up apparently."

"Oh?" That got his partner's attention. "Problem?"

Lytton shook his head. "As far as I'm aware it's just a delay." *It better had be.*

"Matt, delays mean questions. The wrong *kind* of questions," Warwick said with anxiety bleeding through his voice. "We need for this to be put to bed and fast. And if those comedians out there can't do it—"

The strident buzz of his cellphone cut Warwick off in mid-sentence. He fumbled in an inside pocket, eyes still fixed on Lytton's and flipped the phone open without checking the incoming number.

"Warwick."

Lytton saw the way his head ducked sharply and didn't need telling who was on the other end of the line.

"Darling," Warwick ground out, the tone as much threat as endearment, "I've told you not to bother me while I'm working."

He whirled away, began to pace. Lytton tuned it out. He'd heard Warwick and his second wife having too many domestics to willingly eavesdrop on another. He turned back to the window and stared down into the courtyard again.

This time the van's front seats were empty and he saw the two cleaners, re-suited, collecting gear from the back. Whoever it was from, that phone call was good news as far as he was concerned.

Unconsciously his shoulders came down a fraction.

The worst, he thought, might soon be over.

—4—

"I'LL BE HOME when I damned well please!" Steve Warwick snapped into his cellphone and stabbed a thumb onto the End Call button with triumphant savagery.

"Why did you marry that poor girl if you despise her so much?" Lytton asked over his shoulder, not moving away from that damned window like he was glued to the view.

"Who says I despise Yana?" Warwick said easily, tucking the phone away again. He flung himself down into one of the deep-buttoned burgundy leather Chesterfields, draping an arm along the back.

"Be careful with her, Steve," Lytton warned. "You can't afford to pay off another one."

"Yana and I understand each other perfectly. The advantages of marrying a poor girl from the Eastern Bloc." He gave a wolfish grin. "She was brought up in a culture that accepts a man has his appetites and believes it's a wife's duty to cater to her husband's every whim. And I mean *every whim.*"

Lytton didn't smile in return. "She's not living in the nineteenth century—she's here and now," he said. "In a culture where they have anonymous helplines for abused spouses and muckraking tabloid journalists. So, be careful."

Prig, Warwick thought, even as he flashed his teeth. *You and that cold-hearted bitch you married deserved each other.* "You gave Veronica too much free rein my friend," he said lazily instead. *And look where* that *ended.*

"I hardly think you're in any position to lecture me on how I treated my wife," Lytton said, glacial. He turned fully into the room so the light was behind him and Warwick couldn't see his face for shadow. Without expression, his partner's voice seemed cooler. "Tell me, does Yana know about your mistress—the one you're planning to visit on your way back to town?"

How the hell *do you know that?*

But despite his momentary surprise Warwick laughed, automatically smoothing down his green silk tie. "*Mistress* is such an old-fashioned word don't you think?" he asked reflectively, crossing his legs and letting his foot swing. "And you'd be surprised. Yana knows everything I get up to without me having to tell her. You may not think it to look at her but she's a very broad-minded girl."

Lytton continued to stare at him for a moment without comment then turned back to the window. "Just don't let it interfere with the job."

"It won't," he assured.

And by the time it does, my friend you won't be in a position to do a damn thing about it.

"YOU REALLY SHOULD get someone in to handle the books for you Ray. Then you wouldn't have to work late."

Ray McCarron's head jerked up from the quarterly accounts to see Kelly Jacks standing in the office doorway with her hands in her pockets.

She was in her civvies—old cargo trousers and a skinny T-shirt that showed a sliver of taut belly between the two. McCarron tried to avoid a wince. His daughter Allison was less than half Kelly's age and he wouldn't want her going out at night dressed like that.

Mind you, Allison didn't have the same kind of self-possession. There was something about Kelly that made trouble step off the kerb and go round her.

"Had a bookkeeper once. Made the mistake of marrying her. When it came to the divorce she knew what I was worth better than I did," McCarron said sourly. "Of course, it *would* help if I could read anything off the petty cash chits you lot put in." He sifted through another sheaf of paperwork. "It's like working with a bunch of retarded doctors trying to decipher this scrawl. I swear Les writes in Mandarin Chinese half the time."

"Yeah well," she mocked, "they weren't still teaching copperplate when we were at school."

"More's the pity." He leaned back in his chair, letting it rock, and regarded her over the top of his reading glasses as she headed across to the small window. There was a tension in her he saw, a restlessness he recognised of old. "Lytton job put to bed is it?" he asked, his voice casual.

She swung away from the window as if changing her mind at the last moment, hesitated then gave a shrug. "It's done if that's what you mean. Whether it should have been or not is another story," she said. "I tried to call your cellphone when I was on the way back. Leave it in your car again?"

"Aye, probably," he admitted cheerfully. "It's the only way to get a bit of peace." He paused. "But it went all right in the end?"

She fidgeted with the papers on the corner of his desk, her concentration apparently consumed with aligning the edges. "All he has to do now is replace a few busted tiles and no-one will ever know."

McCarron sighed at the bitterness in her tone. "Look Kel, I had a gander at the pictures you sent over and I made some calls," he said gently. "Several in fact. And I was told in no uncertain terms that I'm not on the job anymore and to wind me neck in."

Her lips twisted into a brief smile at that. She looked about to speak but stayed silent, pacing around the room. On the far wall was a line of framed photographs. She began straightening them even though McCarron kept them spirit-levelled anyway.

One showed his younger slimmer self, spit-polished in full dress uniform, frozen in the act of shaking hands with some long-retired long-forgotten chief constable who was presenting him with some equally long-forgotten award. Kelly's eye seemed drawn there longest.

"I looked out the details again," McCarron said. He twisted to face his computer and peered at the screen. "Veronica Lytton. Suicide. Found fully clothed in the bath with one of her husband's guns—an RPA Interceptor if you're interested— alongside her. Fatal gunshot to the head. No other visible trauma. No note, but her fingerprints on the weapon and discharge residue on her hands and clothing. Alone in the house with no sign of forced entry. Husband out of the country. Scene officially released this morning." He sat up and removed his glasses flinging them onto the desktop. "Far as the police are concerned it's an open-and-shut case. With the emphasis on *shut.*"

"Doesn't make it right though," Kelly said.

McCarron sighed again, pulled open his desk drawer and brought out a bottle of vodka—the good stuff. There was a jam jar on the desk holding a letter opener and a collection of pens. He tipped out the contents, gave the jar a cursory wipe and poured slugs into that and his empty coffee mug.

"Aye well sometimes this job stinks Kelly love," he said handing over the jar. "In more ways than the obvious."

"Ain't that the truth," she murmured. They touched rims and sipped in companionable silence.

The office was small, tucked away on the upper floor above the garaging for the vans. No way could he afford to leave them parked on the street overnight. He'd tried it briefly when the business was starting out. The signwriting proved an irresistible attraction for every local toerag with a ghoulish sense of curiosity. After the fifth smashed side-window in so many weeks he'd bitten the bullet and rented somewhere secure.

The loft space above the garaging had seemed an extravagance at the time but as the company had taken off he'd gradually expanded into it. A bit of studding and a dash of plaster and it was now a neat layout of storerooms and offices. He kept a posh executive lair of his own right next door to this one. It was spotless and Spartan with a stainless steel desk that resembled a mortuary table—possibly because that's what it had once been.

That office presented the kind of clean, uncluttered, efficient workspace that clients expected and admired but McCarron found it impossible to get anything done there. So he hid himself away in this untidy little bolt-hole and only nipped through the connecting door when clients had been buzzed in and were on their way up.

He felt more at home this side of the door. The office was cramped and messy but it was reasonably clean. There was even a scuffed sofa that he'd frequently kipped down on when the working day stretched into the working night, when the business was on the way up and his marriage was on the way down like the two facts were on opposite ends of a seesaw.

Kelly sank onto the sofa now, leaned her head back and shut her eyes. She cradled her vodka almost untouched in her lap having taken no more than a taste. And that, McCarron knew was just to be sociable. These days Kelly was careful to the point of paranoia about what she allowed into her system.

Can't blame her for that I suppose.

He'd never known her go out simply for her own enjoyment, to let her hair down. In fact she didn't seem to have any friends outside work—something that had cost her dear in the past, he knew.

Sitting there as close to relaxed as she ever got, McCarron thought she seemed young and frail—both of which he knew were just an illusion. But she also looked tired, he realised. The kind of tired that comes from stress as much as physical labour.

Allison had recently had her nose pierced just the same as Kelly and he resisted the urge to ask what happened when she got a cold.

After a few moments he set down his mug, cocked his head on one side and said, "Want to tell me about it?"

Kelly didn't open her eyes. "Old ghosts," she said simply.

"Should've thought about that," he said, gruff. "Sorry Kel. Never crossed my mind ..." He shrugged. "Sorry. Saw the upmarket postcode and wanted my best team on it that's all."

"Flatterer." She lifted her head, shook it like a dog out of water. "Don't worry about it Ray. Not your problem." But the smile she'd intended to be reassuring came out wan instead. "I just walked in there and *knew* the scene had been staged—and you know as well as I do that it bloody was—and it ... brought it all back."

McCarron tensed. "All of it?"

"Well." She lifted a shoulder, gently swirled the colourless liquid round the inside of the jar without meeting his eyes. "As much of it as I ever remember."

"I'm sorry love but it'll do you no good trying to force it." Even as he spoke he was aware of the hollow emptiness of words. "It's a done deal. You've just got to move on with your life."

For a moment he thought she was going to say more—maybe even confide in him. Instead she glanced up, eyes glinting.

"Yes Mum," she said and stuck her tongue out.

McCarron didn't know whether to be relieved or disappointed. "Well, at least you haven't had *that* pierced yet, I'm glad to see."

—6—

"TELL ME!" THE voice commanded. "Tell me everything!"

As the lash sizzled across his exposed flesh Steve Warwick flinched in pain. He'd sworn that this time he'd take the beating without a sound, like a man, but a traitorous groan forced out past his whitened lips.

His hands were tied over his head to one of the low-slung roof beams. He twisted against the restraint cursing silently but there was no give in the mounting. And although the material itself was soft enough not to mark him it had so far resisted all his frantic efforts to tear himself free.

Blindfolded as well as bound, he strained for every reassuring noise above the hammering of his heart. His tormentor circled with slow footsteps, a deliberate measured pace on the bare wooden floor and he cringed deep inside waiting for the next blow. A hot flood of humiliation had started low in his belly and was creeping outwards. Standing at full stretch like this, naked and vulnerable, he was completely at their mercy.

"I don't *know* anything," he pleaded breathless. "How many more times—"

"Liar!" The woman's voice cracked out synchronised with the whip and he jerked again. She struck harder this time and his groan mutated into a shocked howl, outrage and pain in equal measure.

The woman laughed. A throaty, husky purr of sound. "You are being *very* bad boy," she admonished, her voice tinted with the seductive Russian accent of her birthplace. "You are—how you say?—holding out on me because you know I shall punish you, yes?"

"No! I—"

The whip landed again curling dangerously around his thigh and eliciting a strangled yelp this time. "For God's sake be careful Myshka!" Warwick snapped. "I've a squash tournament this weekend. Not where it will show!"

"Do not presume. To tell. Me. What. To. Do!" The woman punctuated each shouted word with further brutal strokes while he yelled and gasped and shuddered in exquisite agony until his legs buckled and he dangled sweat-soaked from the beam, chest heaving, utterly unable to speak.

She leaned in close enough for her distinctive musky perfume to tantalise his nostrils and whispered against his ear. "You think I am some slut to be ordered around, yes? You think I am like your pathetic excuse for a *wife*?"

"N-no," he managed, still panting as he struggled to get his feet under him again and wincing from the fresh weals that laced across his back and buttocks.

Without warning, she stripped the blindfold from his eyes. Warwick screwed them up against the sudden light. It took a few moments before he could squint past his own eyelids.

The fantasy subsided revealing the neat bare bedroom of the top-floor rented flat in Harrow, with its stripped pine floorboards, sturdy exposed beams and conveniently empty office space beneath. The room was dominated by the huge bed with all-white linen and old-fashioned brass bedstead.

Myshka had stepped back and was watching his recovery through narrowed eyes, still fingering the suede-thonged whip longingly. It stung like a bastard but left no lasting scars and *damn* if she didn't know how to use it to maximum effect. The best he'd ever had. And having taken the traditional path through the British upper-class educational system Warwick could speak from considerable personal experience.

Myshka herself was a well-endowed brunette, her hair a long gleaming collection of shades from polished oak to copper. He'd always had a weakness for Eastern European girls with their mottled English and exotic beauty. And Myshka knew how to dress to make the most of what she had.

Tonight she was wearing a tightly belted raincoat over long glossy leather boots. The little bitch did that just to tease him he was sure—not letting him see the rest until she was good and ready.

He wriggled his fingers experimentally to return the blood-flow but Myshka made no immediate move to release him. He eyed her impatiently.

"Come on darling let me down," he said aiming one of his killer smiles. "If you don't give me a couple of minutes' rest *you* won't be getting your reward tonight."

Myshka pouted and for a moment he thought she was going to refuse. Then she stepped forwards and reached up to unhook his hands, rubbing her body deliberately against his as she did so.

"You promised to tell me all about Matthew's poor dead wife," she breathed into his mouth. "Did you see her body? What was it like? Was there *lot* of blood?"

Warwick pulled a face at this last question, pushing her away far enough to deal with his bonds. "Sorry to disappoint you darling but it was all over by the time I got there. Well *almost* all over, anyway."

Myshka's fingers froze on the knots. "Almost?"

"Yeah, Matt called in some specialist cleaning firm to deal with the mess. They tried to tell him it wasn't suicide." His eyes were on the swell of her breasts beyond the tightly wrapped raincoat. "You ask me it was just a scam to try to squeeze more money out of him."

She finished untying his wrists and Warwick hauled her against the length of him rough enough to make her gasp. As his hands groped her backside he could feel the outline of stocking tops and suspenders under the thin material of the coat. He yanked greedily at the belt.

Maybe this is your lucky night darling and I won't need a couple of minutes' rest after all.

"Did it work?" Myshka asked.

"Oh yeah, I'd say so," he muttered engrossed in his task.

"Pay attention!" She fisted a hand in his hair to drag his head back. "Did he believe them—that she did not kill herself?"

"Ow! Yes, no, I don't know!" he protested, too surprised to be angry yet. "When I got there everything had ground to a halt while they consulted higher authority. Whoever it was must have told them to stop pratting about though. By the time I left they were hard at it. Matt says they've got the place nearly good as new."

Myshka turned her grip into a caress. "Maybe I should ask them to clean up here when I am done with you, yes?" she suggested. "Who were they?"

"McSomebody-or-other, I think. McCarron—that was it. Big white vans with Specialist Cleaning Services on the side. Can't be many of those in the phone book," Warwick said with the beginnings of irritation in his voice. "I wasn't paying attention.

For God's sake—Matt will have the details if you're really *so* desperate to know."

Then with a grunt of triumph he yanked the belt apart and spread the coat wide. Under it she was naked apart from a leather suspender belt and fishnet stockings, her body hair shaved to a minimum. His eyes ran hotly over her perfect pale body, hands following. He wasn't gentle but she never seemed to want him to be.

She stood quietly accepting of his touch and smiled at him. A beautiful woman who became breathtaking when she smiled. In one hand she still held the green silk tie she'd used to bind him, now torn and distorted beyond repair.

"Your poor tie," she said with mocking eyes. "Was it your favourite?"

"No I hated it." He plucked the tie from her grasp and flung it across the room then shoved her backwards until they hit the bed. She went sprawling onto the mattress. He followed her down murmuring against her skin, "It was a present from my wife."

—7—

MYSHKA SAT IN front of her dressing table mirror. She was alone in the flat. Steve Warwick had satisfied himself and left for some meeting he pretended was more important than it was. Later he would go home to his pathetic little mouse of a wife. Myshka was left to smear away the whore-paint and try to scrub the smell of him from her skin.

She took a long inward drag on her cigarette and blew out a thin stream of smoke towards the ceiling. Warwick did not like her to smoke in the flat—it was not allowed. Myshka gave a tight little smile. She did many things that were not allowed.

A long time ago when she was growing up in a small town ten hours' train ride from St Petersburg Myshka's most heartfelt ambition was not to be cold and hungry. Later, when she realised what those things meant, it was her desire not to be poor. After she started to grow in ways that men could not help but notice—

and as a result acquired warm furs, a paid-for apartment, meals in the finest restaurants and a generous allowance—she realised not being poor was no longer enough. She wanted to be rich.

So she had made friendships with rich and richer men but even then it did not satisfy the empty spaces in her soul. Being given a new Mercedes-Benz for no other reason that the paintwork matched her eyes was very nice of course, but she remained as much a possession as the car itself.

And as she grew older and the lavish presents came perhaps a little less often it was then Myshka realised that what she really wanted above all else was power. It was better than money because where power went money soon followed. And it was better than sex—which in her experience was all about power anyway.

The acquisition of power was a challenge that sent her pulses fizzing in a way no sexual thrills had ever done.

She stubbed out her cigarette.

"Soon," she promised her reflection.

She picked up her iPhone, scrolled through the contacts and set it to dial. It took a long time for the call to be picked up with a brusque, "*Da?*"

"Dmitry," Myshka said huskily. "I begin to think you not love me anymore."

"I was in a meeting," Dmitry said. He had learned his English younger than Myshka and so his use of it was smoother.

Somewhere behind him Myshka caught a sudden burst of loud music and raucous voices.

"Where are you?" she demanded sharply. "It sounds like a peasants' market."

She heard him suck in a breath. Dmitry had once worked in just such a market selling cheap western imitations at anything but bargain prices.

"We are at a hotel," he said. "There is a wedding party here."

Myshka sniffed. "And *he* is there?"

"Of course he is here." Dmitry's tone warned her not to start anything. "He is my boss."

"For now, yes?"

She heard him twist as if to cover her words. "Myshka—"

"We may have a problem," she said switching to Russian.

"What kind of problem?" Dmitry stuck to the language of their adopted country. Sometimes she wondered if he did it just to put her in her place. Or try to.

"Lytton called in cleaners."

This time the intake of breath was harsher and more apparent. "Instead of the police?"

Myshka rolled her eyes. "Not *that* kind of cleaners," she said. "Kind that come *after* police. They looked at place where she die and somehow they know."

Dmitry swore low and vicious but she heard uncertainty beneath the anger. "How?"

"I do not know. You make ... mistake, perhaps?" She only phrased it as a question to salve his ego just a little.

There was a long silence at the other end of the line and she knew he would be pacing. When Dmitry was under pressure he could not stay still. "What happened?"

Myshka was reluctant to let him off the hook so soon but she said, "In end, nothing. "They report, wait for a time and then are told to clean anyway. I am merely keeping you—how do the English say it?—up to scratch."

"Up to speed," Dmitry corrected missing the intended irony. "Who are they?"

Myshka lit another cigarette and gave him the details she had coaxed or goaded out of Warwick—and how she had done it. She knew Dmitry did not like to hear such things. He was a man for whom sex and violence did not mix. *A pity.*

"And will your sick little puppy keep *you* up to speed?" he asked when she was through.

"He will do whatever I tell him," she said and gave a throaty chuckle, "just as long also I tell him he is *very* bad boy."

Dmitry swore again. "I have to go," he said quickly. "Keep me informed, hmm?" And he cut the connection without waiting for her to speak.

Myshka pulled a face and put the phone down slowly. "You are welcome," she said. "But next time ... get it right, yes?"

KELLY ARRIVED HOME late to find someone had nicked the low energy bulb in the hallway again. It happened regularly enough for her to keep a small LED flashlight permanently on her key ring. That at least allowed her to navigate the tangled assortment of bicycles and pushchairs behind the front door without breaking anything or impaling herself in the gloom.

Her flat was three flights up on the top floor of a shabby Victorian mid-terrace house. The young letting agent had done his best to extol the property's virtues as he'd walked her up that first day. But by the time they reached the final dirty landing high under the eaves he hadn't the heart or the breath for what remained of his sales pitch. He'd allowed her to wander through the scant three-roomed flat in silence.

Kelly had made his day by taking on the lease anyway.

The place had been lavishly described as a "cosy studio apartment in need of some modernisation" which translated as "crummy dwarf bedsit" in anybody else's language. But it was affordable and a stone's throw from Battersea Park on the south side of the Thames. And besides, Kelly had just been released from somewhere much worse.

After five years in a cell barely ten feet by eleven with cellmates who snored or sneered or ranted—and even one who tried to suffocate her while she slept—the three-hundred-square-foot apartment had seemed like untold luxury whatever its condition.

Her first task had been to tackle the place like a crime scene, suiting up and sanitising every inch, a two-foot segment at a time. She painted it in pale creams and greys and golds that made the most of the modest skylight and the single window. The transformation had taken up an entire weekend and proved a cathartic exercise.

As she slipped inside tonight and re-engaged the locks she reminded herself yet again that she was shutting the rest of the world *out* not shutting herself in.

She dumped her keys in the terracotta pot in the two-pace hallway, along with the rotor arm from her ancient Mini.

Removing it proved the cheapest way to immobilise the car whenever she left it parked on the local streets.

Not that it was worth stealing but people round here were apt to overlook the more rust-than-paint bodywork and the kerbed steel wheels if a vehicle fired and ran.

And Kelly had taken advantage of the prison educational programmes to learn motor-vehicle maintenance, so for all its sorry appearance the Mini was endlessly reliable and nipped through gaps in traffic like a jet-propelled skateboard.

She switched on the shaded lamps in the living area, one either side of the sofa that folded out into her bed. It didn't bother her that the flat was tiny. It was her space, her retreat, her solitude. A place where nobody had the right to roust her in the middle of the night to order her outside so they could pick over her belongings at random.

And it had a priceless feature that the letting agent hadn't been remotely aware of never mind thought to use as leverage on the rent.

Now, Kelly went into the tiny bathroom and opened up the narrow skylight above the sink. She used the edge of the bath as a single step and levered herself carefully through the opening out onto the roof.

The skylight led out onto the interconnected rooftops that had become her secret refuge. A huge rolling contour map of hips and valleys dotted with TV aerial forests and chimney stacks that rose like rock formations towards the sky. She'd taught herself to navigate the slate and tile landscape like a ghost so those beneath never knew she was there.

For a moment Kelly stood balanced easily on the sharp slope and breathed in the night air above London. The smell of freedom.

She picked her way nimbly across the slanted rooftop avoiding loose wires and broken tiles by instinct and familiarity. The end of the terrace butted up against a taller building, its elderly brickwork face providing a relatively easy ascent.

The first time she'd scaled this wall Kelly had shaken with delayed reaction afterwards but now it was almost second nature. She moved smoothly, continuously, using the mortar gaps and concentrating on texture and grip. Free climbing was risky but by ensuring she always had three good points of contact she could contain the risk. And the prize made it worth the effort.

Kelly's favourite spot faced nominally north-east. From there perched on the ridge with her back to a substantial brick chimney she could see the glow of Big Ben, the giant London Eye Ferris wheel, the four huge funnels of the disused power station at Battersea and the glimmer of a thousand lights reflected on the slow water of the river.

Even if she shut her eyes she could point to every landmark in turn, see them spread clearly across the canvas of her imagination. She'd always had an excellent memory, had once been noted for her ability to recite facts and figures in court with absolute conviction and without recourse to notes.

But suddenly six years ago she'd had a blackout. A total void that stretched for hours. And when she'd come back to herself she'd discovered that all the evidence—for which she'd always had such respect—pointed to her being a murderer.

Her victim's name was Callum Perry. She remembered that much. Secretive and cryptic, Perry had called her claiming to have information she *needed* to know about a dead prostitute. That case looked straightforward at first glance but Kelly had run into anomalies. Questioning them had not made her popular in some quarters.

So she arranged to meet him. That was the last thing she knew until she woke next to his corpse.

So for the first time she'd found herself in the dock rather than on the witness stand, assailed by roiling uncertainties. She'd *believed* herself to be innocent but didn't *know* it. Not for certain. And certainly couldn't prove it.

Her friends—ones she'd made through her work and all connected with law enforcement—steadily melted away. Even those who thought she might be innocent were told by their chain of command that if they valued their careers they'd cut her loose.

She thought of David as she hadn't thought of him in years. As she had conditioned herself *not* to think of him. David who had shared her life, her heart, until …

She'd felt him pulling back from her right from the moment of her arrest, had often thought he'd only stuck around as long as he did because it looked worse to go than stay. In the end he'd stayed too long and the wash of associated guilt had almost drowned him alongside her.

David resented her for that she knew. Held her bitterly responsible for the permanent stall in promotion that followed. He'd hoped for chief superintendent if not higher. Now he was likely to see out his twenty-five as the longest-serving detective inspector in the Met.

The police, it seemed, were very quick to turn on their own.

Alone, all Kelly could cling to was faith in the evidence she'd always trusted. That it would somehow come to her aid.

But the evidence had let her down.

Now, she thought back to the scene of Veronica Lytton's supposed suicide.

"I *know* she was murdered," she told herself. Even if the evidence was gone—all bar a few digital images and her tainted expertise. Neither of which were likely to stand up in court. Especially when she had personally helped wipe out all physical trace.

Safe in her eyrie looking out over London she hugged her knees to her chest and shivered despite the balmy air.

—9—

DMITRY SLUMPED IN the driver's seat of his black Mercedes-Benz, watching and waiting.

It was a long time since he'd had to sit like this in silence and darkness waiting for his prey. *Not since the old days*, he thought sardonically and half-smiled. In some ways he almost missed it.

But since he had left his homeland Dmitry had tried hard to acquire western sophistication. Take the car for instance. The ten-year-old S-Class coupé was all Dmitry could afford but he'd made up for the age by kitting it out with huge chrome alloys and heavy tint on the glass. Very classy. Back home it was the kind of motor that would have brought people out onto the streets to stare as he passed. In London it didn't warrant a second glance.

But for something like this the car's anonymity was a good thing.

He'd been waiting for three hours. Three hours without a cigarette and with nothing to occupy his hands. Nothing to occupy his mind either except idly wondering how far to go with the message he had come to deliver. A little further with each passing hour most likely—something had to make up for this boredom.

He was parked in a side street near the Tube station at Stonebridge Park in north-west London. As he arrived he'd caught glimpses of the arc of the new Wembley stadium in the distance. It was an area more industrial than residential which was a good thing. Not that people were likely to look when they heard noises outside anyway.

Such a *polite* race the British. So careful not to get involved even to the point of allowing a stranger to be beaten to death on the very steps of their home. Besides, he was a stone's throw from the North Circular inner ring road. The constant traffic flow even at this time of night would mask any small sounds. Dmitry prided himself that he was good enough for there to be little else.

In fact his only brief worry was the Ace Café just a little further along the road. It seemed to be a local bikers' haunt and there was a lot of coming and going, and groups of people milling around outside. He shrugged it off. If anything the bad press bikers usually got meant they could well be blamed for his actions.

And then finally the lights flicked off in the office window above the line of roller-shutter doors.

At last!

Dmitry was out of the car and across the road in a few seconds, moving fast without seeming to hurry. He made sure to blip the locks on the Mercedes as he walked away from it. It would be bad news if the car was stolen while he was otherwise engaged.

He was only a few strides away from the main door to the building when it opened. Dmitry tucked in close to the wall so he merged with the shadows. The light that flooded out of the doorway briefly illuminated the figure of a man, just enough to confirm his target.

Dmitry already had one hand wrapped around the short baton in his coat pocket. Now he pulled it out and extended it with a sharp upward flick of his wrist. The sound of the baton's segments telescoping outwards and locking into position was designed to resemble that of a shell being racked into the chamber of a pump-action shotgun. The sound alone made most people freeze but this guy ducked and swung on a reflex.

The first blow landed short. It was still enough to send the man back and down, grabbing hold of the door frame in an attempt to keep his balance. He gave out a grunt and brought his left arm up instinctively to protect his head. Dmitry aimed for the exposed elbow, hearing the muffled crack as the joint exploded.

This time the man let loose an enraged bellow as he collapsed onto the laminate floor, rolling to escape the pain. Dmitry followed him inside, kicking the man's legs clear of the door so he could close it behind them. No point doing this in full view of the empty car park.

Now he could take his time to coldly and scientifically deliver blows that inflicted misery as much as lasting damage. Killing the man would be counterproductive he knew. All he needed to do was scare him into silence.

When Dmitry figured he was scared enough he stood over him staring down as if to read meaning in the jerky spasms of his limbs. The man's cries had dribbled away to groans. He lay with his face against the wall in a greasy puddle of his own spittle and blood.

Dmitry nudged him over onto his back with his foot, leaned in close.

"You see me?" he demanded.

The man opened the eye that wasn't completely swollen shut, swallowed before he could speak. Even then he hesitated as if this might be a trick question.

Dmitry sighed. "Remember my face, friend. You have poked your nose into something that's none of your business and my boss is very upset. So let it lie—or you will be seeing my face again for sure. Yes? And next time I will not ask so ... politely."

There was another hesitation, then a slow fractional nod.

The hesitancy might have been due to pain or confusion but Dmitry did not leave that to chance. Just in case, he repeated his message with several more, brutal blows and followed them up with another verbal warning, laying on a dose of extra threat.

When he was done he carefully wiped the baton on the man's clothing and forced it shut against the powerful spring in the base.

Then he walked out of the building and pulled the door neatly closed behind him. Halfway back to the Merc he lit his first cigarette of the evening and inhaled the smoke deep into his lungs.

A job well done, he considered.

Yes, perhaps after all he *did* miss it.

Getting back to central London took less than an hour. Dmitry cruised with the stereo on and didn't go out of his way to attract attention.

As he pulled up to the underground parking garage the transponder behind the Merc's front grille sent out a signal that opened the security gates. A few minutes later Dmitry had slotted the car into its bay and was taking the plush lift to the penthouse apartment high above.

He let himself in and pocketed his keys. Voices came from the living area. When he pushed open the doors he found Harry Grogan sitting alone at the head of the dining table with one of the twenty-four-hour news channels playing on the huge flatscreen TV on the far wall. Grogan was eating a steak so rare it still bled onto his plate.

He was a big man wearing a three-grand suit and a hand-finished shirt that Dmitry felt did a passable job of disguising the middle-aged slide of muscle into fat. When his hair started to grey and thin he'd shaved his head down to the scalp. It gleamed now under the ceiling spotlights.

"You're late," Grogan said.

Dmitry bowed his head briefly. Partly in acknowledgement of the rebuke and partly to hide the flare in his eyes.

"I am sorry boss," he said. "I was dealing with a … minor problem."

Grogan stared at him steadily while he chewed another mouthful then picked up his wine glass. "Anything I should know about?"

Dmitry shook his head. "No," he said stonily. "It is nothing I cannot handle."

—10—

TYRONE CAME TO with a start and realised groggily that he was lying face down in something wet. He must have drooled something awful while he'd slept because his pillow was soggy as his football shirt after a tough Wednesday night game.

He rolled over, his eyes going to the bright figures of his alarm clock on the chest of drawers. It took him a moment to work out that the 4:06 on the display was AM not PM and he stifled a groan.

There wasn't even a sniff of daylight outside. Tyrone rubbed his hands across his face and tried to work out what had woken him. Then his cellphone bleeped again to tell him he had a waiting text.

He scrabbled for it so as not to wake his little brother Brendan who shared the same bedroom. Tyrone flipped open the phone and stabbed the buttons to retrieve the message. It was from Kelly—brief and to the point.

Ray attacked. Bad way. Central Middx Hosp'l. Pk Royal.

"*Shi*-ite," Tyrone murmured.

"Tellin' Ma on you," came the mumbled response from somewhere under the far duvet.

"And *I'm* telling Ma *you* was awake when you wasn't supposed to be, yeah?" Tyrone shot back in a harsh whisper. "Go to sleep."

The walls in the flat were paper thin and he didn't want to wake his mum or his sister as well. His mum cleaned other people's offices half the night. Less messy than the jobs Tyrone tackled but hard slog just the same. She didn't deserve to be woken by something like this.

He threw back the covers, grabbed his clothes off the chair at the end of his bed and slipped out of the room. In the bathroom he splashed cold water on his face and dressed hurriedly, stabbing out a brief return message while he cleaned his teeth.

On way.

He scribbled a note and tacked it under a fridge magnet where all household messages were left then grabbed his bike helmet from the hall.

His mum hadn't wanted him to get a motorbike—had been well against it at first. He'd talked her round. It was cheap transport and faster for getting through London traffic. No congestion charge either, and though the bastards were trying to bring in parking fees at least you were never short of a space.

At home he kept the old Honda 250 chained to a concrete pillar under the flats next to the wheelie bins. He let it be known that if anybody messed with it, it he had easy access to chemicals that could dissolve a body down to *nothing* in a couple of hours. Pure bullshit, but so far the local toerags had kept their thieving hands off it.

Now he unchained the bike and fired it up, letting it warm through while he zipped up his jacket and got himself together.

Someone had attacked the boss. Bad, Kelly had said. The idea left him shaky. More shaky maybe because he saw the after-effects of violence every day. He'd helped clean up after domestics and home invasions that ended in a bloodbath.

Where? he wondered, buckling the strap on his helmet. He didn't ask why. He'd long since stopped looking for reason. A funny look, a spilled pint, a nice pair of trainers. All good enough cause for a fist or a quick blade.

But Ray McCarron wouldn't be an easy target. He'd been a copper—still had that way about him. And he was fast for an old guy.

Not fast enough.

Anger pushed the shakiness aside. Tyrone toed the bike into gear and accelerated out onto the main road.

This time of the morning he could go straight down the Mile End Road, then head west through Shoreditch, past King's Cross, and skirt the bottom end of Regent's Park to hit the A40. That would take him straight out to Park Royal. It was a route he knew well enough—he went that way to work sometimes if it wasn't rush hour.

Tyrone had been riding a bike ever since he was old enough. Before then if truth be told but he wouldn't admit as much to his mum. He'd always been big for his age and the local coppers were more interested in valid tax and insurance than they were with checking the face and the licence matched up.

It was only since he'd started working for the boss that he'd seen another side of the cops. The right side, he supposed. Before then they'd been the enemy swaggering into his home territory like invaders, all cocky, ready to swoop on one of his mates. Sometimes they were justified but it could just as easily be a random thing. Like they didn't care who they picked up as long as they picked up somebody.

Now he saw most of them as pros who dealt with the worse side of life with dedication and more care than they let on. His jaw clamped under his visor. He just hoped they cared enough to get a result on this one.

Or Tyrone would be looking to do their job for them.

—11—

KELLY SAT ON a wooden bench in the hospital courtyard garden staring at the swirling pattern of slate in front of her.

It was a sculpture as much as a piece of landscaping and was supposed to represent an echogram of the heart laid out in different coloured cobbles that spiralled inwards to a central point.

She'd watched the texture of the piece solidify as the sun rose slowly over the city and filtered down into the garden. Called 'Echoes of the Heart' it was intended to provide an oasis of tranquillity for patients and visitors but all Kelly felt was an overwhelming sense of sadness.

Ray McCarron had been rushed in an hour ago with a shopping list of injuries that frankly dismayed her. Shattered elbow, cracked ribs, concussion, possible fractured skull and internal bleeding as well as cuts and bruises just about everywhere.

The only way she could hold it together was to think of it in coldly clinical terms. Whoever worked him over had done a very professional job. Nothing bad enough to be fatal—she clung to that thought—but plenty that would afford a painful lasting reminder.

She put her head in her hands. If she'd been a weeper she would have wept but tears were a luxury she'd dispensed with a long time ago.

"Kel! How is he?"

She twisted to see Tyrone barrelling towards her still clutching his bike helmet. He came straight over the top of the cobbled artwork without noticing it was there.

So much for deeper meanings, Kelly thought and something of her self-pity seemed to collapse with the pretence.

"He's out of surgery," she said forcing optimism into her voice. "Going to have us waiting on him hand and foot for weeks after this I bet. We'll be lucky if he puts the kettle on and makes the rest of us a brew ever again."

Tyrone nodded like he knew exactly what she wasn't saying and asked hesitantly, "Do they know who?"

Kelly shook her head. "The police have asked for the CCTV from the office but I doubt it will tell them much. He was in the hallway so the car park camera won't have caught much and we've no coverage inside the building."

"This happened at *work*?" He frowned. "I thought he was, y'know mugged or somethin'. How did you ... I mean ... who ...?"

"I found him." Kelly looked down at her hands. "The security company rang me. Apparently he set the code but then didn't shut the outer door within the time and the silent alarm triggered. They couldn't raise Ray as the main key holder so they called me as secondary."

Tyrone swore softly under his breath. "Bastards. Did they take much?"

"No. Upstairs was untouched." She paused unsure how much to put onto Tyrone and decided it wasn't fair to lumber him with anything—not until they knew for certain. So she hedged. "Maybe they were disturbed."

"I'll disturb 'em if I get hold of 'em."

She put a hand on his arm, a gesture of comfort and solidarity. She felt him tense under her fingers then he shifted, leaning down to envelop her in a big hug. A warning note sounded in the back of Kelly's mind. She disengaged herself gently and offered Tyrone a sympathetic smile. He wouldn't meet her eyes.

Across the courtyard a door opened and a nurse stuck her head out. "Miss Jacks, is it? Can you come? Mr McCarron's asking for you."

Kelly lurched to her feet, aware of Tyrone edging closer as if he expected her to faint. She had never fainted in her life and wasn't going to start now.

She put out a hand to stay him, asked instead, "Is he …?"

"Oh, sorry love it's not like that," the nurse said breezily. "He's as comfortable as can be expected for what he's been through. If you'd like to follow me?"

She disappeared leaving Kelly to hurry after her. Tyrone tagged along behind, shoulders hunched into his bike jacket.

Kelly caught up with the nurse halfway along the corridor. "I didn't think he'd be allowed visitors," she said. "Not yet anyway."

"He shouldn't by all accounts but he won't settle—not 'til he's had a word with you he says." Her tone suggested she doubted the urgency of this request and was humouring the pair of them by going along with it.

Kelly's heartrate stepped up. What was so urgent that it couldn't wait?

As much for Tyrone's benefit as the nurse's Kelly said blandly, "Work I expect."

"Hmm." The nurse let her eyes slide up and down Kelly's figure as they bustled towards the ward. "Of course love."

Eventually she led them to a doorway and stopped with a decisive squeak of soft-soled shoes on polished lino.

"Here we are. One of you only, if you don't mind," she said sternly. "And no more than five minutes please."

If anything, Kelly thought Tyrone seemed relieved not to be going in there. She couldn't blame him for that. She didn't want to see her boss—her mentor, her friend—like this herself.

"I'll wait out here, yeah?" Tyrone said jerking his head towards a row of plastic chairs. He slouched off without waiting for a reply. Kelly bit her lip as she watched him go, then stepped into the room the nurse had indicated.

Inside Ray McCarron lay very quiet amid the sheets. He presented a grey figure, suddenly an old man, helpless and vulnerable. In all the years Kelly had known him she'd never seen him like this.

They'd fastened together the cuts on his face and arms with Steri-Strips rather than stitches and immobilised his left arm. His hand just peeped out from below the dressing. It was swollen and angry, the fingers beginning to blacken. They could do little for the other bruises that had bloomed into a swirling mass under the surface of his skin, spreading and darkening even in the short time since she'd last seen him.

"Hi Ray," she said softly.

McCarron opened one eye—the one he still could. "'Lo Kel," he mumbled.

"Ray I'm so sorry—"

He swallowed with obvious difficulty. "Don't be," he said more firmly this time. "No' your fault. Bas'ard got the jump on me s'all."

"Who?" Kelly urged. "*Who* got the jump on you?"

"Dunno," he said his voice almost dreamy. The puffy lips attempted a smile. "Don't need to. Got the message. Loud an' clear."

She resisted the urge to shake him but only just. "What message?"

"'Bout turning over rocks, Kel. Never know what might be unnerneath 'em." His eyes were starting to glide and he refocused with an effort. Even then she couldn't be sure who or what he saw.

"I wasn't intending to turn over any bloody rocks."

"Good girl. Keep it that way." He nodded, winced, nodded again sagely. "She's not worth it. Don' wanna see you like this. Can't trust anyone ..."

"Wait! Ray is all ... *this* because I queried the Lytton job?" Kelly leaned over him, smelled the iodine and antiseptic wipes they'd used to bathe his minor wounds. "Ray?"

But he'd drifted off into a drug-induced doze. Considering the painful alternative, Kelly hadn't the heart to wake him.

—12—

TYRONE SAT IN the hallway outside the boss's room with elbows on knees and his head sunk. He didn't like hospitals, never had. Not since his dad anyway. They were places connected with temper and sorrow. No facts, just feelings. Even the smell was enough to set off the memories, none of them good.

His dad had died of bowel cancer when Tyrone was just a kid and it hadn't been quick. His childhood was stained with long periods spent on chairs like this while his mother sat by his father's bedside and listened to him rage against the pain and the unfairness of it. It had been a long slow downhill journey with no possibility of reprieve. The old bastard had taken it with ill grace and a large amount of morphine. Just being inside the building was giving Tyrone the jitters.

Being here because of what some thieving sod had done to the boss—that was even worse.

Tyrone's hands were loosely clasped but every now and again his fingers would tighten, stretching the skin taut across his knuckles.

He wanted to hit someone. Hit them hard and keep hitting them. He'd done his share of fighting as a kid. First on his own account and then for his younger brother and sister. The standard threat of "I'll set my dad on you!" hadn't been an option. If you wanted you-and-yours left well alone you had to show them you weren't an easy target, weren't to be messed with. Nobody messed with the Douet kids after that.

But this was different. There was nobody to fight, nobody obvious to blame. And he was getting a weird vibe from Kelly like she knew what was going on and was afraid to tell him.

Or maybe it was because he'd given himself away he realised, flushing painfully. That brief contact had been enough to send his pulse bounding into overdrive. In the far recess of his mind he knew Kelly viewed him just as a workmate but that didn't mean he couldn't dream. And tonight she'd looked so vulnerable, like she needed someone to protect her for once, not the other way around.

Maybe she thought he couldn't handle it whatever it was. Tyrone's hands flexed again. *There ain't much I can't handle.*

Growing up in a tough area had taught him how to handle plenty. The first lesson was spotting trouble at fifty paces. So as soon as the big guy in the leather jacket walked in asking for Ray McCarron's room Tyrone's instincts screamed that here was all the trouble he could wish for.

The guy had dark hair and a young-but-old face with a nose that had been broken more than once. He carried himself with an aggressive muscular stance that had Tyrone launching out of his plastic seat. *If you think you've come to finish what you started mate you gotta get past me first.*

Since he started playing football, rugby and ice hockey up at the club in Walthamstow Tyrone had learned to use his size to best advantage. Now he ducked his shoulder intending to bounce the newcomer off the wall nearest the boss's room. It was the kind of vicious body check that would have had him sent off the ice for half a game. The guy should have gone down hard and stayed there. Those with any sense usually did.

Tyrone wasn't expecting to be expertly flipped somewhere in mid-tackle so it was his own back that slammed up against the wall with an explosive thump. Before he knew what was happening a rock-hard forearm was wedged against his throat.

"For God's sake children, if you're going to play rough take it outside." Kelly's voice was a low growl. Tyrone's eyes slid sideways—the only part of his head he dare move—and found her glaring up at the pair of them from the doorway. She suddenly filled it like she'd fluffed up her fur.

Tyrone's would-be opponent released the choke hold with some reluctance.

"Tell it to him," the man said mockingly, not even out of breath. "He's the one who jumped me."

Tyrone saw the way Kelly's eyes jerked, wondered what the guy had said that made her look so haunted. His ears grew hot. "He was asking for the boss's room," he protested, "and I just—"

"—wanted to protect him," Kelly finished kindly, her voice careful. "I'm sure the nice detective will forgive your burst of enthusiasm for making a citizen's arrest."

Oh great—the Old Bill. Just what I need.

The man was staring at Kelly with the kind of dark assessing gaze the boss used when he was checking over crime scenes.

"Have we met?"

Kelly shook her head. "We don't need to," she said shortly. "Trust me—I recognise the type."

—13—

HE EVEN SMELLS like a cop, Kelly thought. What was it about these guys that made them favour aftershave with the same curiously musky overtones? Either way she felt her pulse rise as her body primed for flight in some kind of associated response.

"DI O'Neill," the man said now by way of introduction, flashing a warrant card like sleight of hand.

"Ah," Kelly said. "And what interest does CID have in a simple mugging?" She caught the way Tyrone's mouth opened then closed again quickly as he registered the flicker of her eyes.

"Ray McCarron is a retired police officer," O'Neill said not giving any sign he'd noticed the exchange. "We look after our own."

"Is that so?" She allowed her voice to drawl a little with contempt and watched the faint flush steal up past his shirt collar.

He took a breath as if to stay his patience, asked, "And you are?"

She bypassed the obvious invitation. "We work for Ray."

"Dedicated," O'Neill said dryly. "I need to talk to him."

"Talking *to* him would not be a problem. But if you're expecting him to talk back you're out of luck." Pure stubbornness forbade her to add, *for the moment.*

He frowned. "I understood his injuries weren't that serious."

Kelly regarded him a moment, bristling. *How crass can one man be with only one head?* "Try having a baseball bat or whatever it was taken to *you* with a vengeance and then define 'serious' why don't you?"

"I wasn't trying to make light of the situation," he said grimly. "I was told he was conscious at least."

"He *was*," she allowed. "But now he isn't." Kelly was aware she was out of line. *Way* out of line. But the anger and guilt were welling inside her and he was a convenient target. "I'm afraid this is one occasion where a blue flashing light and a siren will not make things happen any quicker."

He put his hands on his hips, glancing from Kelly to Tyrone at her shoulder. A smile twisted his lips.

"You two got a problem with authority?" he asked. "Wouldn't have thought that's an asset in your line of work." He paused. "Maybe I should ask you both to turn out your pockets."

"Maybe you should have 'just cause' first," Kelly shot back.

He sighed, tiring quickly of this game. *Unworthy opponents,* Kelly judged.

"Cut me some slack would you? If not for me then for him." He nodded towards the room behind her causing a twinge of additional guilt that did not make her like the man any better. "Mr McCarron called us yesterday about something. I'm here simply to check this is not ... related."

You and me both.

But even as the thought formed, Kelly noted the careful choice of words. *Mr McCarron* not *Ray* as a friend or former colleague might refer to him. And *called us* rather than *called me.* O'Neill might simply be the one who drew the short straw when it came to follow-up at this time in the morning.

She kept her voice cool as her eyes. "Do you have any reason to suspect it *might* be related, detective inspector?"

He hesitated which was an answer in itself even before he matched his tone to hers. "Not right at this moment, no."

"What? I mean, this is the Lytton thing, yeah?" Tyrone broke in suddenly, up on the balls of his feet like a boxer. "The boss tells you lot no way it was suicide and then he gets the crap beaten out of him and there's no connection? That how it works now?"

Kelly struggled not to take an audible breath. Not only that Tyrone had put it all together—her own thoughts and fears—but that he'd voiced them in front of a copper.

O'Neill frowned again, went dangerously still.

"If you take my advice," he said heavily, "that's not the kind of speculation you want to be indulging in."

Kelly recalled Ray's own words about not turning over rocks because of what might lie beneath.

"Can't trust anyone ..."

She knew she should have backed off then. Backed right off and stayed there but maybe she was just sick and tired of always being on the retreat. Maybe it was time for a reckless stand. She was only partially aware of the tension in her neck as her shoulders went back, head tilting.

"And if we *don't* want to take your advice?"

O'Neill fixed her with a brutal stare, one there was no way through and no way around.

"I remember you. You're Kelly Jacks," he said abruptly, his voice silky enough to send ice through to her bones. "Well, Kelly Jacks, you don't want to go there."

Not again.

He didn't add it but he didn't need to. Kelly shivered. *Much like Ray*, she thought bleakly, *I get the message.*

—14—

ABOUT THE TIME Kelly Jacks was heading across the river home from the hospital Dmitry was having a leisurely breakfast at South Mimms service station at the junction between the A1(M) and the M25 London orbital.

Whatever its drawbacks his time working for Harry Grogan had taught him to appreciate the finer things in life. The old man had shown real pleasure when Dmitry's uneducated palate had finally developed enough to distinguish a properly aged steak or a favourable year for a grape.

"If you're ordering the best you've got to *know* you're getting it and not being ripped off with a cheap substitute," Grogan had told him. "Don't trust nobody not to have their hand in the till."

And he was right. The last waiter who'd taken one look at Dmitry's longish tangle of hair and leather jacket and decided he wouldn't be able to tell shit from toothpaste had ended up with both hands rammed repeatedly in the drawer of the cash register. After that word got around.

But now, rather than some high-class restaurant—not that he had any choice here—Dmitry was up sitting at a table by the window in the service station's open-plan food court.

Western junk food had not been a part of Dmitry's experience growing up. He had only made the glorious discovery when he first arrived in the UK. Of course he quickly realised that to live on nothing else would be bad for his health but Dmitry was nothing if not a man of utter control. So he treated the occasional greasy burger and extruded potato-starch fries as an indulgence, a reward for good behaviour or a job well done.

Last night's work he considered qualified as both.

As a compromise he ate slowly, chewing every mouthful and keeping his elbows off the table. He was early and in no hurry. Around him his fellow diners fell on their food with disgusting gusto, stuffing their faces like the pigs they were.

Dmitry allowed nothing of his disdain to show on his features. He didn't need to. Disdain was an impotent emotion whereas he had the ability and the temperament to beat any one of them to death for no better reason than their table manners offended him.

He sat with his back to the security cameras out of habit although he was confident that his face would not set any alarm bells ringing. He'd always been very careful about that.

The man he'd come to meet however, that was another matter and Dmitry had no wish to come to official attention merely by association.

So he kept a close eye out for the make and colour of vehicle he'd been told to expect and spotted the dark blue Land Rover Defender the moment it swung into the car park.

He glanced at the time display on his iPhone. The man was only a couple of minutes late which—if not exactly pleasing Dmitry—at least did not put him in too black a mood.

Without appearing to hurry he wiped his fingers fastidiously on a paper serviette and strolled out leaving the debris of his meal on the table behind him. Important men did not clear up after themselves—not food wrappers anyway.

Despite the steadily climbing sun there was still a residue of night chill outside which did not encourage people to linger. Nevertheless Dmitry gave the surrounding area a casually thorough survey as he walked across the car park.

He approached the stationary Land Rover from an oblique angle in the blind spot to the rear. When he rapped his knuckles on the side glass the driver started in his seat before opening the window a crack.

"Whatever you're selling I'm not buying," he said, his voice abrupt. He was a big man with fleshy jowls and the lacework of thread veins across his cheeks that indicated a lifetime spent outdoors in all weathers. Even through the small opening Dmitry could smell the earthy odour of animals and wet cloth.

He kept his face stony. "It is fortunate then that I am buying."

But as he stepped back to let the man climb out from behind the wheel Dmitry saw the beginnings of a shift in his expression, the sly calculation blossoming in his eyes.

Like a snake Dmitry launched against the Land Rover door. It cannoned into the big man's bulk bursting a grunt of pain and surprise from his lips and pinning him there by his shins, half-in half-out.

Dmitry leaned his body weight a little more onto the edge of the door, watching the man's annoyance turn to fear as his discomfort leapt another notch.

"Your brother vouched for you. We are here to do business my friend," he said quietly, ladling on the Russian accent because he knew the effect it would have. "Let us not have any ... unpleasantness that may come back on your family, yes?"

"Y-yes!" the big man said, his voice a gasp as if he daren't take a breath. "I mean no! No unpleasantness—you have my word on it."

Dmitry eased back, opened the door wide and gave a mocking bow. "This is good," he said smiling. "You have the ... merchandise with you of course." It was not a question.

If the big man had been thinking of trying to cheat him Dmitry reckoned he was now too unsettled and flustered to follow through. Instead as he slithered down onto the tarmac he clutched the door frame with hands that trembled slightly.

The two of them moved around to the back of the Land Rover and Dmitry waited while the man opened the rear door. As he did so the man glanced round in a way guaranteed to draw attention to the pair had anybody been watching them. Dmitry suppressed a sigh. He hated dealing with amateurs.

"There you go," the man said gesturing inside with nervousness surging through his voice. "It's all there—just as we agreed, eh?"

Nestling amid the junk-filled interior was a stained coolbox. Suppressing his distaste Dmitry dragged the coolbox out into the centre of the gritty straw-crusted floor and opened it. The big man leaned in alongside him as if to make sure Dmitry would see what he was supposed to.

Dmitry surmised that, having initially planned to double-cross him in some way, he was now anxious everything should go according to plan instead.

The young Russian pursed his lips as if disappointed by the amount or the quality or both. In truth there was more than he'd anticipated.

Excellent.

Still they engaged in a half-hearted round of haggling which ended with Dmitry paying a little less than he'd expected and the big man able to kid himself he'd driven a hard bargain.

Dmitry handed over the cash still wrapped in its bank paper bands and had to stop the man counting it there and then right out in the open. He pointedly withdrew to the Land Rover's cab leaving Dmitry to transfer the coolbox across to his Mercedes.

By the time he returned the man was back out lighting up a noxious pipe that reminded Dmitry of the old men back home. In the bad times they smoked just about anything they could shove into the bowl and set on fire. As a child it had made him feel nauseous. Now it made him slightly sentimental.

Perhaps that was why he didn't kill the big man when he gave him a sideways glance and remarked, "Lot of stuff there. Want it for something *special* do you?"

Dmitry lit a cigarette of his own, bending his head to his lighter and taking his time about it. Then he gave the man a long stare through the smoke, cold enough to make him shiver.

"Unless you wish to find yourself on the receiving end," he said, "then it is best for your continued good health if you do not ask such questions, yes?"

—15—

MATTHEW LYTTON PRESSED the call button for the lift but didn't hold out much hope of a response. It looked like someone had tried to pry the buttons out of the wall and taken a cigarette lighter to them when that failed. The steel lift doors themselves were scarred deep with penknife graffiti.

As he waited, the young kid he'd been aware of furtively watching him for the last couple of minutes finally sidled into view.

"S'not workin' mister."

Lytton looked over and saw a miniature scally-in-the-making complete with baggy sweatpants tucked into his socks, a knock-off designer baseball cap and a roll-up pinched inside his cupped hand. He had the thin slightly rat-like features of a kid born premature doubtless due to the amount of booze his teenage mother put away while she carried him. They were told stunting the baby's growth made for an easier delivery.

Lytton gazed at him without expression. *Your life was over before it began.*

He had no illusions that the kid was being friendly. He knew he'd been sent either to scout him out or distract him so the heavy hitters could make their move. For those reasons he pointedly looked around before replying.

"Tell them it wouldn't be worth their while," he said keeping his voice flat and even.

The kid took a long seasoned drag of the roll-up and squinted through the smoke as he exhaled. He might not yet be in double figures but he'd spent a lifetime on the street—long enough to recognise the advice as a genuine warning.

The kid flashed him a dimpled grin then flicked the dog-end towards the gutter and swaggered away. A moment later two larger boys slipped out of the shadows and followed suit.

Amateurs.

Lytton watched them go and then headed for the stairs.

The flat he was after was on the fourth floor. The climb was enough to tell him all the units were rented rather than owned. Once the tenants were safely locked inside nobody gave a damn what was happening to the neighbours or the rest of the building. Still, the proportions of the place weren't bad and the area was beginning to level off before what Lytton predicted would be an upswing. He made a mental note to check out the finances of the current owner.

Maybe he'll want to sell—especially now.

Most of the numbers were missing but Lytton counted the doors to the one he wanted. It had been forced open and crudely secured with a hasp and staple but the padlock to connect the two was missing. The door was already ajar and something about that sent the hairs riffling at the back of his neck. There was a strong chemical smell leaching out through the gap, something astringent he couldn't immediately identify. He pushed the door open with his fingertips, stepped quietly inside.

Straight ahead along the hallway was an open door with light beyond. Lytton poked his head cautiously through the gap and found a living room with misted double-glazed doors standing open onto a tiny weather-beaten balcony. The room itself was overpowered by an ugly sofa and cheap bookcases. The empty shelves sagged as if still exhausted by the memory of books. The kitchen was off to one side separated by a narrow breakfast bar. The cupboard doors on the units badly needed realigning. Apart from an upturned plate rack on the drainer the room was devoid of the usual clutter of occupation.

Lytton turned back towards the front door. As he did so a figure moved out of one of the other rooms off the hallway. A woman, but unlike the boys near the lift there was nothing amateur about her. In her right hand was a tightly rolled magazine which she gripped like a relay-runner's baton.

"Miss Jacks," Lytton said gravely, eyeing her. "Do we shake hands or are you going to beat me into submission like a badly behaved dog?"

There was a long pause. "That depends if you're planning to make a mess on the carpet," she said. "I've spent all morning cleaning up."

Her voice was light but he caught the way her body uncoiled.

"I'm sorry. I didn't mean to alarm you," he said more sober now. "And don't worry—I'm reasonably well house-trained."

"I'm glad *somebody* is," she murmured.

He looked around. "What happened here?"

"Junkie suicide," she said distractedly. She was frowning. "What are *you* doing here?"

"I wanted to speak to you again."

Lytton watched her face as he spoke. There was no coy reaction and if anything her frown increased and became overlaid with wariness. Whatever value she put on herself it was not in her powers of attraction.

"How did you find me?"

"Via the woman in your office."

Kelly groaned. "It's an answering service. I will *so* have words with her later," she said. "No way is she supposed to give out that kind of information."

"I was at my most persuasive."

Kelly's glance told him she doubted that very much but she didn't say so out loud. She folded her arms, making her oversuit rustle like disapproving whispers.

"So … talk."

Lytton tried a smile. It bounced off.

"First off I wanted to say how sorry I was about your boss."

She stiffened—not the reaction he was expecting.

"'Sorry' how?" she demanded. "Sorry to hear what happened to him? Or that it was necessary?"

"Hey I—"

"And how did you know about it anyway? It only happened last night and I can't believe our office blabbermouth told you any details about *that*."

Temper flashed through him and died away just as fast.

"Don't you bloody start," he said tiredly. "I've just had the third-degree from some snotty policeman called O'Neill, that's how. And whether you choose to believe it, that's not how I do business." *Not if I can help it.*

She subsided slowly, almost with reluctance as though she'd been spoiling for a fight and was disappointed to be denied.

"I'm sorry," she said shortly. "Was that all? Only I'm on a bit of a deadline here."

"No it wasn't all. But don't let me stop you working while we talk. I'm sure a woman of your many talents numbers multi-tasking among them."

She skimmed her eyes over him briefly as if looking for any sign of mockery.

"Well, if you can stand the smell you're welcome to stay."

She put the magazine down next to the phone on the side table in the hall and jerked her head for him to follow. Lytton nodded to the gradually unfurling pages.

"Not the most lethal means of self-defence I've ever seen," he said.

Kelly's only response was a raised eyebrow, maybe the faintest quirk of the corner of her mouth. "You can punch one of those things through an internal door," she said in a voice that suggested she'd either seen or done it herself.

Probably best not to pursue that.

Inside the bedroom the chemical odour was so pungent it almost made his eyes water.

The room had been stripped clear. The walls glistened from wipe-down and even the skirting boards had been levered off. Close to one wall was an oval stain on the floor that had darkened to black.

"Is that—?"

"Blood? It was. Don't worry—it's all scrubbed and disinfected now."

"When you said this was a dead junkie I assumed he'd overdosed or something."

"He set off by swallowing, snorting or injecting his entire stash," she agreed. "But then he took a razor to his wrists and managed to slice through his radial artery. That's when he either panicked or changed his mind. He started out in the bathroom, searched the kitchen for a First-Aid kit." She nodded to the phone on the hall table. "He tried to call for help—forgetting his phone had already been cut off for non-payment—then collapsed on his bed and finished bleeding-out into the mattress."

Her matter-of-fact tone was more shocking somehow than the words themselves.

The landlord in Lytton compelled him to ask, "How long before he was found?"

"Two weeks," she said. "By which time the smell and the flies were too much for the neighbours to ignore any longer, even round here. They called the letting agent and he came round with a couple of guys and broke in." She paused and he thought he detected the vaguest hint of a smile. "We had to clean up their vomit as well."

"Speaking of 'we', where's your young apprentice today?"

The twinkle of amusement snuffed out and the caution was back. "Tyrone's taken the mattress and the rest of the contaminated waste for disposal. We have to use sites licenced for biohazardous material—it's not exactly the kind of thing you can dump in your local landfill." She peeled back her sleeve to glance at her watch. "I *was* expecting him back by now."

He looked at the oval stain again.

"It's a far cry from being a CSI, Kelly," he said quietly and noted the fractional pause.

"Not really. They're opposite ends of the same road wouldn't you say? As a CSI I'd be one of the first at a scene and working for Ray I'm one of the last." She shrugged. "Still the same scene though. The same tragedy."

"But it's no longer your responsibility to work out what happened is it?" he asked. "So what was it yesterday—old habits?"

She regarded him with steady eyes. They were nominally hazel he saw, but that didn't begin to describe the flecks of amber and gold and grey that radiated out from the centre.

"You've been digging, Mr Lytton."

When he'd had time to think about her name—about why it was familiar to him—he'd certainly had some digging done. There was plenty of info to go at. "Please, call me Matthew."

She gave a hollow laugh and drawled, "Oh yes, because first-name terms make insults and innuendo *so* much more civilised."

He leaned his shoulder against the door frame. "I didn't come here to insult you."

"Really?" She picked up a plastic drum with a hose and spray nozzle attached to the top of it, forced him to move aside so she could transfer it into the hall. "So why exactly *did* you trek all this way into London?"

"You saw things at the scene of my wife's death that all the other so-called experts missed," he said. "That made me curious."

Kelly picked up another chemical drum and brought it back into the bedroom. The drum was clearly full but she hefted it with practised ease. She might appear small, even delicate, but she had a deceptive strength that intrigued him.

"It's standard procedure to photograph the scene and email before-and-after pictures back to base for every job," she said at last. Her voice was both evasive and strangely bleak. "You may be giving credit where it isn't due."

He shook his head. "Your sidekick let it slip yesterday that *you* were the one who saw something and reported back, not the other way around. Why try to deny it now?"

She slammed the drum down so hard Lytton heard the contents slosh around inside. He hoped whatever was in there wasn't as volatile as Kelly herself.

"Because since then somebody beat the crap out of my boss—who also happens to be one of the few true friends I have—and in no uncertain terms warned him off. The only people who knew anything about it were us, the police, and you. So tell me, *Matthew,* in my position what would *you* do?"

—16—

HE COCKED HIS head on one side and regarded her with cool eyes that seemed to see right through her skin and lay bare all the insecurities beneath.

Then after a long lingering inspection he gave a crooked smile.

"Deny all knowledge and keep a low profile, probably," he admitted. "Is that what you're doing?"

Kelly tried to ignore the disappointment in his words—as if he'd hoped she had more spine.

Easy to think that way if you've never had to face the consequences.

She'd struggled hard not to show shock and anger at him turning up like this. Since her release she'd worked hard to guard her privacy. The thought of being so easily uncovered was … unsettling.

She turned away, unscrewed the cap on the drum and inserted a spray nozzle with a hand pump, tightening it down.

"You might want to suit up or stand well back—either that or leave," she said. "This sealant is strong stuff. Get it on those nice clothes and it won't come out."

If it had been her hope to make him go that was dashed when he retreated one small token pace and stopped on the far side of the threshold. For a moment she considered giving him an 'oops-sorry' squirt to see if that would get rid of him.

"Please—Kelly," he said then. "All I want is a few minutes of your time."

Just before he spoke she caught the brief swallow and something about the vulnerability of the gesture beneath all the cool bravado made the decision for her. Besides, if he had any funny ideas he'd very quickly discover that she was not an easy target.

Not anymore.

"You've got until I've finished up here," she said pumping the handle to pressurise the drum, not looking at him.

"To tell the truth I don't know where to start," he said. "I was hoping you might."

"My job as a CSI was to gather and interpret physical evidence—to work out *what* happened, not why it did."

"Even so, you're far closer to the process than I've ever been."

She began to spray the sealant in even strokes across the floorboards, starting in the far corner and working across.

"I might have been once but not anymore," she said and tried to keep the bitterness out of her voice. "I'm sorry. I can't help you. Now, if that's all ...?"

"No, it isn't." He let out his breath in an audible hiss and she tensed automatically. "I came to apologise," he said gently and Kelly felt her mouth fall open. The taste in the air was enough to shut it again fast. "For being brusque. Yesterday was a bitch to be frank, but that was no excuse to take it out on you and for that I'm sorry."

"Apology accepted," she said quickly. "I—"

"My wife is dead, Kelly," he said, pinning her with those mossy grey green eyes. "The police were convinced it was suicide but then you came along." He paused, chased and caught her gaze. "*You* came along telling me a different story. I think you know the truth about her. And I need to know what you think that is."

Kelly's mouth dried as her brain put instant interpretations and reinterpretations on his words.

Threat or plea?

"What if you don't want to know the truth?" she asked, scanning his face for another sign of his humanity. *Damn* but he was difficult to read. "Not really. Not deep down. Sometimes knowing for certain can be worse than not."

Lytton folded his arms and put his head on one side as he regarded her.

"Is that personal experience talking?" And when she shrugged he added, "I read the reports on your trial."

"What? How the hell did you—?"

"Google," he said shortly and once again she couldn't tell if that was a flippant answer or the truth. "Does your defence at the time still stand?"

Kelly's spine went rigid. She dragged the chemical drum across the floor so the spray nozzle would reach the far corner.

"That I simply have no memory of taking a life you mean?" She fought to keep her voice even and her mind objective. "That I don't know how—or why—I stabbed to death a complete stranger?"

He gave a fractional nod. "And are you still sure that not knowing is better?"

No! Kelly wanted to scream. *Because if I don't know how can I be sure it will never happen again?*

But instead she gave him a level stare as she pumped the pressure back up again. "If it turns out your wife was involved in something—something that led to her death—what then?"

Lytton was silent for a moment and it seemed to Kelly that his eyes lingered on the scrubbed and disinfected bloodstain across the old boards. She laid on another even coat letting the nozzle drift back and forth like a metronome.

"That I can only tell you once I know the answer," he said. Another twist of his lips that mocked himself as much as her. "And then, of course, it will be too late."

Kelly stopped and straightened. "So, what *was* she doing before her death? Was she stressed about something? Upset? Under pressure?"

He ran a hand through short dark hair that she could tell would start to wave if it was allowed to grow longer. His hands were big, wide across the palm from manual labour but long-fingered to give them proportion. He wore no rings.

She gave herself a mental shake, brought her concentration back on track.

"The police asked me all this at the time," Lytton was saying. "Veronica was organising the hospitality for a racing event we're sponsoring—horse racing," he added before Kelly could ask. "It's a major undertaking but gala dinners and hunt balls were part of her upbringing. She thrived on that kind of stuff."

"Did she?" Kelly challenged, hearing the hint of derision in his tone. "Perhaps that was your perception—your projection even. You needed her to do it so you convinced yourself she could cope."

His eyes narrowed. "She didn't *have* to do anything but *she* convinced *me* to let her take it on. I was going to contract the whole thing out—which is what I've subsequently done, before you ask."

"What else?"

"What else what?"

"What else did she do?"

"Charity work mostly. Worthy causes. And she did bits and pieces in the office—arranging my travel plans, sorting out company insurance. Just enough to justify being on the payroll and keep the taxman happy. Steve's wife does the same."

"Steve?"

"My business partner."

"But Steve's wife isn't involved in the hospitality for this race meeting?"

Lytton half-smiled. "English isn't Yana's first language and she's shy. I wouldn't even have suggested it," he said shortly. "She does a bit of filing, that's all—makes coffee, goes to the post. That kind of thing."

"Who benefits from Veronica's death?"

He laughed outright then and it was not a happy sound. "If you think I offed her for the insurance think again," he said. His tone had not only sharpened but hardened a little too, taking on a fine serrated edge that grated against Kelly's nerves. "Between us Steve and I have more life insurance than we know what to do with but they don't pay out on suicides. If that had been my angle I would have fixed the brakes on her bloody car, not—"

He broke off as if suddenly aware of what he might have been about to say. The silence stretched thick and dark between them.

"Did you love your wife, Matthew?" Kelly asked softly.

His head snapped up and he stared at her directly. Kelly met his gaze without flinching, refusing to be the first to look away.

62

Again she saw that haunted glimmer she'd picked up in the bathroom at his country house.

"I suppose so—in a way. But if you'd asked was I *in* love with her then ... no. It was mutual," he said tightly although with a candour that surprised her. "But I didn't wish her dead and as far as I knew that was mutual too."

"Was there anyone else in her life?" Kelly asked carefully but he just nodded as if he'd already considered the question and could do so again without heat.

In the time it took him to think about it she made the last couple of passes with the sealant spray-nozzle and moved the drum past him into the hallway.

"If she was having an affair they were being very discreet about it. Vee hated gossip."

"That doesn't necessarily mean whoever she might—or might not—have been involved with felt the same way," Kelly said. "Jealous rage is an age-old motive."

Lytton nodded, his face impassive. "I very much doubt Veronica was capable of inspiring such emotion but I'll make some enquiries," he said reminding her suddenly of the policeman O'Neill. "Anything else springs to your expert mind?"

A picture of Ray McCarron lying bruised and broken in his hospital bed. Of Ray telling her not to turn over rocks. She took a breath.

"As far as you know she wasn't stressed or desperate or having an affair. You didn't love her and you didn't hate her, and nobody else wanted her dead," Kelly murmured almost to herself. "Which only leaves ... you."

"Me?"

"Mmm," she said. "Have you thought that Veronica might have been killed to send you a message?"

"Really." His raised eyebrow denied it. "What kind of a message?"

That was as far as he got before thc front door of the flat swung open and two big heavyset men shoved their way inside.

TYRONE BOUNCED UP the stairs to the fourth floor taking them two at a time and not feeling the strain. He was pleased to note he even managed to whistle while he was doing it. All those early mornings spent pounding the running track at the Mile End Leisure Park were paying off.

He jogged along the corridor leading to the flat where they'd been working all morning hoping Kel wouldn't think he'd been loafing. He couldn't slice through traffic in the van quite like on the bike. Still, he couldn't get a blood-soaked mattress on the back of his old Honda either.

It was only when he got near the door that he heard voices inside the flat. Deep voices gruff from smoke and booze. The kind that came from men with thick necks and knuckles scarred from dragging along the pavement when they walked.

And Tyrone remembered what had been done to the boss— by big men who knew what they were about—and he slowed to a cautious shuffle along the cracked concrete.

Kelly!

He nudged the door open with the tips of his fingers and edged through suddenly wishing he was armed with something more than just the keys to the van. When he swallowed he found someone had sucked all the saliva out of his mouth when he wasn't looking.

A man stepped out of the open doorway to the bedroom and Tyrone almost thumped him in shock and reflex. The man seemed as surprised as he did.

Out of context it took Tyrone a second to place him as the Lytton guy with the massive country place who'd kicked up a stink about the bathroom where his missus blew her brains out—or had some help doing it, according to Kelly. Tyrone had no reason to doubt her word.

"What *you* doing here?" Tyrone asked roughly. "Where's Kelly."

"I'm just leaving," Lytton said. He jerked his head towards the bedroom. "She's in there."

As he brushed past Tyrone managed to register that whatever Lytton had come for he probably hadn't got—not if the scowl on his face was anything to go by.

So what was you after then?

Tyrone didn't stay to watch the man exit. He threw himself into the open doorway to the bedroom with the blood pumping hard in his ears and arms flexed to take on all-comers.

The occupants of the room jerked up fast as he burst in. The voices he'd heard belonged to two men who suited them—hard cases in black cargo pants and bomber jackets like nightclub bouncers. They were bent over Kelly who was crouched on the floor between them. Tyrone started forwards.

"Ah there you are Tyrone," Kelly said calmly getting to her feet. "Any problems?"

"Erm … no. All sorted."

"Good." She nodded, turned her attention back to the men. "As I was saying, you can't get blood out of floorboards but we've scrubbed and disinfected it so the floor structure won't be affected and as you can see with the coat of sealant I've sprayed on you can't tell it was ever there. Or more to the point your future tenants won't be able to tell. I'd leave it twenty-four hours before you put new carpet down just to let it harden completely."

"You've done a great job," said one of the men. "Couldn't believe the state of this place when the boss had us break in, could we Gary?"

"Shocking—it was rank in here," Gary agreed. "You've even got rid of the stench. No-one'd ever know."

"I'm glad you're satisfied," Kelly said. "I've checked with the office and the fee's already been transferred into our account so as soon as we've cleared out our gear you can re-secure the door."

"Cheers," said the first man. "You need a hand?"

"We can manage thanks," Kelly said when Tyrone would have taken them up on the offer. He didn't miss the pointed look she jabbed in his direction as she swung the drum of sealant up into his arms and gathered the rest of the stuff.

Uh-oh.

She didn't say nothing until they were back in the van and she was cranking up the motor. Then she sat back in her seat and sighed.

"Look Tyrone I know you're only looking out for me but you were lucky those two didn't rip your arms off when you came charging in like that. What were you thinking?"

He stared down at his hands and mumbled, "Dunno."

She sighed again.

"You're upset about Ray," she said. She put her hand on his arm and gave it a squeeze. "I am too. But you can't go for the clients Ty-ger or we'll be out of business in no time."

He nodded. Pleasure at the nickname warred with shame at the feeling he'd somehow let her down. He didn't speak again 'til they were cruising through traffic a few minutes later.

"So what was he doing back there—that Lytton guy?"

"To be honest I'm not entirely sure." She glanced across frowning. "He said he wanted to know what really happened to his wife."

Tyrone's head came up. "And you believe him?"

Kelly shrugged, her focus on changing lanes without swapping paint with the pushy courier who zipped alongside. "Believe him? Maybe," she said then. "But trust him?" She flashed a brief smile. "Not as far as I could throw him."

—18—

LYTTON WAS IN his Aston Martin DBS and north of the river heading through Belgravia before his cellphone rang. He touched the Receive button on the hands-free kit.

"Matthew Lytton."

"Matt!" Steve Warwick's voice boomed inside the car. "Where are you?"

"Near Victoria heading back to the apartment," he said. He checked the time on the classic analogue clock in the Aston's centre console. "Problems?"

"Just wondering how it went that's all," Warwick said breezily. "Come on, you can't yank me from my bed at an ungodly hour in the morning to run Internet searches for you on some mystery woman and not have me itching to know what came of it!" He gave a bark of laughter that sounded unduly harsh through the Aston's speakers. "So let's have it—did the lady succumb to your wicked charms?"

"Unlike you, Steve I'm not looking for submission in a woman," Lytton said dryly. "And if you're itching for anything you should try a course of antibiotics."

"Ha. Don't knock it 'til you've tried it old son."

Lytton braked hard to avoid a ubiquitous white-van man who swerved into his lane. It took a moment's continued static silence for him to realise Warwick was still on the line.

"Was there anything else Steve?"

"Not really," Warwick said casually. "It's just ... well, we can't afford to have anything rocking the boat—not right now. So if this bloody Mrs Mop is going to cause trouble do you want me to—?"

"Kelly Jacks won't be a problem," Lytton said. He changed down viciously and launched the big car through a closing gap between two buses that it had no right to make without a scratch. "Leave it to me—I can handle her."

—19—

ABOUT THE TIME Matthew Lytton was going hand-to-hand with the thickening rush of traffic near St James's Park—and Steve Warwick was sitting alone at his desk—the glamorous Myshka was still in bed.

She lay quietly luxuriating in a dockside penthouse that gave just as panoramic a view of London as Kelly's rooftop aerie, minutely aware of the silk sheets against her naked skin. And Myshka remembered a time when she'd been forced to don every piece of clothing she owned before climbing into bed at night. When not to do so was to risk freezing to death in her sleep.

She had vowed never to be cold like that again.

She stretched enjoying the sensuality of her surroundings. The bedroom was decadently large and decorated in a palette of muted creams and mushroom greys from the glossy doors of the wardrobes that stretched across one wall to the ridiculously deep pile carpet.

On the wall opposite the king-size bed hung a fifty-inch flatscreen TV. This, Myshka felt was an unnecessary indulgence. She had never got a kick out of porn—either watching it or taking part. So who needed a television that size in the bedroom where there were so many other avenues to be explored? But it was a small price to pay.

She turned her head on the pillow towards the wall of glass that looked out onto the immaculate roof garden and beyond over the river and the city. Lying between her and this magnificent view, snoring gustily, was the man she'd had sex with last night.

The price.

Myshka was ambivalent about sex, was neither enthralled nor appalled by it. It was simply a physical activity like Pilates or using a step machine—something that might be a little boring to undertake but the results were worth it. She'd learned to fake a convincing reaction she could never feel and viewed it simply as a means to an end.

On the bedside table her iPhone lit up and began to vibrate. She rolled over carefully and checked the display.

Dmitry.

Myshka slipped softly out of bed and thrust her arms into the sleeves of a thin emerald green kimono as she hurried out into the open living area with the phone still buzzing in her hand.

Dmitry sat at one end of the huge dining table, a copy of one of the financial papers spread out in front of him. He glanced up briefly and cancelled the call he'd made from his own phone.

Myshka hid her outrage and finished putting on the robe without hurry or embarrassment. She was after all used to men seeing her naked. Dmitry, to her amusement—or was it irritation?—studiously kept his eyes on the newsprint in front of him.

"Let yourself in, why do you not?" she said haughtily as she swept past him into the ultramodern stark white kitchen area. "Make yourself at home."

"As *you* do," Dmitry fired back. He indicated the closed bedroom door with a sullen jerk of his head. "You'd rather I rang the doorbell?"

Just because he had a valid point that didn't mean Myshka was prepared to let him off the hook. "Why are you here?"

He showed his teeth, more snarl than smile. "Duty calls. I answer."

Her annoyance waned. She crossed to him put her arms around his neck and kissed the top of his head, rocking him to her breast. He gripped her arm and squeezed tight for a second and she felt the tension go out of him.

"I do not like to think of you ... with him," he said at last, his voice muffled against her chest.

"Soon, Dmitry," she murmured.

He stiffened, frowning. "Myshka—"

"Hush." She bent her face close to his roughened cheek and put a finger to his lips. "Soon this will all be over and we will be free together I promise."

He twitched and she let him go, straightened. For the first time she saw doubt in his eyes and with a flash of intuition knew the cause. Whatever faults and flaws Dmitry might possess, disloyalty was not one of them.

"He does not appreciate all that you do for him," she said then, fiercely. "He wastes your talents."

Dmitry raked a hand through his hair and stared back down at the newspaper columns. A bitter smile twisted the side of his face. "Perhaps you could speak with him—put in a good word on my behalf then it would not be—"

"If I thought for a moment he would listen to me I would do so."

Dmitry gave a short laugh. "If you do not have his ear who does?"

"You know as well as I do that he listens only to the sound of money," she dismissed. "And he thinks only of how to increase it."

Not entirely true but true enough for this purpose. Besides it *was* entirely true that Dmitry was being taken advantage of. His contacts had been plundered, his authority frittered away until all he could be was his new master's lap dog.

She moved back into the kitchen area partly so he wouldn't see the sudden clench of her fingers and busied herself with the espresso machine. While it gurgled through its cycle she picked up her cigarettes and gold lighter from the countertop, headed for one of the huge sliding panels of glass. There she turned, struck an imperious pose, flicked her fingers.

"Come."

Dmitry raised his head and looked at her with the blank cold stare of the killer she knew him to be. She shivered in glorious relief.

"Good," she said with a short nod. "So you have not yet acquired the spine of a jelly baby."

For a moment he stiffened then a gradual smile widened his mouth. And although he made an annoyed sound in his throat she knew the moment of strain between them had passed.

"Do you not mean jelly*fish*?"

He folded the paper neatly, rose with the economy of movement she'd always admired and opened the window for her, standing aside with a mockingly gallant bow.

She gave him another slight regal nod and stepped out onto the roof terrace. It was too chilly to be comfortable and she shivered again with less enjoyment this time and wrapped the kimono closer to her body.

Dmitry shrugged out of his leather coat and draped it around her shoulders. She took it as her due, folded herself into one of the cushioned rattan chairs and reached for the cigarette pack. Dmitry lit for both of them.

As the first hit of nicotine curled into her lungs Myshka regarded him through a whisper of smoke.

"The danger from Veronica Lytton may not be over," she said.

Dmitry raised an eyebrow. "I do not think McCarron will pursue things," he said easily. "I was very ... persuasive."

"He is not the problem. The bitch who works for him, *she* may be."

"London can be a dangerous city for a woman to live in," Dmitry said meaningfully, sitting back in his chair. "Anyone can become a victim of violent crime. It's shocking."

Myshka smiled. Sometimes Dmitry had such a simple answer to every question. If she wasn't around to rein him in, she mused there would be a trail of blood behind him wherever he went.

"It cannot be handled like that. Not this time." She shook her head, regretful. "There is a policeman—how do you say?—sniffing around her. Another 'accident' and even *he* may become suspicious."

Dmitry showed his teeth. "Being a policeman can be a dangerous job also," he offered.

Myshka laughed out loud, put a hand on his knee briefly. "There is no need," she said. "Certain *information* has come to light about the woman. If we are clever we can use it to deal with everyone involved at one time."

She leaned forwards in her chair tilted her cigarette into an ashtray and told him, keeping her voice low and focused, everything that Steve Warwick had uncovered about an ex-CSI called Kelly Jacks. And about the plan that had come to Myshka after she had climbed back into bed this morning and lay sleeplessly alongside her lover.

When she was done, her cigarette had smouldered into ash and Dmitry's face was creased in concentration.

"It's too complicated," he said doubtfully.

"No—don't you see? Is simple," she argued, conviction in her voice. "Dmitry, is *perfect*. There will not be a better way."

He was silent, staring downward into empty space. She knew him well enough to let him think it through in his own time. So she rose, leaving his leather coat on the chair, and went back indoors closing the sliding window behind her.

She was pouring coffee when Dmitry opened the glass and stepped back inside.

"You are right—as always," he said without expression. "It *is* perfect. But—"

"What is?"

71

The voice made them both turn. Harry Grogan stood in the bedroom doorway, his skin still pink from too hot a shower, fastening cufflinks at the wrists of another handmade shirt.

"A gift," Myshka said smoothly. "Dmitry has a special girl. He asked my advice on what would ... please her."

Grogan regarded the pair of them for a moment unsmiling, adjusted his tie. "Well you should know sweetheart." He nodded to Dmitry. "Tell Viktor to bring the car round and wait," he said. "I'll be down in ten minutes."

Dmitry nodded, his own face carefully expressionless. "Of course."

But Grogan's eyes were on Myshka. She had allowed the front edges of the green kimono to slide provocatively apart almost to her naval. "Is that coffee fresh?" he asked. "Bring me a cup into the study there's a love. I've a couple of calls to make." And with that he disappeared back into the bedroom.

Myshka tightened the thin robe again, aware of an aching stab both of relief and disappointment.

Dmitry gathered up his newspaper from the table and nudged her under the chin with his forefinger as he came past.

"Do not worry," he murmured. "I know what needs to be done and I will see to it."

And if there had been any lingering uncertainty in his tone when he had come back in from the roof terrace it was gone now.

—20—

KELLY LIFTED THE steam vacuum into the back of the van and peeled off her nitrile gloves. Behind her, Tyrone appeared in the doorway leading to the flats carrying a drum of enzyme cleaner and the sharps' bin.

He swung the two items easily up into the back of the van and hopped in after to secure them. Kelly noticed he'd split the back seam of another Tyvek suit. She really would have to speak to Ray about getting hold of a better range of sizes.

Her face clouded briefly at the thought of her boss. They'd kept him in awaiting surgery on his shattered elbow. She'd been to the hospital to see him again this morning. He was still groggy and in a lot of pain although they were talking about letting him out at the weekend. She made a mental note to go round if they did, take him some food. He wouldn't be up to looking after himself for a while.

The letting agent hovered from foot to foot while she filled in the paperwork for him to sign. He was far less appreciative of their efforts than Gary and his mate at the flat south of the River. Kelly didn't need to be told that he was desperate to get them out of here now the job was done.

The flat they'd just sanitised had not been the scene of a crime other than bad judgement. It had been mistakenly let to a pair of drug addicts who had eventually trashed the place before scarpering, several months behind on the rent.

Normal cleaning firms baulked at dealing with contaminated needle debris. The letting agent had admitted—eventually—that he'd discovered one of the tenants was positive for either HIV or hepatitis. He claimed not to know which.

Kelly made a guess that he'd failed to report any of this to his superiors or the building owner and was paying for the clean-up out of his own pocket. Hence the undue haggling about the price.

Even now he had a nervous twitch about him that Kelly recognised.

"You've agreed you're satisfied with the job and we specified payment on completion so I'll take that now OK?" she said offering him the clipboard and pen. "Cash or credit card will be fine."

"Look if I don't need an official receipt surely we can ... come to some kind of arrangement about the price eh?" he said with a nervous laugh. "I mean you guys aren't cheap but if it's cash you must be able to do better than the estimate."

Without taking her eyes off him Kelly said over her shoulder, "Tyrone take the sharps' bin of contaminated needles back upstairs and empty it out will you?"

"No problem Kel," Tyrone said cheerfully. "I'll spread 'em around the place just like we found 'em. You want me to dump the lot?"

"That depends on how much discount we're being asked to give," she said.

The letting agent stared in horror as Tyrone stepped down out of the van carrying the container plastered with large yellow warning labels for blood-borne infection.

"Now wait a minute—"

Kelly held up a finger cutting him dead. "A hundred percent of the price *you* agreed to gets you a hundred percent of the job," she said firmly. "Any less and you'll need to get your rubber gloves out and hope your shots are up to date. Your choice."

The man was small and thin, narrow-featured except for his ears which stuck out far enough to glow pinkly when he stood with his back to the light. He scowled furiously but couldn't take his eyes off the additional stickers on the bin that warned of serious health risks from the contents. He scrabbled for his wallet and waited impatiently while Kelly ran his credit card details.

As soon as she was done he snatched back the card and hurried away to lock up, looking over his shoulder furtively as he did so.

Tyrone heaved the sharps' bin back into the van and grinned at her. "Don't think we'll get much word of mouth from this one, yeah?"

"Oh, I don't know," she said sitting on the edge of the load bay to strip her own suit over the booties, making sure it stayed inside out as it came off. Ray was fanatical about ensuring not just his licences stayed unblemished but that his staff protected themselves from infection as well. "You'd be amazed who he might come into contact with."

Tyrone's own gear went into the bin for biohazard waste disposal too. "Might have been talking already," he said then quietly leaning towards her. "There's a guy sitting in an old Merc across the road—been watching this place all day."

Kelly followed his casual nod and noticed a pimped-up black Mercedes coupé on wheels so large they barely fitted under the chrome spats on the arches. The limo-black tint on the glass made it impossible to see the driver but as she turned to follow Tyrone's gaze the engine fired and the car pulled out sharply into traffic.

She stared after the disappearing taillights, frowning. The car was distinctive and she could have sworn she'd seen it earlier in the day as they headed out towards Dartford but hadn't caught the reg number.

Coincidence?

She felt cold fingers walk slowly and deliberately down her spine.

What else could it be?

"That us done for this afternoon, is it?" Tyrone asked then, trying and failing to keep the hopeful note out of his voice. "Only, I'm playing in a pub league five-a-side this Sunday. I said I'd try and get to practice early tonight."

Kelly checked her watch. "You can scoot off as soon as we get back to the office if you like," she offered. "I'll put the report in and restock the van."

He grinned. "You're a real star Kel, y'know that?"

She cocked her head on one side. "What—very dim and far away?"

Traffic was bad on the way home and driving the large van took up most of Kelly's concentration. She kept a watchful eye out for the black Mercedes but decided that either it was indeed a coincidence or the driver had been more interested in the property they'd just cleaned.

Either way, she didn't see it again.

—21—

DMITRY HAD NO need to observe the two cleaners more than he had done. He'd seen enough to know they turned up together and worked without outside supervision.

What more did he need to know?

So he waited until it was dark before heading out to the East End listening to hip-hop on the Merc's expensive stereo. He kept the volume at a level where it would not intrude outside the car. It irritated him to sit next to some vibrating boom-box at traffic lights, the occupants' baseball-capped heads bobbing in time with the distorted music.

Back home he'd have killed them for such an intrusion.

But he liked driving at night through the darkened streets of the city. It made him feel like some kind of avenging angel searching out the weak and the damaged.

In this case the weak and damaged were to be found on waste ground near the river on the Isle of Dogs, huddled round perforated oil drums filled with scavenged timber lit for warmth. The homeless, the hopeless, the repossessed and the dispossessed. They shuffled together after dark like the walking dead to remember old stories and forget new ones with any kind of brew that would fire them from the inside out.

As he approached on foot across the rough ground the smell of the derelicts was acrid in Dmitry's nostrils even from a distance but he had smelled worse. He waited a long time in the shadows for suitable prey to make itself apparent. To split from the herd.

He wanted an older man so he'd be easy to overpower, and skinny enough that he'd be easy to carry. And already drunk so it wouldn't take long.

In his jacket pocket Dmitry had a half bottle of Bacardi 151 overproof rum which at more than seventy-five percent ABV was enough to have an effect even on the most hardened of drinkers.

Just in case, folded up inside his jacket was a plastic body bag.

Over by one of the oil-drum braziers an argument of sorts broke out. Raised voices and shoving until one old guy with straggly grey hair and a long matted beard found himself scuffled out and away from the fire. He made a couple of half-hearted attempts to regain his place but soon gave up the fight. As he shambled away into the shadows he continued to curse and gesticulate wildly.

Watching from the darkness, Dmitry smiled.

—22—

THE FIRE WAS called in anonymously from a public call box—one of the few still functioning in that area of Millwall—and logged at 2:26 AM. The caller was male with what the operator judged to be a slight eastern European accent. Maybe an asylum seeker? It was no surprise that he rang off without leaving a name.

A single appliance was dispatched to the address given which turned out to be a partially completed warehouse conversion near the River Park Trading Estate. There firefighters discovered the burning body of an elderly male sitting propped against a steel pillar in an unfinished office on an upper floor of the building.

He was firmly ablaze but the lack of combustible materials nearby prevented the spread of the fire which was quickly extinguished. Broken glass alongside the charred corpse was identified as a container for a particularly potent brand of rum so highly flammable it came with a flame-arrester on the bottle.

The police were called in as matter of course but the uniformed officers who attended were not about to launch an investigation for one dead tramp. As far as they were concerned the spilt booze, tin of tobacco and dog-eared book of matches found told the story.

After a cursory examination by the pathologist the body was scraped up and removed. A lone constable was left at the scene with the task of trying to track down the owner of the building—some faceless development company.

The following morning he eventually managed to find a number for a real person instead of an answering service and received assurances that somebody would be down immediately to secure the building.

By 8:30 AM upper management had been copied in on an email regarding the damage.

At 9:00 AM, after consulting with the development company's parent corporation in Sweden, a recommendation for a firm of specialist cleaners was passed down.

At 9:15 AM the phone on Ray McCarron's desk began to ring.

"BLOODY HELL, HOW can you not notice you've set yourself on fire?" Tyrone wondered aloud as Kelly indicated and turned into the approach road leading to the trading estate.

"People fall asleep and start fires with dropped cigarettes every day," she replied. "And when you've pickled yourself in industrial-strength alcohol beforehand ..."

"Yeah but if he was *so* drunk he was like, passed out, how did he manage to be lighting up a cigarette when he went boom?"

He glanced across from the passenger seat of the McCarron van and noticed Kelly frowning again the way she had done when she'd first looked at the bathroom at the Lyttons' country place.

She pulled up outside the old warehouse where the dead guy had been found and leaned forwards to gaze up at the largely glassless windows. "Maybe we're about to find out."

They climbed out, suited up and gathered their gear.

As they walked in, began to climb the stairs to the upper floor, Kelly asked, "How was footie practice last night by the way?"

"Stormin'. We're gonna *murder* them next weekend I'm telling you," Tyrone said turning back to flash a satisfied grin down at her. He paused, took a breath. "Hey Kel, you should maybe come and watch."

"Be some kind of cheerleader you mean?"

"Oh yeah!"

She gave a self-deprecatory snort. "I think I'm a bit old for a short skirt and a set of pompoms, don't you?"

"No way!" Tyrone protested unable to entirely keep the longing out of his voice. "You'd look *well* spanking."

Kelly grinned back at him, a kind of teasing sexy grin. "You say that like it's a good thing."

"'Course it is." Tyrone felt his ears heat and was glad she couldn't see it. He'd had more than one little daydream fantasy where Kelly came and watched him score the victory goal from the touchline and he got to take her home on the back of his bike after.

OK so *that* wasn't going to happen he thought ruefully, shouldering open a fire door on the landing. The closest he'd got to her was a slow dance at the office Christmas party. But it would still be cool if she *could* make it to a game. In fact the only reason it might *not* be a good idea was because he'd never keep his mind on the ball. Saying that, none of the opposing team would be able to either, so—

The blow took him completely by surprise. To begin with he wasn't even aware of being hit, only a fierce jolt of some kind and the bare concrete floor coming up fast to smack him across both knees.

He felt something serious give way inside the left joint and his only thought was, *Ah bollocks. There goes Sunday's match.*

Then he was down on his side, grit scouring his cheek. The whole back half of his skull felt as if it had shattered and the pieces were pressing into his brain, building up into pain so bad it paralysed his limbs.

He blinked slowly and saw a world operating at ninety degrees out of kilter. It looked like Kelly was standing on the wall like in some bizarre sci-fi movie. She was locked in dirty hand-to-hand with a couple of guys who also seemed to be wearing Tyvek suits.

This puzzled him. Surely the only people who wore those disposable suits were the good guys? He knew Kelly shouldn't be fighting with them or they'd never get the job done and then the boss would be annoyed. And Mr McCarron was definitely one of the good guys.

He wanted to yell at the men that he and Kelly were the good guys too but his voice was outside him, too far to call back.

Either way they had her on her knees now and he could see her mouth working but could hear no sound coming out. He saw one of the men rip back her sleeve baring her arm and if anything Kelly's thrashing increased. Tyrone was aware of admiration despite his haziness. She was a tiger all right was Kel.

But even as he silently cheered her on she seemed to fade, losing coordination and focus, the fight going out of her.

Come on Kel, don't let the bastards beat you!

A pair of Tyvek legs and bootie-clad feet momentarily blocked his view and Tyrone even found himself feeling vaguely annoyed about that. Then he noticed the blade of the knife lying flat against the newcomer's leg. His gaze swivelled sluggishly upwards and saw a distant face above. A cold calm face that he knew would show no mercy.

Tyrone felt tears of fear and frustration burn his eyes, tried to get his hands underneath him to press upwards and found nothing worked.

As the man with the knife stood over him the others dragged Kelly over, her feet bumping loosely against the concrete. They put her on her knees alongside him, hands slack in her lap.

Tyrone's eyes sought her face in desperation but the Kelly he knew wasn't inside the face anymore. There was nobody he recognised behind those glazed golden brown eyes.

Terror clawed into Tyrone's chest scraping it raw from the inside out, bubbling up his throat, but there was nothing he could do.

The man with the knife bent over him and Tyrone discovered right in his last moments that death *did* faze him, after all.

—24—

KELLY WOKE TO the smell of blood, a knife in her hand.

—25—

"EMERGENCY SERVICES. WHICH service do you require?"

"Police," said a man's voice. Voice analysis experts would later identify his accent as Russian. "There has been a death—a man has been stabbed."

"OK sir, stay on the line. I'm putting you through—

"There is no time. If you hurry you may catch the person responsible, yes?"

"Where are you sir?"

"Don't waste time. I am in a call box and the number will be on your screens. I have just seen a murder."

He gave the address and rang off resisting all efforts to extract his name or keep him talking.

An exploded gas main and a minor coach crash had local resources tied up longer than they anticipated. It was not until seventeen minutes after the triple-nine call that a patrol was dispatched.

—26—

KELLY SAT BACK on her heels, gazing down stupidly at the knife and the blood.

Part of her brain was screaming at her to move, to *do* something. Another part registered the characteristics of the weapon with an almost clinical detachment. A combat survival knife with an eight-inch blade partially serrated along the back edge. Small rips of flesh and skin from the victim still clung to those serrations.

And yet another part of her mind cried over and over *No no. NO! Not again …*

It took longer than it had any right to for Kelly to get her feet under her. Her balance was shot. Upright, swaying, she realised she was still clutching the knife tight in her right hand. She bent and put it down with ingrained care for the evidence it contained. The floor tilted crazily underneath her. She staggered and almost fell.

Oh God what have I done?

Fragments came back to her, a disconnected vision of blonde girls in college shirts performing high kicks on a sports field. Kelly frowned. What the hell did that have to do with anything? But a moment later the association of words clicked in one after another like the tumblers of a lock.

Cheerleaders. Football. Wrong football—soccer.

Tyrone.

"Ty?" she called, her voice rising raspily. "Tyrone! Where are you?"

She managed a couple of steps reaching for one of the pillars and leaving a bloody smear across its crumbling paintwork. She was, she recognised casting a trail of physical evidence that was a CSI's dream.

"Tyrone?" she shouted again, fear making her tone sharper, more desperate. A couple of pigeons scattered in fright at the sound of it.

Across by another pillar she saw a blackened mess, making her heart bound into her throat and pump there ferociously. Something had burned with a fierce intense heat, greying at the centre and leaching out towards the edges so that tatters of material remained along with zippers and a belt buckle.

A man died here. It came back to her suddenly, a whole formed idea. And with it a partial sequence of events. Of her and Tyrone arriving in the van, just another job, of climbing the stairs.

We came through the doorway talking about football ... What happened next?

And then she saw him.

Tyrone was lying on his back near the doorway to the stairwell. He was very still.

Kelly stumbled across to him weaving drunkenly. She didn't need to drop to her knees alongside him to know for certain he was dead but she did it anyway.

What have I done?

Tears welled in her eyes blurring her vision but she would not allow them to fall. It had been a long time since Kelly had wept for anyone or anything. She had thought herself all cried out.

"No," she said aloud her jaw bowstring taut. "No I did *not* do this. Not to Tyrone. No way."

Why not? Do you think you could kill a stranger but not a friend? Who are you trying to convince?

She bit her lip, forced herself to look at Tyrone's body. His Tyvek oversuit was slashed and torn in at least a dozen places across his torso and upper thighs. The placing and number of the wounds was horribly familiar. A frenzied attack by someone possibly out of their mind. Someone suffering a psychotic episode.

The blood had pooled and spread until the front of Tyrone's suit had a solid dark red sheen already shading to black. It had haloed around his body, leaching into the dusty concrete particularly around his head.

There's another injury there. The realisation came almost automatically. *Blunt-force trauma?* Tyrone was not the type to go down without a fight but he had fewer defensive wounds than she would have expected. So they'd hit him first—hard enough to put him down where they could do with him as they wished.

Just because he didn't fight back might mean he didn't want to not that he couldn't whispered a vindictive voice inside her. *Like maybe he didn't believe someone he thought he knew—someone he worked alongside every day—would try to kill him.*

"Concentrate dammit," Kelly muttered.

She examined every inch of the floor surrounding Tyrone's body noting the extent of the blood pool, the level of clotting.

She crouched and tentatively touched the backs of her fingers to his cheek. His skin was cool to the touch.

Too long. Too late …

She took a couple of attempts to rise again and made it only then because she clung to the wall by the doorway. Her hand slipped, snagging at her palm. When she looked she found it already grazed from—

A jagged image flashed into her mind of trying to grab at the rough surface and being dragged away by a fist wrapped in her hair. She reached up, found a tender patch on her scalp.

"I did not do this."

The words echoed in the blank space, but this time—for the first time—they held conviction.

—27—

THE PATROL DISPATCHED in response to the anonymous triple-nine call sat in traffic within sight of Tower Bridge.

Behind the wheel was a veteran called Ferris with an undistinguished twenty-three-year career behind him of quietly doing as little as he could get away with. He liked the uniform and the weight that came with it but had long abandoned any kind of ambitions for advancement.

Alongside him twitching in the passenger seat was an overly keen probationer called Jacobson who was still desperate to make a name for himself. Probably—as Ferris had commented cynically in the canteen only that morning—by doing something heroically daft that would read out in glowing terms at his memorial service.

"Come on mate. Use your blues and twos can't you?" Jacobson protested now. "It's an emergency isn't it?"

"And where exactly are all this lot going to go to get out of our way?" Ferris rolled his eyes and flapped a hand towards the line of brake lights visible head. "It's not like the movies son."

Jacobson huffed out a breath. "I know that but—"

"When you've been on the job as long as I have you'll know that half these supposed emergency calls are hoaxes anyway. Relax. Cop a load of that little darling in the scarlet mini-dress. I wouldn't mind doing a stop and search on her."

"If half the calls are hoaxes that still means half of them are genuine," Jacobson said stubbornly through his teeth.

"All right, all right. No need to get your knickers in a twist." Ferris grinned. "If it makes you feel any better ..." He hit the lights and the siren.

The car in front lurched forwards and to the side maybe two feet before it came to a stop unable to go any further.

"See?" Ferris said. "Now we've just pissed everybody off. They think you just want to get back to the station for your tea break." Which, he thought, was not a bad idea.

In the passenger seat Jacobson fumed silently.

—28—

THE REALISATION OF her own innocence brought Kelly far closer to weeping than the fear of her own guilt.

She fought not to let it out, not to break down and let the shakes take her. Because if she had not killed Tyrone in a rabid attack then somebody else had.

84

And that somebody had left the murder weapon in her hand.

It did not take a genius to work out that whoever had set this up so carefully to mirror her earlier crime would hardly then leave it to chance for her to be caught.

I don't have much time.

Kelly pressed the back of her clenched fist to her forehead willing clarity of thought but her mind still seemed to be functioning with a wretched slowness. Otherwise, why did it take her so long to come to another obvious conclusion?

They gave me something to knock me out—to make me forget.

Her defence counsel had insisted on a tox screen last time but it had been carried out with obvious reluctance after a long delay and the testing had been stingily brief. That it came back negative for any illegal substances which might have explained her actions came as no surprise to anyone. By that time not even to Kelly herself.

This time she swore there would be no such delays. Carefully she let go of the wall and tried an unaided step. Then another, and another.

Her legs still did not feel as though they entirely belonged to her but it was getting better.

And if it's getting better that means whatever's in your system is disappearing fast.

She turned. Their clean-up kit was still lying where they must have dropped it when they were attacked. She made it across and opened the handles. Inside was a roll of clear plastic ziplock bags which they used for collecting biological debris. Would it be strong enough?

Kelly shrugged. It was all she had. But when she searched through the kit she couldn't find any kind of a blade. Then she caught sight of the bloodied knife still lying where she'd put it down and made an instant decision.

She picked up the knife and took a sterile wipe out of the kit. It grieved her to do this but she had no choice. With great care and attention to detail she cleaned every scrap of Tyrone's blood and tissue from the blade.

Then she gripped the handle firmly in her right hand, opened up one of the bags and drew the tip of the knife sharply across the exposed skin of her left forearm before she lost her nerve.

For a moment there was only a thin red line then the blood began to swell out. It ran around her arm and dripped into the bag she quickly held below it. The wound burned and stung but she flexed her fingers to maintain the flow. It felt disturbingly hot against her skin.

By this clumsy and highly unscientific method she managed to fill a corner of the bag with her own blood. More than enough, she thought fiercely, to test for Rohypnol or something similar.

What makes you think they'll go that far? After last time do you think they'll bother wasting resources on lab work to tell them what they think they know already?

No, she realised. *They won't.*

Kelly had never thought of herself as squeamish—it wasn't a luxury she'd ever allowed. But even she could not suppress a small shudder when she unpeeled a fresh bag from the roll and forced the clotting wound open for a second time.

—29—

IT TOOK CONSTABLES Ferris and Jacobson thirty-four minutes to arrive at the location. It was an unpromising-looking warehouse building obviously in the midst of renovation into offices. The only commercial vehicle parked at that end of the estate was a big van belonging to some cleaning company.

Still, they'd had the additional information on the way over that there had been a death at the same place only the day before. That one was all done and dusted and the scene handed back to the building owner.

"This'll be just another wino most likely," Ferris said with a dismissive sniff as they pulled up outside. Jacobson, he noticed with a sneer, screwed his peaked cap firmly into place as soon as he stepped out of the car.

You'll learn.

Despite his casual comments Ferris kept one hand on the baton at his belt as he entered the building. The crunch of his boots on the gritty surface was much too loud.

"Police officers," Jacobson shouted behind him, a slightly squeaky note in his voice betraying his apprehension. "Show yourself!"

"Oh yeah 'cause *that* works every time." Ferris abandoned the quiet approach and stumped up the concrete stairs. On the first floor landing was a fire door. Ferris kicked it open and peered through without immediately going in. It swung shut again on a self-closing mechanism.

Nobody launched any kind of attack but what Ferris saw in that brief closing snapshot made him hesitate before trying the door a second time.

This was no hoax.

"Call for backup," he told Jacobson in an urgent whisper. "Do it now!"

Behind him he heard the youngster fumbling through the radio message.

Not so bloody keen now are you mate?

Ferris didn't want to go in there either but at least he'd never pretended any different. He drew the baton, flicked it down and away so it locked out fully extended, then nudged the door open again.

Despite his hopes for an optical illusion the slashed corpse was still lying where he'd glimpsed it. He tore his eyes away and gave the rest of the open space a thorough scan just to be sure they weren't about to get jumped themselves. Apart from a couple of pigeons scuttering up around the rafters like grubby flying rats the place was deserted.

Jacobson came in behind him with all the enthusiasm of a man edging out onto a narrow ledge above a long drop.

"Aw ... Jesus Christ," he gulped when he saw the body.

Although Ferris knew he'd be giving Jacobson some stick for a long time to come over his reaction, deep down he couldn't blame the lad. It was a bad one, no doubt about that, with the gaping wounds and the blood. Like the work of a madman.

Death made it hard to put an age on what had once been a person but he realised this guy had probably been no more than a teenager despite his size.

"Drug deal most likely," he declared, taking in the dead kid's race. Jacobson was studiously checking out everywhere but the body.

Next to it lay the knife that had made such short work of the victim, the blade gleaming like evil chrome.

"Wiped clean by the looks of it," Ferris said, more to make Jacobson look than anything else. *No surprises there—all the little scumbags watch the TV forensics' shows these days.*

But what did make him rock back, shocked, was the object that had been placed on the corpse's ragged chest.

"What the ...?"

It was a clear plastic bag containing a greasy puddle of blood like you sometimes got around vacuum-packed meat in the supermarket. And on the bag was scrawled a message in black marker pen. A confession? Or a denial?

I DID NOT DO THIS.

—30—

BALANCED ON A couple of inches of protruding brickwork outside one of the glassless windows with her fingertips wedged into a crumbling mortar joint Kelly listened to the policeman's shocked exclamation.

She closed her eyes, tried to relax to regulate her breathing and control her panic. Not easy when she was suspended between her outstretched arms, one leg crossed behind her for balance, foot pointed. It was twenty feet or so to the ground—a dangerous distance. Not far enough to kill her unless she was unlucky, but injury was a certainty.

The only way to go was up.

Still she hesitated, aware of the muffled squawk of the police radios just inside the building. All her life she'd thought those in authority knew best. She had trusted them to do the right thing by her.

Until she'd put that trust to the ultimate test and they had failed her.

Nevertheless her first instinct when she'd heard the car draw up below and seen the policemen emerge to head so obviously in her direction was to give herself up.

That instinct lasted for only a few seconds and was disregarded by her scornful inner voice of reason.

Yeah, because look how well that *worked out for you last time.*

Kelly opened her eyes, carefully unclamped the whitened finger ends of her lower hand from the edge of the brick and stretched up for the next handhold.

She had already jettisoned the bloodstained Tyvek oversuit, letting it go from the window before she'd climbed out of the aperture. The breeze coming up from the river had caught it almost instantly, semi-inflating it like some weird balloon and sending it billowing skywards.

Inside her shirt, still warm next to her skin, was the second bag of her own blood. She needed to hang on to that at all costs.

She'd bound up the gash on her arm with the heavy duty duct tape they always carried in the cleaning kit. The last thing McCarron's reputation could afford was to leave a trail of decomposing fluids as they carted disposal bags out to the van and duct tape was sure to seal any leaks.

Right now Kelly was more worried about remaining at liberty until she'd had the opportunity to get the blood independently tested.

She moved with desperate caution knowing any slip would send loose grit and dust scattering down the outside of the building. With no glass to damp out the sound they were bound to hear her.

But she climbed almost every day—not rock but urban faces like this one. She willed herself to stay calm, to pretend there was nothing more at stake than gaining a high place from which to enjoy the view.

Who are you trying to kid?

With a grim twist of her lips that became more grimace than smile she reached the sagging line of the gutter. And from below she could see that the rusted fastenings were mostly loose in the powdery brickwork. There was no way she could use it to lever herself onto the roof.

Kelly bit back a groan of frustration. She was running out of both time and options. The tension was making her muscles quiver with the effort of holding herself flattened against the wall. That and the after-effects of whatever muck they'd pumped into her system. She couldn't stay here much longer.

She glanced quickly each way and saw a threaded rod sticking a few inches out of the wall about three or four feet to one side—part of a steel tie put in some time earlier to stop the old building bulging out of shape.

With the last of her strength Kelly swung for it.

—31—

"WHAT WAS THAT?" PC Jacobson demanded, jerking round.

"What was what?"

"I dunno. I heard something—from outside I think."

PC Ferris gave a dry chuckle. "You're getting jumpy my son," he said. But when Jacobson still faltered he waved a hand towards the open windows. "Go on, have a gander if you're so sure you heard something."

"Probably nothing," Jacobson muttered but he went across to the line of windows in the back wall of the building. Anything was better than standing around trying not to look at the dead body while they waited for the promised reinforcements.

He stuck his head out with great care, only enough to expose one eye. There was no fire escape or other means of easy egress. He even craned his neck to look up and saw nothing but yet more pigeons squabbling over window ledge territory rights above him. Jacobson drew his head inside quickly. He'd no desire to get dumped on even if it *was* supposed to be lucky.

"Well?" Ferris said with a distinct taunt in his voice.

"Nothing," Jacobson admitted. "Must have gone well before we got here, eh?"

And if both men felt a sense of relief at this thought neither was prepared to admit it to the other.

—32—

DMITRY SAW THE flashing blue lights in his rearview mirror and pulled the big Mercedes coupé over as far as he could on the crowded street.

The full-dress squad car came bowling past him, the sound of its siren fading rapidly into the distance as it was swallowed up by the buildings and the other vehicles. Still, it didn't take a genius to work out where the car was heading.

Dmitry checked his mirrors again and sedately pulled back into the traffic flow.

He hit one of the speed-dial buttons on the cellphone sitting in its holder on the dash. In the ear-piece of his Bluetooth headset Dmitry heard the call connect and begin to ring.

It was answered with a short female, "*Da?*"

"It is done," Dmitry said by way of equally short reply then hit End without waiting for a response. He smiled into the empty car.

"And now it begins."

—33—

GETTING DOWN FROM the roof did not present Kelly with as much difficulty as getting up there. Rooftops were her playground and she knew how to pick her way across fragile slate and tile using the timber skeleton underneath. In this case, staying low and avoiding the skylights she shadowed the ridge line to the end furthest away from the entrance.

The next building was butted up against the one she'd escaped from but was one storey lower. Kelly dangled herself carefully over the gable and edged her way down the brickwork by fingers and toes until she was on the lower level. Her arm throbbed fiercely all the way.

This building was occupied so in a better state of repair. It was also reasonably compliant with the current regulations regarding fire escapes—in this case a sturdy metal staircase.

Fortunately this was mounted on the far side, so while the occupants gaped out of the windows at the activity below, Kelly was able to slip past on the opposite side of the building without being noticed.

Good job too, Kelly thought. Even without her tattered oversuit she knew she must present quite a picture of a fleeing fugitive. She half-ran, half-tiptoed her way down the old cast-iron treads, moving as fast as she dared.

The pull-down ladder at the bottom was rusted closed and refused to open out all the way to the ground but jumping the last few feet and rolling through the impact was a small price to pay for freedom.

Kelly dusted herself down and walked quickly east trying not to look guilty as another police car came barrelling into the estate. She crossed the road, trotted past a modern-designed junior school and yet more developments of high-rise flats. Half a glimpse of the river and the prices rose accordingly, even out here.

All the way her mind keened for the dead boy she'd left behind. He'd been gauche as a puppy in some ways but as close to a friend as Kelly allowed herself these days, and fervently loyal. She remembered his attack on DI O'Neill at the hospital in defence of Ray. Had he tried to protect her too or was he always the intended victim?

Aware of Tyrone's crush on her she'd tried to be gentle of his feelings. *And now he'll never know what it is to fall in love— properly truly in love.*

Eyes blurring, Kelly turned down the first available side street and headed along its length, past the doorway to a small swimming baths that let out a damp belch of heavily chlorinated air across the pavement.

The street was long and straight enough for Kelly to keep a wary eye out for anyone following. As far as she could tell, she was alone.

An abandoned shopping trolley next to the fence at the far end sparked an idea. She hurried through a half-empty parade of new shops and crossed over the Inner Dock using the Pepper

Street bridge, making for the supermarket on the other side of the railway line.

She grabbed a bottle of cola and ducked into the customer toilets as soon as she was inside the store, locking herself into the disabled cubicle which had its own sink. The blood on her bare arms and hands had dried and without an abrasive cleaner the cola was the most effective thing she could find.

She was thankful that she always kept her wallet in a back pocket rather than a handbag which would most likely have been left in the van. At least she had a bit of cash on her even if it wasn't enough to get her much beyond south Croydon—never mind South America.

Even the thought of exile made her sink down onto the closed lid of the toilet, her knees suddenly rubbery.

I am not running away, she told herself sternly. *This is a tactical retreat.*

She made sure she brought the empty cola bottle out with her to pay for. No point in getting nabbed by in-store security. In the clothing section she picked up a cheap baseball hat and a hooded sweatshirt discarding the labels in the first waste bin she came across once she was through the self-service checkout and back outside.

The disguise, such as it was, would not hold for long. As soon as they ran her prints and DNA through the system it would light up like Bond Street at Christmas. All she needed to gain was a little time and distance to find somewhere safe to hide at least until she could get her own blood sample tested—and by someone she could trust over the result.

She bought a Day Travelcard from one of the machines in the Tube station at Coldharbour and boarded the first northbound Docklands Light Rail train that pulled in.

Kelly sat next to the window, swaying to the motion as the train briefly picked up speed again. Her face was turned to the glass so that she watched her own reflection more than the shifting scenery outside. She wasn't sure she either liked or recognised who she saw there.

She watched the reflections of the other passengers as they got on and took the seats around her, too. Nobody seemed to be paying her undue attention.

Good, so they haven't put it together yet or they'd be screaming it from the rooftops.

The DLR train was heading for Bank station. There she hopped across onto the Central line for West Ruislip and rode it out to Hanger Lane, close to the McCarron office.

She had hesitated briefly over going back there but by the time she'd changed trains her mind was made up.

It's not like I have many options.

She walked the short distance from the station down to the office keeping her cap pulled down, her hood up and her hands stuffed into her pockets. Her arm under the makeshift dressing had subsided into dull painfulness and she still had a vile headache. It had receded with the adrenaline of evading capture but now it was back with a vengeance and making up for lost time.

Kelly reached the office doorway and let out a long shaky breath as she slipped the keys from her pocket. She hoped the place was empty, weighed up the risk and thought it likely. The chatty woman who'd given her location to Matthew Lytton worked from home. With Ray in hospital the rest of his crew had been working flat out, taking it in turns to pick up messages from the answering service while they were out on jobs.

Today, she recalled it was the turn of Les and Graham. They were Ray's most experienced team and specialised in what were referred to round the office as Hoarding Houses which made up a big chunk of the firm's business. They should be down in Purley clearing a place that had belonged to an elderly eccentric who didn't seem to have thrown anything away during the thirty years leading up to his death. Les's estimate had run to five one-ton skips needed to cart away the accumulated rubbish. This had included what seemed to be at least twelve months' worth of the old guy's own faeces, carefully bagged and labelled.

They'd be gone some time.

Kelly locked the door behind her. Ray, she remembered, had been jumped at the very spot where she was standing.

Is this a vendetta against all of us rather than just me?

She shook her head—a mistake—and wearily climbed the stairs to the upper floor.

There she stepped into the small galley kitchen and lifted the bag of blood out from under her shirt. The seal had proved up to the job. For want of anything better Kelly slid the bag into the fridge. She'd already written the date, time and her name on it in indelible marker. It wasn't quite chain-of-custody, but it would have to do.

She raided the office First-Aid kit and properly cleaned her arm. Removing the duct tape hurt like the devil and peeling away the adhesive made the whole thing open up again. It took Kelly a while to slow the bleeding enough to close the edges of the wound with four or five Steri-Strips and wind a sterile dressing in place around it. At least working this job she knew all her jabs were up to date.

She was tempted by the heavy duty painkillers in the kit but in the end settled for nothing stronger than a couple of paracetamol just to take the edge off it. She thought briefly of the bottle of vodka in the bottom of Ray's desk but rejected that too.

If there was one thing she needed now, above all else, it was a clear head.

Just to sit for a few minutes and catch her thoughts she sank slowly onto one of the chairs around the table where the team gathered to eat their lunches, discuss jobs and write up their reports. Her eyes slid to the places where Tyrone and Ray always sat.

"Two down," she said out loud. "Who's next?"

Stupid question. It was supposed to be me.

Reluctantly she got to her feet. If she was going to stay ahead of the police long enough to find answers of her own she was going to need money—of the kind that could not be obtained via a photographed and instantly traceable hole-in-the-wall cash machine.

The petty cash tin was in the bottom drawer of Ray's desk next to the vodka bottle. It was secured by a spindly padlock that Kelly had never had the heart to tell her boss could be picked in seconds. As she finessed the tumblers with a safety pin and re-bent paperclip she was thankful she'd spared his feelings.

There were some skills Kelly had learned in prison that she would be forever grateful for.

The cash tin held a couple of hundred in mixed notes and maybe twenty quid in loose change. Kelly took the lot, folding it into the leg pocket of her cargoes. She was just looking round on Ray's cluttered desktop for a scrap of paper she could use to write an apologetic IOU when her eye lighted on a familiar name on the top of a pile of invoices.

Matthew Lytton.

She picked up the invoice slowly. It was marked 'Paid in Full'. Kelly noted the amount Ray had charged Lytton for the clean-up after his wife's alleged suicide and calculated he'd taken one look at the scope of the country place and doubled the number he'd first thought of.

But what really caught her attention was the address on the invoice. The country house with the luxury bathroom, it seemed, was not Lytton's only residence. He'd asked for the paperwork to be sent to another address—in central London.

Suddenly her next move was clear. Not sensible by any means, but definitely clear.

Kelly memorised the address and put the invoice back—not on top but a couple down in the stack. After all there was no point in leaving *too* many clues for the likes of DI O'Neill to follow.

—34—

AS SOON AS Matthew Lytton opened the door to his apartment, he knew something was wrong.

For one thing it had been daylight when he left so there would have been no reason to switch on the lamps in the living area. And for another he was pretty sure he would have remembered leaving the VH1 music channel playing on the TV, even at low volume.

His first instinct as he paused in the hallway with one hand still on the open front door was to retreat to a safe distance and call the police. He quickly dismissed that option.

One way or another he'd had his fill of the police lately.

That and the fact he'd never heard of burglars who broke in and then made themselves at home to the point of cooking up a meal. The distinctive smell of frying onions drifted out from the kitchen. It was all he could do to stop his stomach growling.

Lytton cautiously checked his watch. It was close to 2:00 AM. He'd put in another eighteen-hour day at the office and it seemed a hell of a long time since lunch.

Silently he closed the front door behind him. He kept his car keys and cellphone in his hand as he ventured further inside, moving softly on the hardwood floor.

As he reached the kitchen he heard the sound of rapid chopping, the sizzle of something fresh being added to a hot pan.

He edged an eye around the door jamb. Kelly Jacks was cracking eggs into a glass mixing bowl. Her back was towards him but still he recognised her. She was wearing a skinny halter top over baggy cargoes and her feet were bare. He knew he should have been furious at the sheer arrogance of the woman. Instead he found himself admiring her audacity.

Lytton slipped the keys and phone into his jacket pocket and stepped into the room.

"I don't suppose there's enough for two is there?" he asked tapping her lightly on the shoulder.

She gave a gasp and spun round. The next thing he knew, the hand he'd laid on her was grabbed, wrenched away and twisted up his back hard and fast. He felt the tearing graunch of over-stressed ligaments in his elbow and wrist.

The force of it drove him down to his knees in an attempt to yield. All that did was allow her to put the lock on more firmly. The spike of pain took his breath away.

"Christ! What the—?"

She froze, finally recognising his voice, relaxed her grip then released him altogether and stepped back quickly.

"I'm sorry," she said sounding shaky. "You startled me."

Lytton got to his feet slowly, rubbing his wrist. "Yeah well that makes two of us," he said warily. "Where the hell did you learn that?"

"Prison."

He'd frightened her, he realised and she'd reacted instinctively—almost without conscious thought.

"I'm sorry," she said then, unable to meet his gaze. "Not just for that ... I know I'm being bloody cheeky coming here like this but I didn't have anywhere else to go."

Lytton pulled a wry face, flexing his fingers experimentally. "Flattery will get you everywhere." He nodded to the debris-strewn countertop aware that he was still teetering on the far reaches of anger. "I see you've made yourself at home."

"I'm sorry," she muttered again. "I waited but when you didn't come back after normal close of play I sort of assumed you weren't going to and—" she shrugged, "—I haven't eaten."

She sounded beaten-down weary. Lytton sighed, moved further into the room. "Well now you've started keep going." Out of the corner of his eye he saw the way she tensed as he came past her. He merely went to the cooler and pulled out a bottle of Beck's. "Drink? I certainly need one after that."

She shook her head. He dug out an opener and flipped off the lid then drank from the neck not bothering with a glass. "How did you get in by the way?"

She'd turned back to the hob, answered over her shoulder. "Not difficult with the security you've got."

"I had the front door locks changed only a few months ago when ... when Veronica lost her keys. The guy told me they were nine-lever, whatever that means. He reckoned they were fairly secure."

Her lips hitched upwards and almost made it to a smile. "Should have got him to change the ones on the sliding windows at the same time then," she said. "They're a joke."

Lytton didn't point out that the balcony onto which those sliding doors opened out was on the fourth floor because he'd heard the cracks in her voice despite the light hearted words. He put down his beer and studied the strain in her face.

"What's happened Kelly?"

She had been holding herself rigid but the gentleness of his voice seemed to crumple her. She looked away sharply, took a deep breath before she raised her head again.

"Remember Tyrone?" she asked.

He frowned, was about to ask but then an image of the big black kid she'd been working with opened up in his mind. He nodded.

She took another breath shaky this time. "He's dead," she said flatly. "He was murdered today at a crime scene we were supposed to be cleaning in Millwall."

"Christ," Lytton said. "When did you find out?"

She fussed for a moment with the pan on the hob turning down the gas to a low simmer before the onions turned to caramel. "When I woke up," she said in a voice so low he thought for a moment he'd misheard her.

"When you ...?" he began then stopped. No wonder she'd overreacted when he came in. "My God ... you were there."

And crowding in on that thought came a bunch of others. He'd read the trial reports after her manslaughter conviction—about the blackout and the murder. That there'd been no previous history or medical evidence presented to suggest Kelly might be prone to such traumatic lapses. Nothing to say she wasn't lying about the whole thing.

Clearly judge and jury had believed she was.

So why should he trust her now?

"It happened again," he said but she shook her head and raked a distracted hand through her short choppy hair. He noticed the bandage on her arm as she did so. Had her victim fought back this time?

"No," she said more determined now. "I'm beginning to think it never happened in the first place."

She waited fiercely for his incredulity. He schooled his face not to present any, leaned his hip against the countertop and folded his arms. "So, what did?"

"I think I was framed," she said twisting restlessly away and beginning to pace. Lytton's eyes fell onto the knife she'd been using to cut the vegetables. It lay casually on the chopping board in full view but he made no moves to stop her getting back to it.

"I think they gave me something—Rohypnol maybe," she went on. "Something to make me compliant and make me forget. Then it was just a case of sticking the knife in my hand and leaving me in the wrong place at the wrong time."

"Didn't they test you for possible drugs last time?" he asked.

"Eventually," she agreed. "And—surprise, surprise—nothing showed up. That's why I took this."

She yanked open the fridge door and pulled out a small ziplock bag. One corner was filled with liquid that was a dark rich red.

"Please tell me that isn't what I think it is?"

She nodded to the bandage on her arm. "I improvised before I left the scene. I was out for half an hour or so and got away from there just before the cops showed up. Maybe whoever did this miscalculated the dose or whatever. Or maybe they couldn't afford to have me actually unconscious when the cops arrived. Too many awkward questions."

"And you want to get that tested—independent of the police this time?" he guessed.

She nodded and he saw her desperation in the way her shoulders had begun to sag. If what she said was true he realised she must be in shock to some degree and close to nervous exhaustion. Not to mention suffering a chemical hangover to rival anything induced by alcohol.

But ...

Lytton put his head on one side. "Why did you come here Kelly?"

She gave him a tired smile. "Process of elimination," she said. "All this kicked off because I asked questions about your wife's death. Either you killed her and tried to set me up because I spotted it or you're completely innocent and you'll want answers just as much as I do. More, perhaps."

He met her eyes. "And how do you know which is the truth?"

"By what happens next."

"GOOD EVENING VINCE. You're pulling a late one."

DI O'Neill glanced up from signing the on-scene log to see the lead CSI approaching.

"Hiya Bob," he said. "I just heard we ID'd the victim. Kid called Tyrone Douet. That makes it one of mine."

Bob Tate, a tall cadaverous Scot, lifted the crime-scene tape for him to duck underneath. O'Neill was already wearing booties and gloves. "Oh aye?"

"Douet worked for a specialist cleaning crew—McCarron's," O'Neill said. "Couple of nights ago the boss was beaten up pretty badly. Now this."

"Poor sod," Tate said, pushing his glasses further up his long nose with the back of his own gloved hand. "I knew Ray McCarron when he was one of us. I hadn't heard." He paused. "You think there's a connection?"

"Doesn't hurt to look."

Tate sighed. "Well it's going to be a wee while before we're done here I'm afraid. The scene suffers from an embarrassment of riches as it were. It doesn't help that there was another death here only yesterday."

"Oh aye?" O'Neill said, echoing him. "Anyone I should be aware of?"

Tate waved a hand towards a dark oily stain around and up against one of the steel support pillars. "Homeless man," he said. "Managed to set himself on fire with a cigarette and a half-bottle of overproof rum. Bacardi 151 according to the fragments of label. Lethal stuff in more ways than one it seems."

O'Neill vaguely recalled that Tate was a Presbyterian and a teetotaller.

"Accidental?"

The CSI shrugged. "Not the first time it's happened and I daresay not the last."

"But where did a derelict get hold of something that not only just so happens to be highly flammable but also sells for around seventy quid a bottle?"

Tate paused again. A tick of irritation crossed his features, eyebrows drawing down. "It wasn't my call," he said grimly. "But I'll be making it my business now." His eyes drifted back to the burn marks. "At least the cleaners hadn't begun to sanitise the scene before young Tyrone was attacked. I'm sorry you missed the body by the way."

"I spoke to the pathologist on the way in," O'Neill dismissed. "As you're only too aware, he never likes to commit himself but he reckoned the fractured skull would have done for the kid. The fourteen stab wounds just made sure of it."

Tate pursed his lips as he eyed the patch of blood-soaked concrete that had until recently been Tyrone Douet's final resting place. "And then there's the blood bag of course," he added.

"Blood bag?"

"Oh aye. Didn't they tell you about that?" Tate shook his head. "When the uniforms arrived on scene they found a little sandwich bag with blood in it and a note saying 'it wasn't me' or some such nonsense." He glanced at O'Neill, his amusement dying as he realised the other man did not share the joke. "A red herring surely?"

"Maybe not."

"Well it could be worth running a full tox screen on it I suppose." Tate pulled a face. "Depends on the state of the budget I expect and how seriously you take this person—whoever they are."

"Kelly Jacks," O'Neill said, almost under his breath.

Tate paused. "Now that name I *do* recall," he said. "Bad business when one of our own turns bad." He frowned. "Didn't she claim to have some kind of mental breakdown when she stabbed—what was that laddie's name?"

O'Neill had no time for reminiscences. "Jacks worked with Douet," he said. "According to McCarron's the two of them were scheduled to come out here and clean up the tramp's death yesterday morning. Nobody's seen or heard from Jacks since."

"But—" Tate's mouth opened and closed. With his slightly protruding eyes behind the glass O'Neill was unkindly reminded of a goldfish. "What about the blood? And the message?"

O'Neill was already striding away stabbing a number into his phone. "Maybe," he threw back over his shoulder, "she's just getting her defence in place a lot earlier this time."

—36—

KELLY WOKE WITH a start, body snapping upright and her heart pounding like a fist.

For a few moments she had no clear idea of where she was or how she got there. The blank caused an instant burst of panic that pierced her chest and seized her lungs until she was gasping for breath.

She was in a bedroom, she saw, in one half of a double bed. The other half was empty.

Well that's good, at least.

The curtains were not drawn at the long windows. Through the glass the soft-hued glow of pre-dawn washed in allowing Kelly to take in the details of the room.

Off to her left was an adjoining door through which she could see a sliver of en suite bathroom. Expensive glossy tiles and a glassed-in shower cubicle with a rose the size of a dinner plate. She looked around the bedroom itself, frowning. The art on the walls looked genuine if a little bland, giving it the impersonal feel of a seldom-used guest room. It was certainly no cheap motel.

Memories returned slowly, layer on layer like falling snow. By the time each of them had settled she began to wish for the amnesia that had once seemed such a curse. She sat, hugging her knees through the fine sheet.

Tyrone's dead and they're going to come after me for it.

She remembered her flight from the scene, her brief foray to the office, and finally coming here to the apartment of Matthew Lytton. A man who owed her nothing. A man she'd attacked by way of greeting as soon as he walked into his own home.

"I must have been mad."

Maybe I was. And maybe I still am.

There was a digital clock on the side table. A glance at it told her it was a few minutes before 5:00 AM. At least she'd managed a couple of hours without the police breaking down the door and dragging her out in chains.

Which means he hasn't called them.

The realisation gradually released its grip on something that had been clenched tight beneath her ribs.

Does that mean he didn't set me up? she wondered. *Or does it simply mean that he wants to deal with me in his own time?*

Soundlessly, she slid out of bed. She was still wearing a thin undershirt and her knickers. When he'd shown her the room Lytton had told her in a neutral voice to make use of anything she found there. A long silk dressing gown was draped over a chair and after only a moment's pause she slipped it on, knotting the sash around her waist. The material whispered around her legs, cool against her bare skin.

Before climbing into bed she had locked her bedroom door. Now she took a breath and untwisted the key. She paused in the hallway, listening tensely. She had no idea which was Lytton's own bedroom and she had no desire to disturb him.

But as she stepped out into the open-plan living area she spotted his outline at one end of the low sofa, sitting facing the wall of glass with his back to her. She froze. He was in shirtsleeves, the cuffs rolled back. Loosely in one hand he held a squat glass of what might have been whisky.

She was on the point of retreating when his voice floated back to her. It came disembodied from the shadow of his silhouette against the lightening sky.

"Can't sleep?"

Kelly was silent for a few elongated seconds. She saw his head turn as if to sense her position. Feeling suddenly gauche she moved around the sofa and into his field of view. She told herself that the ungainliness of her limbs was due to nothing other than delayed shock from the day before.

"I managed a couple of hours," she said with admirable calm. "You?"

"Not a wink," he admitted, lifting the glass and taking a sip.

"Why?"

The question came out more starkly than she'd intended. It hung between them, glossy with intent.

"Because you're here," he said at last, a certain dryness to his tone.

She stiffened. "If I'm making you uncomfortable, I'll go," she said quickly, turning away. "I'm sorry. You should have said. I'll get dressed."

But as she passed him he reached out and caught her wrist. Everything jolted at the touch. Kelly felt the warmth from his fingers glowing across the surface of her skin. This time her first instinct was not to fight her way free.

She faltered, stared at him wordlessly.

He looked up at her. She felt his gaze soft on her face, her hair, her shoulders. She swallowed.

"Sit with me a while," he coaxed. "Nothing more. Just ... sit with me."

Kelly would have pulled back but she heard something in his voice. Not seduction but a need for comfort, for a kind of mutual consolation and she remembered that he too had lost someone. He had as good as told her that his marriage was more partnership than romantic bond. Nevertheless, Veronica was someone he'd known, cared for and lived alongside. And he'd lost her to an act of shocking violence he had neither understood nor been prepared for.

She stood there unable to find the words to express her sorrow for both of them. After a moment he let her arm drop with a quiet exhalation that could have been a sigh.

Kelly moved around the arm of the sofa and sank onto the cushions next to him, tucking her feet up. She felt his surprise in the brief hesitation. Then his arm went around her shoulders and very gently he drew her closer.

This is a bad idea, she thought. *But I need this—and so does he.*

She allowed herself to fold against the side of his body, her head resting on his shoulder. She put one hand on his chest for balance. Beneath her palm his heart beat strong and steady. He carried the faint trace of good cologne.

Lytton inhaled and then exhaled unsteadily as if letting go of more than simply spent air. He turned his head slightly and his breath stirred her scalp. His hand began to drift along her upper arm in a smooth, unthreatening caress.

Gradually Kelly felt knots she hadn't even realised were there begin to untie themselves. She sank deeper into him as everything slowed within her. It was a long time since someone had just held her like this, apparently without expectation. A long time since she'd wanted or needed such human contact.

Hazily she wondered, *why him?*

And then she slept.

* * *

When Kelly woke the light had solidified into morning. She found herself alone on the sofa, curled up like a cat with the duvet from her bed wrapped carefully around her.

She had no recollection of how long Lytton had stayed with her or when he'd edged out from underneath but she hoped she hadn't snored.

From somewhere behind her in the apartment she heard the sound of a shower running. To avoid any awkward hellos she stumbled to her feet and hurried back towards the bedroom she'd been given, bundling up the duvet as she went.

She indulged in a long shower. The water was hot and plentiful and she took full advantage of it. The prospect of climbing back into yesterday's clothes held little appeal.

Although Lytton had told her to make use of anything she found in the room, she hesitated before pulling open drawers.

To her surprise, the second one she checked held a selection of classy lingerie. The bras were too big but Kelly had never considered herself over-blessed in that department and often went without anyway. She found camisole tops instead and knickers to match.

The wardrobes held suits, blouses, dresses and coats, all with a rake of designer labels. Kelly dithered briefly then took a plain white silk blouse off a hanger and shrugged it on. It didn't quite go with her grubby cargoes but what the hell. She knotted the front tails rather than tuck them in. Too formal was not her style.

Then she took a deep breath and went in search of her host.

Matthew Lytton was in the kitchen, expertly preparing grapefruit. There was a smell of toast and coffee. In the corner was a muted TV tuned to one of the twenty-four-hour news channels.

Lytton was dressed in suit trousers and a formal white shirt with the collar and cuffs yet to be buttoned. His dark hair was still damp from his own shower. He looked remarkably relaxed for a man whose home had been invaded by a fugitive who'd assaulted him and then more or less passed out in his arms.

He greeted her with a guarded smile and gestured to the coffee pot.

"Help yourself."

She lifted the knotted tails of the blouse. "I already did. I hope you don't mind?"

"No, that's fine," he said, his eyes flickering over her. "Vee rarely wore half the stuff she kept in her room."

Her *room? You mean you didn't share?*

Kelly hunched a shoulder. "I'll get it back to you."

"No need. It looks good on you." The toast popped up. He fished the slices out of the big chrome toaster and piled them on a plate, adding over his shoulder, "I was going to send the whole lot to Oxfam anyway."

"In that case tell me which shop. I may stage a raid."

Her attempt at levity hung heavy between them where last night—early this morning—things had seemed so easy. Perhaps it was because they both knew that if things turned out badly she might be wearing prison garb for the foreseeable future.

"Eat." He pushed the grapefruit and the plate of toast towards her. "You look better for some rest."

That brought heat rushing into her face. She busied herself pulling out a stool from the breakfast bar, perching on top. "I *feel* better. And thank you."

"What for—breakfast?"

For being there. For holding me.

"Of course," she said lightly. "Food is the way to a woman's heart, not just a man's. Didn't you know?"

He paused and just when she thought he was going to say something profound he said instead, "Well, I better make sure I feed you well then. There's juice in the fridge if you'd like some?"

She didn't but nodded regardless. As he turned away she used the distraction to quickly swap the grapefruit dishes. Lytton put the juice container on the breakfast bar with no sign he'd noticed the substitution.

As he took the stool opposite it struck Kelly that they must have seemed like any normal domesticated couple eating breakfast together. The air of intimacy was unfamiliar and unsettling.

She found herself minutely aware of the size and the shape of him, the way the muscles in his arms shifted as he hooked a slice of toast from the stack. Of the mobile dexterity of his hands. Hands that had stroked her into trustful slumber.

And she was also aware that, for all the veneer of civilised sophistication, here was a man who'd started out at the physical end of the construction business. He still had that tough capability about him and she sensed he would be capable of great ruthlessness to get what he wanted.

Did that extend to killing his wife, she wondered? Or having her killed? The wife he no longer shared a bed with or seemed to mourn?

They ate in silence. Kelly found herself too jittery for it to be a comfortable one, tensing whenever he reached across for the marmalade or to refill his coffee cup. There was a pressure building in the air that made it buzz between them.

She could see the faint bruise braceleting his wrist from the lock she'd put onto him last night. One thing about prison, if you pissed off the guards they gave you an excellent practical demonstration of pain compliance at work.

It was a shame she hadn't been able to use more of what she'd learned when she was at the warehouse.

"Tell me what you meant last night," Lytton said suddenly, breaking into her reveries, "when you said you came here because you had nowhere else to go."

Kelly shrugged. "Just that."

"No friends? No boyfriend?"

An image of David sprang into her mind, the twist of disgust on his face during that final visit when she was on remand, telling her he couldn't keep up the pretence. That he couldn't stand by her—couldn't *stand her*—any longer.

She pushed it away, took a sip of her coffee and said calmly. "I always tended to make friends through my work. When the job went bad, the friends went the same way."

He didn't press her on that. She remembered that he'd looked up the reports of the time. The tabloids had a field day with David's abandonment. If even her lover—another copper—didn't believe she was innocent, they cried, who would?

"No family you could turn to?"

Kelly put her cup down before responding. Was he making small talk or trying to find out if she would be missed? Should she lie?

"I was always the odd one out, the cuckoo," she said, opting for the truth without quite knowing the reason. "The bright one, the one with her head stuck in a book. The one who had fancy ideas about wanting to go to university."

"The one who thought she deserved something better than being stuck in a dead-end job for the rest of her life, you mean?" Lytton asked. And when she glanced at him surprised at the insight, he gave a crooked smile. "Been there. Done that."

"Yes, I suppose you have. And you're right. I went away to study and was so wrapped up in the course I didn't see what was happening back home, that they were turning against me in my absence."

"People despise what they don't understand."

She nodded. "I left it too long. I came home qualified and expected them to be proud of me. Instead, all I got were sneers."

"So they couldn't wait for you to fall on your arse, you mean?"

If only it were that simple. "When I was arrested my mum had her first stroke," she said quietly. "They said it was the shock ..."

Her voice trailed off and there was a beat of loaded silence between them.

"Ah, you've made the news," Lytton said. He picked up the remote for the TV and thumbed up the volume.

Kelly twisted on her stool just in time to see DI O'Neill's sombre face appear on the screen. A rolling banner hotline number scrolled past underneath him.

"... vicious and unprovoked attack on a young man of good character who was well-liked in the community," O'Neill was saying. "It's vital we speak with young Tyrone's colleague, Kelly Jacks. According to our information she was apparently ... with him at the time of his attack."

The pause was artful, Kelly thought bitterly. Nobody hearing it could fail to get the hinted meaning even without the interviewer's next question.

"Is Kelly Jacks a suspect?"

O'Neill stared at the earnest female interviewer for a couple of seconds. "We would advise anybody with knowledge of Ms Jacks's whereabouts to contact us immediately," he said. "But not to approach her themselves."

"Jacks has already served a prison sentence on a previous manslaughter charge. Does she present a danger to the public?" The interviewer made another stab, hardly troubling to suppress the excitement in her voice. She was young, a little brash, only just promoted to the crime beat and no doubt keen to catch the eye of the big networks.

"Let's just say we have concerns for Ms Jacks's state of mind at this time," O'Neill said dryly.

He nodded to someone past the camera and the report came to a rapid close. The interviewer did a solemn round-up with the crime-scene tape fluttering behind her. Kelly's picture appeared in the corner of the screen.

It was the one from her records, taken at the time of her original arrest. Her hair was longer then, the style curving around her face making her look younger, more feminine. Or maybe it was just that five years inside had robbed her of whatever innocence she might have once possessed. Kelly could see the bewildered desperation in her own reflected image, the sheer panic and disbelief.

She swallowed, looked away. Lytton was watching her over the rim of his cup. There was something brooding in that observation that suddenly unnerved her.

"Well, that answers *that* question I suppose," she said, aiming for wry and not quite bringing it off.

Lytton lowered his cup and raised an eyebrow. "Which is?"

"If O'Neill was going to keep enough of an open mind to look elsewhere," she said, absently brushing the toast crumbs left on her plate into a pile at the centre. "It seems he's going for the easy option. Surprise, surprise."

She thought of the bag of her own blood in the fridge a few feet away. She was glad she'd taken the second sample and at the same time disappointed to be proved right to have done so.

"Not necessarily," Lytton said. "Even if he was pursuing other avenues you'd still be his first port of call. He either has to break you or clear you. Until then he can't move on."

"You're defending him now?"

He took another sip of his coffee and shook his head as he swallowed. "Hey don't get me wrong. I didn't like him much either. I'm just trying to see both sides." He paused, fixed her with a straight level gaze. "You have to face it though, Kelly. The longer you stay on the run, the more guilty it makes you look."

Kelly drained her own cup and got to her feet. "I'd better not waste any more time then, had I?"

—37—

ACROSS THE OTHER side of the river, lying alone in bed in Harry Grogan's luxury penthouse, Myshka watched the same news report and smiled.

Dmitry had done well she decided with a flush of pride. But he had been well taught. The secret of a great man was not simply to avoid mistakes but to recognise them for what they were and deal with them effectively—simply, quickly—once they had been made.

She would have to think of a special way to reward him.

She picked up her iPhone and flicked through the contacts until she came to Steve Warwick's number and hit it, longing for a cigarette. Even *she* daren't smoke inside while Grogan was away and that fact rankled.

The call was answered—Warwick's slightly petulant tone demanding, "Where the hell have you *been*? I've been calling!"

"I've been busy," Myshka said carelessly. *Deal with it.* "Tell me again about the hospitality arrangements. Which entrance will the caterers use? Not the basement?"

She heard his gusty sigh—that of a cranky child made to perform in order to receive a treat. "We've been over all this a dozen times. The basement car park entrance will be closed off the day before. They'll come in at ground level and use the service lifts from there."

"Good boy," she said her voice turning husky. "There, that wasn't so hard was it? But if you can tear yourself away from your desk I will make it hard for you, yes?"

Warwick gave a groan. "I'm due at the venue this morning," he said in an agony of indecision. "I could always cry off but—"

"No!" Myshka let her voice rap him smartly then dropped it again to a soothing purr. "I will deal with you ... later. The anticipation will make it worth the wait, I promise."

Another groan. "Good God, Myshka—what the hell did I do before I found you?"

He ended the call. Myshka lay back against the sheets and smiled up at the ceiling.

"You suffered," she said.

—38—

AN HOUR LATER Kelly took a deep breath and dialled a number from her own contacts list.

She almost lost her nerve in the time it took the phone to connect and start to ring at the other end, and again with every unanswered second.

"This is such a bad idea," she muttered.

But then the receiver was lifted, a mumbled greeting given and it was too late to go back.

"Mrs Douet?" she said. "Please don't hang up. This is Kelly— Kelly Jacks."

She heard the woman's sharp intake of breath and rushed on. "I just wanted you to know that I didn't hurt Tyrone. He was my friend. I know what they're saying but I wouldn't do that. Not to him—not to anyone." She heard the break in her own voice and took a breath to steady it. "Please believe me."

There was a long pause, to the point where Kelly feared Tyrone's mother had let go. She had a brief remembered image of a careworn woman with a permanent stoop that added a decade or more to her probable age. Kelly wondered how much extra weight Tyrone's murder would add onto her shoulders and her throat tightened.

"Why you running then child?" Mrs Douet asked almost gently. "Why don' you just give in—talk to the policeman—let the law decide?"

"Because I've been here before and the law decided wrong."

"You know? Or you think?" she asked, her voice slightly disconnected as if she'd been given something to take the edge off her grief. "I can't talk to you now child. I should, I know ... but I can't. I'm sorry."

Kelly wondered almost angrily about the woman's friends, neighbours and family who were letting her field calls at all in that state ...

Oh shit.

"Look I know you have to go," Kelly said quickly. "I just wanted to tell you—that I'm innocent. I *did not* do this to Tyrone. And I don't believe I killed anyone before, either." She spoke past Mrs Douet to the people she knew were also listening. "That girl who was beaten to death all those years ago. It wasn't random bad luck—she was murdered to silence her. Nobody would believe me and when I kept asking questions they found a way to shut me up too. Well it won't work again. And if the police won't find out who *did* do this to your son, I will."

—39—

DI O'NEILL REACHED across very gently and took the receiver out of the woman's nerveless fingers. Her dulled eyes, red-rimmed from weeping, swivelled in his direction.

"I'm sorry," she said. "I know you said if she called to keep her talking but I just couldn't ..."

"It's all right Mrs Douet," O'Neill said. He looked to the technician sitting at the dining table. The man gave him a brief thumbs up. "You did enough. I know how difficult this must have been. We're very grateful to you."

She nodded vaguely. "I met her a few times—Kelly I mean," she offered. "She seemed so ... nice. And she say Tyrone is her friend. Why would she—?"

"I see people hurt—killed—by their closest friends all the time."

She nodded again, starting to fade as the nervous energy receded. One of the neighbours, a big strident woman, glared at O'Neill and hustled across to envelop Mrs Douet in a protective cloud of shawl and scent. She guided her to the floral sofa where the other children sat—a younger boy and a girl. They were huddled together watching with wide eyes every move of the police personnel around the cramped flat. At the moment they were scared and maybe even a little excited. Only later, O'Neill knew, would it sink in that their big brother wasn't ever coming home.

He moved through to the tiny dining area. "Where is she?" he demanded of the technician, keeping his voice low.

"Just the other side of Battersea Park," the man said scrawling down an address and handing it over.

O'Neill glanced at it, his brows drawing down. "You have to be kidding me."

The technician wisely said nothing to counter this disbelief in his abilities, just gave a quick shake of his head. "She didn't even withhold the number."

O'Neill reached for his phone, stabbed at the buttons with growing anger.

"Dempsey!" he snapped when the call was answered. "Where the hell are you?"

"Sitting outside the bird's flat boss. Where else would I be?"

"And you haven't been off for a slash or a kebab—even for five minutes?"

"Of course I haven't." DC Dempsey's voice was righteous. "There's been nobody in and nobody out since I got here."

"Well how come she's just made a phone call here from her home number then?"

"What? There isn't a back way boss. I checked."

"Well check again. Get yourself up there—right now!"

—40—

KELLY SCANNED UP and down the street before opening the door and sliding into the passenger seat of the Aston Martin, dumping a small backpack into the footwell as she did so.

Behind the wheel Lytton turned down the radio and twisted towards her, his eyes hidden behind slim designer sunglasses. "How did it go?"

Kelly tipped her head back against the leather and let out a long breath. "Better than it might have done," she said. "She didn't call me a murderer outright if that's what you mean."

"But?"

"She wasn't alone."

"You think the cops are watching your place?" Lytton glanced over his shoulder automatically.

"I imagine so."

"Did they see you?"

Kelly smiled. "Not unless they were watching by helicopter or satellite."

Lytton raised an eyebrow. "Where now?"

Kelly sighed. He'd already put on hold his plans for first thing this morning in order to swing past the forensics lab in Lambeth. It might have been Kelly's old ties that called in the favour to begin with but it was Lytton's cash that secured the promise of a fast-track service. She picked up the backpack, suddenly wary. Was this bout of helpfulness merely a way of keeping a close eye on her?

"Look it's enough that you gave mc a placc to bunk down last night—not to mention paying for the lab tests," she said awkwardly. "I can hardly expect you to play taxi driver for me all day as well."

"One of the nice things about being the boss is that I'm answerable to myself for how I spend my time," he said. "Besides, if I get some answers about Vee from all this it will be worth it."

Kelly was aware of that stab of doubt again. If he was involved he was good at maintaining a convincing facade. She found herself unwillingly believing him, believing *in* him.

"Even so," she argued, stubborn, "you must have commitments on your time."

He checked his watch. "I'm supposed to be meeting with my business partner at the racecourse after lunch. Vee was organising corporate hospitality for us." He paused. "Why don't you come with me? It would give you a chance to see what she did—get a feel for how she worked. You saw things at the house that the police missed. Maybe you'll do the same again."

Kelly glanced down at herself ruefully. She had taken the opportunity to grab some more clothes from the flat. The borrowed silk shirt, beautiful though it was, was folded neatly in the backpack ready to return to him. She was now wearing a set of desert cam combat pants and a clean halter top under the hoodie. On her feet were old Red Chili climbing shoes.

The contrast with Lytton's quiet affluence was marked. She was aware that anyone glancing in at the pair of them could be forgiven for the assumption she was carjacking him.

She ran a hand through her choppy hair, scowled. "Yeah 'cause I'll fit in *so* well with corporate hospitality."

"We can soon fix that." He twisted in his seat and smiled at her. "Besides, I could point out that I've done you some favours and now I'm calling them in."

"But you wouldn't do a thing like that," she said gravely, hiding the jolt his words provoked.

"You might see the surface trappings of success and mistake me for a gentleman," he said and Kelly remembered again her first impression that here was not a man to cross.

"Aren't you forgetting that I'm a wanted fugitive?" she said, almost a taunt.

"I think of little else," he drawled. "But I can live with it if you can."

"BIT OF A cock-up all round, Vincent, wouldn't you say?" remarked Chief Superintendent John Quinlan.

DI O'Neill hated being called Vincent. Only his mother used his full given name—usually when he'd disappointed her in some way. These days she used it a lot when she reminded him of his increasing age and lack of prospective wife, never mind the patter of tiny O'Neills "while she was still young enough to cope with grandchildren". He wondered if she and his boss had been talking.

"Yes sir," he said stiffly.

The chief super was standing with his back towards him, apparently transfixed by the view out of the narrow window of his office. As soon as O'Neill had got back to the station after his abortive attempt to track-and-trace Kelly Jacks he'd received the summons from on high. Quinlan had a good quality carpet up here and he liked to put people on it.

In truth O'Neill was just as pissed off about the way things had gone this morning. Dempsey had gone straight up to force entry into Kelly Jacks's flat. He'd found clear signs that she'd been there only minutes before, including the clothes she'd undoubtedly been wearing at the warehouse.

The only clue as to how she'd managed to get in and out without being seen from the street was an unlatched skylight. Even that might have gone unnoticed had O'Neill not recalled a snippet from Jacks's conduct record while she'd been inside. About how much time she'd spent on the prison climbing wall.

A climbing wall—in prison for Christ's sake! Why not just let them build a glider in Handicrafts and have done with it ...

Quinlan turned away from the window and caught O'Neill's scowl of irritation. He let his breath out fast down his nose like a snorting horse.

"Oh take that bloody stick out of your arse and sit down Vince, for God's sake. No way could that young idiot Dempsey have known he was dealing with Spiderwoman."

"No sir," O'Neill agreed tightly. He paused. "*I* should have figured it out as a possibility though."

The chief super snorted again louder this time. He was a lean man with the whippet-thin stringy build of a marathon runner and movements to match—quick and impatient. No-one would ever accuse John Quinlan of being handsome but his features had improved a bit with the cragginess of age.

He moved over to the ever-present coffee pot, sloshed liquid dark as coal tar into two cups and handed one to O'Neill.

Quinlan had joined the Met earmarked as a high-flier with a rich wife and all the right social connections to sit in the chief constable's chair. But now only a month or so from retirement he was destined to see out his service at chief superintendent. Rumours said the old man liked to get stuck in to the sharp end of policing too much to ever have ridden a desk all the way to the top. It was hard to tell how Quinlan himself felt about it one way or the other.

"So what do we know about all this business with Jacks?" Quinlan asked settling back into his chair behind the desk. "Was she having a tumble with the lad Douet d'you think? Was it friction over the job—lover's tiff gone bad?"

"He was practically half her age," O'Neill pointed out.

Quinlan grinned from behind his cup. "Since when did that ever stop anything?"

O'Neill shrugged and took a sip himself. The coffee was thick as treacle but twice as bitter. He only just held back a cough.

"That's true enough sir. And Jacks is not looking bad for someone who's done time, I'll say that for her," he allowed, adding lightly, "Maybe claiming innocence kept her youthful."

Quinlan's face was brooding. "You're not going to drag up the Perry case again are you? That kind of thing never reflects well on the force."

"No sir."

"Is that 'no sir' it doesn't or 'no sir' you're not?"

"Either—or both." O'Neil sighed and rubbed a hand around the back of his aching neck. "Still, it's weird that she went so far as to leave a bag of blood at the scene for us to test."

Quinlan cradled his cup in his lap and rocked the chair a little, lips pursed.

"Bit on the macabre side," he agreed. "Do we even know for sure it's her blood?"

"Not yet sir." O'Neill forced a smile. "We *are* always having it drummed into us about the cost of lab work."

Quinlan's answering grin was brief. "Don't get cute with me, sonny," he warned. "OK. Let's get it tested—'get the cat a budgie and hang the expense,' as my old gran used to say. See if we can match it to Jacks before we go any further."

"What about the tox screen?"

"Hmm. The obvious stuff to start with. After all it's pretty bloody clear she was there and it's not as if this is the first time she's gone off the rails." He put his empty coffee cup down onto the desktop. "We tried like hell to prove she didn't do it last time. I know—I was there. But that didn't work out well for any of us in the 'mud sticks' department. And this time around there's racial implications to add to the mix as well. We all need to keep our wits about us this time around—including young Dempsey."

"Yes sir."

Sensing dismissal O'Neill put down his coffee cup and rose.

Quinlan nodded. "All right Vince. Keep me up to speed on this one. The press are already having a field day but I'll keep them off your back as much as I can. The longer it goes on the more they're going to parade out Jacks's record and wave it in our faces. Let's try to put a lid on this thing before that happens and we all end up in the brown sticky stuff, eh?"

"Yes sir," he repeated.

Somehow, O'Neill reflected as he jogged down the stairs, it made it worse that the chief super hadn't chewed him out over letting Jacks slip through their fingers. He hadn't needed to— O'Neill felt bad enough about that without any help from on high and the headache tightening its grip around the base of his skull was proof of that. There was a packet of cigarettes already gripped in his hand like a weapon as he headed for the fire exit prepared to bite the head off anyone foolish enough to get in the way of a nicotine fix.

"Boss?"

O'Neill spun at the call, scowling furiously. From the panicked look on DC Dempsey's face he knew the young detective had just been handed the short straw.

"*What?*"

"Erm, there's just been a phone call for you—"

"Unless it's someone with the precise current GPS coordinates for Kelly Jacks it can wait," O'Neill ground out already moving again.

"Erm, not really, boss."

O'Neill stopped, turned with slow precision and glared at his junior officer. "Oh for God's sake Dempsey, spit it out."

Dempsey swallowed, his Adam's apple bobbing nervously above the knot of his tie. A weedy lad who looked younger than his years, the last remnants of his teenage acne warring with clusters of freckles. "Erm it's someone called Allardice. Claims he knows you," Dempsey said still hesitant. "And he claims he knows Kelly Jacks too."

O'Neill felt some of the anger uncoil itself from his neck and shoulders, the black buzzing cloud lift a little from his vision. Regretfully he put the cigarettes back in his pocket.

Maybe—just maybe—he'd finally caught a break.

"Well, he *should* know Jacks," he said as he strode back along the corridor. "Allardice was the one who arrested her last time."

—42—

"WILL I PASS?"

Matthew Lytton glanced up from his laptop and found his fingers faltering on the keys of his laptop. Kelly Jacks stood in the doorway to the private washroom that came adjoined to all the office suites at the racecourse, one hand on the frame. At his attention she let go and walked sedately into the office itself.

"Wow," he said with quiet awe, pushing back from the desk a little to take in all of her. "Quite a transformation."

And it was. Gone was the loose confident stride, the wild black hair, the stud through her nose. In its place was the sway of heels, a sleeked down style and understated makeup.

The dress was lavender with a short matching jacket. And while the particular shade had complemented Veronica's cool English rose looks, it looked stunning against Kelly's darker colouring. She'd damped down her hair and used a couple of grips to tame it into place.

Earlier that day he'd been fascinated to watch Kelly calmly scale a wall onto a low roof and from there onto an extension, moving up and on without fear or hesitation as she headed for the aerial access to her flat.

When she slid back into the Aston afterwards hardly out of breath he'd mentally pigeonholed her into a category that put her way outside his scope of experience. No man likes to think he's with a woman who can manage perfectly well—if not better—without him.

And yet when he'd persuaded her to come to the racecourse, to take her onto Veronica's turf, he'd known he'd have to disguise her in some way. Perhaps he'd just been experimenting to see if it could be done.

He reflected now the answer to that one was a resounding yes. The two women couldn't have been more different in colouring, height or style but the dress was an acceptable length and fit and the two of them took the same size in shoes.

Now she regarded him with a wary frown as he rose and came forward.

"Are you sure this doesn't feel creepy?" she asked. "Dressing me up in her things?"

He sighed. "Half the clothes Vee bought she never wore. You probably realised that at the apartment. She kept a change here in case of emergency, but if I ever saw her in this I've long forgotten the occasion," he said. "Besides, she was five ten in heels, curvaceous, blonde and one of the coldest women I've ever met." He smiled down at Kelly—lean, dark and fierce. "There's no way I'd ever confuse the two of you."

She frowned as if about to question him further then dismissed it with a light, "Just goes to show I can still scrub up when the occasion demands."

But he sensed a hint of sadness in her and realised for the first time the extent of what she'd lost—and stood to lose again.

Being a CSI must have been a good responsible job and a source of pride to her even if it had served to alienate her family. That exile had spurred her to succeed and from what he'd read she'd been well-respected in her field. Along with that kudos naturally came a nicer flat in a better area than her current address demonstrated, a newer car and no doubt a wardrobe befitting her position.

The woman who'd emerged from her ordeal was far different—tougher inside and out. She might be able to *scrub up* as she put it, but now it would always be make-believe where once it had been the real Kelly. She was even carrying her ordinary clothes with her in the small backpack she'd brought with her from her flat as if not wanting to be entirely separated from her old persona.

"You scrub up very nicely indeed."

"Are you sure this is necessary?" she asked, tugging at the front of the jacket.

"If we bump into racecourse security it's best to look like we belong rather than we're casing the place."

She shrugged. "Isn't that what we're doing in a sense—casing the place?"

"I hope so." He stepped back, inviting her to join him. "Come on. Come and see exactly what Vee got up to and then—seeing as you're dressed up for it—I'll buy you lunch."

As she moved past he put a hand in the small of her back. She stopped and glanced down.

"I can walk," she said. "But keep that up and *you* might not be able to."

—**43**—

O'NEILL SPOTTED FRANK Allardice as soon as he walked into the little tapas place just outside Covent Garden. The retired detective chief inspector was holding court at the bar, a pint of lager half-drunk by his elbow, giving the barman the benefit of his vast experience.

O'Neill paused in the doorway. Allardice was just the same as he remembered. Older maybe, browner of skin and thicker of waist, but still the same arrogant sod he'd always been.

Allardice turned at that moment and spotted him, giving the barman chance to beat a hasty retreat.

"Vince! Good to see you, old son." Allardice thrust out a meaty hand for a bone-crushing shake. "What'll you have—a pint? My shout."

"Just a half, Frank," O'Neill said, disengaging his fingers while they still had feeling. "Some of us have got to work this afternoon." *And the days of turning up half-cut after long boozy lunches went out about the same time you did.*

"If you say so. Hey! Half a lager down here *rápido, por favor.*"

O'Neill leaned an elbow on the bar, friendly but less rooted than taking the next stool along. "So how's life on the Costa Del Crime these days?"

"Flourishing, my son," Allardice said taking a swig of his lager and pulling his lips back in appreciation. "Better than this poxy shit-hole that's for sure. Any time you fancy packing in the daily grind and coming out to run another bar for me, sergeant, you let me know."

"It's *inspector* now," O'Neill said mildly, nodding his thanks to the barman who put down the half-pint and fled again.

Allardice pursed his lips. "Is it now? Well done, old son. Always knew you were destined for greatness—right from when you were a newly minted DC still wet behind the ears and only just old enough to shave the bum-fluff off your chin."

It was hard to tell, O'Neill reflected, if Allardice was being sincere. His style of delivery had always veered between sardonic and outright sarcastic.

"So what can I do for you, Frank?" he asked. "I assume you didn't ask for a meet to discuss my career prospects."

Allardice grinned at him. "Still the same old impatient Vince eh?" he said. "All cut to the chase and no foreplay with you is there?"

"I can dance when I have to," O'Neill said taking a sip of his drink. It was cold enough for condensation to have formed already on the outside of the glass. "But your ego was always plenty healthy enough without any stroking from me."

"You got that right, old son," Allardice agreed amicably. "You must have learned to play the suck-up game though. You're still a bit of a whippersnapper to have made DI."

O'Neill suddenly got the impression he was being sounded out about something. He kept his expression neutral. "Didn't you hear, Frank? Our policemen are getting younger every day."

Allardice laughed out loud at that. "Too right," he said. He slid off his stool and picked up what remained of his drink. O'Neill noticed that the man's hands were starting to liver-spot and although the hair on his head was still suspiciously dark and glossy, the mat visible at the open neck of his shirt was looking decidedly grizzled. Allardice and Quinlan had been contemporaries but the chief super had aged if not better then certainly more gracefully.

"Let's go sit out back while we're still allowed to have a smoke *there* at least," Allardice said with a jerk of his head.

O'Neill picked up his lager and followed the ex-copper out to a tiny yard at the rear of the bar. A couple of rickety patio tables were huddled together under a space heater. An attempt at landscaping had been made with a scatter of half-hearted plants in terracotta pots that had been used as ashtrays. Allardice sat and looked around him with contempt. He fished in his pocket for a red and white pack of Fortuna cigarettes and offered them across.

"Gawd. If they gave me charge of this place for six months I'd double their turnover for them," he remarked, lighting up. "No worries."

"Quite the expert aren't you?"

Allardice grinned and raised his glass. "I've three bars and a restaurant now," he said. "Bloody entrepreneur that's me."

O'Neill tired of the swagger. "Why did you come back, Frank?"

"I heard the news about Kelly Jacks—up to her old tricks again," he said. "Thought you might want all the gen straight from the horse's mouth. Doing you a favour."

"Heard the—" O'Neill began and his eyes narrowed. "It was only released this morning."

"So? Spain's a civilised country. Our EU brothers and all that. Besides, I had a bit of business back home anyway, so—two birds. I pulled a few strings and hopped on the first cheap package jet out of Málaga. Rang you from Heathrow."

"Why the big hurry?"

Allardice regarded him for a moment with that expressionless gaze he'd used to such effect during his years as a copper on a tough patch. "Because I warned 'em when they locked her up that she was one loopy bitch. They should have thrown away the key but she was clever. Clever enough for there to be an element of doubt about *why* she did it."

"The amnesia plea you mean?"

"Amnesia my arse," Allardice snorted. "She did it and she knows full well she did it. That was the best she could come up with to wriggle out of a cast iron murder charge. She attacked and killed Callum Perry and tried to get away with it. End of story."

O'Neill paused. "She keeps bringing up the case she was working on at the time," he said carefully. "I've been looking into the files. A dead prostitute. Remember that one too?"

"I may have gone soft around the middle old son but that doesn't mean I've gone soft in the head. 'Course I remember. Jacks was just trying to make a name for herself—you know how they get. They watch too many TV shows and think it's all about the geeks. It was just another hooker made a bad decision and paid the price for it. End of story. Jacks just couldn't face being wrong."

O'Neill frowned. "Did she even *know* Perry?"

Allardice took a long pull on his cigarette and shook his head as he exhaled. "Not as far as we could work out. He was just a barman up the East End. Jacks claimed he'd asked for a meet but we couldn't find anything to support that. She said she didn't know what he wanted and next thing he's dead." He gave a short laugh. "Difficult to claim it was an accident when she stabbed the poor bugger about eighteen times, so she comes up with all that crap about not being able to remember."

"And you never found out what Perry might have known in relation to the case?" O'Neill asked. He fixed his former boss with a cool eye. "If this is going to come apart on me Frank, I'd like a heads up."

"Not a sausage," Allardice said firmly. "Whatever he knew—if there was anything for him to know in the first place—he took it with him. Kelly Jacks made sure of that."

—44—

"YOU LOOK ... PENSIVE," Lytton said. He sat relaxed, draping an arm along the back of the empty chair alongside him.

"Wouldn't you in my position?" Kelly asked. They were in the members' bar at the top of the modern grandstand. Midweek with no event in progress the place was almost deserted and the view was stunning.

Directly beneath them were the private boxes with their slanted glass walls looking out over the track. The boxes were set slightly forwards of the grandstand seating to give unobstructed sight of the action. Here the privileged could go from expensive lunch to closeted luxury without ever having to mix it with the hoi polloi below.

Kelly glanced at the debris of an excellent meal which had yet to be cleared from the starched tablecloth and admitted, "If this is being on the run I could get to like it."

Lytton smiled, then asked, "You really think you'll get to the bottom of this when the police haven't?"

"I don't think they're trying," she said levelly. "It's too tempting to go for the obvious explanation and forget the rest. And I worked for the police don't forget. I was a crime-scene specialist for nearly ten years so I know the real cleanup rate not just the figures massaged for public consumption."

He nodded and reached for his glass of imported lager. Kelly had started out on sparkling water and was now drinking tea. They sat in comfortable silence until he asked suddenly, "There was something in the news reports about you—from back then—I didn't quite understand." Only his raised eyebrow made it a question.

Kelly forced herself not to tense up. "And what was that?"

126

"Your nickname," he said. "They said you were known as 'the blood whisperer'. It's not a term I've ever come across."

She smiled. "I'm not surprised. It was more a bit of poetic licence than anything else."

He gestured with his glass. "Go on."

She took a moment to find the right words, neither too serious nor flippant. "Evidence speaks to me," she said at last simply. "Maybe I learned how to listen better than most."

"And what did Vee's workspace have to say to you?"

"It tells me the kind of person she was."

"Which is?"

Kelly hesitated again, choosing her words carefully. For all his apparent detachment he still referred to his wife—still thought of her—in the present tense.

"Organised," she said, "maybe to the point of obsession. She seemed to write everything down more than once. There was a diary and a day-planner—both were filled in and kept up to date. So I would say ... good on the details, neat, sharp, vain."

"Vain?"

Again Kelly paused. *How do I say that she doesn't strike me as the kind of woman who'd ruin her good looks by putting the barrel of a gun into her mouth and blowing the back of her head off? Pills yes. Maybe even a hosepipe from the car exhaust. But a rifle? No.*

"This suit as a backup for a start. Spare cosmetics and hosiery in her desk drawer," she said instead. "Clearly she wasn't the kind of woman who'd be happy being seen out with smudged lipstick or laddered tights."

Lytton's mouth twisted. "I'd say you've got her taped," he said. "She never goes ... never *went* anywhere without full make-up and her BlackBerry, like a shield and armour. She loved that thing—said the blue matched her eyes. I swear she'd even have it with her in the bath."

He stopped suddenly aware of what he'd just said. Kelly stepped easily into the awkward moment.

"That would be the ultimate definition of multitasking," she murmured. She lifted the lid of the teapot and gave the contents a swirl. "So where is it?"

"It's ..." His voice trailed off. "You know, I've no bloody idea," he said at last, surprise in his voice. "I've already been through her study at home and it wasn't there or at the apartment. And we didn't find it in her desk today—not that she would leave it here. I've known her turn around practically at the front gates and drive back to town if she'd forgotten it."

Kelly said nothing. Her mind had already jumped ahead but she realised that voicing her suspicion—that if the device wasn't to be found somebody must have taken it—would bring an instant denial. This she had to leave him to work out for himself.

She turned her head and stared out deliberately over the scope of the racecourse while he wrestled with it. After a few minutes he asked, "How long have you known?"

She turned back, found him watching her intently, leaning forwards in his chair. She was almost unnerved by the intensity of those dark grey-green eyes.

"As long as you have, probably," she said. "She was your wife after all. You'd have known her best."

His mouth twisted in a derisive smile that held no amusement. "*Knowing* Vee wasn't easy," he said. "Very little pierced that icy façade. Trust me—I tried. Eventually I had to accept that we had signed a contract not a marriage licence. I gave her wealth and she gave me a certain ... respectability. Anything more wasn't on the table."

She heard the frustration and the sadness, opened her mouth but before she could speak another voice broke in.

"Matt! Thought I'd find you up here."

Kelly heard the annoyed hiss of Lytton's escaping breath. She twisted in her chair to see a man weaving towards them between the largely empty tables. Fair-skinned and blond he was shorter and more squat than Lytton but in no way running to fat. He wore an expensive suit with careless elegance, one hand stuffed into the jacket pocket.

Trailing behind him was a dowdy woman who seemed to walk with her eyes permanently downcast and her shoulders rounded defensively so that she was almost crabbing. She was so plainly dressed it was hard to put an age on her. Kelly guessed forties but she could have been ten years out either way—it was hard to tell. With her face devoid of make-up and her dark hair pulled back severely from her face the woman seemed completely over-matched by her surroundings and company.

With obvious reluctance Lytton rose and shook the newcomer's hand. The woman presented her cheek meekly for his kiss. Kelly got the fleeting impression she did so because she knew Lytton expected it but took no pleasure in the greeting herself.

"Steve Warwick," the man said turning to Kelly and bending over her exaggeratedly as he took her hand. "I don't believe we've met."

Kelly pushed her chair back and got to her feet as much to put some distance between them as for politeness. She gave him a purposely limp grip knowing he was the type to take anything else as a challenge.

"No we haven't," she agreed smiling sweetly. "Nice to meet you Steve."

Warwick looked her up and down like he was gauging the price and frowned, glancing at Lytton.

"My business partner," Lytton said shortly. "And his wife Yana."

Kelly disengaged herself and reached round Warwick towards the woman hovering in his shadow. "Hello Yana."

"Am pleased meet you," Yana mumbled her English heavily accented. She barely touched her fingers to Kelly's before dropping back as if trying very hard not to be noticed.

"Won't you join us?" Lytton said with more than a hint of sarcasm as Warwick was already plonking himself down next to Kelly, ignoring his wife. It was left to Lytton to wave Kelly back to her seat and pull out a chair which Yana slunk into.

"So, who are you?" Warwick asked more baldly, something of his bonhomie disappearing. "Only I couldn't help noticing Matt had signed you in as his PA and I'm fairly sure I know all our staff pretty well." His eyes wandered up her lower legs in leisurely inspection. "So what kind of tasks do you *personally assist* Matt with, hmm?"

"Kelly is simply a friend," Lytton said quickly as if he knew how she was likely to react to this kind of innuendo. Kelly briefly considered smacking Warwick's legs for him like the snotty child he was. She snuck a quick peek at Yana while all this was going on but the woman kept her gaze firmly on the table linen, frowning as if deep in thought.

"A *friend* eh?" Warwick said with something close to a leer. "You dark horse you."

"Steve—" Lytton began warningly but Kelly interrupted him with a bright smile.

"OK let's get this out in the open," she said. "I am not shagging your business partner and have no desire to do so—certainly not within days of his wife dying. Nor, if you'll forgive me for being blunt, do I find you remotely attractive either. And no I'm not a lesbian, since that's bound to be your next question." She caught the eye of a lurking waiter. "Now that's out of the way shall I order more tea?"

Warwick opened and closed his mouth a couple of times then said faintly, "Erm coffee for me."

Lytton quietly saluted her with his glass. Yana continued to stare mutely at the tablecloth.

Kelly ordered from the waiter. Silence formed around his departure and she cursed inwardly. Such an outburst was not going to help her stay below the radar but she'd lost patience with oafs like Steve Warwick a long time ago and learned that life was too short to suffer them when she no longer had to.

She grabbed the handles of her bag, sitting next to her chair, and got to her feet.

"I'm sorry," she said to Lytton, "but I think I need to get back. Thank you for showing me round the place. And for lunch."

"You're welcome," he said rising. "I'll drop you wherever you need to go."

"Thank you." She smiled at Yana, receiving no response, and gave Warwick a cool stare. "Goodbye. Meeting you has been … interesting."

"Likewise," Warwick drawled recovering something of his poise.

She nodded to Lytton and hefted the bag. "I'll just get changed. I'll meet you in the car park."

45

LYTTON WATCHED HER walk away from the table fascinated by the way the heels emphasised the definition in her calves. All that climbing certainly had an effect.

Warwick leaned in towards him. "For God's sake Matt are you out of your tiny mind?" he demanded in a savage whisper. "I know who she *is*. I recognise her from the other day at the house never mind the news reports. What the *hell* are you doing bringing her here of all places?"

Lytton eyed the other man's anxiety without concern. How did he explain? It was probably best not to try.

"She was determined to investigate," he said instead, keeping his voice even, dispassionate. "And in that case it seemed preferable by far to have her on the *inside*."

"One phone call and she'd be on the inside all right," Warwick muttered, "of Wormwood bloody Scrubs."

Lytton linked his hands on the tabletop, put his head on one side. "Isn't that a male prison?"

Warwick made an irritated gesture as if flipping away an annoying insect. "You know damn well what I mean," he complained.

"Of course—but this way she's keeping me informed every step she takes."

"I don't like it. It's a risk."

"Risk of what exactly, Steve?" Lytton asked, his voice dangerously soft. "There isn't anything you want to tell me is there?"

46

IN THE LADIES' room, Kelly changed back into her own clothes with a feeling that was half regret and half relief.

She slid the grips out of her hair, ran her fingers through it vigorously to return it to its usual more comfortable casual style. But as she fastened the belt of her cargoes she glanced at the lavender dress hanging on the back of the cubicle door.

"Nice try," she murmured to herself, "but it's just not me anymore."

She folded the dress as carefully as she could into the backpack aware that it was probably going to need dry cleaning just to get rid of the creases.

She wasn't expecting company so it was a surprise to find Steve Warwick's wife Yana waiting anxiously by the doorway when she stepped out of the cubicle.

"Hello," Kelly said cautiously. A frightened mouse the woman might be but she could still recognise Kelly from the news reports.

Yana ducked her head by way of greeting and hurried over with wide pleading eyes.

"You need go," she said urgently, fingers grasping Kelly's arm. Her nails were short and discoloured. "Please hurry."

"Yana, I ... Why?" Kelly asked flatly.

The other woman looked about to burst into tears. "My husband is bad man," she said as if the information was being tortured out of her. She glanced nervously over her shoulder. "He do things that are ... illegal. I do not know what to do."

"I'm very sorry but—trust me—I'm the last person you should be asking for help right now."

"Help?" Yana said, her face blank. "No, no! You no understand. *I* try help *you*."

"What?"

Yana shook her head as though frustrated by her own lack of vocabulary, accent thickening. "He deal with peoples from my home country. How you say? Bad men."

"Gangsters," Kelly supplied, her mouth going suddenly dry.

"*Da!* Gangsters," Yana said. "That how I came here—as payment. You understand?"

Bastards. "Oh I understand."

Yana nodded, eyes still flitting to the doorway as if expecting her husband to burst in at any moment and drag her out by the hair. "He and Mr Lytton they talk about you just now. Mr Lytton he say he 'want you where he can keep eye on you', yes?"

"Did he now ..." Kelly's voice was cold but she felt something shrivel into a hard tight knot in the centre of her chest.

"I work sometimes for poor Mrs Lytton. I know she hear something bad—something that make her very unhappy—about her husband."

"What was it?"

Yana shook her head. "I don't know. She not tell me. But after two days she dead. And now I scared." She was twisting her hands together until the knuckles showed white. "My husband he send text to someone—I think about you. You need go now! Before he hurt you too ..."

—47—

IN THE CAR park of the racecourse Dmitry shoved his cellphone back into his pocket and climbed out of the Mercedes. Above him towered the modern grandstand, like a giant vee balanced on its side.

He moved without haste across the open tarmac towards the bulk of the stands. As he went he patted the pockets of the leather coat. In one side he had several industrial tie-wraps suitable for immobilising the average adult female without possibility of escape. In the other was the extendible baton he'd used to such effect on Ray McCarron.

Dmitry wasn't happy having the baton concealed there—it pulled the coat out of line. But he wasn't expecting to carry it for long.

—48—

KELLY TOOK THE emergency exit stairs three at a time jumping the last batch to each half landing and using the walls as a springboard. If she'd still been in heels she would have broken both her ankles before the end of the first flight.

It had taken too much time to reassure Yana. The woman had suffered minor hysterics as it sank in what her husband and Lytton might do if they worked out she had tipped off Kelly.

"Tell Matt I was planning to duck out on him all along," Kelly said ignoring the voice in her head that craved Lytton's approval for her actions in some small way. She closed her mind to it, hardened her voice. "Tell him I was taking him for a ride." Her mouth twisted. "Well you just can't trust an ex-con, can you?"

Yana gazed at her with slightly uncomprehending eyes but nodded mutely. Kelly knew the other woman would pass on the message—if only to save her own skin.

"You should get out too Yana," she said fiercely. "Get out while you still can."

"I ... cannot." Yana shook her head vigorously, gave a wan smile. "And he not force himself on me so much now—he take his pleasure ... elsewhere."

That last had Kelly wanting to stay and punch Steve Warwick's lights out for him but what good would that do other than provide a sense of righteous satisfaction? Kelly gave Yana's arm a last heartfelt squeeze, and ran.

She shouldered into the straps of the backpack as she went, hardly able to see for the sudden blurring of her vision.

Uppermost was anger, she realised. Anger at herself that she'd slid into trust so easily. She'd thought after David that trusting a man—being attracted to him—would not happen without a long association. And yet she'd found herself going to Lytton within days of their first meeting. She remembered curling into the side of him on the sofa at his apartment and cursed herself for a weak-minded fool.

She kept heading down, eventually finding an open door that led out onto a walkway at the base of the huge covered stands. In front of her was a set of railings that looked down onto the paddock area. Doors at each end of the walkway were marked EXIT. Kelly hesitated a moment then went left.

As she stepped out she glanced upwards. Somewhere above her Lytton and Warwick were still sitting at the table in the members' bar, hopefully oblivious to her premature departure.

She felt guilty ducking out and leaving him with the bill until she realised she didn't have a hope of paying it anyway.

Kelly paused, looked around. She swore under her breath that she hadn't taken enough note of the way in to have an exit strategy planned. How many times had she listened to other inmates explaining their capture because of just such a mistake.

Sitting there listening to their stories it had seemed so elementary. Now she wasn't so sure.

But Lytton had lulled her into a false sense of security. *Stupid, stupid, stupid!* It echoed in her head to the beat of her own footsteps. *Just because he's charming and attractive, it doesn't mean he's not a monster under the skin.*

She should have learned *that* from being inside, if nothing else.

The sign above the double doors lied. When Kelly reached them they were firmly locked, providing no way out. She turned, began to head for the other end.

If they were locked too she was going to have to go back inside, try and find another way that didn't involve going out past the security man on the desk. She broke into a jog. This was all taking far too long.

As if providing an answer to her prayers the far doors opened and a man came through. Kelly dropped back to a fast walk not wanting to give him cause for a second glance.

He was young, bearded, wearing a black leather coat that bulked out his shoulders. His hair was long enough to wave slightly as he moved.

As he moved ...

Something stabbed into Kelly's subconscious with enough of a jolt to make her gasp. A memory that was somehow deeper than a memory. More an inbuilt sense of fear, a primeval instinct.

Predator.

Her body language must have given her away. At the very moment the word formed in her mind she saw the change in him. He abandoned all pretence of being just another visitor there by chance and became the hunter, arrowing in on her.

He was already closer than she was to the door she'd last come through and she knew the one behind her was locked. It only took a fraction of a second to realise she had only one option left.

Kelly put both hands on top of the railing and launched herself over into the space below.

—49—

DMITRY DARTED FORWARDS and made a grab for the woman's hooded sweatshirt as she jumped. His fingers just brushed the small backpack she carried then she was plunging downwards away from him.

Holy Mary, she has a death wish!

The irony of that thought did not immediately occur to him as he hit the railings leaning out to watch her descent. It was at least five metres to the ground and he expected the worst.

To his amazement she landed feet first, neat as a cat, onto the lid of a big green wheelie bin that was directly below. The plastic deformed like a trampoline to break her fall. She catapulted from there to the ground with hardly a break in stride and took off running.

For a second it was all Dmitry could do to watch her go with his mouth open. He closed it with a snap, slapped the railing hard with both hands in sheer frustration and sprinted back the way he'd come. As he did so he reached for the baton in his jacket pocket.

Nobody had warned him he was after Catwoman.

OK bitch, let's see you dodge this.

—50—

KELLY BOLTED THROUGH the deserted parade ring keeping close in to the line of the building so she'd be harder to track from above. At least she was out in the open although she wondered if that was a good thing or not. Every instinct screamed at her to go to ground.

She'd had no clue when she made her desperate leap what lay beneath. It was entirely by chance that she'd landed squarely on the lid of the bin squashing it inwards as she did so. A foot or so either way and she'd be on her way to hospital by now. Or prison.

Or—if the mystery man had succeeded in getting hold of her—more likely to the mortuary.

A cold shiver sliced across her skin. She'd no idea who he was but at the same time she *did* know him. She just didn't know *how*.

She ducked into a tunnel that led under the stands and out towards the car park and the exits. At the far end was a set of iron gates. Even from here she could tell they were padlocked shut.

She cursed and spun. As she did so she saw a door bounce open further along the stand maybe a hundred yards away. The man in the leather jacket emerged, head swinging as he searched for her.

Kelly retreated into the tunnel again, looked in vain for other doorways leading off it. There weren't any.

Double stupid ...

Looking over her shoulder she ran towards the gates. If she'd any hopes that the padlock might be looped through just for show they were dashed as soon as she got close. The lock was snapped firmly shut and threaded through a hefty piece of chain.

Kelly grabbed the padlock. It was old, oiled but worn. She scrabbled out of her pack and dug right to the bottom of the lining for a couple of the grips she'd taken out of her hair.

She prised one of them almost straight and stripped the blob of protective resin off the end with her teeth, spitting it out. Then she knelt to the padlock trying to remember all the secrets her last cellmate had taught her during long days of boredom about the gentle art of lock-picking.

Awkwardly she wedged the end of one grip against the central tumbler to hold it under tension and slid the straightened end of the other into the barrel of the lock itself, raking the pins. It was a tricky balance of force and persuasion not helped by sweaty hands and the rampant fear of imminent discovery.

"Come on come on!" she muttered as she fumbled, almost weeping as the hairgrip slipped. She wiped her hands on the leg of her trousers and tried again.

Then behind her she heard the grit of approaching footsteps suddenly echoing loudly in the tunnel. The rhythm of them changed, picked up, as their owner began to run.

Kelly risked a glance over her shoulder, saw the man in the leather coat closing rapidly, and gave the lock one last frantic try.

DMITRY BROUGHT THE baton out of his pocket and flicked it upwards to send the inner segments shooting into place.

The woman was on her knees by the gates, facing away from him. He stopped a metre or so from her and laid the baton across her shoulder just at the vulnerable juncture with her neck.

"Stop," he commanded. "Let me see your hands."

She froze. Then very slowly she brought both hands up and out to the sides. There was a piece of crumpled wire of some sort in one of them and he realised what she must have been trying to do.

He smiled, slid the baton under his arm and reached for the tie-wraps instead. *Nice and quiet.*

"Picking locks is not quite so easy as they make it seem in the movies, huh?" he said, leaning forwards to grab hold of her arm. "OK let's go. Up."

She lurched as she rose, stumbled against the gates and put her hands out to steady herself. Dmitry let go briefly. As he did so she whirled, whipping her arm round.

There was a tremendous ringing clatter and something hard and heavy coiled itself stingingly around Dmitry's knees, pinning them. He tried to stagger back, found he couldn't move his legs and fell with a roar, spilling the tie-wraps and baton as he went down.

What the ...?

He realised in a brief flash of intuition that she'd hit him with the chain from the gates. That she had indeed managed to undo the padlock securing it with her makeshift pick.

She tried to hurdle over him but he snagged her ankle and yanked, bringing her down too. The restriction on his legs loosened and he levered up, getting a tight hold of her, pulling her down and rolling her underneath him, using his bodyweight to crush her resistance. She went rigid then began to thrash like a landed shark.

The baton was out of reach but he'd wanted to use it to subdue not kill her here. That would raise far too many difficulties. He'd just have to do this the old-fashioned way.

So he hit her in the face with his closed fist, just once. In Dmitry's experience that was usually all it took to make a woman compliant enough to handle.

She whimpered and went still under him, trembling.

"That's better," he hissed. "Be a good girl and you won't get any more."

He stretched sideways for the tie-wraps to secure her but as soon as his body was off centre, her hand darted up clawing her nails into the soft skin behind his ear, dragging him down and away.

At the same time she bucked her hips, getting one knee up and Dmitry found himself sprawling onto his side. He just had time for the anger to flare before the same knee landed hard in his groin and all such thoughts shrivelled in the face of a sickening pain.

She bounced to her feet, snatching up the chain.

"Bastard," she ground out. "Nobody hits me and gets away with it!" And she kicked him twice in the kidneys. Hard.

Pain encased his torso. For several moments Dmitry lay shallow-breathing around as much of it as he could. He was only dimly aware of the woman snatching up the baton and darting through the gates. On the other side she refastened the chain around them, snapping the padlock shut. He was vaguely aware of her flinging the baton away across the car park with a distant clatter.

Then she was gone. It was some time before Dmitry was able even to consider the possibility of going after her. By then she'd disappeared.

—52—

"WHERE THE HELL is she?" Warwick grabbed hold of Yana's shoulders and gave her a rough shake. "What did you say to her?"

"I s-say nothing!" Yana protested. She was crying, the kind of ugly weeping that afflicts some women whose faces go puffy and reddened and their noses stream.

"Leave her alone Steve," Lytton said tiredly. "It's not her fault." But even as he spoke he could not bring himself to feel utterly sorry for a woman who was so damned *passive* all the time. He couldn't imagine Kelly sitting there sobbing, letting anyone manhandle her.

Kelly.

"She s-say she always plan to run out on y-you," Yana managed, desperation in her voice. "That s-she taking you for ride."

"What?"

Yana flinched back at the suppressed anger in Lytton's voice. Even Warwick flicked him a concerned glance.

"That w-what she s-say!" Yana insisted, hands clutched whitely together around a soggy tissue in her lap, her voice turning sullen. "That she use you."

Lytton straightened slowly, trying to work out if he was surprised or not. *Not*, he realised after a moment. *Just disappointed.*

He turned away, stood by the rail looking down onto the racecourse and sucked up the cold feeling of regret. Behind him he heard Warwick still chastising his wife in low tones, her mumbling replies. He tuned it out.

He'd thought he was good at reading intent. Had to be in this business. People gave you their word and you had to work out instantly whether to take it at face value or not.

But some people you met and just felt a connection. He'd thought Kelly was one of those. Turns out she was little more than a con artist, simply after what she could get and dumping him at the first opportunity.

Question was, why now? What had she learned here or from Veronica's office that made her decide to up and run?

"Matt?"

He turned, found Warwick hovering by his elbow. "What is it?"

Warwick sighed. "Look, I'm sorry chap. I can see you're cut up about this." He paused. "I guess it's better this way though."

"Better?" Lytton asked not turning his head.

"Yeah before you get in too deep with this girl." He glanced around, lowered his voice. "Jesus, Matt she could bring nothing but trouble to us."

Lytton turned. "You never did explain that one did you?"

Warwick shrugged. "This place, Matt. We've got a lot staked on the prestige of this damned race. One breath of scandal and people will stay away in droves. It will finish us."

"You exaggerate."

"Oh really?" Warwick leaned on the rail alongside him, close enough to force himself into Lytton's eyeline. "What is this girl to you? Like Yana says, she was using you and now she's taken off. Well good riddance. Get over it." He took a breath, looked about to say more then shut his mouth into a compressed line and went back to his wife.

Lytton was left standing there looking down. Steve was right, he thought. He should forget about Kelly and be thankful the encounter hadn't cost him more than it had.

So why was that easier said than done?

—53—

KELLY SAT AT the rear of a bus heading back into London, keeping the baseball cap pulled well down over her forehead and her face turned to the glass. Rain was just starting to fall from a darkening sky. It suited her mood.

The adrenaline that had fired her escape from the racecourse had receded leaving her tired, heavy-limbed and aching. Her face felt bruised and tender, already starting to swell around her cheekbone. And her hands shook with reaction like she was suffering a chemical withdrawal. She kept them tightly gripped around the pack on her knee and thought back to events in the tunnel below the stands.

This time he had a weapon and still I attacked him.

Remembering brought on a sense of panic so acute she could hardly breathe.

Wait a minute—this time ...?

The realisation drenched down over her in a slow wash, freezing her skin to shivers. The combination finally slotted into place and the lock inside her mind opened up just like the padlock on the chain around the gates. One moment it was shut fast and she was struggling uselessly and the next it lay exposed in her hands.

The man at the racecourse was the same man at the warehouse on the Isle of Dogs—one of them at least.

She'd known it partly when she saw him walking towards her. The way somebody moved was individual and distinct. Even so that might not have been enough.

But the smell of him ... that was something else again.

Scent is one of the strongest triggers for memory. Coffee, fresh bread, newly mown grass, lilies. They all produced strong accompanying mental images for Kelly. She sometimes focused on them during the nastier clean-up jobs. It was the only thing that stopped her heaving.

But this was a combination of odours—some kind of sharp citrus aftershave mingled with tobacco and another faint mechanical note that was harder to define. Not unpleasant in itself just ... associated with violence in her mind.

The violence of Tyrone's death.

Oh yeah, he was there.

She cursed herself again for not stopping to question him, search him, but at the time her only priority had been getting away from there as fast as she could. It wasn't just the man who'd come after her she had to worry about.

It was who had sent him and why.

She kept circling back to Veronica Lytton's death. Was that the start of all this? Or did it start six years ago with another rigged suicide? She couldn't see what linked the two deaths other than herself. And if someone had indeed set her up the first time around why do it all over again now?

But she couldn't deny the path of evidence—from the Lytton job via Ray McCarron's beating through to Tyrone's death. Ray had warned her not to go turning over rocks and the only person she'd told that she was going to keep looking was Lytton himself, the morning he'd sought her out at the dead junkie's flat.

Kelly swallowed back tears of self-indulgent sorrow. After today there was no denying it. She refused to believe that she'd been followed out to the racecourse by chance. Lytton's Aston might be easily recognisable but nobody had any reason to suspect she was with him.

Not unless he told them.

The thought rose bitter and unbidden but there was no way around it—he was the only one who knew where she'd be. And although she didn't trust Lytton's partner Warwick as far as she could have thrown him, by the time he and his wife arrived in the restaurant there surely would not have been time for the man in the leather coat to be summoned for an abduction. Maybe that was why he'd bungled it?

She remembered the timid Yana's warning and wondered if things had gone as badly for her as the Russian woman obviously feared. *If she's right about them she took a hell of a risk for a stranger,* Kelly thought, humbled.

But still it didn't make sense that Lytton would have arranged to have her snatched from so public a place. She'd been at his apartment all night. There had been any number of better— more private—opportunities.

Get a grip Kel, you're just looking for excuses for him, she told herself. *Face it—you wanted to trust him.*

And she *had* wanted to, she realised with a sour taste in the back of her throat.

Badly.

It was not a mistake she intended to make again.

—54—

TWELVE CROW-FLOWN MILES north-west of Kelly's bus route Frank Allardice sat in a rented Vauxhall outside a nursery school on the outskirts of Hampstead Heath.

His quarry had taken some finding. That he was here at all was a testament to palms greased and backs scratched and favours called in. There were still a few aging coppers left whose memories stretched back far enough to when DCI Allardice was a man worth staying on the right side of.

Allardice humphed out a breath. Those days were fast coming to an end he knew. He shifted in the driving seat and flicked the windscreen wipers to clear the beads of water from glass.

Bloody country. Always raining.

He hunched further into his coat, recognising that four years of living in southern Spain had made him soft as far as temperature was concerned. Anything under 20ºC and he was reaching for an extra layer.

It was a good life out there. He'd sworn he was never coming back but sometimes things you'd thought dead and buried turned out not to be.

Best to make sure.

Across the road a gaggle of parents began to gather around the school gates. A few stay-at-home fathers but mostly mothers, they clogged both sides of the road with their four-by-fours and BMWs. The only ones on foot Allardice judged to be nannies or au pairs. It wasn't just the mode of transport that set them apart—there was a definite distinction in manner and dress.

Allardice saw the girl when she was halfway along the street, approaching from behind him on the opposite side. He recognised her even in the door mirror which he'd tilted out to give him a wider view.

"Well hello there Erin," he said under his breath.

Watching her walk past him oblivious, Allardice reflected that she hadn't changed much. Erin never had looked old enough even when she was in her teens and now she was getting on for mid-twenties he would still have carded her before he'd have sold her alcohol in any of his bars.

Well, perhaps not.

She was looking good—hair cut and coloured, skin clear. Although her clothes were not the designer labels sported by some of the other mothers they were clean and reasonably smart.

She'd come a long way from King's Cross to the verges of respectability.

But not *so* far. As he watched, she gravitated naturally towards the group of nannies rather than the well-to-do mums, exchanged a few smiles and nods but nothing overtly friendly. They were acquaintances by virtue of their kids, he reckoned, rather than friends.

Well that just makes things easier. Nobody's going to stick their nose in.

He climbed out of the car buttoning up his coat and crossed towards them mindful of those cruising soft-roaders. A couple of the mothers watched him approach with wary eyes no doubt primed to expect child molesters at every turn. He smiled at them. They did not look reassured.

Erin was standing with her back to him watching the doors to the school across the playground, checking her watch. He stopped a few feet behind her, waited until something tipped her off and she turned.

"Hello Erin," he said again. "Long time since I've bumped into you … out on the street as it were."

He watched the colour drop out of her face. The breeze sent her hair across her cheek and she pushed it back behind her ear distractedly, eyes never leaving his face.

"Mr Allardice," she whispered. "What … what are you doing here?"

Allardice spread his hands. "Oh Erin, is that any way to greet an old friend?" he asked stepping in close. "Can't I just look you up for old time's sake? How's … tricks?"

If anything she grew paler still at the deliberate choice of words, glancing sideways to see who was close enough to overhear. But as if sensing the atmosphere the women nearest had sidled away.

So much for feminine solidarity.

Erin caught at his sleeve, tugging at him, her face twisting with desperation. "Please," she said low and urgent. "I'm out of all that now. I'm clean. I have a life. A proper job—"

"Receptionist at a fancy hairdressers," Allardice supplied. "Do they know you used to—?"

"Please!" she said again through her teeth, eyes beginning to redden. "Look I did what you wanted didn't I? I kept my mouth shut. What more do you want from me?"

Behind them the school doors opened and children flooded out like an emptying fish tank, all squeals and laughter. The mothers broke ranks and moved to greet them. Only Erin and Allardice remained stationary.

After a couple of beats Allardice gently removed her hand from his arm. "Just a reminder Erin," he said. "That I know where to find you. That you still have a lot to lose. *More* these days I would have said, wouldn't you?"

A tousle-haired little girl came running across the playground, her stride faltering as she picked up on the tension between her mother and the stranger standing alongside.

With a fearful glance, Erin wheeled away from him and bent to welcome her with arms open. The child ran into the embrace and allowed herself to be swept up, cuddled.

Erin turned back with the little girl on her hip, their heads close together. She seemed to regain a little of her courage now she had hold of her daughter. Maybe she was just putting on a brave face in front of the kid.

"I haven't forgotten," Erin swore. "And I won't!"

"Good girl. Let's keep it that way eh?"

As he spoke Allardice reached out and trailed the edge of one finger down the little girl's cheek. Erin flinched but the child just regarded him mutely, eyes grave and huge in a chubby face. He tried a smile. It did not meet with a response.

"Cute kid," he said stuffing his hands into his coat pockets. He began to turn away, paused. "She looks just like her father."

—55—

"IDIOT!"

Myshka's voice rose to a shriek as it lashed across the room, followed half a second later by a vase of roses. The vase hit the far wall at shoulder height and shattered into a splash of fragments, scattering a burst of broken petals like drops of blood.

Dmitry winced. She'd always had a temper and lately it seemed to have worsened.

"Myshka—"

"How could you let a *girl*—a *nobody*—get the better of you?" she demanded, whirling on him with both fists clenched and shaking above her head. "How could you let her get away?"

Dmitry got to his feet painfully. It was evening and he'd come back to Harry Grogan's apartment knowing a showdown with Myshka was on the cards. He was in no mood to fight. His back was already turning purple from where that bitch had put the boot in and he'd been passing blood all afternoon.

Next time ...

"I was there only to look again at the territory—to watch," he said doggedly, trying to keep his voice soothing, reasonable. "And it was too public. Not a good place to take her—"

"It was an opportunity," Myshka cut in sharply. "A *wasted* opportunity."

Dmitry felt his own anger begin to rise but he wisely tamped it down. No point in both of them losing it and wrecking the place.

Besides she was right, damn her.

"It was and maybe I made an error of judgement," he agreed simply. "I'm sorry."

The admission and apology seemed to take her by surprise. She stood for a few moments biting her lip, a war of emotions raging in her face, behind her eyes. Then she let out a long breath, her shoulders slumping. She crossed to him, cupped his face with both palms.

"A great general is a man who adapts to circumstance, yes?" she murmured, smoothing her thumbs over his cheekbones. Her talon-like false nails seemed to come perilously close to his eyes. He forced himself not to flinch at the prospect of being blinded on an impulse. "And we cannot afford mistakes—not when we are so close."

"I know," he said gently. "But this girl is no general—do not forget that. She is, as you say, a nobody. A cleaner who got nosy.

She is on the run. The police are after her." He paused. "Why not let them catch her?"

"Maybe—afterwards," Myshka said, pursing her lips. "Until then it would be better if we have ... control over her, yes?"

"I have put the word out," Dmitry said. "She cannot hide forever." He peeled one hand away, pressed his lips into her palm and curled her fingers around the kiss. "The police already believe her guilty. The longer she evades them the more guilty she becomes. After all she has done this before has she not?"

Myshka smiled, faintly at first then wider. "You are right, of course." She sighed, eyeing the broken vase, the strewn stems and dripping carpet with regret. "Nothing can stop us now."

And if Dmitry heard the faintest trace of doubt in her voice he kept that to himself too.

—56—

BY THE TIME Kelly reached the tower block in Brixton the rain was coming on hard.

The only good thing about that was it kept people's heads down and gave her the excuse to do the same. She had the baseball cap tucked well forwards over her face and was confident she was reasonably safe from discovery.

Besides, nobody willingly went to the cops round here.

Kelly had grown up in an area like this, in yet another overcrowded social housing project that hadn't quite worked. Even so, community spirit had still played a part in those days— the drug-related crime hadn't quite become all-pervading. She hadn't been home in a long time. Not for several years before her downfall and certainly not since her release. Her brothers and sister had made it clear there was nothing for her there.

Few people were out on the street in this neighbourhood and those that were gave her a wide berth anyway. She felt like a stranger but somehow one who had never quite lost the look of belonging. Not only that but Kelly realised she was probably putting out fury in waves that were palpable.

The lift in the block wasn't working but even if it had been Kelly would have walked. After working so many clean-ups for Ray McCarron she knew that she couldn't stand being enclosed with the stink of old urine for more than a couple of floors without a face mask.

Not that the stairwell was much better. She climbed the rancid concrete steps with care but encountered nobody lurking besides a couple of rats. They eyed her boldly and without alarm as she passed.

The flat she was after was on the seventh floor in the south-west corner which meant it was unbearably hot in the summer months. Kelly had never been there but it seemed familiar nevertheless. She'd heard all about it many times—there hadn't been much else to talk about.

The door opened a chain's-length to her knock and a single unknown eye in a white face peered at her warily through the gap. There was a TV or a stereo playing loudly in the background, raised voices. Kelly felt defeat wash over her.

"I'm looking for Tina—" she began, and heard commotion somewhere deep inside the flat.

The door slammed but before she could turn away it was thrust open again—fully this time—and Tina Olowayo towered in the aperture.

"Kel!" she yelped and the next moment Kelly found herself lifted off her feet and spun around, engulfed in a mammoth bear hug that threatened to crack half her ribs.

Tina was six foot in flat shoes with blue-black skin and the sinewy muscled build of an athlete. When Kelly had first met her, in a winter-cold exercise yard up in the North East, the woman had seemed a bitter angry giantess railing at the injustices of the world.

She'd been even more angry at anybody who was—or had been—remotely connected to the police and she'd sought out Kelly as a means of retribution.

Fortunately Kelly had been forewarned of this impending confrontation far enough in advance to do a little homework. So when Tina had stepped forward from the crowd cover provided by other inmates, flexing, and thrown down her challenge, Kelly was ready for her.

She'd simply stood her ground and told Tina outright that her lawyer had been a bloody fool to have missed the obvious forensics cock-up in the case that had sent Tina down.

Tina could easily have ignored this as bravado but she didn't. Uneasily, warily, the two of them sat and talked until their hour outside was up. They talked again every chance they got. Six months later Tina's ten-year sentence was overturned on appeal and she was free.

She left Kelly behind still serving time but Tina told her she wouldn't forget that she owed her big time. She told Kelly that she was always welcome in the dirty little corner of Brixton Tina called home—if Kelly was ever desperate enough to venture there.

It was nice to discover, Kelly thought as she struggled for breath, that some people remembered their promises.

At last Tina put her down and whirled her inside all in the same effortless move. She was wearing a T-shirt with the sleeves cut off. Her hair was shoulder length and in braids. The white kid who'd answered the door silently clipped the security chain across again and sloped past them into the kitchen.

"Hey Elvis—make yourself useful and put the kettle on," Tina called after him. "My friend, she like tea. Try not to bugger it up."

Elvis gave a mumbled reply that Kelly took to be assent.

Tina dropped an arm across her shoulders and steered her into the living room, pressing her down onto the squashy sofa as she muted the TV. Then she stared down at Kelly for a couple of beats, flipping at the brim of the baseball cap and trailing along the blossoming bruise across her cheekbone with one finger. Her grin fell away.

"You in trouble *deep,* girl," she said.

"I swear to you I didn't kill him."

Tina put her hands on her hips. "We talking years ago?" she asked. "Or yesterday?"

"Either," Kelly said with a bloodless smile. "Both."

"Yeah but can you prove it?" Tina asked. "'Cause we both know—bottom line—that's what counts. Everything else is just blowing smoke up your arse."

"I don't know," Kelly said wearily. She waved at the dressing still covering the cut on her forearm. "I think I was drugged. I've put a sample in to a private lab so I'll know in a couple of days. Until then—" she shrugged "—I need to stay out of the way of the police."

"And you only just coming to me now?" Tina sounded offended.

Kelly chose something close to the truth. "I wanted to keep trouble away from you," she said. She glanced up at the woman standing over her, caught something in her face that made her pause. "What?" she asked suddenly tense. "What have you heard?"

"That the filth is the least of your problems right now," Tina said grimly. "There's a price on your head, girl. A big one. And they're not hanging the payout on getting a conviction, if you know what I mean."

"A *price*?" Kelly repeated, shocked. "Who the hell has put a price on my head? Not the police surely?"

Tina shook her head. "Ain't you listening?" she asked. "This is not a reward—it's a bounty. All nice and unofficial. And somebody *much* worse than the cops. What you done to upset a honky gangster called Harry Grogan?"

—57—

DI O'NEILL STUCK his head round the door to the CSI's office and rapped his knuckles lightly on the wood panel.

At his desk by the window Bob Tate glanced up from a report.

"Ah Vince. Good, good," he said beckoning. "Come in laddie and close the door behind you."

O'Neill was briefly reminded of Chief Superintendent Quinlan. Tate was already heading for the vending machine in the corner of the room asking over his shoulder, "Moo and two?"

"Excuse me?"

"Ah sorry—milk and a couple of sugars?"

"Is it tea or coffee?"

"Hmm, that's a debatable point. Nominally coffee I would have said but without further analysis it's hard to be sure."

"In that case, yes to both." O'Neill perched himself on the edge of the desk and waited, trying to curb his impatience until Tate returned carefully balancing a paper cup of steaming dark brown liquid. "So what do you have for me?"

"You'll have seen the pathologist's report on young Douet, I assume?"

O'Neill took an experimental sip and regretted it instantly on grounds of both taste and temperature. He managed to swallow before shaking his head. "I think it's waiting on my desk. I was just on my way back to the office when I got your message."

"Well the gist of it is much as we expected. A nasty wee tap on the back of the skull followed by a few sharp stabs for good measure. Any one of half-a-dozen of them would have been fatal given time."

O'Neill was aware of a sudden deflation, his shoulders weighing heavy beneath his jacket. "Nothing of note then."

Tate regarded him sternly. "Do you think I'd drag you in here just to tell you that?" he demanded.

"Oh?"

The CSI reached across and picked up a single page from the top of his in-tray. "You recall the bag of blood which we suspected might have come from Ms Jacks?"

"Of course," O'Neill said knowing Tate liked to spin things out and trying to hurry him along.

"I called in a favour or two at the lab for a bit of queue-jumping and a comprehensive range of tests," Tate said. He paused, allowed himself a thin smile. "You owe me a bottle of single malt for that by the way."

"You know I'm good for it," O'Neill said tightly. "What did they find? Was the blood from Jacks?"

Tate gave a pained frown at this prompting but nodded. "Her DNA is on file so that part was an easy match but my pal ran a full tox screen as well."

152

"Thorough." O'Neill risked another sip and found the faux-coffee had dropped to a slightly less molten level.

The CSI briefly showed his teeth. "Did I mention it was a very *good* single malt?"

"You didn't," O'Neill said with a resigned note in his voice. "So what do I get for it? She claimed Rohypnol or something similar last time I believe. Any sign of that?"

Tate shook his head but before O'Neill could gloat he added bluntly, "It was ketamine."

"What?"

"Special K, Kit-Kat, Super K—call it what you will. Ketamine is mostly used as a veterinary anaesthetic but it's popular on the club scene, so I understand."

"Would it induce a psychotic episode?"

Tate pursed his lips. "It's a known hallucinogenic if that's what you mean. Might induce a certain level of amnesia depending on the dose. People take it because they reckon it can give them 'out of body experiences' or some such nonsense." He drew little quotes in the air with his fingers to mark his disdain. "But in this case she had enough in her system to fell an elephant. I'm no expert but I would have said she'd be unconscious pretty quickly after administration."

"*Self*-administration?"

"Possible I suppose. Depends how she ingested it. In pill or powder form it would take maybe half an hour to have any effect. Injecting's a lot faster. Looking at the concentration I'd plump for the latter. It would have incapacitated her almost immediately." He frowned. "There was no syringe found at the scene."

"There was no Kelly Jacks either," O'Neill said dryly. "She could have taken the works with her when she scarpered."

Despite his years of experience Tate looked almost shocked. "You're suggesting this wee lassie cold-bloodedly murdered someone she claimed was a friend—I heard the tape of the phone call she made to Douet's mother by the way—and then calmly gave herself a massive dose of ketamine in an attempt to cover it up?" The rising incredulity in his voice made it a question. "For God's sake man, why?"

"Why did she wake up next to Callum Perry's body six years ago?" O'Neill countered. "Who knows what was going on with her back then?"

The CSI paused a moment then said reluctantly, "Her prints were all over the place I admit, although she did have a legitimate reason to be there."

O'Neill heard the catch, raised an eyebrow. "But?"

"We found a bloody handprint on a pillar. The handprint was Jacks's—the blood was Douet's. And the only blood and prints on the knife belonged to the lassie too."

O'Neill rose, put down the last of his coffee undrunk on the desktop. "Well then," he said, "she has some kind of brainstorm—*again*—realises she can't hope to sanitise the scene before we get there so she goes through this pantomime trying to avert suspicion. How else would she know to leave us a convenient blood sample just in case we didn't catch up with her before it was gone from her system?"

Tate let him get halfway to the door. "The blood was unnecessary," he said. And when the detective stopped, turned, he went on, "Ketamine would be present in hair samples—much less painful to extract. These days we can test for it months afterwards. It's a relatively new process of course—one Ms Jacks may or may not have been aware of. Perhaps she wanted to leave us something that was harder to ignore than a few strands of hair, hmm?"

"What's this—old CSIs sticking together?" O'Neill asked softly.

Tate made a gesture of annoyance. "It's called giving the lassie a fair crack of the whip," he shot back. "Besides, how did she get hold of the ketamine?"

"She's an ex-con," O'Neill said, his voice flat. "Trust me there'll be any number of dodgy people she could turn to."

—58—

KELLY WOKE WITH a jerk and found herself propped at the chipped Formica dining table in Tina's flat. Her head was pillowed on her folded arms and she had violent pins and

154

needles in her hands. In front of her, in hibernation, was the borrowed laptop she'd been using to run internet searches on Harry Grogan.

She straightened up cautiously, flexing her fingers. She was suddenly aware that it was daylight outside when the last time she'd checked it was still sodium-lit darkness.

Tina stuck her head round the living room door wearing jogging pants and a skinny top both drenched in sweat. She carried a half-empty bottle of water and a plastic carrier bag. Kelly realised she must have heard Tina returning from her morning run.

"You back in the land of the living?" Tina asked, taking a long swallow of the remaining water. "You was spark out when I left. Didn't want to wake you."

"Maybe you should have done," Kelly said ruefully rubbing a hand round the back of her stiff neck.

Tina bounced over, dumped the carrier on the table next to the laptop. "Cheap pay-as-you-go mobile," she said. "Got it off the market. My treat."

"Thank you," Kelly said, heartfelt. "For everything."

"No sweat." Tina nodded to the pile of obviously unused blankets and pillow on the sofa. "You been at it all night?"

"Yeah," Kelly said. "Thanks for the loan of the computer too."

"Don't thank me—it's Elvis's and I don't ask where *he* got it," Tina said flashing a quick grin. "And thank the dumb fool a couple of floors down who put in wireless without no password. Half the building jumps on the back of it."

"Don't tell me," Kelly said holding up a hand. "I don't want to know."

Tina laughed. "I'm gonna hit the shower," she said. "Then you can tell me what you found out about this guy who's after you." She disappeared, thumping on the second bedroom door as she passed. "Elvis! Get your arse out of bed and down the Job Centre. You know they said they was gonna cut your benefits you idle git!"

Kelly sat back and pressed her fingers against her gritty eyes. The move reminded her painfully of the livid bruise across her cheek. Still, round here half the women went about with black eyes and she'd wanted to blend ...

It was a far cry from waking up in Matthew Lytton's beautiful apartment on the river. She blinked suddenly. Waking up there reminded her of falling asleep there. Of being held close and feeling so safe.

She couldn't believe she'd trusted him. After what happened yesterday—and what she'd found out last night—that wasn't a mistake she'd be making again.

The thin white boy Elvis drifted through on his way to the kitchen giving a duck of his head in greeting. She heard him shuffling about in there while the shower ran in another room. Somewhere nearby a baby cried continuously and a man banged on a distant wall and yelled for quiet with no sense of irony.

Elvis reappeared holding an opened can of Coke and a crumpled roll-up cigarette that Kelly suspected did not contain purely tobacco. He plonked himself on the sofa and fired up his Nintendo, earbuds in place. Whether that was to keep the noise in or the neighbours out she wasn't sure. By the time Tina returned, washed and changed, he was engrossed.

She cuffed him around the head lightly, with affection. Elvis swayed from the blow not missing a beat of his game.

"Hangs on my every word," Tina muttered. "So what you found out?"

That I've been a bloody fool.

Kelly sighed. "That too much staring at a small screen really *does* make your eyes go square," she said. "Apart from that ... More than I wanted to, probably."

Tina put a hand on her shoulder gave it a squeeze and said nothing. Kelly found her silence more encouraging than straightforward encouragement would have been. She took a breath.

"Harry Grogan seems to have done a really good job of sailing close to the wind," she began. "I can find lots of 'rumoured to be' and 'probably' and innuendo but he's never been convicted of anything—never even been arrested for that matter."

"So he's clever," Tina said. "Got to be, to get where he's at."

"There are stories about him having links to drugs, arms, prostitution, trafficking—you name it," Kelly said, suddenly bringing to mind Yana's stumbling explanation of how she'd come to the UK. *A payment. To whom? And for what?*

"He's got a *lot* of property round here," Tina said. "And he uses Russians as muscle—like we don't have enough home-grown thugs of our own."

Kelly tried to raise a smile. "They come over here, taking our jobs ..."

Tina grinned back. "You got that right."

But even as Kelly made the crack something rustled at the back of her mind. *Russians.* The accent of the man who'd attacked her—first at the warehouse and then at the racecourse—could it have been Russian? Kelly shook her head, realising just how stiff her neck had become.

"On the surface he's supposed to be a legitimate property developer," she said. *Just like Matthew Lytton.* "Owns a couple of racehorses, contributes to charities, hobnobs with the great and the good."

"If he's so squeaky why's he put a price on your head?"

Kelly hesitated. "As a favour most likely."

"A favour?" Tina's voice was sceptical. "You know for who?"

"Unfortunately, I can make a good guess," she said. She leaned forwards, woke up the snoozing laptop and nudged it round to face her friend, clicking on an image she'd minimised at the bottom of the screen.

The picture showed two men standing next to a sweat-lathered thoroughbred, obviously still blown from a hard-fought race. The men looked justifiably pleased—according to the caption they were part of a syndicate which owned the winner of some prestigious horse race.

"The fat bald guy, he's Grogan, right?" Tina said. "Who's the other one?"

"That," Kelly said, her voice remarkably level, "is Matthew Lytton." She'd already told Tina all about Veronica Lytton's supposed suicide, Ray's beating, the warning and what had come after. They'd talked well into the night before Kelly had begun her searches.

Now she pointed to the screen. "This proves Matthew and Grogan are in it—whatever *it* is—together."

"All that proves is they each own a leg of some fast donkey." Tina sat back frowning. "Ten large is some favour, girl."

That rocked Kelly. "*Ten thousand?* My God ... are you sure?"

Tina jerked her head towards the sofa. "I sent Elvis out last night, see what noise he could pick up on the street. That's what he say."

Somehow Kelly didn't see the sullen youth as a good intelligence-gatherer but she was prepared to reserve judgement—out loud at least. As if reading her doubts Tina grinned at her again. "Hey don't you go underestimating my Elvis. He don't say much but he knows how to listen." Her face sobered slowly. "And ten grand is a lot of dough."

"Dead or alive?" Kelly asked, only half joking.

"Makes no difference." Tina shrugged. "Round here they'd sell their granny for less."

—59—

BUMPING ALONG A rutted track in the back seat of a Range Rover Vogue, Steve Warwick couldn't help the feeling he was taking his last ride to nowhere.

Of course, he'd gone along willingly—to a point. Harry Grogan had asked for this meeting in as much as a man like Grogan ever simply *asked* for anything. In truth Grogan had told Warwick when and where he'd be picked up without giving him the opportunity to refuse. So Warwick had allowed himself to be whisked away out of London like a lamb to the proverbial slaughter.

He sat back and watched the scenery which had turned progressively greener since they'd left the M4 motorway and struck out across the Downs. He tried to keep his face relaxed, almost a little bored, and hoped the trickle of nervous sweat along his temple wasn't obvious to the two men in the front seats.

The driver didn't worry him so much. He was big, yes, and from here Warwick had a good view of a squat, domed head that widened from ears down to collar into a bull neck like a mastiff. But he had the look of a slow bone-cracker and Warwick had been fast enough on the rugger field to know he could probably outpace him if he had to.

It was the passenger who set his nerve ends tingling with apprehension. The passenger was younger, apparently more languid, with rather girlie hair and designer stubble of a kind Warwick had always despised. But the eyes …

There was nothing behind the man's eyes.

Warwick gripped the centre armrest as the big car lurched through another pothole, as much for comfort as to steady himself. And he wished not for the first time that he'd had the chance for a quick snort before this summons arrived. Something to bolster his confidence. Just a little.

The silent driver had turned off the road about a quarter of a mile back and since then they'd been crawling up this winding track to God-knows-where. It looked for all the world like they were taking him to his unmarked grave.

Warwick let out his breath. It emerged long and slow but shaky. He saw the front passenger's eyes flick to his in the wide-angle rearview mirror, thought he detected a flicker of amusement there, but it was hard to be sure. Warwick swallowed, checked the knot of his tie, shot a cuff and willed himself to calm.

All it takes is nerve Steve old son, he told himself. *You've always had plenty of balls in the past. Don't go soft now …*

At last the Range Rover reached more even ground, the bushes petering out into a wide expanse of lush grass that seemed to stretch for miles, offering a gently rolling view. The driver veered to the right and Warwick saw white rails and the first of a set of brushwood steeplechase fences.

Of course—the man and his damned horses!

Another Range Rover was already parked there together with an old Land Rover, its sides splattered with mud. The driver pulled up alongside them and cut the engine. He climbed out and opened Warwick's door, indicating with a jerk of his head that he should vacate. It was not a suggestion and Warwick wasn't foolish enough to take it as such.

Nevertheless he took his time as if not intimidated, stepping down into the wet grass. It immediately soaked through the turn-ups of his suit trousers. He growled under his breath and caught another twitch of a smile from the guy in the passenger seat.

The other Range Rover had an oversized sunroof over the rear seats. The bulky top half of Harry Grogan was visible poking out through it, a set of binoculars to his eyes. Warwick approached but was wise enough not to speak. Instead he turned and stared in the same direction shading his eyes with his hand.

Standing near the front wing was a whiskery grey-haired man with a face like old wood. He was wearing moleskins and a quilted jacket and battered flat cap. He nodded to Warwick without enthusiasm but didn't speak. Warwick smelt horse on him and didn't move closer.

They heard the pack before they saw them, the thrumming vibration of a dozen three-quarter-ton thoroughbreds at full stretch, each obeying the inherent instinct to get their flared nostrils in front of the others.

On the outside about halfway back was a grey horse that stood out from the rest and not just for the colour. Where the others were wholly extended, the grey horse seemed to be almost idling yet covered the ground with coordinated ease. As they came level, the grey's jockey began to ask and the horse responded at once, accelerating effortlessly on the leaders.

They swept up a slight incline hugging the rails as they thundered past. Grogan tracked them all the way, only lowering the binoculars reluctantly when they'd disappeared from view. Even then he continued to stare after them narrow-eyed across the Downs.

"Well?" he demanded of the old man in the cap.

"He's fit to race," the man said shortly, surprising Warwick with his public school accent. Warwick got the impression he was no more eager to be here than him. At Grogan's nod of dismissal the man hurried to the Land Rover keeping his gaze downcast as if to emphasise how little he'd seen and heard and bumped away down the track.

"D'you know as much about horses as your partner Mr Warwick?" Grogan asked then, offhand.

Warwick thrust his hands into his trouser pockets and glanced up, keeping his voice casual. "I know I'd save that grey colt before all the others in a fire," he said, dismissive. "He's got world class written all over him."

Grogan peered down at him sharply, his expression forbidding. For a second Warwick feared he'd gone too far with his praise, that he'd been horribly misinformed about the man's favourite animal, his weak spot.

If you've sold me a line, Myshka ...

Grogan ducked back down into the car. A moment later the rear door swung open and he was beckoned inside. The privacy glass made the interior darker and the lazing engine kept the temperature even.

"Looks like you *do* know your horses son," Grogan said settling back in a corner. He pressed a button on the armrest and the sunroof buzzed closed, shutting out the sky. The car was a long wheelbase with plenty of room in the back. Warwick crossed his legs negligently and forced himself to wait as if he'd time to dawdle. As if there was nothing at stake here.

"I hope you didn't mind this little ride out into the country Mr Warwick," Grogan said pleasantly. "I like to come and see my horses work out every week rain or shine." He removed the stopper from a crystal decanter in the polished rack between the front seats and splashed a measure of dark amber liquid into two heavy tumblers.

"At the start of it I only bought a couple of horses just to please my Irene," he continued in conversational tones as he handed a glass across. "You know what women are—got to have something to keep them occupied or they get up to mischief. She loved the gee-gees did my Irene." His face betrayed a hint of wistfulness. "Not any more of course."

"I'm sorry," Warwick said awkwardly. "Is she ... no longer with us?" He dipped his nose into the glass and recognised bourbon—not his tipple of choice.

"She's in a nursing home in Southend," Grogan said easily. "Early onset dementia so the quacks tell me. Went doolally in her fifties poor cow."

Warwick took a slug of bourbon anyway just to fortify himself. "I'm sorry," he said again.

"Don't be," Grogan said. "She's happy as Larry out there. Away with the fairies. As long as they keep to her routine and nothing upsets her. Mind you I find as I get older I'm becoming a man less tolerant of ... surprises myself."

Grogan sat back, sipping his drink with satisfaction, and between one mouthful and the next his demeanour turned cold. "I don't like changes of plan for instance—or agreements that aren't followed to the letter. You get my meaning?"

Oh shit. Warwick took another gulp of bourbon, set the glass back in its slot. "Oh, I quite agree," he said, unconsciously letting his voice drawl.

"That's good," Grogan said stonily, "because the latest shipment is on its way from St Petersburg as we speak. It's a big shipment Mr Warwick, even by my standards. One *I've* bought and paid for up front like we agreed when you said you wanted the goods brought in. We clear so far?"

"Crystal."

Grogan nodded. "So you won't have any trouble understanding my *concern* that your interim payment—due as soon as the merchandise was on its way—seems to be delayed for some reason. That sounds like an unwelcome change of plan to me."

"My dear chap you'll have your money," Warwick said willing himself not to perspire further. "You have my word on that."

Grogan sat back and linked his hands together. He had very soft white hands Warwick noticed. The kind of hands that stayed a long way from the dirty work.

"Sadly Mr Warwick, a gentleman's agreement means bugger all to me—not being a gentleman." He showed his teeth, a flash of white like a shark in murky water. "I need cold hard cash in advance or I'll find another buyer. I'm offering top quality merchandise. There'll be no shortage of takers. But if I have to go to that extra trouble there will be … penalties to pay. You *crystal* on that too?"

Fear pulled tight at the base of Warwick's skull leaving him breathless. He felt the ground shift under him, saw opportunity begin to tilt away and fought to keep his balance mentally and physically. He paused as if considering then said, "How about I include a bonus—on delivery? Full payment plus shall we say an extra five percent? To ensure future goodwill."

Grogan continued to stare at him, chin sunk down as if the only thing he was contemplating was a mid-morning nap. "Ten percent," he said at last.

"Seven."

"Make it eight Mr Warwick and you've got a deal," Grogan said giving no sign of pleasure at the extra profit. "*This* time. But I better have it in triplicate from the gnomes in Grand Cayman that the money's sitting pretty in my account before that ship unloads or I will be … upset Mr Warwick. *Very* upset."

"It will be there." Warwick offered his hand to shake on the deal but Grogan continued to stare like a fat reclining toad. After a few awkward seconds Warwick withdrew his hand and climbed out blinking in the unaccustomed brightness. By the other Range Rover the sumo-style driver was waiting with the rear door already open for him. The passenger lounged against the front wing watching.

"Oh, and Mr Warwick?"

He turned to find Grogan had lowered the rear window and was leaning towards the aperture.

"Yes?"

"Muck me about again son, I'll cut off your balls and feed them back to you. Understand?"

—**60**—

DETECTIVE CONSTABLE IAN Dempsey was so engrossed in the information on his computer screen that he only registered DI O'Neill's approach in the periphery of his mind and vision. Nothing snapped into focus until a refill mug of coffee was plonked down next to the cluster of empties already vying for desk space by his elbow.

"There you go," O'Neill said. "You look like you could do with a belt of caffeine."

Dempsey sat back in his chair and stretched both arms above his head. He was abruptly aware that his deodorant was not living up to its twenty-four-hour promise. He rubbed his hands across his face against a rasp of stubble.

"You got that right," he said wearily. "Cheers boss."

The coffee was weak instant but it was hot and wet and for that he was prepared to forgive its shortcomings. Swallowing half of it down in one go he put the mug back on the desktop feeling distinctly more human and glanced across at the huge whiteboard at the far side of the office. A picture of Kelly Jacks was tacked up as the sole candidate under 'Suspects'. Next to it was a snap of the dead kid Tyrone Douet, smiling broadly. The shot had been cropped down from a larger image of the lad with his five-a-side team. Half a football trophy was still visible on his shoulder.

"Any sightings?"

Dempsey shook his head. "She seems to have gone to ground boss. But we've plastered the city with her picture and description so it's only a matter of time." He sounded hopeful rather than confident.

O'Neill perched on the edge of the desk and nodded to the computer. "You find anything?"

Dempsey shook his head. "I've been going over the old reports on the Jacks case, looking for the kinks."

"You think there might have been something off with it?"

The DI's tone made Dempsey sudden cautious. "Not sure boss. The guy in charge—DCI Allardice—was before my time. I mean, he was an effective copper if his record's anything to go by but reading between the lines he took a few short cuts."

O'Neill scowled and, too late, Dempsey recalled that O'Neill had worked under Allardice when *he* was a DC.

Bugger. How the hell do I get out of that?

He was saved from doing so by a new voice from the doorway.

"Just because you were Frank Allardice's blue-eyed boy doesn't mean you were blind to his faults Vince," said the chief super.

O'Neill got to his feet and turned to face John Quinlan.

"No sir," he said neutrally.

Detective Chief Superintendent Quinlan advanced further into the room and Dempsey quickly slid his chair back to get to his feet but Quinlan waved him down again without taking his eyes off O'Neill.

"I hope you're not letting old loyalties get in the way of the job?" Quinlan said.

"No sir," O'Neill said again. "But Allardice is retired and well out of it—has been for a while now. What's the use of digging any of it up unless Tyrone Douet's death somehow relates to Jacks's murder of Callum Perry?"

"And does it?"

O'Neill glanced at Dempsey before answering. "Not as far as we know sir."

"Hmm," Quinlan said. He came to a halt and stuck his hands in his trouser pockets. "When the man who was in charge of an old case jumps on a plane and comes winging over here double quick just to tell you what a slam dunk it was—and how guilty *she* was—it makes my spidey-sense tingle gentlemen."

O'Neill frowned and Dempsey hid a smile.

"I suppose he *could* have said all that in a phone call."

"Indeed," Quinlan said and turned his attention to Dempsey. "So what did you find that's set *your* spidey-sense atingling?"

Dempsey hastily scrolled up the on-screen file.

"Mr Allardice never ordered blood tests on Kelly Jacks first time round," he said. "Nor did he look into her statement that Callum Perry claimed to have information to trade—information which might have given someone other than Jacks a reason to want him offed."

"She was found with the bloody knife in her hands," O'Neill pointed out with a touch of acid in his voice. "That makes for a pretty compelling case. *You* certainly thought so at the time sir."

Dempsey tried not to audibly suck in a breath but Quinlan let the pointed remark whizz past him without ruffling his hair.

"I did," he said heavily. "And if I was mistaken then I want to rectify that mistake—but not loudly and *not* in public." His stony gaze was a warning. "At the moment we don't know how the drugs in Jacks's system got there but we'll find out. Meanwhile concentrate on finding her and bringing her in. Anything else is secondary."

"Yes sir." The assent came from both men.

"And let's be robust about this, gentlemen. Follow up every lead. We can't be seen to be going easy on her because she used to be one of us. Get out there and shake some trees—see what falls out."

He nodded in dismissal and had already turned away when O'Neill asked, "What about Frank Allardice?"

Quinlan paused, considering. "Put someone on him until we know what his game is," he said at last. "He did his best to give the force a bad name while he was still within it. I'm damned if I'm going to let him succeed now he's on the outside."

—61—

MYSHKA UNLOCKED THE flat door and yanked it open. Outside she found Steve Warwick with his fist still raised in the act of pounding to be let in. A couple of workmen were passing by on the pavement behind him, their heads turned to watch his antics. They nudged each other and grinned broadly when Myshka appeared in the doorway.

She pulled the silk wrap—in scarlet this time—tighter around her body and glared at all three of them. Her state of undress infuriated her less than being seen with a complete lack of cosmetic armour.

"What is this? What are you doing here?" She kept her voice imperious. "Where is your key that you have to make all this fuss?"

"I left it at the office," Warwick muttered pushing past her. "I need to talk to you. And no it can't wait, dammit!" he added when she would have protested.

Myshka cursed inside her head in two languages. Sometimes he could be so *stupid*—just like Dmitry. *Men. Hah!* Coming here like this, causing a scene. *Causing people to remember …*

She slammed the door behind him. Warwick slumped against the wall of the entrance hall as if exhausted, loosening his tie. She smelled alcohol on his breath.

"Pull yourself together. Why have you come?" She grabbed his arm, gave it a shake. "Tell me!"

Warwick managed to raise a tired smile at being manhandled. "Well for once I haven't come for *that* darling," he said managing a bitter smile. It faded as he took in her wrap. "You *are* alone, I take it?"

Her head came up, imperious. "You expect me to be?" But instead of a sharp rejoinder she got only a wave of defeat—and fear. She made her voice soften. "I was going to take bath," she said more gently. "Come up."

He looked pathetically grateful to be taken in. But not *so* grateful, she noted, that he didn't poke his nose inside the tiny bathroom at the top of the stairs. Just to check the bath was full and the room was empty.

The Harrow flat was supposed to be a bedsit but Myshka rarely spent any time there except in bed so there was nowhere to sit. In the bedroom she turned to face him as she lit a cigarette, her eyes never leaving his face.

"Tell me," she said again.

"He sent for me this morning."

"Who?"

"Grogan—Harry bloody Grogan! Who do you think?" Warwick raked a hand through his hair, ruffling it out of style.

Myshka hid a smile, pursing her lips. "And for *this* you pee your pants?"

That worked to curb the fear and turn it into a petulant anger instead. "What do you take me for? I played it cool naturally, but it was close—too close," he complained. "He suspects, I know he does. Good God, I thought those goons of his were going to kill me and bury me out there …"

Myshka put her cigarette down into an ashtray and crossed to him. She put one hand on his shoulder and stroked his hair back soothingly with the other. "Hush," she murmured throatily. "If you are here unharmed then he suspects nothing, hmm?"

She would, she determined, find out later just how convincing Warwick had been. Either from Grogan himself, if he was feeling talkative, or from Dmitry. Dmitry might not be great at picking up on subtleties but he could judge Grogan's moods well enough by now.

Besides, if Grogan thought Warwick was becoming a problem it would likely be Dmitry who was sent to deal with him.

This could ... complicate things.

"Relax," she said now, smiling. "Remember what we talked about. A little bravery now and you will be a rich man. A *very* rich man."

For once he twisted out from beneath her hands, his movements jerky with agitation. "The shipment arrives next week," he said. "And I haven't the money to pay for it. Hell, I haven't even the money to pay for *part* of it which is why I had to promise Grogan a big fat bonus on top, which—"

"How much?"

He stopped, looked a little shamefaced as he admitted, "Eight percent."

"Eight?" Myshka laughed. "Oh my darling you drive *hard* bargain. He would usually ask for twenty."

Warwick lightened momentarily as his ego kicked in but it soon passed. "He may as well have asked for two hundred," he snapped. "Don't you understand? I haven't a hope in hell of paying him. I should never have let you talk me into this! Oh God what was I *thinking* trying to cross a man like Harry Grogan—?"

Myshka went to him again, letting the edges of the wrap slip apart as she pressed herself against him. His breath hitched, eyes starting to glaze and this time he didn't push her away. He was so easily distracted.

"You worry too much," she said softly, her own gaze on his slackening mouth. "Is all taken care of. This time next week you will have no cares, I promise." A millimetre from his lips she drew back. "You do trust me, hmm?"

"Hell of course I do darling," he said. "It's just, you weren't there today. It's a big risk." He frowned, unwilling to confess just how scared he'd been, she realised. Instead he said, "I suppose I don't like the idea of … turning against Matt either. We've known each other a long time and—"

Myshka kissed him, long and slow, angling her pelvis into his groin as she did so. "He is holding you back," she breathed. "You do not need him."

"No, no I don't," Warwick groaned as she sank to her knees in front of him. He heard the slow rasp of his zipper and his eyes flickered to a close. "Not like I need you."

—62—

IT WAS LATE afternoon before Kelly finally plucked up the courage to contact Matthew Lytton.

A part of her was aghast that she could possibly want to have anything to do with the man. But another part wanted—no *needed*—an explanation. About why he'd done what he'd done.

If she was going down again at least this time she'd know the reason behind it.

Email seemed like the coward's way but she went for it. He'd spelled out his private email for the forensics lab and Kelly had always been good at remembering details like that.

She set up an anonymous email account and composed a brief message but her fingers stilled with the cursor hovering over the send icon.

Annoyed with herself, she pushed back her chair and jumped restlessly to her feet, shoving her hands into her pockets as if to stop them doing something she'd regret.

"Let it go Kel," she said out loud. How many times had she said those words to herself? They didn't help.

She was glad she was alone in the flat. Tina had a job manning the phones at a local centre for battered wives. Elvis was … wherever he drifted to during the day—when he could peel himself off the sofa. Kelly was still not entirely sure of the relationship between Tina and the silent youth. As far as she was concerned it was none of her business.

Besides if he wasn't encouraging Tina to shoot up, beating her or pimping her out, then he sounded like a real step up on half the male company her friend had endured over the years. It was a pleasure to see her clean and focused.

Still, there were worse things a man could do to a woman. Betrayal came top of Kelly's list.

"I'll regret it if I don't do this," she said, decisive now. And she sent the email winging through cyberspace before she could think better of it.

The laptop displayed a busy symbol for maybe a second or so, during which time Kelly was nearly overwhelmed by the temptation to pull the plug on her impulse. Then it was gone and too late.

For the next half an hour nothing happened and she was filled with a sense of anticlimax.

He might not reply for days, she considered. *He might not reply at all.*

If Tina was here she knew her friend would be giving her stick for reaching out to Lytton. For giving him a second chance.

Would those five years inside have been easier to bear she wondered, if she'd known who and why?

No probably not.

She busied herself activating the phone which had been charging since Tina brought it in. Then she stood by the window gazing down into a tiny paved square that the planners no doubt envisaged as a communal play area between the blocks rather than the windswept No Man's Land it had become.

Below her the figure of a black teenager with a lanky stride walked diagonally across the square, hands deep in the pockets of his sweatshirt, baseball cap slanted to a hip angle. Kelly was reminded—suddenly and painfully—of Tyrone. Of his clumsy affection. A crush he'd never have the chance to outgrow. She felt her eyes threatening to fill.

As if coming to her rescue the laptop let out a subdued ping. She bent towards it and saw one new email waiting for her. The address was anonymous like the one she'd just set up herself but there was no mistaking the sender.

Lytton.

This was what she'd been waiting for but now it was here she was strangely reluctant to open it. She shook herself and punched the key. The message was not what she'd been hoping for. A two-word terse response.

Call me.

A cellphone number followed. Nothing else.

Kelly sank slowly into the chair still staring at the words. True, her own message had not been much longer but she'd expected more than this.

Again she hesitated. She wasn't clever enough with computers to know if staying online was dangerous. The tangible rather than the virtual had always been her field of expertise. Could he backtrack her location?

Somehow she doubted the police would be hovering over his shoulder at this moment as they had been with Tyrone's mother.

As a halfway house measure she switched to instant messaging instead.

KJ—Just tell me why.

He swapped over without a blink, the answer batting straight back at her.

ML—Could ask you the same question. Why run out on me?

Was he testing her to see how much she knew?

KJ—Why did you send him after me? she countered.

ML—Send who?

She paused. *Ah well ...*

KJ—You *know* who—the man at the racecourse. The one from the warehouse.

Again the response was almost instant, with exasperation coming through loud and clear.

ML—I know nothing about this. YOU were using ME remember?!?

Kelly sat back. She'd expected placatory lies not indignation. She'd expected to be able to cling to a righteous anger of her own, not be beset by sudden doubts.

171

KJ—Just tell me WHY Matthew.

She realised after she'd sent it that the words held nothing but a weary defeat.

There was a longer pause before his reply this time. She imagined him sitting frowning over a laptop of his own somewhere—somewhere more upmarket than Tina's Brixton bolt-hole that was for sure. At last another message came through.

ML—We NEED to talk. I'll meet you. You choose where.

He was clever she acknowledged. Somewhere safe would be too public. It would invite recognition and capture. Somewhere remote would do half his work for him.

Damn him.

Kelly picked up the cellphone and stabbed at the keys.

"Matthew Lytton."

"I'm listening," she said. "So talk."

"Kelly! Where are you? No don't answer that," he said before she could do so—even if she'd been inclined. "I don't expect you to tell me."

"Too bloody right," she said crisply.

He sighed. "Look Kelly I don't know what's going on with you but I thought we were in this together. You came to me, remember? Were you really just stringing me a line like you told Yana?"

"No," Kelly said. She opened her mouth to throw more of Yana's allegations back at him then shut it again quickly. What would it achieve beyond a quick pointless release of temper? He was hardly likely to confirm what Yana had said and it could make an already bad situation even worse for the poor woman.

"You're the one who's been stringing *me* along," she said coolly. "Setting me up for your pal Grogan to take care of."

"Grogan?" he repeated with what for all the world sounded like a genuinely blank note in his voice. "What the—?" He broke off. "Kelly what the hell are you talking about? You mean *Harry* Grogan? He's no pal of mine I can promise you that."

"Nice try," she said. "So how come I found a picture of the two of you looking very pally over some champion racehorse?"

"Hell, you're condemning me on the strength of a photo taken God knows *how* long ago?" he fired back. "Yes I owned a part-share in that bloody horse—along with half a dozen other people. Grogan elbowed his way into the syndicate just so he could stand in the winner's enclosure at Epsom. I sold my share soon afterwards and I haven't dealt with him since. I would have expected you of all people to keep an open mind about circumstantial evidence Kelly."

That stung, as it was intended to.

"And is it circumstantial that the same man who was at the warehouse when Ty–Tyrone was killed just happened to turn up at the racecourse yesterday?" She managed to keep her voice firm even though she stumbled over Tyrone's name just a little. "Who else knew I was going to be there, Matthew?"

"I told nobody," he said, brusque. "If I'd wanted to do anything to you I'd have done it the night before while you slept in my arms."

She shivered at the intent behind his words. Here again was the ruthless streak she'd sensed in him, the drive and ambition. How far did he let it command his actions?

This is a huge mistake!

"Kelly," he said quickly as if he knew she was about to cut the call. "Look, I get that we've only known each other a few days but when are you going to realise you can't do this alone? Sooner or later you're going to have to trust someone. Why not make that someone possibly the *one* person who wants to find out what the hell is going on just as much as you do?"

Kelly wavered and hated herself for it. But she still had too many questions. About his Russian dealings mainly. What had his wife discovered which so upset her shortly before her death? And had Matthew Lytton indeed murdered her?

"Clapham Common," she heard herself say. "Near the Long Pond. Know it? You've got an hour."

"I'll be there," he promised. "Just make sure you are."

DI O'NEILL DROVE across London with the chief super's orders to "shake some trees" foremost in his mind. He hoped it would prove a viable defence if his visit provoked some flak.

The connection to Kelly Jacks was tenuous but it was a connection nevertheless and he would be neglecting his duties if he didn't chase it down.

Yeah, and I can just hear you spouting that *pious rubbish at your disciplinary hearing, Vincent old son.*

He'd left Dempsey in the office still working his way down the list of known associates, so far without success. It seemed that anyone Jacks mixed with socially before her conviction—even her own family—had not picked up the threads again after her release. It was hard to tell if it was her choice or theirs.

Of the people she *had* spent time with recently, her boss was still in hospital after a vicious beating by person or persons unknown and her closest colleague was dead.

Proper little Typhoid Mary aren't you Kelly?

O'Neill swung the pool Mondeo into the private car park and saw the figure of a man striding towards a low-slung sports car, arm outstretched to disarm the security system. O'Neill accelerated briefly and pulled up directly behind the man's space, blocking him in.

Matthew Lytton already had the door to the Aston Martin open but he jerked round at the sound of the Mondeo's handbrake being roughly applied. O'Neill noticed, not without satisfaction, that there was a distinct edge of guilty shock in his face.

And just what are you *up to, sunshine?*

"Mr Lytton," O'Neill said cheerfully as he stepped out the car. "Going somewhere?"

The other man stiffened. "I have an appointment, detective inspector," he said pointedly eyeing the obstruction. "If you wouldn't mind?"

"This won't take long sir," O'Neill said keeping his own expression blank and official. "Here or down the station—it's up to you."

Lytton gave a heavy sigh and closed the Aston's door. It shut with a solid expensive thunk. "Let's get on with it then shall we? Believe it or not I have a business to run."

"Of course you do sir," O'Neill said soothingly and watched the slight relaxation of the other man's shoulders before he hit him with the next question. "Kelly Jacks—you wouldn't have heard from her by any chance?"

Lytton was good. If O'Neill hadn't been watching intently he wouldn't have caught the betraying little tells of tension in the other man's face and body, the way he shifted his feet as if for a sudden getaway.

"Why would I?" He should have left it there but was unable to prevent himself adding, "She cleaned part of my house—once. On that basis we're hardly likely to exchange Christmas cards are we?"

O'Neill leaned his hip against the Aston's rear quarter, folding his arms. "I think there's a little more to your relationship than that isn't there, sir?" And he noted with interest the uncomfortable reaction but Lytton didn't make the mistake of bluster. He took a moment to resettle himself and then merely cocked an eyebrow.

"Oh?"

O'Neill glanced around at the upmarket cars surrounding him, at the heavily revamped building they were parked outside and his eyes narrowed, assessing. "This one of your developments is it?"

"Yes it is. And?"

"Made quite a tidy sum out of the property game over the years haven't you Mr Lytton? I understand it's all a question of luck—happening across the right place at the right time for the right money. That so?"

"Yes," Lytton said curtly and this time he didn't try to expand or explain. O'Neill took that as his cue to cut to the chase. No point in playing with someone if they weren't prepared to play.

"Four years ago you bought a warehouse in ..." O'Neill let his voice trail off, making a show of hunting through his notebook for the address and then reading it out. "It's now a rake of luxury offices and apartments. You made quite a killing on it so I hear."

175

Lytton made a gesture of impatience. "I may have bought the building you describe, detective inspector," he said. "My company buys a lot of property all over the world. Without going through the files I couldn't say." He peeled back the cuff of his dark wool overcoat to check his watch. "It doesn't ring any bells."

"Really sir?" O'Neill pursed his lips. "Only, I thought this one might have stuck in your mind for some reason."

A muscle twitched in the side of Lytton's jaw. "Why don't you enlighten me?"

Got you jumpy now haven't I?

"Because that particular building was on the market almost derelict for nearly two years before you bid them peanuts for it," O'Neill said quietly. "Do you recall why that was?"

Lytton had gone very still, his gaze resting coolly on the detective. "Go on."

"Well according to the information that's come to light sir, no buyer had been found because of a very nasty murder that took place there. A young barman by the name of Callum Perry was stabbed to death on the second floor."

"I'm sorry I still don't—"

"He was killed by a woman called Kelly Jacks."

Lytton's mouth snapped shut. He was silent for a long time, brows drawn down into something resembling a scowl.

O'Neill watched him closely. "Ring any bells now sir?"

"I didn't make the connection," he said tightly. He looked up, expression smoothing out, back into confidence and, O'Neill felt, arrogance. "It was a long time ago and like I said, detective inspector, I buy a lot of property."

How very convenient.

O'Neill waited to see how long Lytton would spin out his memory lapse. Not long if the way the man soon checked his watch again was anything to go by.

"I doubt you came all the way over here just to remind me about a time several years ago when my path might have crossed with Kelly's, even at a distance," he said. He reached for the Aston's door handle again. "Now, I'm going to be late for a very important meeting. Was there anything else?"

"Just one thing sir," O'Neill said heavily. "I'd hate you to feel you … owed her anything for any reason. So I'd just like to remind you that if she should happen to get in touch we're open twenty-four hours a day." He handed over a card which Lytton took with obvious reluctance. "Please call us."

"Of course."

"Thank you sir. I'd hate to have to pursue you for aiding and abetting a wanted fugitive. Not on top of your recent … tragedy, that is."

But his subtle warning was lost as Matthew Lytton slid behind the wheel of the Aston and fired the throaty engine. The reverse lights were already blazing before O'Neill was back inside the Mondeo.

O'Neill took his time buckling the seatbelt and starting the engine before he put the car into gear and pulled slowly out of the way. Lytton shot out of his space and chirruped the tyres on the block paving as he dumped the big car into first.

"Wherever you're going sunshine, you're certainly in a bloody hurry to get there," O'Neill said out loud.

He briefly considered tailing the Aston just to make life awkward for its owner. The impulse didn't last long. Lytton was not above making his feelings felt, O'Neill guessed. *One irate phone call to the chief super—or the press—and I'll be down-sized onto shit duty in some godforsaken ghetto.*

Still it hadn't been a wasted journey by any means.

He picked up his cellphone, pressed the office speed dial.

"Dempsey?" he said when the line was answered. "Do me a favour will you? Put in a request for Matthew Lytton's phone records—home, office and cellphone. Let's see if he's been in contact with Jacks."

"You think he might have been boss?"

"Yeah I do." He cut the call, sat for a moment deep in thought. "Why else," he murmured to the empty car, "would you refer to a woman—one you claim to have met only once—by her first name? Only a small slip, Mattie boy, but still a slip …"

—64—

KELLY CHECKED HER watch and shut down the laptop. She knew she was cutting it fine to get to Clapham Common in time to meet with Lytton but the last thing she wanted was to hang around somewhere public. She reckoned he'd give her five minutes' leeway.

She shrugged into her hooded sweatshirt and picked up the backpack which still contained his wife's borrowed clothes. At least this gave her the chance to return them—or throw them back in his face. Her hand tightened on the straps. She hadn't yet decided which.

The slam of the front door to the flat made her start. She glanced up to see Elvis slouch into the living room. He stopped when he saw her, eyes circling to take in the closed-down laptop and the backpack she was holding.

"Tina said you was to stay put," he said sounding aggrieved. "You need anything I'm supposed to get it for you."

"I need to go out—just for a while," Kelly said giving him what she hoped was a placatory smile. "I have to meet with someone—someone who might be able to help me."

Either that or Harry Grogan's thug will be waiting for me again.

Elvis shook his head, emphatic. "Not a good idea," he said, moving forwards so he blocked her path to the door. "Erm, what about after dark? Wait 'til then. Safer, y'know?"

Kelly paused, eyeing his agitation with her own sense of disquiet. "I need to go now Elvis," she said gently. "In fact I'm probably going to be late, so—"

"You can't leave!"

"Why not?" Kelly gave a cool stare at his outburst. He shuffled his feet, flushing but didn't move out of her way.

"You just can't go, all right?" he said, his voice turning belligerent now but Kelly caught an underlying note of panic there too.

She froze. "Elvis, what did you do?"

"Nothing!" But he wouldn't meet her eyes. "You just stay here, yeah? And everything will be cool."

178

"Round here they'd sell their granny for less."

She remembered Tina's opinion on the ten-grand price on her head. Alarmed now, she made to push past Elvis but he gave her an unexpected backwards shove. She stumbled, reaching out for the Formica table to stop herself falling.

When she looked up, Elvis was still in the doorway, defiant. A slim-bladed knife had appeared in his right hand.

"Elvis don't do this," Kelly pleaded, getting her feet back underneath her very slowly. "It's not worth it."

"What do you know about that?" he threw back at her. He swallowed, tried to purge the whiny note from his voice and failed. "Where else am I gonna get hold of that kind of dosh? It'll get me started, y'know? It'll put me on the map."

He wants to buy drugs most likely, Kelly realised. Ten thousand would allow him to buy in as a mid-level dealer without having to claw his way up from the bottom of the pile— if he didn't end up dead in six months from stepping on too many existing toes. Either that or he was going to expand his budding stolen electronics sideline, like the laptop sitting on the table just behind her right hand ...

"You really think they'll pay you?" she asked. "You think that little blade will stop them coming in here and taking what they want and leaving you with nothing except a bad taste in your mouth?"

"Shut it!" He seemed jittery, wired, unable to keep his feet still. Kelly's eyes flicked between the knife and the body behind it, trying to gauge experience and intent. Not much of either, she judged, but an unhealthy dose of desperation made him just as dangerous.

"Put the knife down, Elvis and we can all walk away from this—"

She saw the sudden flare in his eyes. "Nobody's walking away!" he yelled, lunging forwards.

Kelly's fingers closed on the corner of the laptop. She dragged it off the table and flung it round and out, aiming straight for the boy's head.

Then she leapt for the knife.

179

65

DMITRY SHOT THROUGH a set of lights as they flicked up to amber, narrowly avoiding the front wing of a black cab as he did so. The cab driver jumped on the horn. Dmitry barely had time to curse before he was bullying the Range Rover through the choked-up traffic.

I should have used the Mercedes, he recognised. But for this job he needed the extra space not to mention the car's off-road capability. Unmarked graves were much better dug in the middle of nowhere.

In the passenger seat—seemingly unfazed by the wild ride—was Viktor, who'd driven Steve Warwick out for his meeting with Harry Grogan on Lambourn Downs. Viktor sat with his massive arms folded, chewing gum with his mouth open and his brain shut.

Viktor might be stupid as an ox but he was strong as one too. This time Dmitry was taking no chances with that goddamn woman. He'd brought backup.

His phone buzzed insistently. Without bothering to check the caller, Dmitry threw his iPhone across to Viktor to answer. After his low-slung Mercedes the Range Rover handled like a pig, rolling alarmingly under hard cornering even if it did stick to the road. He needed both hands on the wheel.

Viktor fumbled with the phone's touch screen controls.

"Da?" There was a long pause during which time the big man's brow furrowed deeply. He dropped the phone to his shoulder. "How long Brixton?"

"I don't know!" Dmitry snapped. "Traffic is awful in this city. No respect!" As if to demonstrate, he leaned on the horn in response to a bus that was attempting to creep across into his lane. "I only got the call a half hour ago. We are almost there."

66

THE COLD WATER hit Elvis in the face like being thrown into the sea. He surfaced through it spluttering and gasping and found himself lying on his left side on the floor of the flat. He'd know that puke-coloured carpet anywhere. There was a bloodied towel under his head.

What happened came back to him in a shameful rush. Kelly getting the jump on him. He didn't know what she'd hit him with—a truck by the feel of it. He put a hand up to his nose carefully and found it was well mashed.

"*B-bitch!*" he managed.

"So she *was* here," said a man's voice somewhere above him. Elvis heard the Russki accent and his guts cramped instantly. He squeezed the water out of his eyes before cautiously opening them.

The first thing he saw was a pair of shiny black boots, the kind that army guys or coppers wear. He forced his gaze upwards and found a huge guy standing in them with Tina's kettle still in his hand. Good job it hadn't just boiled, Elvis thought hazily. This guy didn't look the type to check.

What he *did* look from down here was enormous.

Aware that his throbbing face was a little too close to those heavy-duty toecaps for comfort, Elvis tried to get his left hand underneath him to lever up. A bolt of pain shot through his wrist. He gave a yelp of surprise and almost ended up back on the floor again. The big guy grabbed hold of the back of his sweatshirt and all but dragged him upright.

It was only when he was on his feet that several things came clear to Elvis. The first was that his wrist hurt like a bastard to the point where he felt ready to throw up. The second was the truck Kelly had used to hit him was actually his best laptop which was now lying smashed on the floor near the sofa. He swore again, longer and more inventively this time.

And that's when he realised the third thing.

The big guy was not alone.

A second man was sitting on the narrow dining chair by the window. He had his back to the light so Elvis couldn't make out his face right away. The build came across—lighter, not so gorilla-like as the guy with the kettle. Brains and Brawn these two, and it was always Brains you had to watch out for.

Elvis knew if he was going to talk his way out of the mess that bitch had left him in this was the guy he had to convince.

"So," the man by the window said again. "She was here, *da*?"

"'Course she was here," Elvis said. He clocked the Russian accent more clearly this time and the fear it provoked lent more of a snappy edge to his voice than was wise. He tried to temper it with an ingratiating grin. "You think I'd try and diss you? No way bro."

The man uncrossed his legs, leaned forward and made an exaggerated show of looking around the tiny living room. "And yet ... I do not see her," he said. "So the effect is the same, yes?"

Puzzled, Elvis tried a shrug that also wasn't wise. The room spun crazily. He staggered and nearly fell. The giant grabbed hold of his shoulder gripping hard enough to make him squirm. Elvis's head was banging and he could feel the sweat breaking out across his forehead, under his armpits. He tried to convince himself it was down to being laid out with a ripped-off Toshiba rather than sheer fright but didn't believe it.

He wished he still had his blade but Kelly must have taken it with her after she'd nicked it. He still wasn't sure how she'd managed that. One minute he was in control, the next it was lights out.

Bitch. Look what trouble you left me in ...

He licked his lips nervously. "Hey bro, I can find her for you. No sweat. She *was* here 'cause she and Tina are tight. She'll be back, yeah?"

The man stared at him without expression. "I think she *might* have been back but you said something—did something—to alarm her, *da*?"

"Hey I—"

"Something foolish," the man went on, "that panicked her into running again."

"She was gonna leave, go out. I just tried to stop her—"

The man gave a snort and muttered something under his breath that Elvis didn't catch but didn't need to. He got the gist.

And then without warning the man surged out of the chair and backhanded him across the face hard enough to snap his head round. The blow exploded his already tender nose into a haze of pain, flooded his eyes and sent his body reeling into shock. His knees gave way, his bladder following. He was only vaguely aware of being hauled upright by the meaty hand at his shoulder, held locked tight, immobile.

"If you had not spooked her she would have come back here. Where else does she have that she can go?" the man said, his voice too close, too soft. "I would have been very pleased with you. And you would now be a rich man, *da?*" He paused. "But instead you are a fool."

"Hey man, she was here like I told you," Elvis mumbled driven by self-pity to his own defence. "Not my fault she—"

"*Not your fault*? So maybe you think *I* am to blame, *da?* For being too slow. Maybe you think *I* am the fool?"

Elvis was hazily aware that things had turned upside down against him. It wasn't fair! It had seemed like easy money. Money for nothing. One phone call and Harry Grogan's boys would come and grab her and Tina would never know he'd had anything to do with it. And now it had gone to shit and it was all that bitch Kelly's fault, of—

The blow to his kidneys didn't feel like a truck. This time it was more like a freight train or one of those big pile-driving cranes Elvis had seen down in the East End. His legs gave out completely and this time the giant didn't try to hold him up.

If things had been bad while he was on his feet, Elvis soon realised they got a whole lot worse once he was down. He prayed for unconsciousness. It seemed to be a long time coming.

—67—

KELLY WAS HALF a mile away from the flat before she stopped running. She ducked into an alleyway between two run-down shops and doubled over gasping, her hands braced against her knees. She was winded, shocky, and shaking with both effort and reaction.

As adrenaline hangovers went this was shaping up to be a doozy.

A part of her couldn't believe Elvis had sold her out. Another part—a more cynical embittered part—was more surprised he'd waited so long.

Paid for it though, didn't he?

The laptop Kelly instinctively flung at him had found its mark with devastating effect. She wondered how long it would be before she could block out all recall of the dull crunching sound that his cartilage and flesh and bone had made as the hefty blunt object struck. That he had threatened her—pulled a knife on her—no longer seemed a good enough excuse for what she'd done.

What the hell am I going to say to Tina?

As little as possible seemed to be the best response.

Slowly, reluctantly, she straightened still breathing hard. She dragged the cellphone out of her sweatshirt pocket and keyed in Tina's number but her thumb hesitated over the dial button.

Eventually she took the coward's way out, composing an apologetic if slightly defiant text message and sending it fast before she'd time to change her mind.

As she slipped the phone away again it clunked against something hard in the other front pocket. She reached in and pulled out the knife she'd taken away from Elvis.

Another blade ...

An image of Tyrone's mutilated body flashed into her mind, hard and strong enough to rob her of what little breath she'd managed to retrieve.

There was no blood on this one but that hadn't been for lack of trying. Elvis had taken a determined if inexperienced swing at her. He hadn't counted on reflexes honed from half a dozen attempts to cut her up while Kelly had been inside.

Attacks using cell-fashioned hidden shivs were as common as they were inventive in there. Some inmates viewed being stabbed as so inevitable they took regular ice-cold showers to try and prepare their bodies for the shock, train themselves to power through it. They claimed it worked. Kelly felt avoidance was the better option but sometimes you didn't have a choice.

Nevertheless, she hadn't survived for five years by running away from trouble. She'd learned to meet it head on. So as soon as she'd seen the knife she had reacted on full-auto with speed and aggression.

Now cooling rapidly, she thought of Elvis and remembered again the strange internal wrenching noise his bones had made as she'd twisted his wrist up and round to break his grip. She had not hesitated, not for a moment.

But she was not in prison any longer. She was back in civilisation and supposed to behave accordingly. It just seemed that there had been no transition between in and out and when she was under threat the lines blurred altogether.

For a moment she felt a hollow churning up under her ribcage and thought she might vomit. She bent over again and leaned her forehead against the brickwork in front of her, cushioned by her forearm. Gradually the sickness subsided.

Her head came up slowly and she realised she'd no clue where she was. She'd fled without thought to direction. It took a few minutes' staring at the nearest street sign for her to place the area and realise she had strayed north into Camberwell. Totally the wrong direction for Clapham Common.

Lytton!

A glance at her watch told her she was already late for their meeting. Would he wait for her? And for how long?

Would he turn up at all?

As her vision cleared she noticed there was a drain a few feet away fed by a fractured drainpipe. The brickwork was grey and furred with damp. Kelly wiped the handle of the knife on the inside of her sweatshirt and dropped it into the broken grid. Looking at the rest of the building it would be a long time before the owner got around to calling Dyno-Rod.

The phone buzzed in her pocket. She pulled it out again and gave the display a cursory glance. She recognised the Brixton code but not the number. Tina's work perhaps? She flipped the phone open with a sense of trepidation.

"Tina?"

"Ah, sadly no," said a cool voice in her ear. A voice that sent a bolt of reactive fear straight through to her bones. "Hello Miss Jacks."

The Russian.

"What do you want?" she demanded hearing her composure rip like silk. "What have I done to you—or Grogan?"

There was a pause then the man said, "Better for all of us if you do not know."

"Better for you, you mean," Kelly shot back.

He laughed, a brief chuckle. "*Da*. This is true. Please be assured Miss Jacks it is nothing … personal."

"Oh and that makes me feel *so* much better."

"Your young friend here, I regret that he is *not* feeling better."

For a moment Kelly was puzzled.

"You mean Elvis? He's no friend of mine," she said, partly because it was true and partly because instinct told her that claiming any kind of relationship with the youth would probably make things worse for him.

"A pity," the man said, his tone brooding. "Then he is of no further use to me."

Kelly found she was shivering, had to wrap her free arm around her body to stop the shakes vibrating into her voice.

"Killing him will cause you more problems than it solves," she said quickly, thinking of Tina—clean and sober and happy. "Not least with the police. They're already looking for you over Tyrone's death. Why make them look harder?"

He was silent for a few long seconds then he said, "A nice try but I think you will find it is not *me* the police look for."

Her brain went numb unable to think of a single argument that might stand a hope of persuading him. The voice sounded again almost softly in her ear.

"Thank you for standing so still Miss Jacks. It makes you so much easier to trace …"

Kelly jerked the phone away as if it had burned her ear. She snapped it shut, cutting off the call and threw it away from her. It skittered across the concrete and disappeared after the knife down the broken drain.

She was running before it hit the murky water below.

—68—

STANDING IN THE living room of Tina's flat over the inert body of Elvis, Dmitry smiled.

186

Of course he had no way to track the cellphone she was using. He was not the police, after all. But the bluff had been worth it for the panic it had so obviously caused.

Once you had an adversary on the run, he had learned, keeping them running until they were too exhausted to run any further was always a good thing. If all their efforts went into retreating they had no time or energy to attack.

And Kelly Jacks was tiring, he could sense it. He may have failed to corner her here but it was one more place of safety now closed off to her. So overall this was not quite the disaster it might have been.

He nodded to Viktor. "Come. We go."

The two men stepped over Elvis's legs and walked out. They left the front door casually ajar behind them.

—69—

LYTTON ARRIVED AT Long Pond on Clapham Common almost half an hour behind time. He was filled with the impotent rage of a man who's tried to hustle through Central London traffic and been frustrated at every turn.

He'd been calling the cellphone number Kelly had used to make contact but it came back 'not possible to connect'. So for the last couple of miles he'd been rehearsing his apologies. By the time he parked up as close to the edge of the Common as he could find a space his edginess at the meeting had twisted through concern into anger.

And to cap it all she wasn't there.

He waited, walked, just in case she'd been delayed too but after another half an hour passed he knew. The anger smouldered beneath the surface. She hadn't had the guts to wait for him not even for a lousy thirty minutes.

"Face it man," he said out loud. "She's stood you up—again."

That kind of thing was getting to be a habit with her.

He sighed, re-checked his watch. Only another minute had passed.

Lytton tried to work out why he was giving her any time at all. She was a convicted criminal, a wanted fugitive and there was compelling evidence to suggest this was a repeat of her earlier crime—a man murdered in a frenzy of reasonless rage.

So why did he feel some kind of pull towards her?

It couldn't simply be sexual attraction. She wasn't his type and with Vee not even buried it was hardly appropriate to give in to a burst of hormones.

No there was more to it than that.

He stood on the asphalt path that ringed the pond, his back to the basketball courts and the skate park, staring across the dark flat water towards the road on the far side. His dad had brought him here sometimes if he was suffering an uncharacteristic bout of fatherliness. They'd bring stale bread to throw at the ducks and watch the richer kids sail their model boats.

His dad had always tired of it first, his patience directly related—Lytton only realised much later—to the length of time the pubs had been open.

Lytton shook himself inside his cashmere coat. A lot of water had passed under the bridge since then, a lot of distance travelled.

And look at me, he thought, *standing here again, all wistful for something else I can't have.*

He shot a cuff, checked his watch and turned his back determinedly on Long Pond with its old memories and new disappointments.

Kelly Jacks, he decided, could damn well fend for herself.

—70—

KELLY WASN'T SURE how she got through the rest of the day or the night that followed. Probably, she coped much the same way as she'd learned to get through her time locked up inside—by thinking only from one moment to the next. No long term plans, no goals. Just staying alert to the here and now, reacting if she had to, coasting if she didn't.

She arrived at the north side of Clapham Common over an hour late for her meeting with Lytton. It came as no surprise to find he had not waited around for her. If she was honest she wouldn't put money on him having turned up in the first place.

She was not to know that she'd missed him only by three minutes.

All the way down from Camberwell, Kelly had cursed the knee-jerk impulse that made her dump the cellphone. It was the only place she had noted Lytton's own cellphone number—stored in the phone's memory rather than her own.

She tried to call Tina but the only phone boxes she came across did not accept coins and she had no other means to pay. The thought of ducking into a restaurant or shop and begging use of their phone did not appeal. Her face had been too widely shown for that to be a safe option.

For the first time she felt truly isolated. Isolated from people she could trust—people she'd believed she could trust. She knew she couldn't reach out to her family even if she knew how to get in touch.

Don't call a number for so long and it fades from the memory.

By the time she had reached the north-eastern edge of the Common itself she'd been almost in pieces, unable to go forwards or back. The realisation that Lytton was not there—might never have been there—was the last punch that knocked the stuffing out of her.

She sat for a long time on the bench furthest from Long Pond, hunched over, staring at the ground in front of her feet. It was covered in fallen horse chestnuts from the trees nearby, cigarette ends and the kind of soft drink ring pulls that were supposedly redesigned to reduce litter.

There were no model boaters on the pond itself, just a resting squadron of Canada geese. The traffic behind her formed a constant drone enlivened only by the regular overhead hum of jets stacking for Heathrow out to the west.

Kelly heard none of it for the insistent voice in her head.

I should have left sooner—if I went there at all.

But she was only too aware that people who are desperate will do desperate things if the price is right. She couldn't find it in her to hate Elvis for what he'd done but wondered if Tina would ever forgive her for breaking the kid's bones. Maybe one day she'd find out.

Besides, Harry Grogan had offered ten thousand pounds to anyone who'd give her up. Money like that was life-changing to half the people who lived in Tina's block. And they were used to keeping an eye out, watching the comings and goings, watching their backs. It was only a matter of time before someone sold her out.

The wind was surprisingly chilly, blowing in all the way across the flat expanse of the Common. Kelly shivered and hunkered down a little further into her hooded sweatshirt, glad of the baseball cap even if it did leave her ears exposed to the cold.

She became aware that the summer, such as it was, had turned definitely into autumn when she hadn't been looking. There was a smell of dead leaves and wet wool in the air. Before long it would be getting dark.

She needed food and a safe place to hide—or at least somewhere she could slip through the night unnoticed by either Grogan's touts or the police.

Wearily, Kelly got to her feet. She headed for the Clapham Common Tube station just as the evening commuter rush was beginning to pick up. Most people were fairly unobservant. Better to hide in the crowds and make her pursuers work for their money.

She rode the Northern Line all the way up to King's Cross tucked in a corner feigning sleep for most of the journey. By the time she emerged from below ground it was dark outside, the notorious surrounding streets garish with shabby lights and crawling traffic. Kelly grabbed a carton of food from a cheap noodle bar whose internal security camera was obviously a fake. She was served by a Korean man whose English was barely adequate to work the till. She hoped she would be one indistinguishable bedraggled white face among many to him. She avoided eye contact anyway, just in case.

The food took away the shakes if not the melancholy. She kept moving, grabbing rest in half-hour snatches in quiet doorways, using her backpack as a makeshift pillow and keeping her arm wrapped firmly through the straps.

Even dressed as she was, Kelly received half a dozen propositions—mostly from nervous middle-aged men in slow-moving cars. She simply shook her head and kept walking. A couple of times, guys who were clearly pimps touting for fresh meat asked if she was OK—did she need food, money, a place to sleep or something to take the edge off? Kelly ignored them too and they didn't push the issue. They knew enough not to force it when another day or two at the most and she would be seeking them out.

What Kelly did a lot of during that long night was try to get her head together.

By the time the first faint smears of daylight appeared in the eastern sky she had decided on a plan of action.

She was tired of running. Giving up was not an option. If she was going to stay out of prison again she needed to find out *why.* Why was she worth that kind of money to this Grogan character? What had she done that he might want her to the tune of ten grand?

And the only way Kelly knew to go about that was simply to gather and follow the evidence, the way she'd been trained to do.

—71—

"MISS OLOWAYO, IS it?"

Even with her eyes closed Tina could guess what she was going to see when she opened them. The owner of that voice, the way the question was phrased, it had *cop* written all over it.

Wondered when you'd *get here …*

She let her breath out slow and risked it. Sure enough the guy hovering in the hospital room doorway carried himself tough, almost cocky. She didn't like the shrewd look in his eye though, like he'd heard it all and seen more. If she had to deal with them at all, Tina preferred her cops dumb.

She straightened in the uncomfortable visitor's chair by the bed not sure if the creak she heard was from the plastic or her bones and jerked her chin towards the newcomer's jacket.

"Let's see it then."

The man sighed as he reached for his warrant card. Tina took it from him and compared the photo to the face, going over it a careful twice. *Detective Inspector Vincent O'Neill.*

She returned the ID as if losing interest, her eyes sliding back to the still figure under the sheets. They'd partially shaved his head in theatre. Elvis was gonna hate that she thought, more than anything. There was a ventilator tube holding his lips parted, dressings covering one eye and his reset nose. His arm was busted so they'd told her, and most of his ribs like he'd been stomped on.

Tina didn't know for sure what had gone down. Elvis hadn't woken up in the ambulance on the short ride to King's College Hospital which had the nearest A&E Department, nor since he'd come out of surgery. They weren't saying if they expected him to wake at all.

She thought about a future stretching away where she was alone again. The possibility hurt like a son of a bitch.

All in all, it had been a long night and it was nowhere near over yet.

"I'm sorry about your friend," O'Neill said, straightforward, without the 'had it coming to him, sooner or later' attitude Tina had been half expecting.

She swallowed. "Me too."

He shoved his hands in his trouser pockets and leaned against the door jamb. Tina took in those wide shoulders and wasn't fooled by the relaxed pose—he was blocking her escape and they both knew it.

"Want to fill me in on what happened?"

Tina took her eyes away from Elvis's pale face for a moment. "He clumsy," she said keeping it just this side of insolence. "He trip and fall."

"Yeah and I would say he hit every fist and boot on the way down."

"Don't know." Tina shrugged, let her gaze fall away. "Wasn't there."

O'Neill fell silent. Tina resisted the urge to look at him, knowing that was what he wanted—a sign of weakness.

And right now I am real *close to giving in.*

She heard him move again, caught a glimpse from the corner of her eye and stole a quick look only to find O'Neill had plonked himself in another visitor's chair on the far side of the bed and was watching her. She snatched her gaze away, scowling.

"You're looking good Tina," he said softly. That got her attention full on.

"Excuse me?" She bristled. "Do I *know* you?"

"No, but I know you," he said. "My DC's been telling me all about you. What you've been up to over the last few years. And I meant what I said—you're looking a hell of a lot better than you did on your last arrest photo."

"I wasn't doing so good back then," she allowed, keeping her voice even. "You track me down just to tell me that?"

"No but even without this—" he gestured to the hospital in general, "—we'd have been having a conversation sooner or later."

"Yeah?"

"Yeah. You see, you fall into the category of Known Associates of one Kelly Jacks. And she is someone we definitely do want to track down."

"Who?"

He smiled and it wasn't a friendly smile. "Come on Tina, I'm trying to be nice. Don't spoil things by trying to play me for a fool. You and Kelly were inside together."

Tina sat back setting the chair bouncing slightly and glared at him. "So I knew her. So what? Knew a lot of people inside. Prisons is overcrowded—didn't they tell you?"

"Just shows we're doing our job."

"Yeah, putting people away who's innocent. That sound like your job?" And just for a moment she thought she saw a flicker in his face like the barb had hit home. Then it was gone.

"I read your case file. It was a cock-up—start to finish," he said frankly. "But Kelly got you out. In fact she did more than that

193

didn't she, Tina? She straightened you out too. You owe her. Big time."

Tina continued to glare. "Debt's paid," she said, her voice gruff to stop it being hurt and angry.

O'Neill's eyes flicked from her to Elvis's bruised and battered face, his brows drawing down. "You mean *Jacks* is responsible for this?"

"Who knows?" But the macho disbelief in his tone smarted enough for her to add, "You don't think she got it in her? Not when she went in maybe. But she learned fast inside—and there was plenty gunning for her. Ex-cop—"

"She wasn't a cop," he said quickly.

"Tech—whatever. Still one of you wasn't she?" Tina flapped a hand. "Try explaining the difference while you're having your pretty face cut up in the showers. See who listens then."

"So why would she do something like this to Elvis?" he asked. "Did he try to cut her up, is that it?"

Tina clamped down on the possibility that Elvis had let his own greed get the better of his judgement. She'd found him spread all over the living room floor when she'd rushed back from the shelter, had called for an ambulance right away. And while it was coming she'd searched just in case for anything nearby that Elvis wouldn't want found.

She knew he carried a blade—for self-protection. Made sense given the area but it wasn't on him. Kelly must have taken it away from him in the fight.

And there had been a fight, of that she was quite sure.

The text message from Kelly that had brought Tina hurrying home still haunted her.

"SORRY 4 ELVIS—BSTRD SOLD ME OUT."

So yeah, she might have owed Kelly for her freedom, for helping her get back some control of her life. That still counted for something but not everything.

Not now.

"Don't know who did this to Elvis," Tina said suddenly weary. "Like I said, I wasn't there."

O'Neill sighed again. "Even if Kelly didn't lay a finger on him, she's still wanted in connection with a murder." He paused. "If

194

you know where she is you need to tell me, Tina. Before anyone else gets hurt."

"I don't know where she is," she said, stubborn now.

He stood, out of patience. "If I find out you've been harbouring a wanted fugitive you'll end up back inside," he promised, cool enough to make her shiver. "And this time the case will be watertight." He turned for the door.

"I don't know where she is," Tina repeated. He heard something in her voice, stopped and turned back. Tina took another long look at Elvis, at the bandages and the breaks and the bruises. "But I know where she'll be ..."

—72—

MYSHKA SIPPED HER espresso and watched Dmitry over the rim of her cup with brooding eyes.

"I did what needed to be done," Dmitry said with more than a hint of defiance in his tone as if he was trying to convince himself as much as her. "I must show these dogs who is master, yes?"

He was sprawled on the long white leather sofa in the living area of Harry Grogan's penthouse apartment, looking very much at home. The man himself was out watching his wretched horses work. Viktor was driving him.

Myshka put down her empty cup and gathered the silk kimono closer around her body. If Dmitry was going to make a habit of calling on her before noon she decided, she was going to have to start rising earlier or he would never treat her as an equal. But Grogan had been out until late and had required *entertaining* before she was allowed to sleep.

Sometimes she was unsure if Viagra was the best or the worst thing that ever happened to old men who kept young mistresses.

Not so young anymore though, are you?

"*Dog*? He was a pup, nothing more," she said evenly. "Beating him half to death was perhaps ... unwise."

"It is not like you to be sentimental, Myshka." Dmitry gave a dismissive snort. "It was necessary. And there have been no reports, so—" he smiled, "—he is maybe not yet dead, hmm?"

"Yes, but—"

His good humour evaporated. He lurched forwards to slap a hand down hard against the top of the coffee table making her start. "Do not question me on this! You know it was right. Would you have me let them disrespect me? Have them laugh behind my back? Say that I am weak?"

She got to her feet without response, turning away from him to hide her surprise at this rebellion and the flare of her own temper. Standing by the glass wall that looked down across the river and wrapping her arms around her body she was aware of a sudden chill in the air.

So it begins, she thought with cold clarity. *Your disrespect of me.*

She did not hear Dmitry get to his feet and move behind her until his hands slipped around her waist, his face in her hair.

"Do not let us fight when we are so close," he murmured in her ear. "I need you, Myshka ..."

To whore for you, Myshka supplied silently and could not resist a final gently chiding reminder.

"It is I who have brought us this far Dmitry."

She felt him tense then relax. "I know," he said. "I will not forget."

He kissed her neck, let her go and a few moments later she heard the apartment door bang shut behind him.

Myshka continued to stand at the window, frowning. She could see her reflection in the glass—a pale hunched figure with a worn face, wearing a borrowed robe, in a home that did not belong to her.

And for the first time the future looked uncertain.

—73—

DI O'NEILL TURNED up the collar of his jacket and shouldered a little closer to the blockwork to keep out of the steady rain.

Behind him was an ugly but otherwise unremarkable office block that housed the Forensic Science Laboratory. Its only distinguishing feature seemed to be the large stone construction at the front which he was using for shelter. As far as he could tell, the sole purpose of this square lump with its flared top was to display in large digits the number of the building he was lurking outside together with a sign warning visitors they were under surveillance.

Like you could ever miss it.

He supposed he'd always taken the odd structure for granted—walked quickly past it on his way in and equally quickly on his way out. Now that he was forced by the boredom to study it up close he wondered if it had some deeper meaning.

The building itself was dirty concrete and brown brick and glass at odds with the surrounding architecture as only public buildings can manage. O'Neill reckoned they sent planners to a special school to learn how to draw such monstrosities.

He had gone to Lambeth straight from his visit to King's College Hospital which was only a few miles away. But morning traffic was already starting to build and the journey had been frustratingly slow. He knew he should have used the time to call Dempsey to update him on his interview with Kelly Jacks's old cellmate Tina Olowayo, but he was strangely reluctant to do so.

He knew it was partly pride that kept him from calling. He wanted to see how the information Olowayo had divulged panned out before he checked in. She was a tough cookie who'd given little away of her real feelings for Jacks. And this despite the distinct impression that Jacks had been responsible—directly or indirectly—for the beating. Still, he couldn't dismiss the chance that she'd sent him off on a wild goose chase just for the hell of it.

Even if it had all sounded entirely plausible.

Which was why he'd been skulking under the overhanging stonework for nearly an hour getting drips from the encroaching tree branches down the back of his neck and stretching his ever-thinning patience further with every passing minute.

I'll give it another half an hour, he determined. *Then I hand it over and it all becomes official—to hell with her.*

No sooner had the thought formed than he heard quick footsteps jogging up the short flight of steps that led to the front entrance. He risked a glance around the edge of the stonework and clocked the slight figure with a baseball cap pulled well down and her hair tucked mostly beneath it.

She had a backpack but no jacket and the shoulders of her hooded sweatshirt were dark with rain. He saw that she had removed the stud from her nose. With the slim almost boyish figure and her fluency of movement she could have passed for a teenage student rather than a forty-year-old ex-con.

No wonder we haven't caught her.

He rolled out of concealment and planted himself in her path, hands loose and ready like the ball was in the air and you never knew where it was going to come down for the catch.

"Hello Kelly," he said softly.

Kelly Jacks lurched to an awkward halt as if her legs had suddenly forgotten how to function in sequence. Her eyes flew to his, haunted and vulnerable. Watching closely, he saw the moment she considered running.

"Don't," he advised. "I've had a good night's sleep and eaten my wheaties for breakfast this morning. You, on the other hand, look like you'd blow over in a strong wind. I'd have you before the end of the street."

Her shoulders drooped a little but her voice was calm.

"How did you know I'd come here?"

O'Neill shrugged. "Because you didn't have anywhere else to go."

—74—

KELLY SAT OPPOSITE the detective at a little corner café only a few hundred yards away from where he'd intercepted her. They were outside at one of the small tables squeezed under an awning between the violently pink outer wall of the building and the busy road junction. The noise and the continuing drizzle were enough to ensure they were alone and uninterrupted.

O'Neill had kept her close while he ordered two cups of hot chocolate and a couple of toasted sandwiches from the counter inside, not giving her the chance to make a run for it even if she'd been inclined to do so.

Kelly's instinct and experience told her this was not how arresting officers behaved if they were following the rule book. That O'Neill had another agenda was obvious. What that agenda might contain, on the other hand, was harder to anticipate.

So for the moment she was prepared to go along with this irregular interrogation. She had nothing to lose and no real choice in the matter.

And besides, as he'd pointed out, she hadn't eaten since the night before. Better by far to let him feed her before making a break for it, if it came to that. She snuck a sideways look at him without turning her head. He was a big guy who clearly spent enough time out of the office to keep a paunch at bay. A decent weekend footballer rather than a rugby player, she judged, despite the broken nose. She had no doubt that he could have made good on his promise to chase her down if she'd tried to bolt.

They moved outside with their hot chocolate. It was loud out there with the rumble of the railway line crossing a low bridge behind them, the constant traffic drone and the intermittent buzz of an air-wrench at the tyre place next door. To complete the set, a police helicopter hovered high overhead.

The songs of the city, Kelly thought wryly. *I'll miss them.*

"You've led us quite a dance," O'Neill said then. His voice was cool enough that she could glean nothing from it.

She held out both hands, wrists handcuffs' width apart. "So what's stopping you?" she prodded. She gestured towards her hot chocolate, the café in general. "Has the Met introduced a felon service-charter I don't know about?"

"Let's talk," he said, needlessly stirring his drink. But he didn't seem in any hurry to start a conversation.

Eventually Kelly sighed. "So how *did* you know where to find me?" she asked, then hesitated. "Someone from the lab?"

"No—your former colleagues were very tight-lipped," he said. "Although having Matthew Lytton pay for the tests gave them a plausible deniability if they'd needed it. Nice touch."

He'd done his research before he'd laid in wait for her. Somehow the thought made her feel better—that she hadn't been caught on an off chance.

"Not intentional," she said with a faint smile. "I simply didn't have the money."

He nodded, accepting the candour. "Your friend Tina, on the other hand, is pretty upset about her toy boy."

Kelly thought again of the slim blade, saw it slicing the air as Elvis slashed at her. "I'm upset about it too, but the little sod pulled a knife on me. He had it coming."

"Really?"

Kelly heard the dry doubt in his voice and realised she was going to have a hard time proving any of it. Even if she could retrace her steps and find the alleyway in Camberwell, the chances of the knife still being lodged in the drain were minuscule. And all practical forensic trace would be long washed away.

"I don't think he'll be pulling a knife on anyone for a while," O'Neill went on. "But overreacting the way you did is hardly going to help your case."

"Overreacting?" She heard the acidic note and throttled it back. "Is that what he told you?"

"Broken nose, cheekbone, right arm, four fingers, most of his ribs, punctured lung, severe concussion and a dislocated thumb. With your previous, Kelly, they could easily bump it up from GBH to attempted murder."

Even though she noted his use of *they* instead of *we* Kelly felt her heart step up. "Wait a minute," she snapped. "Broken ribs? What the hell are you talking about?"

The café door opened and the girl from behind the counter brought out their toasties, molten cheese and ham in a deceptively harmless-looking package. O'Neill waited until she'd gone back inside.

"I'm talking about the fact that having inflicted a catalogue of injuries you're not going to be able to claim self-defence here. Not by anyone's standards."

"I didn't ..."

Kelly's voice trailed away as her brain caught up. She tightened her focus on him, said dully, "It's hardly worth wasting my breath to say I didn't do it, is it?"

O'Neill tried an experimental bite of his food that was hopelessly premature. Kelly watched the steam escape. He grimaced and put the toastie aside to cool.

"I'm all ears."

Kelly took a deep breath, tried to let it out slow and steady. "OK, I *did* break his nose," she admitted. "Probably the wrist too. Like I said—he tried to stop me leaving the flat, pulled a knife on me. I did what I had to, to take it away from him, and then I left."

"And he didn't try to stop you again?"

"He wasn't saying much at that point."

"So the intercranial bleed is on you as well is it?"

Kelly flushed. "I checked his airways and put him into the recovery position with some support under his head," she said, defensive. "*Then* I left, OK?"

He nodded slowly. Kelly couldn't tell if he believed her or was just playing along, trying to give her enough rope for a noose.

"So who finished the job for you?"

Kelly's recall presented her with a snapshot of Ray McCarron, lying weak and suddenly old in his hospital bed. She pushed for objectivity, risked a bite of her own toasted sandwich while she tried to obtain it.

McCarron's assault had been cold, calculated, professional. This was amateur to the point of childishness. Did that mean two separate hands were at work? Or the same with differing motives. The first beating had clearly been a warning. The second, by the sound of it, a punishment.

She looked up, found O'Neill watching her closely.

"Why don't you ask Elvis who did it?" she countered.

"If he ever comes round maybe I will."

Kelly fell silent again, eyes on the traffic. An amphibious yellow duck-tour bus came past on its way to the river, filled with goggling tourists in wet-weather gear.

"It seems somebody's put a price on my head—a kind of bounty," she said without any colour in her voice. "Elvis was trying to collect on it."

"From who?"

She shrugged, unwilling to lay out all her cards. O'Neill leaned forwards.

"I can make this official if you like, Kelly and maybe—just maybe—you'll see daylight again before you're a very old lady." He waited a beat. "But somehow I doubt it."

"So why the cosy little chat? What's there to talk about?" she demanded, provoked beyond sense, hearing the anguish break through when she'd been so desperate to hide it. "If you think I'm so obviously guilty what the hell are we doing here?"

—75—

O'NEILL DIDN'T ANSWER immediately partly because he *wasn't* sure why he was doing things this way.

Maybe because there isn't another way to do them.

"Just tell me who you think offered the reward, Kelly," he said in that quiet almost kind voice he utilised to convince the most hardened criminal they'd feel *so* much better if only they confessed.

"A man called Grogan," she said baldly as if expecting him to know the name.

He did, but that didn't mean it was the one he'd been expecting. "*Harry* Grogan?"

"That was my information, yes," she admitted stiffly. "From what I've been able to find out his veneer of respectability is so thin you could practically read newsprint through it."

O'Neill smiled in spite of himself. "Well that fits I suppose, in a warped kind of way."

"What does?"

"You were dosed with ketamine," he said. "You must have come across it in your time. The trendy young things take it for a real out-of-body experience. It has considerable hallucinogenic properties."

"Well I can vouch for that first hand," she muttered, staring at the scratched aluminium tabletop without seeing it. She frowned then looked up sharply. "Grogan has racehorses. And ketamine is—"

"A veterinary anaesthetic," O'Neill finished for her.

"I don't suppose he has a tame vet on call for his animals does he?"

O'Neill smiled. "One who happens to have a bit of an addiction problem and is therefore open to ... suggestion, shall we say."

"Drugs?"

"No, good old-fashioned drink."

"Ah." Her mouth twisted thoughtfully. "Ketamine," she murmured. "No wonder I had a bitch of a headache when I came to."

"Mm, it was probably a lot stronger than whatever you were dosed with last time," he agreed taking a swig of hot chocolate. He picked up his toastie again—the outside seemed almost cold—and began to eat, watching her while he chewed.

Kelly sat very still, the frown locked in. Only her eyes moved, flicking back and forth as if reading some internal document. Eventually she looked at him with narrowed eyes. According to her official description they were brown but he noted that in reality they were hazel flecked with all kinds of greens and copper and gold.

"'Last time'" she repeated flatly. It was more a challenge than a question.

He nodded, swallowing the last of his food. Hers was barely touched. He didn't think temperature had anything to do with that.

"You didn't need to cut yourself open to prove it Kelly," he said gently. "Traces of ketamine would have been detectable in your hair for months."

Her head dipped suddenly so the peak of the cap hid her face. O'Neill wiped his fingers, reached out and flipped the hat off her head. She flinched but didn't otherwise move.

Under the hat he found her features clenched, eyes tight shut. She looked even paler than when he'd first seen her and more fragile.

O'Neill let it pass over her. He'd seen this kind of reaction from suspects before. Not when they were accused but when they were exonerated. The near-collapse of relief when they realised that finally somebody believed them.

"Why is Grogan after you?" he asked then.

It seemed to take a long time for the question to penetrate. When it did she raised her head slowly.

"I may be wrong and it's not him at all," she said with a weary smile. "There was some youngish guy who tried to grab me yesterday when I was in ... south-west London. And I'm sure I remember him from the warehouse. Not how he looked but his aftershave. And the accent."

"Accent?"

"He sounded Russian, maybe Ukrainian, something like that."

O'Neill felt something spark in the back of his mind, dredged through his memory for the cause and remembered the triple-nine caller who'd reported Douet's murder. *A Russian accent.* He kept the connection from showing on his face.

"What have you done to possibly tread on Harry Grogan's toes?"

"If I knew that ..."

"But you've been trying to find out."

"What else can I do?" She shrugged helplessly. "It's all a bit academic now though isn't it?"

O'Neill studied her for a long time but when he came to a decision he made it fast, on instinct. Call it a hunch.

"Not necessarily," he said.

—76—

"TELL ME EVERYTHING Kelly, right from the beginning. And don't leave anything out."

And because she was too weary to argue, she did—almost. When it came to Matthew Lytton she felt the need to be slightly more reticent and she wasn't sure why. She still couldn't quite decide what she felt about him and because she would struggle to explain that to the detective, she left it out.

Throughout, O'Neill sat without fidgeting, without interruption and let her tell the story in her own way.

At the end of it she picked up half the toastie, now completely cold and finished her lukewarm chocolate. The rain had petered out into indifference leaving behind dirty grey clouds like a sulk.

"I want to offer you a deal Kelly," O'Neill said. His voice was terse as if a part of him disapproved of what he was about to do even as he did it. "All unofficial and off the record. I can take care of the CCTV outside the lab so neither of us was ever there. If you're caught I'll deny this conversation ever took place."

"You make it sound so tempting," she shot back. "What do I get out of this?"

"The chance to prove your innocence—and not just for Tyrone Douet's murder."

Kelly eyed him with mistrust. "OK, let me rephrase that. What do *you* get out of this?"

O'Neill shook his head. "Let's just say I have my reasons and leave it at that. I don't think you're in a strong bargaining position here."

"Why me?"

He shrugged. "Why not? With you on the loose certain people might come out of the woodwork and show themselves."

Kelly gave a short bitter laugh. "You want me to act as bait."

"In a way," he agreed. "But I have to act on evidence as much as instinct. You have a free hand. No restrictions, no rules."

"Not to mention no retreat, no resources and every copper in London on the lookout for me."

"We've taken the watch off your flat," he said casually. "Can't justify tying up the manpower when you'd be an idiot to go back there." He smiled. "At least you'll have a bolt-hole. And transport—if that heap of rust you own actually runs."

Kelly knew this was a trap of some sort but right now she was short on options. And it was better than the alternative which offered no choice at all. Absently she broke a corner off the remaining half of her toastie then let it fall. Her appetite had deserted her.

"I don't know where to start," she admitted at last.

O'Neill clearly took that as a sign of acquiescence. He rose, reached into his jacket and pulled out a photo of an elderly man with a whiskery face threaded by veins, wearing a check shirt and quilted waistcoat that marked him as country rather than town.

Kelly took the picture cautiously. "Who's this?"

"That's Brian Stubbs," O'Neill said. "He's Harry Grogan's resident vet."

She gave the picture more attention, thought she saw a haunted desperation captured in the man's tired eyes. When she went to slide the picture into her backpack O'Neill calmly took it back. Being caught with it she realised would lead to all sorts of awkward questions for both of them.

"Even if I found him I don't have any right to question him and he certainly doesn't have to give me any answers."

O'Neill slipped the picture away and buttoned his jacket. "You're a resourceful girl Kelly. I'm sure you'll work something out."

Girl, she thought. *I'm older than you are sonny.*

"I was a crime-scene tech not an investigator."

"You trying to persuade me to nick you after all?" He cocked his head on one side, stared down at her. "I've read your file Kelly, you were an excellent investigator."

"Nevertheless I don't think I can do this on my own." She wasn't sure as she said it if she was asking for his help personally or simply permission to involve someone else.

His expression flickered. "That's your decision," he said. "Just bear in mind—if you were set up last time—that takes a coordinated effort rather than a series of blunders by people who had access to all the evidence. Not just whoever was in charge of the case but whoever took care of the crime scene." He paused meaningfully. "Be careful who you trust Kelly."

Kelly got to her feet, the dizziness in her mind very little to do with lack of food or sleep and threw him a troubled glance.

"Does that include you?"

—77—

O'NEILL STOOD UNDER the café awning and watched the slight figure hurrying away towards the Tube station at Lambeth North. He thought of the cellphone in the inside pocket of his jacket. If he made the call now he could have her picked up before she went underground.

He let her go.

After all, he'd told Kelly that her flat was a safe haven. Bearing in mind that she seemed able to get in and out of the place without being seen from the street, the chances were she'd take the risk and go back. If it came to it he could always reacquire her there even if it meant laying in wait inside.

But that was a last resort.

O'Neill sighed. He'd taken the risk and planted the seeds. All he could do now was hope something fruitful grew from them.

He turned away, flicked open his phone and hit speed dial. "Dempsey?" he said when the call was answered. "How's it coming with the tail on Frank Allardice?"

"Fine boss," Dempsey said. "A couple of our guys picked him up outside his hotel this morning and they've been on him ever since."

"Well remind them not to get too close. Allardice might be an old bastard but that doesn't mean he's not still a canny old bastard."

—78—

FOR THE LAST ten minutes Ray McCarron had been fumbling with a jar of instant coffee, trying in vain to get it open one-handed. Finally he wedged the body of the jar into a kitchen drawer and leaned his hip against the drawer front while he twisted off the lid with a grunt of triumph.

The effort left him breathless, perspiration sheening his forehead. He sank gratefully onto a stool, chin on his chest, not moving until the boiling kettle caught his attention. He watched it bubbling furiously for a second or two. It seemed more intent on steaming the blown-vinyl paper from the ceiling than clicking itself off.

McCarron eyed the appliance malevolently. "Don't you start," he growled. It was only when he got laboriously to his feet that the kettle took the hint and subsided.

He had discharged himself from hospital that morning, unwilling to put up with the disturbed nights and being treated like a half-witted geriatric for any longer. Just because a man was over sixty didn't mean he'd entirely lost his marbles.

Not that McCarron wasn't grateful—for the most part. The surgeons had done a remarkable job piecing his elbow back together which was the worst of his injuries. It was now encased in a glass-fibre cast that was supposed to be lighter and less cumbersome than the old plaster of Paris, even if it didn't feel that way.

He'd managed to satisfy them that his skull was solid enough to withstand a few knocks without going Humpty Dumpty on them. Although they'd initially suspected internal bleeding, a few nights' observation had proved this fear unfounded. And if his ribs hurt like the devil, it was bearable if he didn't laugh, cough or breathe too deeply.

He was, he told them, a tough bastard who didn't break easily and he had proved this by managing to walk out to a waiting taxi more or less unaided. Then he shook with delayed reaction most of the way home.

Once back in the empty house in Hillingdon he half-regretted his bravado. Sure they'd packed him off with enough painkillers to dose an army but McCarron had never liked taking anything stronger than aspirin.

And besides, all the pill bottles had childproof tops that were more or less impossible to remove with only one working hand.

He shuffled over to the kettle, discovering when he got there that the sugar bowl was empty. He leaned against the counter and closed the eye that wasn't still half-closed from the beating. And he wondered at how such a mundane task—one that he'd normally accomplish while reading a report and with a phone clamped to one ear—could possibly have become so damn difficult.

The loud knock at the front door made him jump which was not a good idea for a number of reasons. The stabbing pain in his ribs knocked the breath out of him again and as he swung around the cast caught against the open jar of coffee. It skittered across the worktop and went smashing down onto the kitchen tiles scattering brown ant-like granules along with splinters of broken glass across the entire floor.

McCarron tried instinctively to save it falling. A mistake. By the time the haze of pain had lifted enough for him to see clearly, Kelly Jacks was standing in the kitchen doorway.

"Kel for God's sake!" he mumbled through stiff lips. "What are you doing here?"

"I heard the crash," she said. "Don't move until I've cleared up this glass. You should have slippers."

McCarron looked down at his rumpled socks. "I do," he said, rueful. "Couldn't get the bloody things on."

But he kept still until she'd found a dustpan and brush from the cupboard under the stairs and swept him a clear path back to the stool. He went meekly, too shocked to put up a fight.

"What *are* you doing here?" McCarron repeated, watching her start methodically cleaning up the floor a square at a time the way he'd trained her to do. He didn't ask how she'd got past the front door which he knew he'd locked behind him. "Not just here in my kitchen but *here* at all?"

There was a fractional pause in her rhythmic brushing. "Aren't I allowed to come and check on my boss to see how he's getting on?"

"I would have thought you'd have been too busy—evading the police and so on," he said bluntly. "I've been in hospital Kel, not incommuni-bloody-cado. They still get news there. They're saying you ... had another blackout."

She sat back on her heels and regarded him with clear eyes. "I didn't do it Ray," she said. "But you already knew that didn't you?"

The words hung between them like a tangible entity, dark and bitter. McCarron froze as if any sudden moves would provoke it to attack. And right then he couldn't quite decide if the weight he'd carried on his shoulders for the past six years had just lifted or grown abruptly heavier.

In his heart he knew that it was all over and a part of him was profoundly relieved. Even so, he put up a token resistance.

"Hey you know I've always had faith in you—"

"But you never needed it," she cut in, her voice cool. "Not when you knew—you *knew*—that I was innocent. That doesn't require any great leap of faith."

He took in a shaky breath and found he couldn't think of a damned thing to say.

After a moment Kelly dropped her gaze away, continued sweeping briskly. When she had the spilt coffee and glass in a manageable pile, she unfolded a newspaper from the stack he'd put aside for recycling and scooped it all into the centre, wrapping it up carefully afterwards.

"Where's your bin?"

"By the back door. Look Kel—" he began, but she was already gone. He heard the lid of the wheelie bin slam shut, the back door close again as she returned.

"If that was your only jar of coffee will tea do?"

McCarron could only nod. He hadn't budged from his perch and now he watched her while she moved easily around his kitchen, digging out teabags, a box of longlife milk he kept in for emergencies and a teapot that hadn't been used since his wife moved out.

"You're looking … well," he managed.

She glanced over her shoulder with what might have been a fleeting smile. "I can't say the same for you. You should have stayed in the hospital."

"I'd have been gaga inside a week."

"Hmm," she said, apparently absorbed in prodding the teabags inside the pot, "it's no fun being detained against your will is it?"

McCarron winced but knew he deserved that—and plenty more besides.

"What do you want Kelly love?" he asked quietly. "An apology?"

"What use is one of those?" She shook her head. "No Ray I want an explanation. Because right now the only reasons I can think of for you helping set me up are threats or bribery." She put the lid back on the teapot and turned to face him, folding her arms. "So which was it?"

McCARRON SAID, "IT started with Allardice—you remember him?"

The name conjured up a face instantly in Kelly's mind. An arrogant copper who'd handled her numerous interrogations and made no secret of the fact that he was convinced from the outset she was guilty as sin.

And a second memory hit her almost in rebound to the first. O'Neill's words back at the café.

"... *That takes a coordinated effort rather than a series of blunders by people who had access to all the evidence ...*"

"There may be many things I've forgotten, Ray, but DCI Allardice is not one of them."

"Well you were never going to be his bosom pal after you argued with him about that dead prostitute case. Know the one?"

"The girl who was beaten to death in that dingy little hotel near Euston," Kelly said. "They put it down to some random customer who got carried away. I still hold that she was deliberately murdered."

They had moved through into the front sitting room. The majority of the floor space was taken up by an old-fashioned floral suite that was so big it stopped the door opening fully. There were old family photographs on the tiled mantelpiece and glass-fronted display cabinets in the alcoves on either side, crammed to bursting with knick-knacks forlorn beneath a layer of dust.

Kelly had been invited round once or twice before but previously the room had always seemed to fade into the background compared to her vigorous boss. Now it was the dominating factor and he looked suddenly very old and vulnerable, swamped by his surroundings.

His condition didn't help and he was clearly tiring. When he lowered himself with great care onto one end of the sofa and leaned his head back it was hard to tell where the greying antimacassar ended and he began.

"Allardice was all over that hooker murder from the beginning even if he kept away from things officially," he said at last, taking a sip of the tea she handed to him. "It was only when it dragged on that he put himself in charge."

"The most basic questions weren't answered," Kelly said, her voice level but with an underlying hint of stubborn. "What was a high-class working girl doing in a dive like that? And her injuries—she'd been tortured before she was killed. What did they want to know? And the place had been not just wiped down but professionally sanitised—"

McCarron held up his uninjured hand in submission. "All right, all right. I remember you weren't convinced."

"Maybe because there was a lot about it that was unconvincing."

McCarron started to shake his head, caught himself just in time with only a minor flinch. "We were there to deal with the *what, where* and *how* not the *why*," he reminded her.

"Allardice didn't seem to give a damn about any of that," she countered. "He just wanted the whole thing closed."

"He wasn't alone there. As you pointed out, the girl was part of a high-class stable. There were plenty of supposedly very respectable people sweating when you wouldn't let it lie."

McCarron shifted uncomfortably against the cushions although whether he was trying to find an easier position for his ribs or his conscience Kelly couldn't be sure.

"Afterwards I heard a rumour Allardice might have taken a kickback from somebody high up to put it to bed—if you'll excuse the pun," he said. "Too much scrutiny from the law being bad for business. And he always did have a very ... casual attitude towards women in general and pros in particular."

Kelly tried to work out if she was surprised by this information. From what she remembered of the chauvinistic detective, probably not. His view of the proper role of women was formulated somewhere back in the Stone Age and had not been updated since.

"Well he got his way didn't he?"

McCarron didn't reply straight away and when he did his voice was strained. "You let it be known you weren't happy to let that one go love," he said. "You kept digging. It became almost ... an obsession."

"She was twenty-three years old," Kelly said stonily. "She deserved justice."

"I'm not saying she didn't. Just that sometimes you have to pick your battles. And that one you were never going to win."

"Did you help Allardice set me up for the Perry murder to stop me digging?" she demanded. "Is that what happened?"

"What? No of course not!" McCarron seemed genuinely upset. "That's not how it was."

Kelly reminded herself that she'd worked for him, alongside him, for eight years before her disgrace and then again for almost a year since her release. She'd thought of him as her mentor and certainly her friend.

Dammit, that *hurt*. It lent a certain acidic bite to her words. "So how *was* it exactly?"

He sighed. "Look, when I got the call to say you'd been found with a body I was as shocked as everyone else," he said. "I was certain you were innocent. I pushed to be lead on it but then I began processing the scene." Another sigh. "It looked pretty damning Kel. Even you have to admit that."

"It was supposed to look damning," she said. "All I know is that Perry called me out of the blue saying how he'd heard my name in connection with the case, saying he could give me information about the involvement of somebody important—his words. He asked me to meet him. That's the last thing I remember until I woke up with his corpse."

"The scene was a nightmare," McCarron said grimly. "Whoever it was who killed the lad, they made a right mess of him. He'd been butchered."

Kelly suppressed a shiver. "I remember," she murmured. She didn't think she'd ever forget the sight that met her eyes when she came round.

"I couldn't believe you could have done something like that," McCarron went on, a pleading look on his face. "I worked every inch of that place looking for something to exonerate you."

"But you didn't find it."

"No, that's the trouble," McCarron said heavily. "I did."

80

IN HIS OFFICE in central London Matthew Lytton found himself too distracted to concentrate on work. The meeting with the detective DI O'Neill had irritated him like an out of reach itch and he was determined to scratch it.

Normally, if he needed expertise he didn't possess he called in a specialist. Today he was breaking his own rule.

But with good reason.

He had never been a big fan of computers. They were a necessary evil rather than a front-line tool to him and he preferred to get out there and make things happen. Warwick on the other hand was completely at home with a keyboard and a mouse so Lytton left him to get on with that side of things—even to the point of asking his partner to help out with his initial background search on Kelly Jacks.

Maybe that was a mistake, he conceded.

Nevertheless it hadn't been too difficult to run a search of the records on the office server for the property O'Neill had mentioned. When he found the file he realised why he hadn't remembered it. Although in theory everything had to be approved by both of them, in this case the property purchase had been handled almost exclusively by Steve Warwick. It wasn't unheard of, but it was certainly unusual.

Rather than read it on screen he sent the whole file to the printer and read the pages as they spat out of the machine. It was only when he reached the financial section that he realised part of the document seemed to be missing.

He checked the file on the computer and found that some of the information was simply not there. Normally for this kind of purchase they would have used their standing arrangement with an investment bank but there was no reference number in the appropriate section. Instead Lytton found the cryptic note that the purchasing had been financed by a "private investor" which was unusual enough he certainly should have remembered it.

Frowning, he carried the printout down the short hallway to Warwick's office but when he put his head round the door he found the desk unoccupied.

Lytton was about to leave when he heard a noise from inside the room. He pushed the door wide and stepped through. There was a figure standing over one of the filing cabinets, who spun with a soft gasp. An armful of manila folders went splashing to the carpet, spilling their contents.

"Oh!" Yana Warwick cried. "I am *so* clumsy. So sorry."

"It's all right Yana," Lytton said hurrying forwards. "It's my fault for startling you. Please don't be upset."

Even so, it took five minutes and loan of a handkerchief before he could calm her enough to ask questions.

"I was looking for Steve. I needed to ask him about an investor for a conversion job we did a few years ago. There seems to be some data missing from the file. Do you know where he's gone?"

Yana shook her head. "He not tell me," she said, so firmly that he suspected she knew and had been instructed not to say. As it was she shrank away from him with anxious eyes as though he might blame her. "He leave me to do filing, yes?"

But her gaze strayed to the mess of paper on the office floor and Lytton felt her agitation rising again.

"I'll help you put all this back together again," he promised quickly.

If anything, the offer seemed to distress her further. "No! No, I must do it."

He gripped her shoulders and forced her to meet his eyes. "Hush Yana, it's my fault so please let me help you put it right." He paused, uncertain how to proceed. "Look, if you're unhappy with Steve. If he ever hurts you or threatens you, you don't have to stay with him," he said at last. "You know that don't you?"

She regarded him mutely for a moment then gave a helpless shrug. "I have nowhere to go," she hedged as if an outright declaration of intent might be held against her later.

Lytton let go, straightened up. "You'd be taken care of," he said. "I'd see to that."

81

IF McCARRON EXPECTED a barrage of questions after his admission he was surprised by Kelly's response. She sat quiet for a long time, frowning, perched on the edge of one of the brocade armchairs his first wife had bought more for their hardwearing qualities than comfort.

When eventually she spoke, her voice was low with a suppressed emotion he couldn't quite identify. "What did you find?"

He cleared his throat. His head was beginning to pulse and he badly needed to sleep.

"A smear of blood," he said at last. "Only small, not even a partial, but it was near the door frame leading out of the room where … out of the room. It looked like a bit of cast-off that someone had tried to wipe up."

"And was it?"

McCarron shook his head. "I don't know," he said. "I typed it, just as a prelim. It was O which didn't tell us much in itself—most of the population is O."

"But I'm A and Perry was AB if I remember rightly."

He began to nod automatically, regretted it as pain spiked his skull.

"For heaven's sake Ray haven't they given you anything for that?"

"Half a pharmacy," he said with a faint smile. "It's in a bag on the hall table. Kidproof bottles. Can't get the bloody lids off."

She got up without a word and he heard the rustle of plastic, a rattle and the splash of water in the kitchen sink. When she returned she was carrying a glass and the open bottle of tablets. He took it cautiously, the way a condemned man might accept a last cigarette.

"Thanks love," McCarron said when he'd swallowed the dose. "I got the sample ready to send off for DNA and went bouncing in to tell Allardice all about it. He was convinced you were guilty and this was the first sign of reasonable doubt we'd found."

"And?"

McCarron glanced at her. There was nothing in her face, her voice, to give him a clue to what she was feeling. Or what she might do.

"To say he wasn't pleased was an understatement." He sighed. "Threw a coffee mug across the office as I recall. As good as accused me of inventing the whole damn thing just to try and get you off the hook."

"Which you wouldn't have done," Kelly said, her voice without inflection.

"I didn't need to," McCarron returned stoutly. "It was there right enough."

"So you calmly refuted his allegation of course."

This time McCarron heard the faintest touch of humour in her voice. "I threw a waste bin back at him if that's what you mean? There we were—having a slanging match right in the middle of the incident room—when the boss walks in and asks what the bloody hell we think we're playing at."

"The boss?"

"Chief Superintendent Quinlan. He'd been told to keep an eye on things from a damage limitation point of view I think. And he wasn't a happy camper either. Nothing personal but if you weren't Perry's killer then whoever did it was still out there and we had no other suspects. That never plays well with the media."

"Allardice seemed determined to believe it was me right from the start."

"Aye well, Quinlan told us both to go home and cool off. Pick it up again in the morning. Privately he told me to give myself a pat on the back."

"But?" she said, sharper this time.

He sighed. "The next morning Allardice told me to run the tests again—just to be double sure."

"And this time—surprise, surprise—the result was different," Kelly guessed. She sounded resigned.

"Yeah it was. When the DNA came back the blood was Perry's after all. I expected him to crow about it but instead he told me not to be too hard on myself. We'd been working round the clock—I must have made a mistake."

Kelly simply looked at him very matter of fact. "You don't make elementary mistakes like that Ray. We both know it."

"Thanks for the vote of confidence." He gave her another weary smile. "To be honest I couldn't believe it either, so I checked and rechecked." He shifted again, winced and took a steadying breath. "I became convinced someone had swapped the samples. I took it to Quinlan. He promised to look into who'd had access."

He saw her quick frown. "Whatever doubts you had, they never made it to court."

McCarron nearly shook his head again, caught himself just in time. "No they didn't," he said flatly. "Quinlan cleared him but Allardice got wind of it somehow. He came bursting into the lab and gave me a gobful—he always was a mouthy sod. Said I'd gone behind his back and I'd make no friends that way."

"I hope you reported that too."

"I never got the chance." McCarron took a breath and went on. "That night I had a phone call—withheld number, disguised voice—telling me if I knew what was good for me and those I was close to I'd stop kicking up a fuss. That shook me I don't mind admitting it, but the real clincher was the next morning. I found a set of photographs pushed through my letterbox."

"Of your daughter?" she hazarded. "Is that how they got to you?"

"No Kelly love," McCarron said gently. "They were pictures of you."

—82—

"GOTCHA!"

Frank Allardice lowered the digital camera and checked the results of his efforts on the screen. He didn't consider himself any kind of a photographer but it always went down well to have a few pictures of landmarks from home to pin up behind the bar. And he was damned if he was going to pay rip-off tourist prices for postcards.

Besides, until he heard any different his business for this trip was done and he *was* simply a tourist.

But the object of his photographic aim this time was not the Houses of Parliament, Buckingham Palace, or a red double-decker bus. He'd been trying to get a clear shot of the two guys who'd been tailing him all morning and he'd just managed to snatch a full-face angle of the second man before he ducked his nose into a news-stand.

"Too late matey," Allardice said under his breath, studying the faces. "I wonder who you are and who sent you? As if I couldn't guess ..."

He'd long decided that much as he missed his old haunts in London the weather was something he could do without. It was getting noticeably chilly over here and he was uncomfortably aware of his joints in a way he never seemed to be when he was back in good old *España*.

He'd got out of the habit of city life which was too crowded and in too much of an all-fired hurry. Too much pushing and shoving.

The press of people had not, however, prevented him from spotting the two guys who attempted to tail him from the little hotel near Earls Court. He supposed they weren't doing a bad job but he'd been too long in the game for them to pass unnoticed.

He had toyed with them for the best part of an hour, putting them through their paces while he strolled around the Embankment area apparently at ease. Eventually his patience wore thin. Beneath it was temper.

So when his cellphone rang and he recognised the number he snapped, "What do you want?" into it by way of greeting.

He listened in silence while the voice at the other end of the line imparted hurried information.

"Thanks, but I've already spotted them. Still, better late than never, eh?"

"PICTURES OF ME?" Kelly repeated dumbly. "Doing what? I mean, when were they taken?"

"Some were of you at work, out in the street, at the supermarket, sitting in a restaurant with that young DI you were seeing," McCarron said. He hesitated. "But the others were taken later—of you on remand."

"On remand ...?" Her voice trailed off as the implications sank in. "How the *hell* did anyone get pictures of me then? Doing what?"

McCarron could hardly meet her eye. "In the exercise yard mainly but there were some obviously taken inside and, erm, one of you in the showers."

"That's sick," Kelly murmured, a shimmy of disgust rippling across her arms bringing them up in goosebumps. "In all kinds of ways."

"I don't think the pictures were meant to be perverted—not in that way," McCarron said miserably. A deep flush had stolen up his neck and was mingling darkly with the bruises on his face. "I think they were just to show how ... vulnerable you were. How easily they could get to you."

"And who is 'they'?"

He sighed. "I wish I knew Kelly love. Trust me, I wish I knew."

She was silent, trying to put the sense of violation behind her. It lingered.

Eventually she looked up and said, "What about Allardice? You must have suspected him."

McCarron's expression was a mix of discomfort and shame. "Of course I did," he said. "But you have to remember that Allardice was a copper's copper. He may have had a reputation for cutting corners but he got the job done and a lot of people respected him for that. If I'd accused him again so soon it would have smacked of a witch hunt. I'd been getting the cold shoulder enough after the first time."

Despite herself, Kelly could sympathise. She knew what the cold shoulder was all about. She thought of David again, standing in her hallway, leaving his key on the side table, demanding the return of the one he'd given her to his own flat. The pain was a distant memory but one that still had the power to hurt. Not love, she recognised now, just betrayal.

"I suppose it never occurred to you that just by showing those pictures in court—obviously taken without my knowledge or permission—it might have been enough to suggest that someone had it in for me. Might have been enough to stop me being sent to prison?"

McCarron opened his mouth, closed it again. "Things happened so quickly. And I never thought you'd be convicted," he admitted. "I was worried about you but I never thought ..."

No you didn't think, Ray. That was the trouble.

"But I *was* convicted." Kelly struggled to keep the temper out of her voice. "And you stood by and let it happen."

For the first time he reacted with anger of his own, driven by anguish. "What the bloody hell else was I supposed to do Kelly?" he pleaded. "They were threatening to hurt you, cripple you, if I tried to intervene. Even if I'd got Quinlan to believe that Allardice might—and it is a *might*—be involved it's obvious *someone* on the outside was pulling his strings—" He broke off, let out a slow breath. "I had no choice but to keep my bloody mouth shut."

"Even if that meant me going to prison where it would be a damn sight easier for anyone to get at me," she snapped.

And regardless of whether McCarron had toed the line they'd tried anyway, she realised. More than once. It was fortunate that she'd been a fast learner and had developed a quick-hardening survival instinct to cope with the early attacks. She'd thought they were random or caused by her connections to the police.

If Tina hadn't come along when she did, hadn't befriended me, I'd probably be dead by now.

And in that moment an image formed like a rapid bubble inside Kelly's head—of Elvis trying to collect the bounty on her head. Maybe that prize money had been up for grabs for longer than any of them had realised.

"You never did get around to telling me," she said casually gesturing to the cast and the bruises, "why Harry Grogan sent you that warning message?"

The colour dropped out of McCarron's face like a pulled plug. Watching him, she realised there had never been any doubt for *him* about who was pulling Allardice's strings. She nodded as if he'd spoken and got to her feet.

"Kelly, I—"

"No Ray don't say it," Kelly interrupted. "But has it occurred to you that if you'd come clean about half this stuff Tyrone might not be dead?"

She reached the door to the hallway and pulled it open before pausing briefly, eyes skating over the defeated figure stooped on the sofa. "I guess you can take this as my official resignation."

—84—

McCARRON LISTENED TO the front door slam behind her. Hard enough to rattle the glass in the bay window.

He laid his head against the back of the sofa again and closed his eyes. Even though he'd known deep down this day might come, as time went on he'd buried the possibility beneath layers of hope and foolishness.

McCarron had nurtured Kelly Jacks from the moment she'd started working under him. He'd recognised raw talent along with stubborn determination and a painstaking attention to detail that had her finding minutiae even he might otherwise have missed.

For a while the cops she worked with had loved her. They'd dubbed her their own private blood whisperer. Someone who seemed to be able to coax evidence out of the most unpromising of scenes.

She looked at things with a cool clear eye and a depth of imagination that enabled her to reconstruct the most complex and baffling crimes. He'd been immensely proud to call her his protégé, never thinking for a moment that the tenacity he so admired would be the cause of her downfall.

Never thinking either that his growing affection for her would be so obviously apparent to others. Or such a useful weapon against the pair of them.

McCarron had always thought of Kelly as another daughter. His own had come late and there had never seemed to be enough time to be a good father. Next time he looked, Allison was a discontented teenager, he and her mother were divorced and he'd lost his chance to do the right thing.

Kelly had been a worthy substitute.

But not anymore.

McCarron felt the loss as a bubble rising through his chest. It reached his throat and was released on an anguished gasp.

He rocked forwards on the sofa, his cast left arm cradled awkwardly in his lap and wept.

—85—

"THE CHIEF SUPER'S been looking for you," DC Dempsey said as soon as O'Neill arrived back in the office from his clandestine meeting with Kelly Jacks in Lambeth. "He was in a right mood because your cellphone was off."

"Bully for him," O'Neill muttered, shouldering out of his jacket. "How's the surveillance going on Allardice?"

"I put a couple of guys on it," he said. "They picked him up just outside his hotel and have been on him ever since."

"Good," O'Neill said but his mind was already galloping on. "Now, do me a favour will you—see what we've got on Harry Grogan?"

Dempsey rolled his eyes and swivelled back round to his computer keyboard. "Anything in particular you're after? Only the last time that name cropped up I practically needed to nick a shopping trolley from Tesco's for the paperwork. There's masses of it."

O'Neill paused. He thought of the conversation he'd had with Jacks about the accent of the man who'd come after her and the voice on the phone reporting Tyrone Douet's murder.

"Yeah—look for any Russian connections."

86

KELLY DROVE WEST along the M4 motorway in an old Vauxhall Omega estate. The car belonged to McCarron as did the cellphone in her pocket and the satnav she'd found stuffed into the glovebox.

She hadn't gone to visit her boss with robbery in mind but on her way out she saw his cellphone and car keys lying on the hall table and had snatched them up almost out of temper.

He owes me.

Once outside, she weighed the objects in her hand and debated the petty satisfaction of throwing both over the hedge into the neighbour's ornamental water feature.

Sense and desperation overcame more frivolous urges.

McCarron's car was parked on the short driveway. He always backed in so it was facing outwards and ready for a quick getaway. Tempting.

Kelly glanced over at her beat-up Mini sitting by the kerb on the far side of the road. She'd been back to fetch her own mode of transport as soon as she'd walked away from O'Neill. It had seemed a good way to test if he was telling the truth about her flat no longer being under surveillance.

Nobody had leapt out to arrest her when she'd clambered in through the skylight which suggested that he might be.

She'd debated on the wisdom of driving around in a car that was registered in her name but it was better than using public transport.

This might be better still. After all, she very much doubted McCarron was going to call the cops. And it wasn't like he was going to be using the car any time soon.

She thumbed the key fob to blip the locks and climbed in before second thoughts could stick their nose in. McCarron himself, she knew was not in any state to come running out after her.

The V6 engine fired first crank. She put the car straight into gear and pulled away without looking back.

Kelly wasn't used to an automatic gearbox and compared to the Mini the old Vauxhall was like driving a low-slung tank on the quiet residential streets.

She headed south from Hillingdon with no initial destination in mind, only wanting to put distance between her and the scene of her most recent crime. It wasn't until she picked up the signs for the motorway at Heathrow that her mind seemed to unknot itself and her thought-patterns smoothed out into a single decisive strand.

O'Neill had told her that she'd been dosed with ketamine. Ketamine was used by vets. He'd shown her a picture of the tame horse doctor Brian Stubbs, who Harry Grogan allegedly kept on a short leash. It didn't take a genius to put together those two facts and form an obvious conclusion.

But if it was so obvious why hadn't O'Neill followed up on it himself?

Evidence.

So far, Kelly knew the evidence was tilted against her like one end of a seesaw loaded with big fat facts. The detective had no doubt been instructed not to waste effort with side theories when the main case looked so solid. She'd been told the same thing often enough when she'd been a CSI and she knew that not everyone wanted to work off the clock to prove a point.

So why did O'Neill?

And why had he told her about Stubbs unless …?

Kelly pulled over to the side of the road sharply enough to warrant a quick blast on the horn from the driver behind her. She waved in vague apology and tapped the screen of the satnav.

The article she'd found on Grogan—the one with the picture of him and Lytton alongside their winning racehorse—had mentioned where his trainer was based and Kelly had always had a good memory for details. She asked the satnav for the centre of the village and when it had worked out the fastest route, checked the Vauxhall's fuel gauge. It was registering about two-thirds full. More than enough for a hundred-mile round trip to horse country, even for a thirsty old smoker like this.

Minutes later, striking lucky with lights and traffic, Kelly was on the motorway being slowly passed by the commercial jets coming in to land at the airport. A constant procession of them hung heavy and awkward in the air overhead, wheels dangling like the legs of a carried dog.

She cruised at a steady sixty-five, keeping pace with the slower vehicles, not fast enough to attract unwanted attention. And all the while she was trying to work out what she felt about the revelations that had emerged from Ray McCarron.

She wasn't sure if she entirely believed him. Not about anything in particular, it was just a general sense of distrust.

She remembered Allardice as if it had all happened yesterday. There had been no light and shade with him. If he couldn't use an axe to crack something open he wasn't interested.

Kelly had spent hours being interrogated by him over and over while he sneered and sniped at every aspect of her life until everything she'd thought she stood for was in ruins around her feet.

And all the time he'd known that McCarron had found something that might exonerate her. Not just known about it, she noted bitterly, but had in all probability destroyed it.

But for what gain?

It all came back to the dead prostitute. The one she had been so naively determined to fight for. Why had Allardice seemingly helped bury that one? And what had Callum Perry done to become the means of Kelly's own downfall?

Maybe nothing.

The thought came jolting in hard. Maybe Perry had committed some completely separate transgression and the method of his demise was just a convenient way of killing two birds with one stone.

She'd need to look closer into Perry's life in a way she hadn't been free to do immediately after his death. And, if she was honest, hadn't had the heart to since her release.

All roads seemed to lead her in the same direction. Kelly shook her head. Allardice could wait. Right now her focus was on a crooked vet with access to ketamine and the man who held all his strings.

87

THE POLICE RECEIVED the call about Kelly's abandoned Mini an hour later. One of Ray McCarron's neighbours rang it in. He lived opposite McCarron's house three doors down, a small fussy man in corduroy slippers and a baggy cardigan with tissues stuffed into the pockets.

He was annoyed with himself for not noticing the strange car arrive. Since he'd been medically retired from his job in the Civil Service he'd appointed himself the guardian of the avenue and was constantly on the phone to various authorities about refuge collection timings, wheelie bin transgressions, litter, dog fouling or infringements of the residents' parking privileges.

In this case he'd taken a surreptitious stroll past the offending vehicle and been mildly disappointed to notice its tax disc was in order. Nevertheless, the untreated rust patches on the bodywork strongly suggested an owner careless enough to be uninsured which presented what he felt was a real risk to the public.

Justified by this logic, the retired civil servant hurried inside and speed dialled the local police station from the phone in his front room. While he waited for the call to be answered he stood on tiptoe in the bay window, peering at the Mini as if the owner might try and sneak it away now they'd been rumbled.

The local nick was used to calls about all manner of real and imaginary petty crimes from this particular concerned citizen, to the point where they drew lots for the hassle of dealing with him.

On this occasion a young probationer picked the short straw. He made soothing noises while doodling on a scrap of paper but did happen to write down the registration number of the Mini, pompously delivered in the correct phonetic alphabet. In the time it took the man to explain his own importance and demand action, the bored policeman embellished the number by adding a sketch of a hot rod Mini with a naked young lovely sitting on the bonnet.

"Well, thank you very much sir," the probationer said when the do-gooder paused for breath. Bearing in mind the next unfortunate who would have to deal with him, he added maliciously, "It's observant members of the public like you that make our job easier. We'll send somebody round the moment they're available."

After he'd hung up the young policeman scrunched the paper up and dropped it into his waste paper basket then paused. He was still new enough in the job not to have had all the enthusiasm kicked out of him just yet.

He reached for the paper, flattened it out and idly ran a quick PNC check just for practice. The result made his eyes pop and had him grabbing for the receiver again.

—88—

KELLY LAY HIDDEN in the long grass at the edge of a small copse of trees overlooking the racing stables where Harry Grogan had his horses in training.

It was mid-afternoon. She'd arrived an hour before and left the borrowed Vauxhall parked up in a lay-by, hiking in across the fields to her present vantage point.

If she closed her eyes she could still conjure the image of the man O'Neill had identified as Brian Stubbs. Sadly, she had no clear idea of how often he made any kind of visit to the stables. O'Neill had described him as Grogan's resident vet but that didn't mean he actually lived on the premises, although with animals this valuable she supposed anything was possible.

Waiting was a frustrating business. Kelly gave it another hour, during which time a young lad made a tour of the loose boxes, looking briefly over each door to check all was well. Occasionally he disappeared briefly inside but otherwise the horses were left undisturbed to while away the afternoon doing whatever it was that horses did.

Kelly realised she was going to have to come back tomorrow morning—preferably early—with something waterproof to lie on, and food and drink to sustain her during the wait. Some binoculars would be a good idea too she decided, shuffling backwards out of her position and scrambling to her knees in the wood.

She began to brush the loose leaves and grass from her clothing when the crackle of undergrowth froze her in place.

She turned slowly. There was a man not ten yards away. He was dressed in a similar style to the clothing Brian Stubbs had been wearing in O'Neill's photograph but the face was younger and the expression had far more steel to it. That impression was reinforced by the battered double-barrelled shotgun he carried broken open over his arm.

"This is private property miss," he said in an ominous tone. "You're trespassing."

"I'm awfully sorry," Kelly said in her most harmless voice. "I'll leave at once of course."

She started forwards but the man sidestepped quickly and snapped the gun closed with a solid metallic click.

"Not as easy as that is it?" the man said. He jerked his head. "Boss wants a word. Then we'll see."

Kelly shrugged but her mind was racing. Despite his obvious familiarity with the shotgun she very much doubted the man was prepared to shoot her in cold blood just for a civil offence. On the other hand, being apprehended could be very bad for her. It would only take someone who'd seen a news report over the last couple of days to recognise her face …

She flicked a quick glance at the man's feet, the deciding factor. He was wearing old black Wellington boots, the tops gaping around his tucked-in trousers.

Nobody could run fast in boots that loose.

Kelly darted sideways and set off like a dodging hare through the trees, keeping her head low. Surprise gave her a head start. She'd worked enough crime scenes with shotgun injuries to know that if she managed to pull out a lead of more than thirty or forty yards, the shot would be too spread and too spent to bring her down. She hoped.

The man bellowed something behind her but she didn't catch the words. His voice sounded distant, growing more so. She risked a quick look over her shoulder just to be sure and saw him begin to falter as though giving up the chase already.

When she looked forwards again, she found out why.

A huge man blocked the path in front of her. He was wearing a suit that strained to contain his bulk, arms forced out from his sides by the slabs of muscle around his torso.

Kelly tried to stop, to change direction, felt her feet skid on the soft earth. She just had time to see the big guy swing one meaty arm—to register a fist the size of a steam iron heading for her face at an alarmingly accelerated rate—and then she ran full tilt into the waiting punch.

The sky cracked open in an astounding blaze of light and pain.

Then darkness fell, and so did she.

—89—

IT TOOK RAY McCarron a long time to answer the front door. He was half-hoping it would be Kelly standing there with that casual tilt to her hips and her hands in her pockets. That by ringing the bell instead of finessing the Yale lock again she was somehow making peace.

Instead when he fumbled the door open he found a uniformed constable waiting impatiently on his doorstep.

"Mr McCarron, is it?" the policeman asked. "Ray McCarron?"

"Yes. Why, what's happened?"

McCarron noted the policeman's eyes track over the obvious bruising on his face, the broken arm and the slow careful movements his injuries forced him to make. "Looks like I should be asking *you* that sir."

"I was mugged at work a few days ago," McCarron dismissed stonily. "There'll be a report somewhere I'm sure."

Any trace of humour disappeared from the policeman's face. "Yes, well we're looking for one of your employees—Kelly Jacks. I'm sure I don't have to tell you why sir. If she's here you'd do well to say so now."

McCarron kept his expression flat. Not difficult when the majority of his face was too stiff and too tender to display much emotion anyway. "Why on earth would you think she'd be here?

"That, sir." The policeman stepped sideways and pointed. McCarron glanced over the man's shoulder and saw at once

Kelly's old Mini parked on the other side of the road. It was surrounded by crime-scene tape and being guarded by two more uniforms while a flutter of neighbours gathered to gawk at the show.

Bloody busybodies.

And just as that thought struck, another followed along almost instantly.

Where's my car?

—90—

"OK—GOT IT thanks," DC Dempsey said and dropped the phone back on its cradle. He glanced across at O'Neill. "Looks like Jacks might have lifted her boss's car—a Vauxhall Omega estate. McCarron's just given one of the uniforms some cock and bull story about it being at his office but it's bloody convenient that Jacks's car turns up outside his house and his wheels are nowhere to be seen."

"Check it out," O'Neill said. "We've also—"

"Detective Inspector O'Neill!" The voice from the doorway was loud enough to make the DC jump, the tone chopping through what O'Neill had been about to say like a chisel. Heads snapped round and froze as if hoping to avoid the baleful glare now sweeping the room.

"My office," Chief Superintendent Quinlan ground out. "Now."

He didn't wait to see if the order was obeyed, just spun and stalked out. From back view his anger was all the more apparent in the bulging compression of his neck.

O'Neill rose with a sinking feeling, marshalled his expression into one of neutral unconcern and followed at a more relaxed pace.

"Good luck," Dempsey muttered as he passed. "If you don't come back can I have first dibs on your swivel chair?"

O'Neill forced a smile. "If I don't come back you can probably have first dibs on my job."

That caused a few answering grins. O'Neill held onto his until he was in the corridor and making for the stairs. Quinlan had disappeared. *Christ, how does someone his age move so fast?*

O'Neill lengthened his stride. The door to Quinlan's office was still open when he reached it. O'Neill knocked as he stepped through.

"You wanted to see me sir?"

The chief super hadn't quite reached his chair and he completed the manoeuvre before glancing up. O'Neill forestalled his next move by coming fully into the office and closing the door behind him. He did not make the mistake of taking a seat.

Something hovered around the corner of Quinlan's mouth. He sat upright, leaning his arms on the desk and linking his fingers together very precisely in front of his computer keyboard.

"The boys you put on former Detective Chief Inspector Allardice," he began with surprising mildness, "still wet behind the ears were they? Still in short trousers with the mittens their mummies knitted for them on strings down their sleeves?"

"It was my understanding they're experienced lads sir."

"Are they really? So how is it that a man who is now a glorified bartender was able not only to spot these covert surveillance experts but photograph the pair of them inside the first day?"

It was phrased as a question and O'Neill foolishly thought he was expected to answer. "Well sir—"

"Don't interrupt me when I'm giving you a bollocking."

"Sorry sir," O'Neill said.

Quinlan regarded him bleakly for a moment. To the right-hand corner of the desk was a flatscreen monitor mounted on a swivelling bracket. The chief super leaned forwards and nudged it round to face O'Neill. Two jpeg files were open on screen, both taken at a distance and not entirely sharp but the faces of the men were still clear enough. The captions "Pinky" and "Perky" had been added to them.

"The arrogant sod emailed them for my attention, courtesy of the Press Office." Quinlan's face twisted into a sour smile. "He's playing with us, Vince," he said at last. "He was infuriating enough before but now he's bloody insufferable. And this—" he flicked his fingers towards the screen, "—this is just showing off, rubbing our noses in it."

O'Neill gave a faint nod. "He knows we can't touch him," he agreed. "Or we'd have done it already."

Quinlan regarded him bleakly for a moment. Then he rose with a sigh, turned his back on the inspector and stepped to the window. O'Neill waited for him to speak. His mind inevitably slid to Kelly Jacks. Had she stolen Ray McCarron's car or had he willingly given her access?

He didn't need to ask why. After all, he'd shown her the picture of Brian Stubbs, told her Stubbs had easy access to the drug that had been found in her system and pointed her in the right direction. After that it didn't take a detective to work out where she was most likely headed.

Still, no reports of any bodies yet.

"I've always hated this view," Quinlan said out of nowhere, catching O'Neill unawares. "I won't be sorry to leave this office behind."

That rocked O'Neill. "I can't think of anyone else I'd rather have in here sir."

Quinlan glanced back at him. "Better the devil you know, hmm?"

O'Neill allowed the barest hint of a smile to lurk around his mouth. "Something like that sir, yes."

"I've been trying not to slacken off and watch the clock tick down to the inevitable 'surprise' retirement party and the gold clock," he said, "but the closer it gets the more on tenterhooks I find myself. I don't kid myself that I'll go out in a blaze of glory but I've no desire to go out in a shower of shit either."

"Sir?"

"That's exactly what Frank Allardice could dump on us if we don't handle this very carefully indeed, Vince. As you so rightly say—he knows where the bodies are buried," Quinlan said. "Frank put a lot of people away who thoroughly deserved to be locked up," he went on, "but sometimes his methods left something to be desired—as I'm sure you know better than most."

"I was his DC for a while when I came up out of uniform sir, if that's what you mean."

"Well then you'll know that Allardice was a great believer in the so-called Ways & Means Act—if he didn't get them for something they actually did, he'd get them for something they might have done instead. Net result was the same."

"Given the way half the little toerags bleat on about being under arrest as a 'violation of their human rights' sir, there are some of us who'd still agree with that today."

"And to hell with the law, Vince?"

O'Neill coloured at the dry tone. "We have to be given some room to manoeuvre sir, or you may as well do away with all the real coppers and employ a bunch of trained chimpanzees."

Quinlan gave a snort and ducked his head towards the two images on the flatscreen. "Sometimes I think we already do that."

"I warned them he was canny." O'Neill paused, chose his words carefully. "In some ways I can't help hoping I was right."

"Oh?"

"Well if it comes out that Frank Allardice is mixed up in anything dodgy we'll have a wave of miscarriage of justice claims to contend with." He wondered if he'd gone too far but Quinlan was way ahead of him.

"And if it all comes out just as I'm leaving then nobody will believe my retirement is voluntary." He returned to the desk, slumped into his seat and leaned back a little. "You certainly know how to put a blight on a man's day, Vince."

"Sorry sir," O'Neill said cheerfully. "Do you want me to recall Pinky and Perky—put some fresh faces onto him?"

"No, you may as well leave them in place. A visible deterrent might encourage him to keep his nose clean while he's over here I suppose, although I'm not holding my breath on that one."

O'Neill nodded, was about to turn away when he felt compelled to ask, "What about Kelly Jacks sir?"

Quinlan's eyes narrowed in speculation. "What about her?"

"Do you think she was a victim of the Ways & Means Act too?"

The sudden stillness told O'Neill he *had* overstepped the mark. "Certainly not," Quinlan said. "I was there, don't forget. I remember how she was found—the state she was in. That's one conviction I'd stand by with no qualms at all."

O'Neill nodded. "Good to know," he said.

—91—

KELLY CAME ROUND to the smell of the sawmill and the violent clatter of iron on wood.

She was face down on a scratchy surface that gave slightly under her when she floundered up to hands and knees. That was as far as she got for a while, blinking as she tried to clear her head.

And all the time a voice in the back of her mind was wailing, *Not again!*

She forced herself to focus past the dull nauseating thump inside her head. Her jaw felt like she'd bounced off a truck and gone back for a rematch. She flexed it from side to side, brought a hand up. Her chin was tender and she'd possibly loosened a couple of teeth but the joint itself still seemed to be in one piece.

A miracle in itself.

She focused on the ground under her. Not soft earth or grass but wood shavings which accounted for the smell she'd recognised. She'd had an uncle out near Enfield—long dead now—who used to potter in his garden shed making furniture. During visits as a child Kelly had been fascinated by the pale curls of wafer-thin wood that fell like snowflakes with each steady pass of the plane.

The sound that had woken her came again, a sharply demanding scrape and thunderous bang. Like someone kicking a heavy wooden door with steel-toecap boots. It took her a moment longer to realise that's exactly what it was.

Only the some*one* was actually a some*thing* instead.

A horse.

Kelly sat upright and scrambled backwards expecting to see some huge animal rearing over her but she was alone.

She was, however, in a stable—a loose-box about fifteen feet square with a bed of wood shavings spread across the floor six inches deep and banked up around the edges.

After another five minutes or so, when her heart rate had settled, Kelly was able to get to her feet and explore the parameters of her prison.

The stable was blockwork construction, lined to about four feet with vertical timber planks. There was a door and a window in one wall. The window had bars every three inches—narrow enough, presumably, to stop a horse getting its nose through.

When Kelly peered out cautiously through the grimy cobwebbed glass she could see a row of similar stables opposite, across a swept concrete yard. Behind the other stables was the roof of a substantial stone house. If she craned into the corner she could just see the back door. It was closed. There were no people about.

She gave the stable door an experimental rattle but both upper and lower halves were bolted from the outside. A bucket of fresh water and a filled hayrack suggested the box was in use or would be shortly.

So this was a temporary holding cell.

Is that good or bad?

Kelly could not remember being transported here from the woods but could only imagine that *here* was the trainer's yard she'd been watching earlier. The buildings she could see looked similar.

And at least she could remember everything that had happened right up to the point she got herself clobbered. She touched a hand to her jaw again and reflected that having to eat soup for a while was a small price to pay.

It could have been worse.

She looked around her. The walls on either side of the loose-box did not go all the way up to the peak. They were flat—level with the eaves—so the row of stables shared a common open roof space. Above the walls were only dust-covered beams and the felt underside of the roof itself. Considering the walls and door were built to keep three-quarter-ton horses from straying, forcing her way out there was a non-starter.

The roof, however, might be a different matter.

Kelly dipped a hand into the bucket and splashed a little water onto her face. It was cold enough to have a wake-up effect. She was thirsty but not enough to try drinking it.

They'd taken her backpack and the keys to the Omega, which had been in a trouser pocket, but they'd left her boots. Not the best outcome but again, not as bad as it could have been.

Kelly stood in the centre of the stable and took stock of her options. Even if she got out of here, she now had no access to her transport. Trying to run might provoke a stronger display of force.

There was always the possibility that they'd locked her up while they waited for the police to arrive but from what she'd learned of Harry Grogan somehow she doubted that was the way he dealt with things.

Noises outside had her darting to the window. Through the dusty glass she saw figures coming out of the door to the house. One was the thin man who'd accosted her with the shotgun. The other was the big guy whose fist she'd run smack bang into. And rarely, she felt, did a description fit so aptly.

Their appearance brought her to a quick decision. She moved to the corner with the hayrack. It was made of plastic-coated metal and clearly secure enough to stand a horse yanking hay from between the narrow bars.

Kelly grabbed it with both hands and swung her feet off the floor, hooking one heel over the top and pulling her body up. By balancing on the top edges of the rack it was an easy job to hoist herself onto the dividing wall.

From there she could see she was in the centre box of a row of five. The next stable along didn't offer anything. It too stood empty with the doors closed and—she assumed—bolted.

But she could see more light at the end of the row. She carefully clambered along the roof trusses until she reached the next wall. Sure enough the top door was open but the stable itself was occupied by a very large grey horse wearing a hessian-type rug. He reacted with a startled snort when a strange woman appeared looming above him.

"Easy now boy," Kelly tried in a reassuring murmur. "I'm only passing through. Nothing to worry about."

Sadly, her voice betrayed her doubt and the horse was tuned into tone not words. As she swung her leg over the wall he skittered away blowing hard through his flared nostrils. His feet scuffed through the wood shavings as he did so and she heard the metallic drag of an iron-shod hoof against the concrete underneath.

The shavings might provide her with a soft landing but that would do her no good at all if the horse kicked her to death out of sheer fright once she got down.

This stable also had a hayrack, and she edged along the top of the wall until she was directly over it. Slithering down into the rack had the grey horse backing into the far corner, white showing all around the iris of his bulging eyes. His ears flicked back and forth sending out semaphore distress signals.

Kelly pulled out a couple of handfuls of hay and held them out to the horse, clicking her tongue encouragingly. He favoured her with a look of absolute disdain.

"Oh sod you then," Kelly muttered, dropping the hay. She lowered herself over the side of the rack and landed lightly enough on the ground that the animal didn't have a fit at having a small human suddenly sharing his boudoir. In fact, now she was down at a level he was used to the horse's curiosity overcame his fear. He took a couple of steps forwards and stretched out his elegant nose towards her, snuffling at her sleeve with a surprisingly muscular upper lip.

The closest Kelly had been before to a real horse was a distant donkey ride on the sands at Margate as a toddler. She found this one much too big and overwhelming by comparison, but when she tried to elbow him away his ears flattened immediately.

"Like to get your own way don't you Dobbin?"

Further along the row of stables she heard a bolt being shot back then voices rising in alarm as they realised she'd gone. The grey horse, ever curious, barged past her and stuck his head outside. By peering through the gap between the top of the door and the underside of his neck Kelly could just see the two men looking round frantically. Their shouts had brought more people out into the yard—stable hands mostly, by the look of them.

She realised that her chances of a successful covert escape had just dropped to nil.

Somebody calmed down enough to start barking instructions for a methodical search. From what she could see, Kelly thought it was the big guy in charge—the one who'd knocked her out. She didn't recognise his voice but she did recognise his accent.

Russian.

Kelly shrank back. Already they were unbolting the loose box next door, slamming the door again with a shout of, "Clear!" The grey horse was leaning against his own door craning his neck round to watch them as if it were the most exciting thing he'd seen in ages.

There wasn't time to hide and nowhere to go anyway. Kelly caught a glimpse of a face appearing, prodding the horse back, then there was more shouting, triumphant this time and the door was thrown wide.

"Got her!"

The horse, startled by the sudden raised voices, took a couple of quick steps in reverse. Kelly had to dart to one side to avoid being flattened and put a steadying hand on his rug at the shoulder.

It was only as she did so that she saw the alarm in the faces crowding the open doorway. Somewhere behind them a man swore.

"Christ, she's in with Mr Grogan's colt!"

Something in his voice tipped it. Acting on pure survival instinct Kelly grabbed hold of a handful of mane. She had to reach up a long way to do it. She lifted her booted foot and placed it, edge on, against the grey horse's impossibly fine-boned thoroughbred front leg, just level with his knee.

"Come any closer and the only races this horse'll be running in future will be three-legged ones," she snapped, injecting as much quiet savagery into it as she could manage. They had to believe her. If they didn't …

The threat had an electrifying effect on her audience who froze horrified. The grey horse merely flicked an ear in her direction and watched her with a calmly trusting eye.

"What the hell are you after?" someone asked, sounding shaken.

It was a good question. For a moment Kelly's mind went blank. "I want to talk to the vet," she said. "Brian Stubbs. Bring him here."

There was some muttering and shuffling and then everybody seemed to take a step back, parting so a newcomer could step forwards. He filled the doorway. The Russian hard-hitter, Kelly noticed, was at his shoulder.

The new arrival was not Brian Stubbs but she had no difficulty recognising him from his picture.

"Stubbs isn't here," Harry Grogan said, his voice a low growl. "Will I do?"

—92—

DMITRY WAS CRUISING Brixton giving shit to anyone he thought might have information about Kelly Jacks. According to all those he'd threatened so far, nobody did. He tried not to think about the stubborn resolve on the faces he encountered. Myshka had been right, he acknowledged with a sour smile. His treatment of the kid in the flat had cost him valuable co-operation.

Dmitry's iPhone rang. *Viktor*. Dmitry answered it one-handed while he drove. He was tired and frustrated and he badly wanted to go home and stand under a hot shower for a long time.

"*Da?*"

"She is here," Viktor said without preamble.

"What?" The tremor though Dmitry's hand made the Merc swerve slightly. He didn't need to ask who. "What is she doing there?" And almost as an afterthought, "Where are you?"

"Still with horses," Viktor said, as always a man of few words. "She is talking to him."

Dmitry checked his watch and the thickening traffic around him and swore.

"I will be there fast as I can," he said. "Stall them."

"How?" He could almost hear Viktor's frown.

"Use your imagination! Don't forget—you were there too." *At the warehouse. You held her down while we killed the boy ...*

But even as he disconnected and threw the cellphone onto the passenger seat he knew with a terrible feeling of constriction in his chest that Myshka's grand scheme might all be over.

—93—

"SO," HARRY GROGAN said, his voice a whisky-dry rumble, "you want to tell me who put you up to crashing in here threatening to nobble my best horse?"

"When it comes to threatening, you damn well started it," Kelly fired back.

Grogan was leaning in the open doorway apparently relaxed but carefully blocking her exit at the same time. He'd told everyone else to make themselves scarce, including the hulking Russian who'd clobbered her. Kelly wasn't sure whether to be reassured or not by his desire to banish potential witnesses.

Now Grogan sighed and fixed her with an implacable stare. "I think you'd best explain that—while there's still a chance we can sort this out ... amicably."

Kelly felt laughter bubbling up in her throat, recognised a wisp of underlying hysteria and swallowed it back down again.

She had taken her foot away from the grey colt's foreleg and he'd twitched himself out from her grasp to stretch towards his owner near the doorway, hopeful of some treat or other. Grogan rubbed the animal's sleek head without taking his eyes off Kelly.

"Where do I start?" she queried. "How about with the warning you sent to my boss Ray McCarron—to keep his nose out of your business? A warning that came wrapped in a beating bad enough for him to need surgery."

"Ray McCarron? Never heard of him," Grogan said flatly. "Next?"

The blatant denial shocked but at the same time didn't surprise her. She pressed on. "What about setting me up to take the fall for Tyrone Douet's murder?"

"Now *that* does ring a bell. I believe I saw it on the news," he said without a flicker. "But I believe the police were fairly sure *you* were the one they were after. So how exactly did I manage that little party trick?"

"By having one of your Russian thugs stick the knife in my hand after they'd dosed me with ketamine—probably supplied by your crooked vet."

"Ah that's why you were asking for Stubbsy," Grogan said. "Who happens to be a very good vet I'll have you know. He may have one or two personal weaknesses but as long as he indulges them in his own time then quite honestly I don't give a monkey's."

"I notice you don't deny the Russian thugs are yours."

Grogan shrugged. "I have offered employment opportunities to a number of people from the former Soviet Union," he agreed blandly. "And if they're lacking in the social niceties, shall we say, that's only to be expected. Practically a Third World country these days isn't it?"

Kelly thought of Steve Warwick's wife Yana who'd apparently been traded like a chattel. *Third World* was too advanced, she decided. *Medieval* was more like it.

"Are you trying to tell me you have no control over your own men?" Kelly demanded. "That you let them rampage around London beating up whoever they like and using your name as justification for it?"

The grey colt had taken another step forwards and was nuzzling Grogan's pockets now, impatient for his due. Grogan ignored him.

"My name carries weight in certain circles," he said. "If people choose to bandy it about without my knowledge that doesn't mean I'm responsible."

"I suppose you're not *responsible* for the ten grand price you put on my head either?" she threw back at him.

The mention of money finally seemed to have some effect. Grogan raised an eyebrow, looked her up and down. "What is it you're supposed to have done that makes you worth *that* kind of money?"

Kelly knew she should take her time about replying. That now she had actually provoked a response, however slight, she should make the most of it, play her cards close to her chest. Instead she allowed him to exasperate an answer straight out of her.

"What have I done?" she repeated. "I spotted the botched job your men made of Veronica Lytton's so-called suicide. And ever since then you've been trying to shut me up—one way or another. Well, it may have worked last time but there's no way anybody's putting me away *again* for something I didn't do."

Grogan took a breath. She saw his chest rise, his mouth open, then a large figure stepped suddenly into view, grabbed him roughly by the shoulder and yanked him away, spinning him against the outside wall of the loose box.

The grey colt scuttled backwards swinging his hindquarters dangerously close to Kelly. She jumped out of the way.

When she looked back at the doorway the big Russian who'd thumped her was standing firmly planted in the aperture. The double-barrelled shotgun Kelly had seen earlier was pulled up hard into his shoulder. He was aiming it square at Kelly's chest.

She watched dumbfounded as the knuckles of his fingers began to whiten around the first of the triggers.

—94—

DMITRY FLASHED AN Audi saloon that was dawdling in the outside lane of the M4, muttering furiously under his breath as the offending vehicle moved over with leisurely arrogance.

He had pushed and bullied his way out of London in record time and was now heading west at slightly over a hundred and twenty miles an hour. It was the kind of speed where other traffic was constantly in his way and his temper was in shreds.

But he had told Viktor to use his imagination when it came to dealing with Kelly Jacks and that, he realised, could well turn out to be a huge error of judgement on his part.

Viktor was a man whose imagination usually leaned towards extreme violence.

Dmitry took his hand off the wheel just long enough to stab the redial button on his iPhone but Viktor was still not answering. Dmitry's own imagination painted all kinds of nasty pictures about why that might be.

He pressed his right foot down a little harder on the accelerator.

—95—

HARRY GROGAN STOOD in the stable doorway staring down at the inert figure lying face down in the horse's bedding. There was surprisingly little blood but what there was, the shavings were doing a good job of soaking up.

"Is he dead?" the girl asked, her voice strangely composed.

Grogan gave her an assessing glance. "Take more than a shovel round the back of the head to kill old Viktor," he said. "Stupid bugger, waving a bloody shotgun around near my colt."

He set the shovel down to one side of the doorway and glanced at his horse. The animal was going spare, clattering against the kickboards at the back of the box as if trying to climb out over the walls. Grogan winced at every knock against those priceless legs.

The grey colt was not happy about being approached. His fear translated into a display of temper with ears laid flat and back hunched, stamping his feet down. Sweat darkened his coat in patches, the veins popping through.

There was movement in the stable doorway and the lad who looked after the colt elbowed Grogan aside as he went to his charge, making soothing noises in his throat. Any other time, Grogan would have sacked him for behaviour like that, but the way the horse was immediately reassured made him hold his tongue.

"We need to move him out of here sir," the lad said over his shoulder. Grogan couldn't tell if he was the one being addressed or the trainer, who'd reappeared also.

"What about him?" the trainer asked nodding to Viktor's body sprawled in the entrance to the stable.

"What about him?" Grogan asked brusquely. He turned to the lad. "Just get on with it son. If the horse tramples all over the big daft bastard while he's about it, maybe it'll teach him a lesson."

Between stable lad and trainer they managed to get a bridle onto the colt's aristocratic head and led him out. The horse made a big production of needing to sniff at Viktor before he'd step over him then lifted each leg exaggeratedly high and bounced away across the yard alongside the lad, up on his toes and still blowing hard.

"This might be enough to put him off his game for the big race," the trainer muttered as he hurried after them, not waiting for a response.

Because he had a bloody good idea what that response might be ...

Grogan pulled out a large white handkerchief to clean his hands. "Nothing like making your excuses before you begin is there?" he said dryly.

The girl gave no reply. He looked over and found she'd picked up the fallen shotgun and was now aiming it in his direction with a certain degree of competence about her.

He carried on wiping his hands, apparently unconcerned. "Know what you're about with one of those things do you?"

"I've fired a few in my time."

He grunted. "Shooting into some water tank in a ballistics lab is not the same thing as into flesh and blood though, is it?"

"Hadn't you heard?" she asked tightly, almost a taunt. "Killing people isn't a problem for me."

Grogan paused, staring at her. "I've met some killers in my time sweetheart," he said. "But you're not one of them."

She smiled. "Want to put that to the test?"

No he didn't. He tucked the handkerchief back into his pocket keeping his movements nice and slow and said instead, "Why did you come?"

"I wanted to talk to Brian Stubbs."

"Like I told you, he's not here," Grogan said. "You want to talk? Fine, let's talk." He glanced down. "But I'm not standing around up to my knees in horse shit out here to do it, so either we go inside and sit down like two adults or you can sling your hook."

And with that he turned and walked out of the stable, stepping over Viktor's unconscious figure a lot less carefully than the colt had done.

It wasn't until he'd made it unmolested across the yard that he felt the tension go out of his neck.

—96—

INSIDE THE FARMHOUSE was old-fashioned and slightly scruffy. Kelly took one look at the cluttered worktops, the overflowing sink and the soot stains above the ancient Rayburn and decided that the trainer probably lived alone.

The walls were largely covered with pictures of horses. Black and white shots of old victories going back forty years.

The kitchen itself was empty apart from a couple of ancient Labradors sleeping close to the front of the Rayburn. One dog raised its head when Kelly entered, gave a wide yawn and settled down again.

She moved quietly across the dull tiles, still clutching the shotgun. Only one door out of the room stood open and she could hear movement beyond. She hesitated just outside then stepped through quickly as if expecting an ambush.

The room was a small bare sitting room with French doors leading out onto a mown but otherwise bare garden. Kelly could see the post and rail fence bordering the driveway beyond. The room boasted a large boxy television set and a video recorder stacked with tapes labelled for old races. Racing papers formed decorative stacks at either side of a well-worn armchair.

Harry Grogan was standing at a sideboard on the far side of the room with his back to her, pouring a stiff Scotch on the rocks. He turned as she came in, lifting the bottle.

"Join me?"

Kelly shook her head.

"You can put that thing down," Grogan said nodding to the shotgun. "I've said we'll talk. I like to think I'm a man of my word. You'll not get any more out of me that way."

Slowly, reluctantly, Kelly let the twin muzzles droop until the only thing they menaced was the ugly floral pattern on the carpet which, she felt, probably had it coming.

"I have to hand it to you," he said sipping the drink and watching her closely while he did so. "There's not many people would have the guts to beard the lion in his den as it were."

"I think you'll find it's the lionesses who do all the hunting."

Grogan raised his glass in salute. "And the lion who gets to muscle in on the kill afterwards and take the best for himself without the work."

Kelly sighed. "Shall we stop waving our dicks around here?" she said. "Because I think that's one contest you're always going to win."

His face didn't register anything but she thought she caught the faintest glimmer in his eyes. They were small and deep set, seeming to dominate within his shaven skull. She had the impression of a man who knew his own strength on many levels. And not just so he could crack open a man's head with a shovel.

"I don't know about that sweetheart," he said at last. "You may not have a dick but you've certainly got balls."

He moved round the armchair and sat down, ignoring the way she darted back as he approached.

"So," he said, "you think I've put a price on your head for interfering in my business in some way, is that it?"

"More or less."

Again there was no immediate reaction. He took another sip of whisky, swallowed and then let out a low chuckle.

"Care to share the joke?" Kelly asked, aware of a tart edge to her voice.

"The joke?" Grogan said. "The joke is sweetheart that I'm just a simple businessman—have been for years."

"*Businessman.* Is that a euphemism?"

He smiled more fully now, the kind of smile she guessed was not supposed to be entirely reassuring. "One-hundred percent legit."

"Doing what?"

"Corporate takeovers, property development, import/export—import mainly. I source goods overseas, bring them in, sell them on and make a profit. Same as a thousand other entrepreneurs—only probably a damn sight more successful than most of them. Even Customs have given up tearing apart every load looking for contraband."

Kelly frowned. "So what's with the Russian thug outside?"

Grogan shrugged, an expansive gesture. "I have a lot of dealings with Russia. It makes sense to employ some locals. They have a lot of fine craftsmen over there in need of international markets and I provide one of those markets—at great financial risk to myself."

"Yeah and no doubt great financial reward also."

"Fortune, as they say, favours the brave." He paused, eyed her and took another sip. "You should know."

Kelly felt her certainties crumbling and her focus with them. She shook her head. "I don't get it. Everybody thinks you're some kind of gangster."

"My dad was a gangster—ran with the Krays." Grogan leaned back, almost reflective. "I had a quite a few interesting 'uncles' as a kid. But he died an old man in prison and I decided a long time ago I didn't want to go out the same way."

"So, miraculously you've lived an innocent and blameless life?"

"Like you, you mean?" he shot back. "Everybody thinks you're a murderess sweetheart—tried and convicted once, time served. And now it looks for all the world like you've run true to form and done it again." He cocked his head regarding her, waved the hand with the glass. "Want to take a quick poll and find out how many members of the Great British public believe you didn't do it?"

"No," she said at last, voice stark. "Why are you telling me all this? Won't it blow your fearsome reputation?"

"Maybe it would." He chuckled again, a throaty rasp of sound. "But who are you going to tell?"

RAY McCARRON WAS struggling one-handed again. This time he was attempting to manoeuvre a metal box-file out from its entangled corner of the spare bedroom upstairs. The room was too small to fit anything other than a child-sized single bed and had long since been consigned to a junk store for things waiting in vain to be taken up to the attic.

Without his wife to nag him to carry out the second part of this task the room had gradually filled so the door would barely open wide enough for him to squeeze through with his cast.

By the time he'd uncovered the box and wrestled it from its dusty hole Ray was exhausted, sweating and light-headed. Then as he backed out carefully—but not carefully enough—he bumped his bad arm against the door handle and the box-file spilled from his suddenly nerveless fingers.

This time Ray did not make the mistake of trying to catch it. He could only watch as the file landed upside down on the tiny landing, bounced once and disappeared round the newel post. The clatter and crash as it hit random treads on the way down the staircase seemed horrendously loud inside the empty house.

"*Bugger*," he said, not having the breath for anything more.

As he edged to the top of the stairs he found an avalanche of spilled paper and torn manila folders. His shoulders drooped in defeat. Sorting through it all had been a hard enough prospect before and now it would be ten times harder.

Very slowly and with much wincing he sat down on the top step and reached for the nearest folder. Lifting it caused more of its contents to slither further down the slope but half the pages still remained clinging to the over-stressed paperclip inside.

Ray dragged the folder onto his lap. On the front cover was the familiar crest of the Metropolitan Police. Above the crest was a date more than six years ago and in stark underlined block capitals the words:

MURDER OF CALLUM PERRY

"I'm sorry Kelly love," McCarron murmured. "But better late than never, eh?"

He took a deep breath and opened the file.

"IF YOU'RE NOT after me then who is?" Kelly asked. It should have been a demand—she formed the words that way inside her head but by the time they emerged it had fallen more to the level of a plea. "They murdered my friend, almost crippled my boss, put a young lad into a coma." She looked up more fiercely now. "And they're using your name to do it."

"Oh I'll take care of that, sweetheart don't you worry," Grogan said, his voice rich with a grim promise that contradicted his earlier claims. The glass was empty in his hand. He glanced into the bottom, rose out of the trainer's armchair. "Sure you won't join me?"

Kelly shook her head.

It wasn't until he'd refilled his drink that he said, "Tell me what you meant about Veronica Lytton's 'so-called' suicide."

Kelly didn't reply immediately, just watched him regain his seat with a wary eye. She remained standing although she had put down the shotgun—it now rested barrels-up against the hinge side of the door frame. The gun was within easy reach but would be hidden from anyone entering the room.

Back when Kelly had been a CSI she'd once found a rifle left in just such a position—after a firearms team had supposedly cleared the building. The memory lingered.

As did the memory of the blood spatter in the bathtub at Matthew Lytton's luxurious country house. And because she couldn't think of a good reason to withhold the information she told Harry Grogan what she'd found and the warning that had been impressed on Ray McCarron afterwards.

"An interesting tale," Grogan said when she'd finished, without giving any indication from his face or voice if he found it fanciful or not. "Funny thing is, Lytton always refused to have anything to do with me while his wife was alive." He regarded her with solemn humour. "I don't think she approved of my breeding—unlike that grey colt you were threatening outside."

"I probably wouldn't have gone through with it," Kelly returned, matching his tone. "Probably."

He rolled his eyes and went on calmly, "But now Lady Muck is out of the way suddenly I find myself able to do business with Lytton and his partner—what might prove highly profitable business for all of us at that."

Kelly frowned, remembering the vehemence in Lytton's tone when he'd talked about Grogan. Was he really a better liar than she'd given him credit for or had she just *wanted* to trust him to the point it had coloured her judgement completely?

"I don't believe he'd kill his wife just for that." But the strange twinge of guilt she'd seen in Lytton—the day she and Tyrone had gone to clean the place—remained obstinately in the back of her mind. And there was no doubt he hadn't seemed devastated to find himself suddenly a widower.

"Maybe not, sweetheart but his greedy partner just might— and *he's* the one who's been making all the running."

"Steve Warwick?"

Grogan must have been watching her face as she said the name. Amusement plucked at his mouth. "Make a pass at you did he?"

"I didn't give him the chance," Kelly said, acidic. "But his wife was with him. Maybe that cramped his style a little."

Grogan chuckled again. "Doesn't normally stop him. Not from what I hear."

Her tartness only increased. "Well I gather she's not in a position to say much considering he practically picked her from a catalogue."

The chuckle became an outright laugh. "That what he told you?"

Kelly didn't get the joke. "No—she did."

That seemed to sober him. "Did she now," he murmured. He seemed distracted for a moment then fixed her with a focused eye. "If I tell you I'll look into this, sweetheart will you let me do that without going on the rampage—at least until after my horse has run his big race this weekend?"

Kelly hesitated a moment and almost regretfully shook her head. "I could be dead or arrested by then."

He gave a long sigh. "Let me reach out to a few people—people who owe me favours," he said. "You got a cell number I can reach you on?"

"Yes—if you give it back to me."

He humphed out a breath and put the drink down on the arm of the chair long enough to delve in a pocket for the phone she'd taken from McCarron's house as well as the Vauxhall's keys. He shook his head a little as he did so, as if he couldn't believe he was going to all this trouble over her. Kelly had a hard time believing it herself.

There was an awkward pause. Then the silence between them was broken by the sound of a car engine revving hard as it approached along the driveway.

Kelly glanced out of the French door in time to see a Mercedes braking hard at the entrance to the yard. She glimpsed the driver and her heart leapt into her throat and lodged there.

"Ah about time. That'll be Dmitry," Grogan said with satisfaction. "He'll take care of you."

—99—

DMITRY BARGED THROUGH the farmhouse kitchen and into the small sitting room, fast and aggressive. The trainer warned him the girl had the shotgun on his boss but threats were not the same as actions.

He knew from his own painful experience that she was not to be underestimated. Maybe if Kelly Jacks had shot her last victim he would have used more caution but she hadn't. Besides, if there was a certain amount of ... collateral damage during the struggle, Dmitry reckoned he could probably live with that.

Better than facing the awkward questions that would undoubtedly arise if she and Grogan had a chance to talk.

So he hit the door with his shoulder and kept on coming, aiming to knock aside anyone standing within the arc of its swing or startle her into immobility for those vital few seconds.

Harry Grogan sat alone in the trainer's old armchair, a glass of whisky in his right hand. Despite the violence of Dmitry's arrival he seemed unsurprised by it, lifting the glass without a tremble.

"She's gone," he said not even turning his head.

Dmitry straightened out of his pounce, saw at once that the French windows were standing open.

"I will go after her," he said striding forwards.

"No you won't," Grogan said. "She's no problem to us—for the moment. We got other things to deal with that are ... more pressing."

Dmitry paused as much at the tone as the words. He scanned around carefully and noted the position of the shotgun only a metre or so away behind the door. He stepped back almost casually to lean against the wall where the gun was within easy reach.

"What is it?" he asked roughly.

Grogan finished savouring his sip and relaxed his arm again. Only then did he look at Dmitry for the first time since he'd entered the room.

"Somebody has been taking my name in vain, Dmitry," he said. "You wouldn't know anything about that would you?"

Dmitry kept his face still even as his mind began to race. What had Kelly Jacks told Grogan? What did she know for certain and what might she have guessed?

"Who?" He tried not to hold his breath.

Grogan gave him a long cold stare. "That's what I'm trying to find out," he said at last. "Any ideas?"

Dmitry frowned. He knew he should come up with a convincing scapegoat but could not bring himself to do so. Myshka, he knew, would berate him for not being ruthless enough. For not standing on the heads of others to reach the top of the pile. He shook his head.

Grogan nodded as if that was the answer he'd expected. He levered himself out of the armchair, leaving the whisky glass balanced on the racing papers alongside and headed for the door. As he passed Dmitry, he clapped a hand on the younger man's shoulder.

"I had to give old Viktor a little tap on the head—he seemed just a bit too keen to shut young Kelly up before she'd had a chance to talk to me," he said, nothing in his face or voice to betray his emotions on the subject. "Sort him out would you? There's a good lad."

He didn't wait for Dmitry's agreement. But when he reached the door he stopped, turned back. "And where the hell has Stubbsy got to?"

—100—

BRIAN STUBBS SAT in a police cell and alternately cursed and sweated.

"Harry's going to kill me," he muttered under his breath.

It was not the kind of thing Stubbs would normally ever say out loud—not if there was the remotest chance of being overheard anyway. In the past Harry Grogan had been fairly forgiving of his vet's little foibles but this time he might just draw the line.

Oh Grogan had bailed him out of trouble before, saved his licence a time or two by parachuting in some high-priced silk to argue in his favour.

Without self-flattery, Stubbs knew this was solely because he was a bloody good horse doctor.

The best veterinary surgeons in the country tended to naturally gravitate towards the racing centres of Newmarket or the rolling Downs out past the Chiltern Hills west of London. That's where the real money was to be made.

Brian Stubbs had once counted among the best of them.

But his father had been a drinker. His mother too, now that he thought back. All too soon the odd glass of wine with dinner had become a bottle for breakfast.

And now it had landed him in the biggest mess of his life. He wasn't just looking at a temporary ban this time. He was looking at prison.

Sitting on the edge of the thin bed Stubbs rocked forwards and buried his unshaven face in his hands. It didn't help.

He could still see the old woman on the bonnet, the way her shock had turned into one giant flinch, eyes screwed tight shut, just before she hit the windscreen. It seemed to be permanently imprinted, hard-wired into his brain even with his own eyes closed.

Of course he'd called for an ambulance immediately. And inevitably the police had turned up along with them. They'd been admiring at first, the way he'd calmly taken care of the compound fracture of the old lady's leg, stemmed the bleeding from a nasty scalp wound.

That admiration hadn't survived the mandatory breathalyser test.

Trouble was Stubbs never felt drunk. OK, his hands might not be as rock steady as they'd once been but that was simply down to advancing middle age. And if his memory wasn't quite as sharp in the afternoons, or certain words escaped his tongue, that was because he put in long hours. Dedication, nothing more.

But for some reason his client list had been shrinking over the past few years. There'd been a run of bad luck of course— everyone lost animals occasionally. Couldn't be avoided.

Looking after Harry Grogan's horses were now his main— make that only—source of income. So when Grogan's trainer called in a state, claiming his mollycoddled prize colt was acting up after an intruder had got into his stable, Stubbs knew he couldn't make excuses not to turn out. Not this close to the big race.

Now, sitting in the cell of the police station where they'd taken him after his arrest at the scene of the accident, he wished he'd thought of something.

"What the hell am I going to do?" The words echoed off the painted walls and bare floor, coming back to mock him. He was not a brave man, he recognised in a sudden epiphany of self-awareness. He would not do well in prison.

But what have I got to bargain with?

The answer came at him so fast it left him breathless. He lurched to his feet, started to thump on the cell door with a clenched fist.

"Hey I want to talk to someone," he shouted. "I want to make a deal!"

—101—

"I DON'T GET what the deal is," DC Dempsey said. He was trying to shovel sweet and sour king prawn out of the foil container and into his mouth without dripping most of it down his tie in the process. "Why did we take the watch off Jacks's place? I mean, she must have gone back there to pick up her Mini or how did it end up parked outside McCarron's place? Shouldn't we put someone on the place again just in case?"

O'Neill dug into his own pork foo yung like a man a long way from yesterday's supper. Which he realised was the last time he'd eaten properly. "We haven't got the budget for a round-the-clock on the off chance—unless you're volunteering?" he said. He couldn't resist adding, "And she was pretty good at slipping past you last time anyway."

Dempsey pinked a bit round the ears at that and doggedly applied himself to his food while the blush subsided.

They were alone amid a sea of empty desks with a late ordered-in Chinese that would have incurred Chief Superintendent Quinlan's disapproval if he'd still been in the office at that hour. O'Neill reckoned they were fairly safe from discovery.

"Erm, can I ask a question boss?"

O'Neill suppressed a sigh. "You're not back in school sunshine. Just spit it out."

"Right, erm. What do Harry Grogan and the Russians have to do with Jacks?"

For a moment O'Neill froze. As far as he knew, the only person apart from him who knew Kelly had been threatened by Russian thugs—or that Grogan had put a price on her head—was Kelly herself. How had Dempsey got onto it?

He glanced across at the detective constable sitting on the other side of the desk. The kid might look like a geek but there was a brain lurking under the surface after all. O'Neill forced himself to chew and swallow with every appearance of calm.

"Go on," he invited.

"Well I was reading through the file, and the emergency call about the dead wino at the warehouse where Douet was later found, it came from a Russian. Then the tip about Douet came from another guy with an eastern European or Russian accent. In fact, listening to the tapes, it could even be the same guy. And then you ask me to check if Harry Grogan's got any Russian connections ..."

His voice trailed off, misinterpreting the scowl of concentration on O'Neill's face.

O'Neill registered his alarm and hastily rearranged his features. "No, no—it's a good point," he said. "We thought there was something hinky about that second call. The floor where Douet was found isn't readily visible, so how did our mysterious good citizen just so happen to witness the murder?"

"Ah—unless he was there."

"Shame Matthew Lytton doesn't have any Russians on the payroll."

"No, but his partner Steve Warwick is married to one."

O'Neill let his eyebrows climb. "You mean somebody actually opens those spam emails pretending to be from lonely young Russian girls who dream of love and marriage to a man with a nice handsome British passport?"

"Ha, the only spam I get are the ones offering fake Rolex watches and cheap Viagra." Dempsey wiped his fingers on a paper serviette then leaned across and rifled through the paperwork balanced on the corner of his desk. "You know you asked me to pull Lytton's phone records?"

"Anything crop up that might have been to or from Jacks?"

"I didn't find anything direct to Jacks's flat or work cellphone but there was a call to Lytton's office from a throwaway cellphone the day you went to see him." He handed across a printout with a list of numbers, one of which was highlighted. "Mean anything?"

O'Neill squinted at the sheet and shook his head. "Have you tried calling it?"

257

"Yeah—not available. If it is her she could be anywhere."

O'Neill scanned the rest of the numbers briefly but nothing popped. The office was quiet except for the distant droning vacuum of the night cleaning-staff and the whine of an overhead fluorescent tube just about to fail.

"Any of these turn out to be interesting?"

"Well, funny you should ask that," Dempsey said, diffident. "I mean, it might be nothing but—"

O'Neill fixed him with a hard stare. Dempsey broke off and then grinned at him a little sheepishly.

"OK boss—short version. You wanted me to go through the files on Grogan and look for Russian affiliations, yeah?"

"And?"

"Well lately he's been getting involved in importing a lot of stuff from all over the former Soviet Union. Craftsman-built furniture, mainly. Artisan rugs, ceramics, that kind of thing."

When O'Neill still looked nonplussed, Dempsey took a nervous sip of his Diet Coke. O'Neill wondered why he bothered with no-sugar soft drinks. The young DC was as skinny as a park railing. "When I say 'a lot' boss, I mean it," he went on. "Like, by the container-load. Upmarket stuff too. I had a quiet word with a mate of mine who works for Sotheby's. He reckoned it was worth a fortune to the right buyer."

"So what's he doing—smuggling it in?"

Dempsey shook his head. "All above board and legal according to Customs. But—and this is the interesting bit—Grogan employs some guys from that part of the world who are *not* exactly all above board and legal. They're listed as 'advisors' but I'm not sure what kind of advice they'd hand out unless it was which leg to break first."

So the Russians were working for Grogan. O'Neill thought of Tina Olowayo's boyfriend Elvis lying immobilised in his hospital bed. *They hadn't needed to ask which leg to break there.*

But what he didn't understand was why Harry Grogan should be involved in chasing down Kelly Jacks—or setting her up, for that matter. She'd claimed he wanted her badly enough to put up a reward. A man like Grogan had a lot to lose but what secrets did he think Kelly Jacks might be able to expose?

258

He looked up. "Why 'funny'?"

Dempsey was concentrating on fumbling for his last battered prawn. He gave up on the conventional chopstick approach and speared it instead. "Huh?"

"You said, 'funny you should ask' about Lytton's phone records. Why?"

Dempsey put a hand to his mouth before he spoke as if not wanting to spray his senior officer with half-chewed food. "Ah, there's been quite a bit of phone traffic between Lytton's office and numbers associated with Harry Grogan, that's all." He shrugged. "I had to ID the numbers for the trace."

"So Lytton has been doing some kind of a deal with Grogan. That *is* interesting."

"Could be a coincidence boss. After all, Lytton's into property. For all we know he's simply buying a shedload of furniture for a new development."

O'Neill shook his head slowly, aware he was tired and his brain was going round in circles without making much forward progress. He reached for his cup of coffee hoping a hit of caffeine might do the trick.

"Kelly Jacks queries the suicide verdict on Veronica Lytton," he said. "She and Douet report back to her boss. Next thing, McCarron's been professionally worked over, Douet's dead and Jacks is in no position to make any kind of fuss because she's got enough problems of her own."

"When you put it like that," Dempsey murmured, "I suppose it doesn't seem much like coincidence, does it?"

The phone rang on the desk, unexpected enough to make both men start. Dempsey reached for it. As soon as O'Neill realised from his noncommittal tone that it wasn't a scramble emergency he tuned out the conversation, letting his mind pick over the information without direction as if hoping something would present itself more clearly from the shadows.

Eventually Dempsey dropped the handset into the crook of his neck, eagerness all over his face.

"Erm, fancy a ride out to Reading nick boss?

"What—now? Why?"

"Well, you know the lab identified a vetinerary anaesthetic in Jacks's blood?"

O'Neill made a get-on-with-it motion with his chopsticks. "And?"

"Well I've got Thames Valley on the phone. They just picked up Harry Grogan's vet DUI after an accident and he reckons he's got information we need to hear."

—102—

IN A QUIET corner of Reading Services eastbound on the M4, Kelly Jacks grabbed a couple of hours' rest. Just another tired late-night driver dozing with the seat reclined and her sweatshirt bunched up behind her neck.

She had the car doors locked to keep out the unwanted world but in the end the disturbance came from inside anyway.

The raucous clamour of McCarron's cellphone jerked her upright, momentarily disorientated and rife with panicked guilt.

She recognised the incoming number and almost didn't answer at all, her hand lingering over the keypad. Eventually she let her breath out with a hiss of annoyance and snatched up the phone.

"What do you want Ray?"

Ray McCarron matched her stony voice. "Callum Perry had a girlfriend."

"I don't remember anyone coming forward after his death," Kelly said after a moment's silence. "Something else Allardice forced you to sit on?"

She heard his sharply indrawn breath and felt a complete bitch.

"I know I can't begin to make up for anything I've done—or not done—in the past Kelly but I'm telling you now," he said tiredly. "If you want me to shut up and go away you only have to say so."

She struggled not to apologise, instead giving him a brusque, "Go on."

There was a pause, then he read out a name and address. Kelly scrambled for a pen in the door pocket and a scrap of paper, her head still muzzy with sleep.

"How did you get this?"

"I copied some of the paperwork and case notes," McCarron admitted. "I suppose I thought … well I don't know quite *what* I thought to be honest."

Kelly decided to let that one go. "Was she interviewed at the time?"

"I don't know," McCarron said. "I dropped the bloody file down the stairs and it's going to take me a while to put it back into any kind of order."

"Don't you remember?"

"I was sidelined in pretty short order if you recall," he pointed out. "And I would have been kicked out if they'd caught me taking this stuff. I shoved it through the photocopier as fast as I could and hightailed it out of there."

Kelly swallowed as much to keep her silence as to clear her throat.

McCarron waited a few moments for her to speak then sighed again. "Look Kelly love, why don't you let me help—"

"It's a bit late for that," Kelly said and cut the call. A few minutes later she pulled back out onto the motorway and headed for London.

—103—

"WHERE WE GO?" Viktor demanded. "Is middle of night." He was leaning forwards slightly in the passenger seat so he could hold a towel-wrapped ice pack against the back of his head and he still sounded groggy.

Anyone else hit that hard with a shovel would have a fractured skull or be dead, Dmitry thought from the driving seat. *Not Viktor.*

"I told you," Dmitry said, his own voice terse. "The boss wants us to pick up Myshka."

"Why?"

Dmitry shrugged. "He was in a pissy mood. I didn't ask."

Viktor considered this for several miles.

"Is shame," he said at last. "I like Myshka."

Dmitry took his eyes away from the road for long enough to flick him a quick stare but saw nothing in the other man's face. "So do I," he agreed. "She's clever—maybe more clever than the boss, eh?"

Viktor turned to look at him, an incredulous frown creasing his brow. "She's a woman," he said in such a tone of finality that Dmitry knew there would be no arguing with him.

"I noticed," he snapped. "And keep that damn towel over your nose. I don't want blood on the leather."

They were in Dmitry's Mercedes heading deep into the Berkshire countryside, the lights cutting swathes through the narrow lanes, startling the occasional fox and rabbit that scuttled for the verges as the big car flashed by. At one point Dmitry saw the flutter of huge pale wings at the periphery of his vision—an owl perhaps—disappearing into the moonless night.

He wished himself anywhere but here.

He waited for Viktor to query what a sophisticated woman like Myshka was doing out in the wilds but it never seemed to occur to him. Viktor was a good foot soldier, Dmitry thought. He followed orders without question, broke heads when they needed to be broken. His lack of imagination made his loyalty without question—he could not be bribed, threatened or reasoned with.

"This is it," Dmitry said catching sight of a reflective marker in the tumble of brambles by the side of the road. He braked and swung the Merc carefully along a narrow track. The tree branches clawed in alongside and overhead, lending the darkness another eerie suffocating layer.

Dmitry had been brought up on folk tales of ghosts and wolves and demons. Tales designed to keep a child frightened and in line. He was not a child any longer but he would have taken the most dangerous ghettos of the city over this untamed wasteland.

Viktor showed no signs of alarm about his surroundings. That lack of imagination sometimes had its advantages.

"We walk from here," Dmitry said switching off the engine and climbing out. He turned the collar of his coat up against the cold, hunching his shoulders down.

"Soon be winter, eh?" he said over his shoulder, pulling on gloves and retrieving a powerful flashlight from the Merc's boot. "What passes for winter here anyway."

"In Moscow the winters freeze a man's breath still in his mouth, remember?" Viktor asked solemnly. He lifted the ice pack away from his skull and something twitched around his mouth. "You grow soft Dmitry."

"I do, my friend," Dmitry agreed. "But not so soft." His eyes slid past Viktor's face. "Hello Myshka."

The big Russian turned. Myshka approached out of the gloom, dressed in a long black coat with a fur collar and a hat to match. She carried a flashlight in her gloved hand and lifted her booted feet carefully over the uneven ground.

She stopped a few metres away and set the flashlight down on its end. It was the type that doubled as a lantern. For a moment none of them spoke. She fished in her pockets for cigarettes, lit one and inhaled deeply until the end glowed like hot coals.

"So he sends you for me and you come, yes? That's how it is between us?"

Between us? Dmitry wondered sharply. *Surely she hasn't ...?*

"Yes," said Viktor simply.

She gripped the edges of her coat as if about to strip. "And nothing I can ... offer you now will change your mind?"

Viktor paused a moment, regretful, then shook his head slowly.

"Am sorry," he said.

Myshka's eyes sought Dmitry's face, cocked an eyebrow to ask him a very different question. Dmitry hesitated then gave a tiny shake of his own head.

Myshka sighed. "So am I," she said.

Her voice was cold and clear. Something about it must have penetrated Viktor's brain. His head lifted like a dog suddenly catching the scent of danger. He started to turn, not towards Myshka but to Dmitry, bewildered questions forming in his eyes.

And as Viktor turned away from her, Myshka pulled out a squat black pistol from inside her coat and shot him through the neck.

The sudden noise and light and heat in the darkness was astounding. Dmitry staggered sideways as if hit himself, disorientated by the report that thundered away through the trees and blinded by the flare from the muzzle.

When he looked back, Viktor had dropped to his knees in the dirt, hands clasped weakly to his ruined throat. The round had passed straight through and carried on into the night, tearing a pathway of wanton destruction. Blood gushed between the big man's fingers, pulsing out at a rate that was clearly unsustainable.

His eyes were fixed on Dmitry's, his gaze gentle and uncomprehending when it should have been enraged. Viktor tried to speak, producing only a muted gurgle. He collapsed very slowly onto his side, chest heaving as his lungs flooded, and lay there shuddering.

Dmitry had seen enough gunshot wounds to know there was nothing to be done for him even if he'd wanted to. He caught movement and realised Myshka had moved to stand next to him, the gun held loosely at her side. She was staring down at Viktor with only mild curiosity in her eyes.

"He is too stupid even to know when he is a dead man," she said, her voice breathy. She raised the gun, aiming for Viktor's head this time. Dmitry caught her arm.

"No," he said. "We are not so far from civilisation that gunshots won't be investigated."

Myshka pursed her lips. The light from the makeshift lantern seemed to make her eyes appear very bright. "You would let him suffer?" she asked, something almost triumphant in her tone.

If you had been more careful he would not be suffering. Dmitry glared at her but held his tongue. "Give me the gun."

Now it was Myshka's turn to hesitate. "It was necessary—we agreed," she said, losing some of her certainty. "You said you would talk to him but if he would not join with us then—" a shrug, "—he must go, yes?"

"Yes," Dmitry agreed in a low voice. "That doesn't mean I have to like it."

Myshka dumped the pistol into his outstretched hand. It was a Glock, the barrel still warm even through his gloves.

"Grogan will blame Viktor for whatever the girl has told him has been going on. It will seem he has run away." She nodded to the gun. "You will bury that with him?"

"Yes." Dmitry looked the gun over briefly, saw the serial numbers had been professionally removed. "Where did it come from?"

She shrugged again, said carelessly, "I asked Viktor to get it for me."

There were a thousand questions Dmitry could have asked but he watched her walk away into the trees with all of them unspoken. Her own car would be parked somewhere nearby. She would be back in London in an hour and providing Viktor's body was never found, no-one would ever know.

Dmitry retraced his steps to the Merc and removed the shovel he'd previously stowed in the boot. He took his time about it. When he returned, Viktor had ceased to gurgle and shudder. The woods surrounding them were suddenly very still and very quiet.

Despite any lingering childhood superstitions, as he struck the blade of the shovel into the earth, Dmitry was glad both of the darkness and his own isolation.

At least there was no-one here to see the tears that ran freely down his face.

—104—

AFTERWARDS ERIN COULDN'T be sure exactly what had woken her. One moment she was soundlessly dreamlessly asleep and the next she found herself lying eyes open and scared in the darkness, gasping.

She collected her breath, strained to hear for the repeat of some faint scuffling that must have disturbed her but the flat was apparently quiet as the grave.

She shivered. *Why did I have to think of it like that?*

For a minute or so she lay primed, ready to launch out of bed but praying she wouldn't have to. Erin had long ago recognised that she was easily frightened. But children change all that—they bring out courage you never knew you had. Eventually it was the thought of something happening to Jade that had her slipping out from under the warm security of the duvet and groping for the towelling robe she'd dumped across the foot of the bed.

As she crept out into the tiny hallway she could see the faint glow of the night light spilling out through her daughter's bedroom doorway and her heart rate snagged.

She always closed Jade's door at night.

Jade was a self-contained child who rarely woke demanding attention but she was also a light sleeper. Erin had treated herself to a chick flick on DVD after she'd put her daughter down and she was certain she'd closed her bedroom door so the low volume didn't stop her getting off. It was a school night after all.

But now the door was standing ajar.

Erin hovered in an agony of indecision. Maternal instinct won out. On trembling legs she edged closer but as she drew level with the doorway leading to the living room, next to her own bedroom, a figure whirled out into her path and grabbed her.

She would have screamed out of sheer fright but a hand clamped over her mouth to prevent her loosing off anything more than a strangled squawk.

For a moment she was utterly paralysed. But as her attacker began to drag her back towards her own bedroom that was enough to kick-start Erin's sense of self-preservation. She bucked against the hands that gripped her, struggling ferociously with fists and heels.

"Be still," hissed a voice in her ear and what shocked her into obedience was the fact it belonged to a woman. "I came to talk, that's all. Do you want to give your little girl nightmares?"

Mutely Erin shook her head. She allowed herself to be bundled into her bedroom and set free with a shove that had her staggering. The door closed behind them and the overhead light snapped on, dazzling her. Erin cowered against the wardrobe, shielding her eyes from the light and the stranger in equal measure.

"W–who are you? What do you w–want?"

"You know who I am," the woman said quietly enough for Erin's curiosity to overcome her caution.

She opened her eyes a sliver and immediately wished she hadn't. The woman was right—Erin *did* know her. Not personally, but she certainly recognised the face. Impossible not to if you'd watched the TV news or seen a newspaper in the last few days.

"Oh God," Erin moaned.

Kelly Jacks.

The woman nodded as if she'd said the name out loud. "Then you'll know why I'm here."

"Please! I don't know anything! He never told me."

She regretted the words as soon as they were out. Even to her own ears they smacked of evasion if not of outright lies.

Kelly Jacks stared at her for what seemed like a long time. She was dressed in a hooded black sweatshirt and baggy cargoes. The fact that her clothes looked as if she'd worn them to roll around in the dirt made her appear more dangerous, more desperate, than if she'd been clean. Not to mention the bruises on the woman's face.

Erin remembered seeing bruises like that in the mirror.

Her bag was sitting on the chair next to the bed where she'd dumped it before she undressed. Kelly Jacks stepped across and upended it onto the duvet, giving the spilled contents a cursory skim and eventually picking up her purse.

"You're after money?" Erin said, surprised into speech. "There's not much in there but take it. Take it and get out!"

Her bravado was treated with disdain. But instead of the carefully folded notes, Kelly Jacks eased her bank card out of its slot and studied the raised letters on the front. On the whole, Erin would have preferred it if she'd taken the cash.

"Just checking I'd got the right person," Kelly Jacks murmured. "Six years ago you were Callum Perry's girlfriend. And if he didn't tell you what he was about, who did he tell?"

Erin cringed, the fear pressing down deep in her belly. "He never talked about work—"

"But you didn't work at the bar with him did you?" Kelly Jacks said then shook her head. "No, I would have known about you if you had. Your name would have come up. But you *were* involved with him—I mean, that is his kid lying asleep next door, isn't it? So why didn't your name come up, Erin?"

"I–I don't know."

"Your name didn't come up," Kelly Jacks went on, relentless, "because somebody made sure it didn't. Now why was that I wonder?"

Erin's shoulder twitched into a jerky shrug. "Could have been a mistake."

Kelly Jacks came across the room in two fast strides, fisted her hands in the front of Erin's robe and lifted her bodily off the floor. She was slim and barely came up to Erin's nose. The show of strength shocked her, constricting her belly, her chest, making it hard to breathe.

"Do *not* mess with me," Kelly Jacks said. "I spent five years in prison for something I now believe I didn't do. And if I wasn't capable of murder when I went in, believe me—I certainly am now." She relaxed her grip slightly. "Want me to prove it?"

"No!"

"So talk. Whatever they threatened you with Erin, or promised you, that's a long way from where we are right here, right now. All I want you to think about is what I will do if you don't tell me what I want to know."

Erin whimpered. Kelly Jacks spun her round and dropped her onto the duvet. Erin's cellphone, spilled from her handbag, was less than a foot from her hand but she wasn't brave or stupid enough to try for it.

"You don't understand," she begged, "what will happen ... to me. To Jade ..."

Above her head she heard Kelly Jacks's breath rush out like escaping steam. Then she swore, short, crude and heartfelt. Erin felt the mattress give suddenly. She darted a quick sideways look and found Kelly Jacks sitting alongside her, leaning forward with her forearms resting on her knees and her head low.

"I'm sorry," she said. "I'm no bloody good at this strong-arm stuff—and certainly not on somebody who's obviously been beaten with the shitty end of the stick too many times before." She lifted her head and a pair of brandy-coloured eyes met Erin's with a startlingly frank gaze. "I thought I could pull it off but I find I can't do that to you. Sorry for the scare. You're quite safe from me."

Erin could only gape at her. Kelly Jacks flicked her eyes away and stood up, stuffed her hands into her pockets as if she didn't quite know what else to do with them. "All I will say is, I think whoever's put the frighteners on you so badly is probably responsible for your boyfriend's death. I'm out to get him. And if I manage it you'll be able to stop looking over your shoulder for the rest of your life."

She turned for the door, had almost made it when Erin's voice finally came back to her.

"Wait," she said.

—105—

KELLY SAT ALONE at the tiny table in the kitchen of Erin's flat. She had both hands wrapped round a mug of tea tight enough to stop them shaking.

She was aware of a vague nausea like a kind of dull pressure high up under her ribcage. She put this down partly to lack of food and the possibility of concussion from her earlier blow to the head. And partly down to the fact that she had just tried to mould herself into the kind of monster she'd always despised. The kind that preyed on the weak.

Is that what it's come to?

The kitchen was small and cluttered, bland cabinets with a microwave taking up a quarter of the available worktop space. A child's crayon drawings randomly peppered the fridge door, held in place by alphabet magnets. Every item of furniture or bric-a-brac had come from IKEA. At least it was bright and cheerful. At that moment, Kelly felt neither. She took a sip of tea which was loaded with sugar but didn't help.

Through the thin wall she heard the flush of a cistern, running water and then the hollow click of an overhead pull switch. The bathroom door stuck slightly as it was opened, no doubt warped by years of steam. A moment later Erin appeared hesitantly in the kitchen doorway.

"Sorry," she said. "Always do need to pee really bad when I get nervous."

"Is your daughter all right?"

"Yeah—still sleeping, bless her." Erin came forwards, fiddling with the tie of her robe and flashed a smile that came and went like cheap neon. "She'd be ever so upset if she knew she'd missed the chance to show off her dollies to someone new."

"Look, Erin—"

"Yeah I know," the younger woman said quickly. "You didn't come here for that."

She crossed the room and slid into the chair opposite hardly able to meet Kelly's eyes. "I still blame you, you know," she said, her voice suddenly quiet and colourless.

Kelly shook her head. "I realise you believe that—even I believed it for a while—but it's not true. I didn't kill him. I was framed."

"Isn't that what they all say?"

"I've no reason to lie. I've been tried and convicted. I've served my time. Think about it—what do I have to gain by claiming innocence now?"

Erin took a breath and tucked a stray strand of blonde hair back behind her ear, looked Kelly right in the face with pale blue eyes. "What do you want to know?"

Kelly gave a helpless shrug. "Everything, I guess."

An almost eerie calm had descended over her. Kelly wondered if Erin had taken something out of the medicine cabinet while she'd been in the bathroom. *Valium, maybe. Something to round off the sharp corners of her fear.*

"You're right, of course," she said. "Callum and me, we were going out. He was a lovely guy—a rarity in my line of work I can tell you. He knew what I was and didn't care. Said he loved me anyway."

"Your line of work?"

270

The colour rose in Erin's cheeks. "I was on the streets, on the game, hooked on smack." She gave a harsh little laugh. "He thought he could save me."

Kelly regarded her steadily. "I'd say he managed it."

Erin shook her head. "Having my baby did that," she said fiercely. "I've been clean since before Jade was born. Don't even smoke anymore. That was harder to give up—I still crave a fag every now and again."

Kelly thought of the occasional glass of wine she'd enjoyed … before. Champagne on special occasions, perhaps brandy or a finger of single malt after a meal. It had been a long time since she'd willingly allowed anything intoxicating into her system. It was no longer a craving, she thought—more a sadness.

"How did you two meet?"

"At the wine bar. He was serving," Erin said. "We used to go in—me and some of the other girls. Bit of Dutch courage before work."

She might have been talking about a factory job.

"Wine bar?" Kelly queried. "I thought Perry worked at a club?"

"He did, but a mate of his owned a wine bar opposite St Pancras. Bit of a dive but all right you know? Callum helped out in there sometimes. That's how he met …"

Her voice drifted off.

"Who did he meet, Erin?"

She flushed again, her attention suddenly fixed on a few stray grains of salt that had lodged between the table and its fold-out flap, chasing them along the crevice with her fingernail.

"No-one," she said. "Just a friend. She died—somebody beat her to death. 'Occupational hazard' was how your lot described it to me. Jesus, her own mother wouldn't have known her after what they did."

"In a little hotel near Euston station," Kelly supplied, the memory reaching forwards to wrap itself clingingly around her. "They tortured her and left her body in the bathtub." And when Erin glanced at her, alarm spiking, she added, "I wasn't always on the run Erin. I worked that case. If it helps, I never stopped looking for answers."

271

Erin sat up abruptly, glared at her with eyes that had begun to redden. "No! No, it doesn't *help*. You just don't get it do you? The more you people poked into it, the more Callum got the idea into his head that there was a cover-up going on."

Confused by her vehemence, Kelly said, "I think he was right."

She'd aimed to calm her but had the opposite effect. Erin shot to her feet, scraping her chair back, paced over to the sink and turned to lean against it, restless. She had bunions on both feet, Kelly noticed, the big toe squashed over into the others. A throwback deformity from all that time spent loitering in killer heels.

"He *was* right—that was the whole point. But Callum decided it was a good way to make some easy money. Bonus pay he called it, so I could get out of the game—especially ..."

"With a baby on the way," Kelly finished for her.

Erin's eyes dulled down, lost some of their fire. "Yes," she whispered. She looked at the fridge directly across from her with its coat of artwork. Some of the pictures had 'For Mummy' across the bottom in an uneven childish hand.

Not 'For Mummy and Daddy' then ...

"He didn't understand who he was dealing with—not regular punters who could be squeezed for cash so their wives didn't find out. These were people further up the food chain. People with influence and more to lose."

"They wouldn't pay him to go away," Kelly guessed. "Because they couldn't afford to have him keep coming back."

Erin shook her head, her face screwed up with the memory. "It all got turned around on him somehow, so instead of Callum having something over them, *they* had something over him. He was so scared. And then ... he was dead."

Kelly watched her rock silently for a minute, then asked carefully, "Who's 'they', Erin?"

"Callum always swore there was some shady Mr Big lurking in the background but I only know one—one of yours," she said, bitterness creeping in now. "A copper. Who else could arrange to have him killed like that—as an example to the rest of us?"

"Who?"

She hesitated as if even now the threat lingered, distant but no less disturbing. "Allardice," she said at last. "Detective Chief Inspector Allardice."

No surprises there then.

"And he's the one who threatened you—and Jade?"

"Always was a cold-blooded bastard," Erin said. "I mean, who else would take down one of their own to get rid of Callum?"

Somewhere deep down it was the name Kelly had been expecting but it still hit her with a jolt to hear it out loud. Maybe that was why it took her a moment to catch up with the significance of the rest of it. "You *knew*?" she demanded. "You knew I was set up?"

Erin nodded. "Callum was coming to you because he thought you might actually *do* something with what he had, even if he daren't do it himself. He thought you were on the level. He thought he could trust you."

It was Kelly's turn for silence. Relief warred with outright bloody anger that yet another person had *known* she wasn't a murderer and had done nothing about it.

She was a junkie hooker with a kid on the way, argued her reasonable half. *What* could *she have done? Who would have taken her seriously?*

"Allardice is gone," she said. "Retired. I don't even think he's in the country anymore."

Erin gave her a cynical glance by way of response. "Gone, huh? Well he was here a few days ago, trust me. Large as life and definitely twice as ugly."

"What—here in your flat?"

"No, even he wouldn't go that far," Erin conceded. "He turned up outside Jade's school when I went to collect her." She shivered, wrapped the towelling robe a little tighter. "Just to let me know he could still get me any time he liked. To remind me to keep my mouth shut. So—you were never here and I never spoke to you, right?" Her mouth gave a twist that might have been intended as wry but came across bitter. "Sorry, but I've got my daughter to think about …"

"I understand."

Kelly pushed back her chair and rose, suddenly needing to be out of the suffocating little flat where Erin had burrowed with her child—knowing it wasn't entirely safe but staying anyway.

As she passed on the way to the back door with its easy-pick lock and no inside bolt, she paused, waited until Erin looked at her.

"I didn't kill him but I'm very sorry," Kelly said softly, "for everything that happened."

An expression of stubbornness settled across the younger woman's features. "You made him think he could get something out of it. It was like waving a bottle of drink at an alcoholic," she said. "You might not have put the knife in yourself but you put temptation in his way and he ... couldn't resist it."

—106—

O'NEILL HAD LET Dempsey drive to Reading, reckoning the DC was still young enough to enjoy a fast run along the M4. It was late by the time they left London and traffic on the motorway was sparse.

Before they hit the road, O'Neill had pulled together what they knew about Brian Stubbs. It came to the sum total of not a lot. Name, age, profession, marital status (divorced, no kids), immediate family and address. Apart from a couple of brushes for drink-related affray offences—for which Grogan's slimy brief had successfully argued extenuating circumstances—it seemed Stubbs slept with a clear conscience.

How he'd sleep from here on in was anybody's guess. And, if the state of the man who was led into the interview room was anything to go by, things were unravelling for him pretty fast.

Even after spending a relatively short time in the cells, Stubbs was dishevelled and off balance. O'Neill had been told he'd refused legal representation and found that intriguing. Like he didn't want anyone to know.

Now the vet peered past the accompanying uniform as if fearful they'd called his brief anyway. When he caught sight of

O'Neill and Dempsey sitting waiting for him, his relief was obvious.

O'Neill let Dempsey go through the introductions and formalities, leaving him to observe the shaky hands and bloodshot eyes on the other side of the table. He knew at once what lay behind them.

"Like something to drink Mr Stubbs?" O'Neill offered, and noted the man's twitch of confirmation. "Tea or coffee perhaps?" he went on blandly. "I believe the machine here even makes a creditable stab at hot chocolate, if that's your poison?"

Stubbs let his head hang, shook it once. "No—thank you," he mumbled. A residue of good manners.

"All right," Dempsey said bright and brisk. "I understand you have some information that may be relevant to our current enquiries, sir?"

It took Stubbs a moment to gather himself. He took a deep breath that appeared to reinflate his sense of self-importance.

"I need some assurances," he said. "A deal—freedom from prosecution."

Dempsey glanced at O'Neill. "Sir, we can't make those kinds of promises without knowing how you're involved in, whatever it is—"

"Involved?" Stubbs seemed outraged. "Of course I'm not *involved*. I barely know the man."

O'Neill sighed. "So what exactly are you hoping for immunity from?"

Stubbs cleared his throat. "The, erm, unfortunate incident this afternoon," he said rubbing a hand around his neck as if hoping to massage away the flush that was rapidly forming. "With my car."

"Want us to fix any parking tickets or speeding fines while we're at it?" O'Neill asked with deceptive mildness.

"You can do that?"

O'Neill cursed inside his head, exchanged a fleeting look with Dempsey that told him his DC was thinking along much the same lines.

Waster.

"Mr Stubbs. You knocked down a little old lady in broad daylight with almost three times the legal limit of alcohol in your bloodstream," O'Neill said pushing his chair back and getting to his feet. "We could practically bottle the sample you gave us."

Dempsey followed his lead and rose also, but before the two of them could step away from the table Stubbs blurted out, "Explosives!"

Both detectives froze.

If Stubbs had been asked to pick one word in these terrorism-heightened times guaranteed to grab a copper's attention, O'Neill considered that was probably pretty much at the top of the list.

"What kind, what quantity, and where?" he rapped out.

Stubbs floundered for a moment, drew himself together. "And what about my deal?"

O'Neill leaned into him across the table, resting on his knuckles and jamming his face up close. "Mr Stubbs, I am half a beat away from arresting you under the Prevention of Terrorism Act unless you tell me what you know. Right now."

Stubbs flinched back from the controlled venom, his darting eyes searching for an escape route.

His gaze fixed on Dempsey who did not provide one. "This is not just about losing your licence anymore, sir," he said. "This is serious jail time."

"All right, all right," Stubbs muttered, scowling. "Here I am, trying to do my bit and what do I get but—"

O'Neill straightened to his full height slowly enough for it to be a threat, let his voice simmer. "What kind of explosives, Mr Stubbs?"

"I don't know—I'm hardly an expert am I?"

"So how do you know about any of this?"

Stubbs hesitated. "Look, I happen to, erm … know a chap who does a bit of demolition—blows up tree stumps, that kind of thing. All perfectly legal of course. So when another chap asked me if I knew where he could get hold of some explosives I simply … made the introductions that's all." He tried an ingratiating smile.

"Who was buying and who was selling?"

"I'd really rather not name the seller if you don't mind. It's not really relevant anyway is it?"

O'Neill dredged through the facts of the report he'd read before they set out. "Probably not," he said mildly. "I seem to remember that you have a brother who does a bit of land clearance though, don't you? Maybe we ought to have a little chat with him."

He could tell by the way Stubbs sagged that he'd guessed correctly. "And the buyer?" he nudged.

"Look, this could put me in a very awkward position—"

"You're not a stupid man Mr Stubbs," O'Neill cut in, a trace of doubt in his voice. "You must have known you were going to have to tell us the details."

He saw the indecision. Stubbs had not thought any of this out, he realised and was just lurching from one crisis to the next. O'Neill's object was to keep him teetering until he fell just the way they wanted him.

"You're only doing your duty, sir," Dempsey added. "I'm sure it will look good to the judge when your driving offence comes to court."

"Harry Grogan," Stubbs mumbled. Dempsey met O'Neill's look and raised his eyebrows. O'Neill shrugged in reply. Stubbs, with his gaze averted, missed the exchange.

"Why would a respectable businessman like Harry Grogan want explosives?"

"The man's a crook—a gangster!" Stubbs protested.

O'Neill shook his head. "Not in the eyes of the law he's not. Clean as a whistle. Of course if we had a witness who would testify to his personally obtaining explosives that might all change."

"Ah well, it wasn't Grogan himself you understand. A man like him doesn't get his hands dirty does he? I mean—"

"Who was it then sir?"

"One of Harry Grogan's bodyguards—Russian chap called Dmitry although strictly speaking I believe he's perhaps Ukrainian. Nasty piece of work either way," Stubbs said. "Dmitry is usually the one who relays Mr Grogan's orders or instructions. Turns up at my house, lets himself in like he owns the place!" He throttled back his indignation. "I assumed this time was no different."

O'Neill felt Dempsey glance at him again but refused to let Stubbs know the importance of what he'd just said. "Dmitry have a last name?"

The vet shrugged. "Something totally unpronounceable. They all are in that part of the world aren't they?"

"I don't suppose this Dmitry mentioned what his boss wanted the explosives *for* by any chance?"

Stubbs shook his head. "I didn't ask. I've worked for Harry Grogan for long enough to know one doesn't question his orders." He gave a weary smile, more genuine this time. "If I'd done so this afternoon—refused to turn out to see his damned precious colt before the big race tomorrow—I wouldn't be in my current predicament."

That, O'Neill thought, was a matter of opinion. But aloud he said, "So, if your only contact was with Dmitry, you can't actually say for definite that it was Grogan who wanted the stuff?"

Stubbs looked astounded. "Who else would it be for?"

—107—

BACK IN HIS cell an hour later, Brian Stubbs still felt shell-shocked by the whole experience.

He was not, as the older of the two detectives had pointed out, a stupid man, but he recognised that he'd been woefully naïve. He'd thought he could dangle a few little titbits and have them turn him loose. Now he was in it up to his neck. Worse in fact than when he'd started.

Stubbs slumped onto the thin mattress and raked both hands through his unkempt grey hair.

"Why couldn't you have simply kept your big mouth shut?" he wailed in the empty room.

Unsurprisingly, he got no answer.

They'd made him go over and over it, about how he'd arrived home one day a week or so ago to find Dmitry had somehow broken in and was lounging in *his* armchair, drinking *his* booze with that smug, arrogant look on his face. The trouble was, Stubbs was frightened of him and Dmitry knew it.

If they'd stuck to the explosives, those two, maybe that wouldn't have been so bad. After all, he knew nothing beyond what he'd told them. Dmitry asked for the introduction, presumably on Harry Grogan's behalf, and Stubbs had provided it. End of story.

But they hadn't left it there. The older one, O'Neill, had that same predatory air as Dmitry, that same ability to smell blood in the water and home in on it. It was O'Neill who'd led him gently, sneakily, into talking about his professional life and encouraged him to boast, just a little, of his prowess as a veterinary surgeon.

And then the bastard had dropped the smiling act and said, "Tell me about your supplies of ketamine."

Stubbs had known right then that he was well and truly screwed. He'd no idea how they'd found out he'd been letting a little of the drug go out through the side door or that the last lot had been acquired by Dmitry. It was only after Stubbs had spilled everything he knew that he discovered it had been little more than a lucky guess.

Bastards!

Stubbs clenched his hands into fists in his lap. Only when they were curled tight did the habitual tremors become unnoticeable.

They'd got him every which way. Not just for being drunk behind the wheel and running down that stupid dozy old woman but half a dozen other charges relating to conspiracy to cause explosions and, to cap it all, possession with intent to supply.

No two ways about it—he was going to prison.

It was only then as the weight of it all piled down and began to crush him that Stubbs recalled a final indignity.

A few years previously, when his reputation had not yet begun to tarnish quite as badly, he'd been working for a trainer with a considerable string. There had been a few mistakes—maybe even the start of the downward slide—and he'd been let go. The trainer had given him an expensive bottle of booze to soften the blow.

It was only much later Stubbs had realised the irony of the parting gift—that he was fired because of his drinking. On principle he had put the bottle away and never opened it.

After Dmitry's last visit though, Stubbs had noticed the gift was gone and he knew the damned man had stolen it.

Perhaps I should have told those two about that.

He quashed the thought as soon as it rose. They'd probably have tried to pin something else on him. Shame though—the way he was feeling at the moment, drowning his sorrows with a few healthy shots of Bacardi 151 overproof rum was a bloody good idea.

—108—

"I COULD KILL for a decent cup of Earl Grey."

Kelly spoke the words to her own reflection in the Vauxhall's rearview mirror. She could see only a narrow slot of her face across the eyes, strobed by the passing streetlights and the flare of oncoming cars. Apart from the shadow of bruises around her cheekbone she looked no different from a week ago, before all this had begun.

Before the world at large assumed her capable of killing for a far lesser reason than a good cup of tea.

She headed west from Erin's flat on the borders of Hampstead Heath and skirted Golders Green. It was only when she got onto the North Circular and saw the distant bright arc of the new Wembley stadium that she realised she was on autopilot heading back to the McCarron offices.

After a moment's surprise Kelly shrugged and kept going. The Vauxhall was getting low on fuel and she didn't want to risk filling up. Not in a garage that was covered with CCTV and staffed by people who had nothing to do between customers but stare at the front covers of the newspapers. Her own face had been made uncomfortably familiar over the past few days.

No, she knew the car had outlived its usefulness and taking it back to her boss's house in Hillingdon was probably not a wise plan. Ray had mentioned his nosy neighbours often enough for her to know the chances were the Mini had been reported by now. If the police had any sense they'd be watching out for her return.

Besides, Ray hadn't yet shopped her to the police for nicking his car or his cellphone. So the least she could do was park the old Vauxhall somewhere it wasn't likely to be towed or stripped within a day.

She left the North Circular just after The Ace Café and pulled up carefully on the road outside the office, peering up at the darkened windows. Kelly crawled into the car park, stopped nose-in to one of the up-and-over doors and climbed out. Nothing stirred. It had rained earlier in the evening and the concrete glistened under the streetlights. The smell in the air was of diesel and winter.

Kelly unlocked the main door using the key on Ray's set, punched in the alarm code and wound the garage door up from the inside without turning on the overhead lights. The ratchet mechanism seemed very loud in the gloom. Kelly was glad to shunt the car inside and drop the door again.

She lifted her backpack out from behind the driver's seat and gave the controls a cursory wipe down. She'd had plenty of legitimate reasons to have been in her boss's car but not as the last person behind the wheel. If the techs wanted to drag the vehicle in and go over it with a fine-tooth comb she knew they'd find plenty of evidence. Shed hair, skin cells, fibres, footprints, dirt, sweat or some other source of her DNA.

Every contact leaves a trace.

Locard's Exchange Principle had been one of the first things they'd taught her when she began her training as a crime-scene investigator. It had fascinated her—how hard it was to eradicate all possible remainders of yourself.

Ever since her first scenes Kelly had this image in her head of the different strands of evidence swirling around the place like coloured mist. All you had to do was be able to see it.

But in this case the evidence was not physical. It was hearsay and conjecture. Full of *might be* and *what if*. She had never felt so lost among it.

Weary, she climbed the stairs to the upper floor. There was enough light bleeding in from outside for her to make her way without bumping into anything. Upstairs had the nutty smell of burnt coffee left too long too brew in the filter machine, mingled with the enzyme cleaner they used at scenes and furniture polish.

She dumped Ray's car keys on top of his in tray where she'd seen him put them himself a hundred times before. It was only as she turned to go that she saw a dark shape rising from the sofa on the far side of the room.

Heart bounding, Kelly dropped into a crouch. There was a second's buzzing silence and immobility then a calm familiar voice spoke out of the darkness.

"No need to panic Kelly. I've been waiting for you."

—109—

RAY MCCARRON REACHED out with his good arm and switched on a small lamp next to the sofa. It spread soft fingers of light across the comfortably untidy office. His domain. Across the other side of the room Kelly was still poised for flight, tense on the balls of her feet. She looked different—and not necessarily in a good way.

"I suppose I really should ask for your keys, seeing as how you've resigned," he said casually and watched her gradually uncoil.

"I suppose you should," she agreed.

He could almost get both eyes open again but even so the light was too dim for him to read her face clearly and he could glean little from her voice.

She asked, "How did you get here?"

"Without my car you mean?"

"I was more thinking without two working arms. Taxi?"

"Les gave me a lift," McCarron said.

She raised an eyebrow at that, glanced around. "He locked you in and left you here alone in the dark?" she said flatly. "What happened—did he resign too?"

"I asked him to do it," McCarron said. "Not the first time I've slept on this old sofa and you know as well as I do the alarm sensors only cover the ground floor."

So I knew I'd be safe up here.

It had still taken some mental girding to set foot in the place so soon after ... so soon. But of all his employees Les had been with him the longest—almost since the start. He was the one most likely to speak out if he thought McCarron was taking a wrong turn. McCarron was heartened by the fact Les agreed to drive him over without protest. Neither of them mentioned Kelly, as if by some tacit agreement. McCarron was heartened by that too.

Les told him to stay in the car while he opened up, ostensibly to keep him out of the rain. McCarron watched from a distance while he disabled the alarm and briefly checked the building before he came back to help him out. McCarron thanked him profusely but Les had shaken off the gratitude like beads of water from his waxed cotton jacket, given him a gruff goodbye and departed.

Two hours later McCarron listened to Kelly arrive.

"Want to tell me about it?" he invited now.

She let out a long breath. "Not really," she said.

But she did, going through it from the moment she'd taken his car until her return to the office. It took about forty-five minutes and he interrupted her account as little as he could. There was weariness about her rather than anger, but that was OK. McCarron was angry enough for both of them.

"That bastard Allardice," he growled when she was done. "If—"

"Don't, Ray," she said, her voice muted. "Believe me, you can't say anything I haven't already thought, but louder and with a whole lot more expletives."

He swallowed the bile. "So what do we do now?"

"*We*'?" Kelly said. "To be honest I don't know what anyone can do. Allardice retired with a farewell party, a gold watch and a pat on the back, and I left in chains. You really think anyone's going to take action now against one of their own?"

"You were one of their own too, Kelly love. Didn't seem to stop them back then."

"And now I'm a fugitive and a murder suspect." She sighed. "I've no chance of proving who really did what six years ago. Too much water under the bridge. Best I can do is hand over what I know to DI O'Neill and let him figure it out."

"O'Neill ...? Not Vince O'Neill?"

Kelly went still. "You know him?"

"I know *of* him."

"But didn't he come to see you in hospital—after you were attacked?" she asked. "Ty-Tyrone and I met him there that first night."

McCarron noted the way she stumbled over the boy's name but didn't comment. Instead he lifted the cast an inch or two. "Kelly love, the amount of morphine they'd given me you could have told me the Dalai Lama had arrived with his ukulele to give me a medley of George Formby classics and I wouldn't be able to contradict you with any certainty."

"And he didn't come back later? O'Neill, I mean."

"No. If he had, well I would have said something when I saw you earlier today." He glanced at the clock on the far office wall. It was a little after one in the morning. "Yesterday," he corrected.

"Come on Ray—I know that tone of voice. What is it about O'Neill?"

McCarron hesitated. "He worked with Allardice."

She frowned. "So did you."

"Yes but not like that, Kel. There was a bit more to it than that."

Her only reply was an eyebrow so arched he had no trouble making out the gesture.

"Allardice always liked to have a blue-eyed boy under his wing—no, nothing like that," he added catching her cynical sniff. "A kind of sidekick."

"Robin to his Batman?"

"Not quite. More like Igor to his Dr Frankenstein. Someone he could build up, who'd owe him and be grateful later down the line."

That produced a fleeting smile. "And O'Neill was the chosen one?"

"Aye. Allardice started to groom him while he was still in uniform. A word or two in the right ear. A favour or two called in. You know how it goes."

"Oh yeah," she murmured. "And how it doesn't."

"Look, it might just be coincidence love, but after you were arrested O'Neill made the jump to CID and he's been rising fast ever since."

"Even after Allardice retired?" Kelly said. "Perhaps he's just a bright boy."

"And perhaps," McCarron said grimly, "he knows where the bodies are buried."

—110—

KELLY STOOD NEAR the office window cradling a mug of lukewarm tea. She watched the colour of the sky over the rooftops changing slowly from sodium orange to the pale pink of sunrise.

Behind her, Ray McCarron stirred fitfully under the blanket she'd laid over him when the pills and the pain had finally caught up. She glanced across at the bruised and beaten features, his hair ruffled into a peak like a mini mohican.

Kelly hadn't slept but spent the remainder of the night in restless contemplation of what to do. What she *could* do. There weren't exactly a lot of options open to her.

Give up. Run. Fight.

She'd tried the first option before—surrendered to the authorities. That hadn't worked out so well. Running wasn't much of a long-term prospect either. Might be feasible if she were a criminal mastermind with half a dozen secret offshore bank accounts at her disposal. But Kelly had less than twenty quid left from raiding the petty cash tin in McCarron's desk. That wouldn't get her to Southend-on-Sea, never mind the South Seas.

She tried to look at her situation with a cool and logical mind. She knew she couldn't stay ahead of the police for much longer.

285

Whatever O'Neill's motives in letting her loose, she wasn't naïve enough to think it was anything but a temporary reprieve.

Kelly sipped her tea and frowned. She still couldn't work out what the detective's motives *were*. If he was Allardice's young apprentice as McCarron suggested then why hadn't he simply arrested her outside the Forensics building in Lambeth?

An answer—maybe even *the* answer—arrived so suddenly, so fully formed, that she jerked from the force of it then tensed, holding very still as if to move would scare it away again before she had chance to totally appreciate the nuances.

She must have made some sound though, because Ray McCarron shifted on the sofa and said groggily, "Wassup, Kel?"

"Nothing ... I don't know."

He struggled upright awkwardly, hampered by the stiffness and the aches he hadn't quite learned to compensate for. He pushed the blanket aside and rubbed his good hand—carefully— across his face. She heard the scuff of stubble against his palm.

"Care to elaborate?"

Still feeling her way, Kelly hesitated. Marshalling her thoughts was akin to rounding up hyperactive sheep with a lame collie. The more she tried to get them in order, the more they scattered.

Eventually she said, "O'Neill let me go. He had the chance to arrest me and he didn't do it. In fact he pointed me in the direction of the person who probably supplied the ketamine I was dosed with."

"So you're wondering—if he's in bed with Allardice—why would he help you?"

"Supposing he did it because he knows I was innocent. Because he knows who killed Callum Perry and it wasn't me." It still felt good to say the words.

Grumpy from sleep McCarron gave a small tic of impatience. "We've been over all this, Kelly love—"

"But *supposing*," she interrupted, "what O'Neill *doesn't* know—and what he *needs* to know—is the identity of the copycat. Who copied Perry's murder to set me up a second time?"

McCarron drew in a breath as if to begin an argument that never quite made it into words. He frowned, as much as his wounded face would perform such a manoeuvre.

"I don't get it," he said at last. "Why would they care?"

"Because it means somebody else knows their secret. Somebody else knows I was framed successfully once and they've tried to do it again."

"But this time it didn't go according to plan," he murmured. "You didn't wait around to be arrested and even if O'Neill magically vanishes away the blood evidence you collected, you can still prove you were drugged."

It was her turn to frown. "But I didn't know about traces staying in my hair until O'Neill himself told me," she said. "Why would he do that?"

"Because he needed you to do his legwork for him," McCarron said. "He can't go at this from anything other than the official angle—that you've gone off the rails again. Anything else opens him up to too many difficult questions. Clever bugger! He feeds you just enough for you to go crashing around in the undergrowth while he and flaming Allardice sit on their backsides and wait to see what breaks cover."

"By that you mean they're waiting to see who manages to kill me, I assume," Kelly said surprised by the note of calm in her own voice. She thought of the two attempts by the Russian she now knew as Dmitry—first at the racecourse and then via Elvis at Tina's flat in Brixton.

If the law didn't get her first then sooner or later he was going to catch up with her. And then what? He was Grogan's man but Grogan had fed her a little info too.

It's like a game of tactical tennis and I get the nasty feeling I'm the ball.

"I could always give O'Neill what he wants—where to find Dmitry," she said. "After that it's up to him to follow the trail of who hired him and why."

McCarron regarded her steadily. "And what happens to you in the meantime?"

Kelly allowed herself a small smile. "Ah, now that one I hadn't quite thought through," she admitted.

She turned away from the window and put her empty mug down on the corner of the desk. "I can't help wishing you'd sent Les and Graham to do the Veronica Lytton job." Her smile was small and tight and sad. "Useless, I know, but if I'd been just that bit slower, Tyrone would have made a start cleaning the bathtub and I would never have seen anything amiss."

"Aye I know, lass," he said softly. He lifted the cast arm an inch or so off the sofa. "If wishes were horses beggars would ride, eh?"

Horses.

Matthew Lytton and his racehorses.

Racehorses he'd owned at one point or another with Harry Grogan.

And when Lytton had come to her flat the morning after McCarron's attack he'd known all about her past. All about the trial and how it had gone down.

What else had he known?

What else had he used?

Kelly blinked, looked away from McCarron's suddenly intent gaze. "I better go," she said quickly. "If I know Les, he'll be in soon."

"It's barely six o'clock on a Saturday," McCarron said. "We do call-outs only at weekends, remember?"

She gave him an arched look. "Do you really think he's going to leave you here supposedly alone all night and not 'just happen' to pop by and check on you?"

McCarron's own smile was rueful as he heaved himself upright. The effort left him swaying. "You're right," he said, "but I can call him on the way and tell him not to bother. You'll have to drive, after all."

With a feeling of sinking futility, Kelly asked, "On the way where?"

"The racecourse," McCarron said with apparent innocence. "Today *is* this big shindig of Lytton's isn't it? And while you're beating some answers out of him Kelly love, I can be having a nice little flutter."

HARRY GROGAN STOOD in the stable yard watching his heavily padded grey colt bound up the ramp into the waiting horsebox. The colt was on his toes and dragged the lad alongside him in his eagerness to be off.

Standing next to his owner, the trainer nodded approvingly and said, "Knows what's coming and can't wait to get up and at 'em you'll see, Mr Grogan."

Grogan heard the unforced confidence in the man's voice and silently echoed it. The colt was the best he'd ever had. A man could spend a lifetime searching for such a horse and never find it.

The lad tied the colt up in his narrow stall and secured the partition behind him before jogging down the ramp again. There was a buzz in the yard even this early, the rough breath of animals and people mingling under the floodlights.

Grogan stood back and watched the scene—part of it and yet apart from it. He squinted up towards the sky. The sun was just beginning to inch over the horizon, promising a fair mild day. Good going, not too warm. Perfect.

"He'll do his best," he said. "Can't ask for more."

The trainer flashed him a quick relieved smile, acknowledging miracles hoped for rather than expected, before he nodded and hurried away. Grogan watched him go. They'd almost finished loading the horsebox, swinging the ramp closed, starting up the rumbling diesel.

Grogan heard the grit of boots on the concrete behind him and turned to find Dmitry waiting at a respectful distance.

"We should go," Dmitry said shortly. "Traffic."

Grogan took a last glance around, refusing to be hurried, before turning at last towards the Range Rover. Dmitry had left the engine running, the heater on.

As they walked, Grogan skimmed his eyes over the younger man. "Viktor?"

There was a small hesitation before Dmitry shook his head. "Gone."

Grogan said nothing, just waited for the rear door to be opened and climbed inside.

Almost as soon as he had settled himself in the warm leather and the car moved off, his cellphone rang. Grogan checked the display before he took the call.

"Sweetheart. To what do I owe the pleasure?"

"Darling," Myshka's voice drawled in his ear. "How do I not call on your big day?"

Something about the way she said it gave Grogan the feeling he was being mocked, but with Myshka it was hard to tell.

"Where are you?" he said instead.

"Getting ready," she said. "I want to make myself beautiful for you."

Not you I'll be looking at, sweetheart. Not today. He grunted. "Don't be late."

"Do not worry." Her voice was a breathy purr. "I would not miss it for world."

Grogan ended the call and slid the phone back into his pocket and he wished, not for the first time, that his Irene was still with him. Like the old days.

But he allowed nothing of this regret or nostalgia to reach his impassive face.

—112—

"BASTARD!"

Myshka slammed the phone down and stared at herself in the mirror. She was fresh from the shower, hair wrapped in a towel and face bare.

She felt tired and looked old. Perhaps that was why she had called Grogan, in the hope that he might offer some throwaway reassurance that she need not go to any special effort. Something like: *"You'll always be beautiful to me sweetheart."*

She should have known better than to expect flattery from a pig like that.

Myshka sat very straight and stared at her own reflection. She didn't need to lean close anymore to see the lines around her eyes, across her forehead and beginning to ring her neck like an old chicken.

She would always have a striking look she knew, because of the way she'd learned to carry herself, the way she'd been taught to dress. But soon people would speak of her in the past tense— "*she used to be such a beauty*"— in hushed tones. As if she hadn't the sense to die young before everything began to leave her and she was left only with her memories of faded glory.

Dmitry will not leave me.

The conviction was strong, overwhelming. Dmitry had always stood by her. He would always do so.

After today he would be able to do nothing else.

—113—

STEVE WARWICK HAMMERED on the door to the en suite bathroom.

"Hurry up in there, can't you?" he called sharply through the panelled oak. "What's taking so long?"

"I want make myself pretty for you," Yana's wavery voice called back.

But Warwick was already halfway across the bedroom raking a hand through his still damp hair as he yanked a dress shirt off its hanger and shoved his arms into the sleeves. "Matt's used to how you look," he shouted casually over his shoulder. "And he'll kick up a stink if we're late."

"Am coming."

Warwick sighed impatiently as he fastened his tie in the full-length mirror on the bedroom wall, turned back the cuffs and slipped on cufflinks.

He tried out his trademark killer smile and hoped that nobody would see past the urbane confident appearance he presented to the trembling man beneath. The deadline with Harry Grogan was rapidly approaching. Warwick had no more hope of paying what he owed now than he did when he'd made that absurd deal—never mind the extra eight percent on top.

He felt himself begin to sweat with remembered fear. *Perhaps another squirt of antiperspirant wouldn't be a bad idea.*

"Yana, come *on!*"

As he crossed the room again he glanced at the drab black dress she'd laid out on the bed. Anyone would think she was going to a funeral he thought, not a race meeting.

—114—

O'NEILL LOOKED LIKE death.

That was DC Dempsey's first thought when his boss came hammering through the office door. He had a manila folder in one hand and a cardboard cup of vending-machine tea or coffee in the other.

Dempsey wondered if maybe last night's Chinese hadn't agreed with him. Or maybe it was something to do with the six-pack the DI had cracked open when Dempsey dropped him off at his flat on the way back from Reading.

O'Neill had tried to get Dempsey to stay and help drink it but judging by the state of him this morning he hadn't needed any help on that score.

Dempsey wasn't much of a drinker which was still something to be ashamed of in today's police force. He hid it well though, getting more than his share of rounds in just so he could slip over to non-alcoholic lager after the first couple of pints.

This morning he'd already been out for a run alongside the Thames in Putney, where he shared a flat with his sister, before he'd bounced into the office.

He was early he knew, but this was his first murder enquiry since coming up out of uniform and he didn't want to blow it. Nobody, surely, could have predicted that Kelly Jacks was going to climb back into her flat via the damn skylight but he was still anxious to shake off the sting of that failure.

DI O'Neill, on the other hand, looked like this was the last place he wanted to be on a Saturday morning with what appeared to be the mother of all hangovers.

As Dempsey eyed him warily, the DI took a slug from the cup, winced predictably and dumped the whole thing into the first waste bin he passed.

"All right Dempsey, let's hear it," he said by way of greeting, dropping into his chair.

And it had better be good. Dempsey heard *that* bit as clearly as if it had been voiced.

"Um, morning boss," he said making an effort not to look or sound too healthy. "I've dug out what I can on Lytton and Warwick's company. Not much, unless we've reason to get a warrant, but I've tapped up Companies House and the Revenue—"

O'Neill held up a warning hand with enough authority to stop traffic. "Impress me with your reasoning later sunshine," he said. "For now, just cut to the chase will you?"

"Yes boss." Dempsey flipped through the top few pages of the printout on his desk. "There's not much out of the ordinary. They make a pretty bloody healthy profit, file their returns on time and pay their taxes. The only thing I found that *might* be interesting is their insurance. They're both directors of the company and apart from a few office staff everything else is done via subcontractors. I mean, both the wives were on the books as well, but I think that was just a ploy to offset some tax liability—"

"What *about* the insurance?"

"Um, well, they've got a key-man policy each. Or I suppose I should call it key-*person* these days. Basically, because there's only really the two of them they're both considered crucial to the running of the company. So if either or both of them kicks the bucket there's a huge payout to compensate ..."

His voice trailed off as he registered the hard stare O'Neill lasered in his direction. The effect was spoilt only by the puffy bloodshot eyes.

"OK, OK," Dempsey said quickly, suppressing a grin. "Basically, they upped the policy amounts, boss. Back end of last year it went up to ten million apiece."

O'Neill stopped glaring and leaned back in his chair, clasping his hands behind his head and closing his eyes. For a horrible moment Dempsey wondered if this was some kind of elaborate put-down. *Your information is so boring it has sent me to sleep.*

But after a few seconds O'Neill straightened up. The glare was gone. "Who benefits?"

"Well, essentially—the company benefits."

"Ah, but if anything happens to Lytton or Warwick themselves, who benefits then?"

"Well, we know from looking into the wills of both Lyttons after the wife's death that if he'd died first she stood to inherit all his worldly goods, *including* a good chunk of his half of the company. But as she died before him—and Lytton doesn't have any other relatives—the company goes lock, stock and two smoking barrels to the remaining director, Steve Warwick."

"So it wouldn't be out of the way to assume that the same arrangement is true for Steve Warwick and his wife—he dies, she gets the lot?"

"His wife?" Dempsey queried blankly. He looked up to catch O'Neill actually smiling. "Boss?"

"We've been looking at the wrong man," O'Neill said. "We've been looking at Lytton when we should have been looking at Warwick."

Mystified, Dempsey knew the DI was waiting for him to give in and ask so he gave in and asked, "Why? Looking at him for what?"

O'Neill made him wait a beat longer then said, "It was bugging me. I knew there had to be some connection but I couldn't see what. You were the one who pointed me in the right direction, as it happens."

Impress me later with the reasoning—just cut to the chase, Dempsey thought savagely and wished he had the balls to say it out loud.

O'Neill nodded to the manila folder. "I was up half the night going over the files and I finally hit on the connection."

Chastened, Dempsey reached for the folder, flipped it open to find photocopies of two passports. He recognised the first as Dmitry Lyzchko, a Ukrainian-born Russian employed by Harry Grogan.

The second face was unfamiliar to him but he read the details and it only took a moment for the implications to sink in.

"Holy hell," he murmured. He glanced up. "What are they up to?"

"Well, we've got a shitload of explosives, family connections—or a lack of them—and a sudden increase in life cover. I could hazard a pretty good guess."

—115—

MATTHEW LYTTON STOOD on the balcony of the racecourse restaurant looking down at the gathering throng. Behind him was the same table where he'd sat with Kelly Jacks on the day he'd brought her here.

Lytton gripped the smooth polished rail in front of him. He wasn't going to think about that—wasn't going to think about Kelly. There were other things he needed to worry about today. Even if he *was* having trouble getting her out of his head.

Outwardly, he knew he presented a picture of the successful entrepreneur. He even had a buttonhole pinned to his lapel—a tight combination of lilac and blue rosebuds to remind people of his absent racing colours. Veronica's idea, subtle but clever like the woman.

Behind him, the waitresses hurried efficiently between the tables, setting up. He ignored them. For the racecourse staff this was just another day. For him it was momentous.

And Steve Warwick was late.

Nothing entirely unusual in that, of course. Steve always did like to be a law unto himself but today of all days ...

A voice from inside the restaurant filtered out to him. "Hey sweetheart, any chance of some fresh coffee down in the private boxes?" Lytton hadn't heard that voice for quite a while but it was one he recognised immediately. "The amount you're charging for them, I'd like a pot—make it hot and strong."

He turned just as Harry Grogan stepped out on the balcony in an immaculate grey suit with a pale tan overcoat unbuttoned over the top. All he needed was a slanted trilby on his shaven head and he'd be the archetypal gangster.

"Matthew old son," Grogan greeted him. "Not brought that nice little filly of yours today."

"Grogan," Lytton returned calmly. "I didn't think it was sporting to enter her in a race where I'm the main sponsor."

"Probably best—not enough bone," Grogan dismissed. "Wouldn't stay the distance." A glimmer of something that might have been humour flickered in those flat grey depths. "Should have thought of that when you were setting up this race of yours."

"A mile and four furlongs is the same as the Derby."

"Got your sights set on the classics have you?" Grogan pursed his lips. "Ambitious. I like that in a man."

"You should know." He looked over into the man's eyes and could read nothing there.

"Oh, I think between you and your partner there's more ambition than I'd want to have." Grogan stepped forwards to the railing and looked down at the massing crowds. "Going to be an interesting day," he said. "Let's hope we all come out of it winners, eh?"

With that he turned and walked away leaving Lytton with the feeling he'd just been given a message—a warning.

He pulled out his cellphone and punched in Warwick's number. It rang without reply, eventually clicking over to voicemail.

"Come on Steve," he muttered under his breath. "What the hell are you playing at?"

—116—

"I DON'T KNOW what you're planning, Kelly love, but it had better be good."

Ray McCarron was staring out of the side-glass of one of the works' vans at what seemed to be an inordinately large number of coppers patrolling the area immediately surrounding the racecourse.

296

"When I think of something," she murmured from behind the wheel, "I'm sure it will be."

She was wearing logoed coveralls that were far too large and had a company baseball cap pulled down low over her face. The hat didn't do a bad job of disguising both her features and the bruises she'd picked up over the past few days. They were just blooming to full glory. McCarron was sure she was only too aware that the marks on her face alone would cause people to take a second glance. A second glance that might make them realise who she was.

Between the two of us we look like we've been worked over by professionals.

Sometimes, it seemed, appearances were not deceptive after all.

He eased himself in the seat and recalled the parting advice of the doctors at the hospital when he'd prematurely discharged himself. *"Get plenty of rest Mr McCarron—nothing too strenuous."*

He wondered how this ranked.

"Head for the service entrance," he said. "It's just behind the stands."

Kelly put the van into gear. "You've been here before," she said.

"Once or twice," he admitted. "A few times as a punter and then we got called in to deal with a vermin problem a couple of years ago."

"You mean rats?"

"Well rats and horses tend to go together, what with the feedstuffs and all that." He smiled. "Some bright spark put down poison and when they came in a couple of days later, the rats had not only trailed the poison everywhere, they'd corpsed it all over the place. Must have been fifty—big buggers some of them. We had to sanitise the whole lot."

"Does that mean you have friends in high places?"

McCarron shook his head somewhat sadly. "The manager got the boot as soon as it was dealt with," he said. "Shame really, I would have enjoyed a season ticket for our trouble."

Kelly swung the van towards a gate. "So apart from the fact you know the layout, how does that help us?" she asked, eyes fixed on the security guard who stepped out to meet them.

"We'll see," McCarron said, winding down his window as the guard approached. "Morning mate," he called in a booming cheery voice. "Where do you want us?"

The guard looked about twenty, with a prominent Adam's apple above the pinched knot of his collar and tie. He trailed down his clipboard with a forefinger, frowning.

"You sure you got the right place?"

McCarron looked up at the stands looming over them. "Only one racecourse round here isn't there?"

"Yeah I guess," the guard said. He squinted at the name on the side of the van. "Cleaning? I thought all the cleaning was done last night."

"Normal cleaning, yes," McCarron said not letting his cheerful demeanour slip. "We're more in the nature of an emergency crew. For your unexpected nasty stuff."

The guard almost took a step back. "Like what?"

"Don't know until we get in there. We were just told it was bubbling or something, giving off some noxious fumes." He smiled. "You should be all right down here though. Unless the wind changes direction."

"I dunno." The guard hovered, looking round as if hopeful of more senior intervention. "You're not on my list, see."

"Won't be—nobody expects an emergency do they?" McCarron said. "Tell you what, don't you worry." He patted the van door casually and didn't miss the way the guard's eyes were drawn to the bold-font list of services written there. "We'll stick this in the public car park and take the gear in the front door. We'll be suited up of course but it shouldn't cause too much of a panic."

"No, no!" Alarm flared in the guard's face. "Don't do that. They'll have my guts for garters. Come in this way. Just park it somewhere out of sight will you?"

"'Course we will," McCarron said, smiling more broadly now. "Discretion is my middle name."

"Thanks," the guard said. "Oh, what happened to your face?"

"Mugged—just round the corner from here as it happens," McCarron lied just for the hell of it. "Not safe anywhere nowadays is it?" He gave the guard a wave. Kelly drove the van through the gate and threaded it across a car park filled with exhibitors' vehicles.

"You're a dark horse Ray," she said, parking up near the rear of the building. "That rather nice piece of bluff might have got us past the gate guard but I have a feeling it may not get us much further."

"Didn't expect it to," McCarron said. "I'm going to pay my money at the turnstiles like a good little punter."

"And what about me?"

He smiled again. "You, Kelly love, are going to do one of the many things you do best."

—117—

O'NEILL LET DEMPSEY drive again. The way the kid sliced through traffic anybody would think he spent all his spare time playing *Grand Theft Auto*.

O'Neill wedged himself between door handle and centre tunnel and spent most of the journey on his cellphone trying fruitlessly to reach someone higher up the food chain. Chief Superintendent Quinlan was taking a weekend off and nobody else wanted to handle this particular hot potato.

"There's no guarantee anything's actually going to kick off at this race meeting, is there boss?" Dempsey asked, taking his eyes off the road for a second, during which time it seemed to O'Neill that about half a mile of scenery zipped past.

"We've got all the players in one place and a quantity of unaccounted-for explosives," O'Neill snapped back. "You think?"

"Even so, we could cause a panic for nothing—"

"But if it turns out to be *something* and it comes out that we knew about it beforehand, we're going to get our arses handed to us," O'Neill said. "Can't this crate go any faster?"

"COME ON, COME on!" Kelly grumbled as she jogged around the outside of the main building, aware this was all taking far too long.

She'd abandoned her coveralls in the van and left McCarron to make his own more legitimate way inside. Now she had to find an opening herself.

The ground floor yielded nothing accessible, nor did the floor above. It was only when she lifted her gaze up to the high second level that she spotted a small window slanted open.

"Oh you have to be kidding me ..."

But the main stand was a striking modern design, its outside walls constructed of a composite material that could have been metal or plastic. Either way, it was smooth to the touch, each panel measuring roughly one metre by two, but the fixing system left a sizeable recess between one panel and the next. The gap was big enough to hook her fingers into and the narrow toes of her Red Chili shoes.

Despite herself and the situation she was in, Kelly smiled. She shifted the backpack more securely onto her shoulders and went for the first hold.

Once she got off the ground her biggest fear was being spotted. There was no way she could explain away climbing up the outside of the building. Not for any legal purpose.

As if I wasn't in enough trouble.

She kept moving smooth and slow but making deceptive progress, always maintaining three points of contact, always reaching for the next gap for fingers or toes.

After a minute or so all her attention was focused on what she was doing so that even if anyone had called out from the ground she would barely have heard them, but her luck held. Nobody called out.

Nevertheless, by the time she reached the window her limbs were tight with the effort. The open pane was unlatched but the aperture was much smaller than it had appeared from the ground. Kelly realized that, still wearing the backpack, there was no way she could fit through. She dangled perilously while she struggled to remove it, thrusting it inside first.

She squeezed herself through after the pack and just caught a glimpse of a cloakroom of some kind before dropping hands-down onto a bench in semi-controlled descent.

Kelly forward-rolled onto her back on the floor, staring up at the utilitarian lighting in the ceiling while her chest stopped heaving and her pulse rate slowed to something approaching normal.

After maybe a minute she sat up. Her initial impression of the cloakroom was confirmed but this had the look of a staff sanctuary and—judging from the clothing hanging on pegs on the wall in front of her and the scattering of shoes—she'd had the luck to land in a female domain.

Kelly propped the window back on its latch and lifted the backpack onto the bench beneath it. She still had the suit she'd borrowed from Lytton. If she changed into that she might just manage to pass for one of the guests. It was a weak plan but she didn't have anything better.

No sooner had the thought formed than she heard the faint rattle of the door handle behind her. Kelly spun in time to see the door beginning to swing open. There was nowhere to hide, and no time to do so.

Looked like her luck was just about to change.

—119—

DMITRY OPENED THE door. Standing outside was one of the restaurant waitresses carrying a tray holding an insulated cafetière of coffee and all the paraphernalia to go with it.

"Sorry sir, we're short-staffed so we're running a bit behind," she said, flashing him an anxious smile. "I've brought you some to be going on with and we'll get the filter machine going as soon as we can."

Dmitry did not return her smile. He jerked his head towards the table and the girl hurried forward to put down the tray.

Harry Grogan was standing at the full-length sloping window, staring down onto the track. He did not turn round when the waitress entered. He had no need to, Dmitry acknowledged, when he had someone he trusted to guard his back.

"Would you like me to pour?" the girl asked, reluctance in her voice.

Dmitry was just about to make her do it but without turning from the glass Grogan ordered, "Leave it. Just make sure we've got our proper supply like we're supposed to, sweetheart, before things get going."

"Y–yes sir," the girl stuttered, plonked the tray down and bolted for the door. Dmitry reached across her when she went to grab the handle and saw the fear jerk in her eyes. It didn't abate when he handed her a tip, even if it was a generous one for somebody earning close to minimum wage. She pocketed the folded note with a brief mutter of thanks and scurried away.

Is this how I want people to behave towards me? Dmitry brooded. *Is this success?*

He let the coffee brew and poured a cup the way he knew Grogan preferred it, putting it down near his boss's right hand.

"Make yourself scarce will you Dmitry?" Grogan said then over his shoulder. "I'm expecting company."

Dmitry felt something dig deep into his gut but was careful to keep his face expressionless. He knew Grogan could see his reflection in the glass and was watching for some unguarded gesture.

"Of course," he said. "Call if you need me."

Grogan picked up the cup and sampled the contents with a grunt of approval. "Why don't you go and seek out our noble sponsors?" he said. "Perhaps you could remind Mr Warwick of his ... obligations."

"Of course," Dmitry said again, only this time there was a touch more enthusiasm in his tone.

—120—

"AM I GLAD to see you!"

Kelly gaped at the girl who stood in the open doorway, her mind a complete blank.

The girl didn't seem to notice this reaction right away. She was slightly on the plump side with skin the colour of strong café latte and an air of bustle about her as she hurried into the cloakroom. "Oh, please tell me you're the new girl?" she blurted out as Kelly remained frozen with surprise. "We are *so* short-staffed it isn't true. Today of all days, and then we were told you couldn't make it. I mean, disaster or what?"

Kelly saw the girl's eyes flick over her features and instinctively put a hand up to her discoloured face. "I nearly didn't," she said, rueful. "But I need the work, you know?"

The girl rolled her eyes. "Don't I know it," she said. "I'm Shula by the way. You?"

"Ellie," Kelly invented quickly.

"Did they explain anything to you?"

"Erm, no," Kelly said. "They just dumped me here and assumed somebody else would tell me."

Shula rolled her eyes. "Typical. Well, we'll soon get you sorted out." She pointed to a rack of clothing. "Pick out something that fits—white shirt, waistcoat and either black trousers or skirt, whichever you prefer."

Kelly thought of the climb she'd just made and her leap from the walkway last time she was here. "Trousers, I think."

"Don't blame you. I don't have much of a choice—don't have ankles, see, just calves that go all the way down. About a size eight are you? Lucky girl."

Spending time in prison had rid Kelly of whatever inhibitions she might once have had about undressing in front of a stranger. She stripped down to her underwear without a qualm and was soon pulling on the uniform Shula helped her select.

"We're supposed to have the wife of one of the sponsors helping organise the hospitality but she hasn't deigned to put in an appearance yet," Shula said rolling her eyes. "Losing Mrs Lytton was a disaster—she was originally taking care of things and there wasn't nothing she didn't know."

"What happened to her?" Kelly asked innocently.

Shula pulled a face. "She died suddenly. Not here," she added quickly as if worried about scaring Kelly off. "And the other bloke's wife was supposed to take over but she's been a non-starter I can tell you. Scurried around the place like she was counting the silver and never showed up again after that."

Kelly nearly asked more about Yana Warwick then realised she shouldn't even know the name and shut up.

"What happened to your face—boyfriend?" Shula's eyes lingered with a certain amount of sympathy. When Kelly just gave a shrug she added, "Don't worry—we've all been there. Tell you what, the girls are always leaving their make-up bags lying around. Let's see if we can't steal you a bit of foundation, take the edge of those bruises. He caught you a belter didn't he?"

And five minutes later, when Kelly stepped out of the cloakroom with her newfound friend, she realised she was wearing a far better disguise for helping her blend in on the racecourse than anything she could have borrowed from Matthew Lytton's dead wife.

—121—

STEVE WARWICK WAS sweating inside his suit as he walked from the VIP car park towards the main racecourse building. It had nothing to do with the exercise and everything to do with the woman on his arm.

Her face a mask of cosmetic perfection and dressed in a voluptuous but politically incorrect fur coat, Myshka was looking her mysterious very best.

"Matt's going to flip out," he complained, flicking her nervous little glances. "He's expecting to see me with Yana not—"

"It will be nice surprise for him then, yes?" Myshka said, her voice as sultry as her walk.

Warwick swallowed. "Darling I thought we agreed it would be best—"

"No!" Myshka interrupted. "*We* did not agree. *You* made decision. *I* did not agree."

And Warwick finally realised with a feeling of panic in the pit of his stomach that by allowing Myshka to dominate him in the bedroom he'd also allowed her to take too much control of things outside of it.

"Look darling, let me at least go and have a talk to him before he sees us together—explain things, hmm?"

He held the door open for her, ushered her through. Myshka waited until they were in the lift gliding upwards before she turned him to face her. The way she let her eyes focus on his mouth had his breath hitching in his throat. Damn, she could always do that to him with just a look.

She trailed one of those deadly red-tipped acrylic nails along his cheek, gripped his chin just a little too hard. Lust began to curl through his belly.

"He will understand soon, and we still have a *little* time," she murmured. She leaned close to his ear, her breath stirring the delicate hairs on his lobe as she whispered, "And I do not have on *any* underwear ..."

—122—

McCARRON'S MUGGING STORY did not gain him free entry to the racecourse but it did see him escorted through the disabled entrance by an elderly steward with too kind a heart for the job.

It did not take much after that to feign a weakness that required a brief rest at the First-Aid post, located in the main building. The steward walked him in and delivered him into the care of the uniformed paramedic in charge who'd been drinking a cup of tea and reading a racing paper.

"Ah, first customer of the day," the paramedic said jumping up. He let out a low whistle as he cast a professional eye over McCarron's healing wounds and intricately cast arm. "Coming out today in this state, you must *really* like to put a bet on, old man."

"Well Matthew offered to send a car, bless the lad, but I told him I'd rather make my own way," McCarron improvised, shrugging off the jacket he'd only managed to get half on in the first place.

"Matthew?" the medic asked. He slipped an inflatable cuff around McCarron's good arm and began to pump it up.

"Hmm? Oh, Lytton, of course."

The medic faltered. "Lytton as in the Warwick-Lytton Cup—that Lytton?"

"Aye lad. Why else do you think I'm here 'in this state' as you so rightly put it?"

The medic flushed. "I'm very sorry sir. I didn't realise ... you should be wearing a tag, see, to show you're a VIP."

"And that makes a difference to how you treat people does it?" McCarron asked with ominous calm.

"Well no, but—"

"I'll be sure to mention that to Matthew," he said. "Now, where would I find him?"

—123—

THE POLICE PRESENCE around the racecourse was being organised by a uniformed chief inspector called Cheever. Initially he didn't take kindly to a couple of plainclothes cowboys from north of the river trying to ride onto his patch and start any kind of a ruckus.

He explained this to O'Neill and Dempsey in terms that left them in no doubt of his feelings on the matter. O'Neill mentally labelled him an arse within moments of meeting the man. The mental picture was completed by the fact Cheever was almost entirely bald and had a cleft chin.

"So, you've no hard intel there are explosives at my racecourse—or anywhere within a hundred miles of here for that matter, hmm?"

"No sir," O'Neill said with a scrupulous politeness he tried hard to maintain. "But we've been watching this drama unfold and we can't ignore the fact that all the players are here—in one place. Today. If Warwick really *is* planning to get rid of his partner then—"

306

"Ah but that's exactly my point, hmm?" Cheever interrupted. "It's all a big 'if' isn't it? You know—if you'll pardon my saying so—jack shit for certain."

O'Neill felt the muscle in his jaw hinge clench, heard the squeak as his teeth clamped together.

"No sir."

Cheever nodded. "Well then. I am not prepared to evacuate this facility, causing disruption and no doubt panic—not to mention a world of bad press—solely on the basis of your gut instinct."

"Sir, surely public safety is—"

"*My* concern," Cheever snapped. "And I'll thank you not to try and tell me how to do my job detective inspector!" He paused, glowering. "If you can provide one iota of hard evidence I'll act on it. Until then I'd thank you to get out of my command post and stay out of my way!"

O'Neill turned away, Dempsey silently on his heels, and stepped down out of the Portakabin Cheever had commandeered. The door wasn't quite slammed behind them but it was a close-run thing.

"Bloody tin pot dictator," Dempsey said sourly once they were outside. He hunched his shoulders. "What now, boss?"

"We find him his bloody evidence," O'Neill declared. "And make him eat it."

—124—

STEVE WARWICK SHOULDERED his way into the private box with his fist wrapped in Myshka's hair and his mouth clamped onto hers. As soon as they were inside he groped for the key to click over the lock and backed her roughly against the wall alongside the door. She gasped in pleasured pain. Warwick's hands dived for the hem of her dress, gathering it up towards her waist.

"Stop!" she commanded, before he could discover for himself if her boast about a lack of underwear was true.

But he stopped anyway. Experience had taught him that Myshka's games might be cruel, but they were always *so* satisfying in the end. He let the edge of the dress fall back into line, smoothed his hand across her hipbone and cupped her, not gently, through the material instead.

She gasped again, her eyes bright with a feral excitement he didn't think he'd ever seen in her before.

Hell, if horseracing turns you on this much, darling, I'll take you to bloody Ascot every week.

She batted his hand away, drew herself to her full imperious height. "Strip," she ordered.

Warwick glanced at his watch even as he reached to unknot his tie, his expression wolfish.

"Whatever you have in mind, darling, we'll have to make it quick," he said, shrugging out of his suit jacket. "The race will be—"

Myshka moved in closer, pinched his chin between a steely forefinger and thumb. "Silence," she rapped. "Your clothes—take them off. All of them."

He fumbled in his haste to comply, but at least still had enough of his wits to hang the jacket on the back of a chair and fold his trousers to avoid creases. No point in making it *too* obvious what he'd been up to when he got back out there—especially not to Matt.

Myshka strolled over to the big slab of a conference table which stood near the slanted glass front wall of the box. He tried to make a grab for her as she past him, but she jinked her hips out of reach and smacked his hand away again.

"On the table—now," she said, patting the smooth surface. "Face down."

He glanced down pointedly at his rapidly growing erection and gave her a lascivious smile. "That might be … hard."

"But I will make it *much* harder on you, yes," she promised in the slightly fractured English that zapped straight to his groin. Her voice was so sultry it should have come with a blood pressure warning.

Warwick didn't wait for a second invitation. He hopped up onto the table and rolled obediently onto his stomach, sucking in a breath at the cold against his flushed skin.

Myshka opened her bag and brought out the suede-thonged whip he knew so well, along with a skein of silk scarves. She deliberately placed the whip close to his head while she fastened the first scarf from the nearest table leg to his wrist, stretching first one arm and then the other out wide.

In moments, it seemed, he was spread-eagled at her mercy. She picked up the whip and stood in front of him, trailing the thongs through her fingers. It was all he could do not to groan out loud.

"You really have been very, *very* bad boy," she said solemnly.

I know, I know, so do your wonderful worst, darling. Don't keep me hanging!

She moved out of his line of sight and he trembled at the fleeting brush of the soft suede along his body from shoulder to calf. Then he heard the warning swish. He just had time to tense before the whip landed across his upper thighs and buttocks and a bellowed cry escaped him at the unaccustomed force of the blow.

"I told you *silence*!" Myshka hissed and she hit him again—if anything, harder this time.

"Christ, woman! What the devil d'you think you're playing at?"

He heard her stride across the room and when she returned she had his tie bunched in her hands.

For the first time, a prickle of unease came to him.

"Myshka, what the—?"

But as he opened his mouth to protest she stuffed the balled-up tie inside. It was Hermes and not only would such treatment see it ruined, but she shoved it so deep he started to choke at once. He shook his head angrily, tried to regurgitate the tie without spitting on it too much. What the bloody *hell* was the mad bitch playing at—today of all days?

"What is matter, darling—not having fun?" she asked, her voice icy. "Maybe it is not so nice having something pushed down throat, yes?"

309

He snarled his fury behind the gag.

The sudden staccato knock on the door made him jerk in panicked surprise. Suppose it was Matt? Or, worse still, someone from the racecourse?

He heard Myshka's footsteps again, heading for the door and his protests rose in pitch and volume.

Don't let anyone in, you stupid bitch. I'll die of embarrassment, being caught like this.

She opened the door and a man walked in without showing any apparent surprise at what lay before him. With a cold wash of shock Warwick recognised the young thug with the dead-cold eyes who'd scared him so badly that day he met with Grogan out on the Downs.

"You remember Dmitry, of course," Myshka said.

The young thug stared at him without expression. After a moment he reached inside his jacket and pulled out a long black cylinder which he handed to Myshka.

A throaty murmur of appreciation emerged from between her lips. She flicked her wrist sharply to extend the baton to its full, lethal length and admired it with chillingly sensual delight in her face.

She tried an experimental slash and the air zizzed with the power of this new weapon.

"All this time we are together you think you are big dog, in control," she mocked. "Now *I* am big dog, yes?"

For the first time since he'd entered the private box and delivered himself into her hands, Steve Warwick realised he might just have made the biggest mistake of his life.

Or the last one.

—125—

"OH STEVIE BOY, I'm going to make you suffer for this!"

Matthew Lytton uttered the threat under his breath as he stalked the corridors of the main building. He and Warwick should be out in the paddock, mixing with the VIPs, glad-handing and hobnobbing and doing all the rest of the things they'd originally conceived this damned event *for* in the first place.

But still there was no sign of the man.

Lytton tried Warwick's cellphone for the twentieth time. Switched off. The answering machine on his home number picked up after half-a-dozen empty rings.

Lytton thrust his own phone back into his inside pocket and let out a fast annoyed breath.

"Something troubling you Mr Lytton?"

Lytton turned to see the cocky DI O'Neill approaching from the direction of the stairwell. With him was a younger man who also had "copper" written all over him.

What the hell *are you lot doing here?*

"I'm the main sponsor for this event," Lytton returned with creditable calm. "You'd expect a few hiccups."

"Anything you'd like to share?"

"No. Anything *you'd* like to share?" He glanced from one detective to the other, letting annoyance win out over concern. "Why are you here?"

O'Neill pursed his lips for a moment, clearly debating how much to tell him. Lytton saw a twitch of consternation cross the younger detective's face as if he thought O'Neill might withhold something vital. Lytton waited, not patiently but refusing to be manipulated.

"Big day for you then," O'Neill said at last. "Where's your partner—Mr Warwick isn't it?"

So they were not here to tell him Warwick had been involved in some kind of accident. Lytton's relief turned back to irritation. *Where is he?*

"That's one of the hiccups," he said, deciding nothing would be gained by evasion. "I'm trying to find him. I supposc hc could have been caught in traffic."

O'Neill pulled a face. "We had no problems on the way down," he said. "Mind you, DC Dempsey here thinks he's the next Lewis Hamilton so maybe that might have had something to do with it."

Lytton stepped in close, getting in O'Neill's face.

"I'm busy, detective inspector. Get to the point." He didn't miss the way the younger guy Dempsey shifted to intervene if he had to.

"Get on all right with your partner do you, Mr Lytton?"

That rocked him back. "Well enough. Why?"

"What about his wife?"

"Yana? I hardly see anything of her. She helps out in the office sometimes—she was giving Veronica a hand to organise the hospitality for this event."

"They get on?"

Lytton sighed, could tell from O'Neill's stubborn expression that asking questions of his own was not going to speed things up. "Veronica thought Yana was a little mouse who needed to stand up for herself more. She thought Steve bullied her."

"Russian, isn't she? One of these mail-order brides?"

"Russian, Ukrainian—something like that," he agreed shortly. "I don't know how they met. Steve was in Russia for a time looking at property deals, trying to cultivate some contacts. When he came back he brought Yana with him."

"You suspicious about that?"

Lytton gave a short laugh. "Wouldn't you have been? I thought she was after him for a passport and would be off like a shot as soon as they'd made it legal."

O'Neill and Dempsey exchanged a look. "Maybe she was after him for more than that."

"Meaning?"

"You and Mr Warwick have company life insurance on each other don't you?" O'Neill said. "Quite sizeable sums."

Lytton shrugged. "Key-man policies are standard business practice for companies like ours with a small number of vital personnel," he said. "And it's the company that holds the policies, not us."

"But not so long ago you upped the payout from half-a-million to ten, I understand. Whose idea was that?"

"Steve's. He said we should keep up with inflation although I don't see what the hell business that is of yours," Lytton snapped. "It's all perfectly legal."

"I've no doubt," O'Neill said mildly. He paused and then added in an almost careless tone, "Now your wife is deceased you have no living relatives."

"No, I—"

"And Mr Warwick?"

"What? He's an only child—parents died in a car accident years ago."

"What about his wife's relatives?"

"Yana? I don't know," Lytton muttered. "I think she has family but we've never talked about it."

"You might like to bear in mind sir, that your value to your business associate might have undergone a fundamental shift, shall we say."

"You're joking," Lytton bit out, anger rising out of fear like smoke from fire. But his mind spun away in a hundred different directions. All of them left a cold trail of sickness through his belly. He thought of his smiling cocksure partner, sometimes infuriating but with the charm and the banter.

Not Steve, not ...

He looked up, met O'Neill's gaze. "You're talking like Steve's going to try and bump me off, for Christ's sake."

"In our experience Mr Lytton, most people are killed by people they know—people they're close to."

"So you're telling me what—that I should check the brakes on my car on a regular basis? Get someone in to taste my food?" And he thought suddenly of Kelly Jacks, so convinced she'd been drugged that she'd taken a bag of her own blood for test.

It was uttered with a smile, an attempt to lighten a mood that was oppressive but O'Neill gave him no reassurance in return. "Know anything about explosives do you?"

—126—

KELLY STUCK HER head round the restaurant door where Shula was placing cutlery on the tables with all the dexterity of a casino croupier dealing cards.

313

"Hey Shula, I've just been asked to take a tray of coffee and stuff along to a Mr Lytton," she said with as much casual innocence as she could squeeze into the lie. "Any ideas who he is or where I find him?"

"Ooh, he's one of the bigwigs. Didn't you see the signs everywhere? He's got an office on the next floor down, with the admin people, or he might be in his private box—one of the posh ones they use for conference meetings right at the top."

"Ah," Kelly said managing to look sheepish. "They didn't say and I didn't ask. Sorry."

"Never mind. Here, I'll give you a hand."

Shula abandoned her table setting and hurried across to the serving area, quickly assembling a tray of cups, saucers, spoons, sugar, cream and a handful of foil-wrapped mints on a plate. She splashed coffee from the filter machine into an insulated cafetière and fastened the lid. Her movements were fast and sure. Almost as an afterthought Shula added a small vase containing a single carnation.

She caught Kelly's raised eyebrow and grinned at her. "Well he's a bit of a looker—and he tips all right."

Kelly picked up the tray, got the balance of it. "Office or private box," she murmured. She glanced at Shula. "If it was you, where would you try first?"

—127—

THE EMERGENCY STAIRWELL at the east end of the stand was glassed in and afforded a reasonable view down into the VIP car park. Lytton stood on the top landing looking down at the blanket of car roofs parked in serried rows like some bizarre arable crop.

And there in the next-to-the-end line was Steve Warwick's yellow Porsche. Even allowing for there being more than one yellow Porsche, Warwick could make out the first couple of letters of Warwick's private registration just to clinch it.

He swore again and spun on his heel. So Warwick *was* here. Lytton had been mad enough at Warwick's lateness even before his conversation with the police. Now he was fuming.

Lytton had skated close to the wind quite a few times in his career one way or another and his previous contacts with the law and its officers had not always been happy ones. He was aware therefore that O'Neill and his crony could simply have been trying to drive a wedge between him and Warwick. Why, he didn't know.

So in some ways he was relieved to recognise Warwick's car down there among the others. Because that meant this story about insurance payouts and explosives was likely to be bullshit. Why would Warwick turn up at all if he was planning something like that?

On the other hand, arriving without letting anybody know and sneaking off for a quickie with his mistress was *just* like Stevie boy. And in that case Lytton had a pretty good idea where he'd be doing it.

And he was just in the right roiling bad temper to break up the party.

—128—

DMITRY CAUGHT MYSHKA'S arm as it was upraised for yet another strike. His fingers dug in hard enough to register through the bloodlust that consumed her.

"That's enough," he said quietly.

Breathless and glittering, she tried to wrench free but his grip was steel. Her head—her eyes—whipped to meet his.

"It will never be enough," Myshka said through her teeth. "Years I have been nothing but plaything to this—this *svoloch*. Now is *my* turn."

Dmitry was silent for a moment, staring down at her. She saw nothing in his gaze and that alone made something of her passion ebb away.

"There is no point beating a man who is past feeling any of it," he said then as if speaking to a child.

Myshka could have told him the beating was as much her reward as it was a punishment for the man tied to the table but she realised it would not serve her purpose to admit to such emotion. It was … self-indulgent.

She relaxed her muscles. He let go and stepped back, peeling the extendible baton from her hand as he did so. He wiped the length of it carefully on Steve Warwick's carefully discarded jacket. Warwick did not object.

He would never object about anything again.

It was only then, without the fire in her belly, that Myshka looked at what she had done and a cold fear spread slowly up through her. She shrugged it away but her eyes were drawn fascinated to the seep of blood edging across the polished surface.

"It will not spoil things," she said with more confidence than she felt.

Dmitry twisted the baton's inner sections back into place with a rough shove that might have signified anger.

"This," he said with a jerk of his head, "will not look like an accident."

Myshka dragged her eyes away and turned to him, stroking both hands down his cheeks. "Do not lose heart now, Dmitry. By time we are finished, nobody will be able to tell."

Dmitry was still frowning when into the silence that hummed between them came the rattle of the door handle being turned.

—129—

LYTTON FUMBLED IN his suit pocket for the box key the racecourse people had given him and jammed it into the lock.

He'd already been into the box several times so he knew the door should be open. But having seen Warwick's car was here he had a pretty good idea what his partner was probably up to and who with. Barging in unannounced and catching them at it would just about satisfy his bubbling righteous anger.

He pushed the door open and strode through … and faltered, still gripping the handle as if to let go would be to have his legs buckle under him.

Warwick was there, all right, up on the broad conference table stark naked. But he was not indulging in some furtive sexual coupling.

Lytton's mouth dropped open. He tried to tear his eyes away and found he utterly could not. Tiny details imprinted themselves on his brain as if to focus on the whole would send him spinning into hysteria.

Warwick's ankles were bound. One heel sported a piece of sticking plaster as if to cover a blister. The man's fingers were curled, relaxed inside the material that held his wrists fast. The onyx and diamond signet ring he always wore gleamed under the overhead lights. Half his face was visible, turned towards the doorway as if seeking rescue. Lytton read a petulant bewilderment in the open lifeless eye.

It was only then as the shock rolled over him and Lytton's vision widened out that he realised there was a woman sitting in the chair at the head of the table. She was wearing an extravagant dark fur coat. Her legs were crossed elegantly.

Lytton's mind reeled, overwhelmed by this latest shock. He stared, incredulous.

"You?"

It was as much as he managed before something very hard, travelling very fast, hit the back of his skull. The ceiling cracked open above him in a shower of light and sparks swiftly followed by intense pain, a sense of falling, and darkness.

—130—

DMITRY STOOD OVER the inert body of Matthew Lytton, the baton in his hand. He was breathing hard.

Myshka stood up, unfolding herself like a model. She strolled over with an exaggerated sway, assured and back in control. Then she took hold of Dmitry's face again and, when he continued to stare down at the man on the floor, she kissed him hard on the mouth.

He reared back, eyes a little wild.

"Don't!"

Myshka simply smiled at him.

"Is time," she said.

—131—

KELLY JABBED A finger onto the call button again, eyes flicking between the floor indicators above each of the two lifts. For a building that only had five storeys it seemed to take forever for the damn things to arrive.

She had flipped a mental coin and chosen to go down to the office first instead of up to the private box. A mistake, she acknowledged. The office door was locked and she heard no signs of movement inside.

Of course there were no guarantees that Lytton was even in the building but it was somewhere to start. And besides, her disguise only worked in here. As soon as she went outside her waitress garb would make her stand out.

The lift indicator on the right rose slowly from the ground floor and reached her level. The doors opened and she had taken half a step towards the opening before she recognised the man inside.

"Ray!"

"Hello Kelly love," McCarron said giving her a weary smile. He was leaning against the back wall looking dog tired. He took in her change of attire, the tray and the concealing make-up in a single brief survey. "You've made yourself at home I see."

She moved into the lift and the doors slid closed behind her. "How did you get in?"

"As Matthew Lytton's mythical guest. I suppose I don't need to ask you the same."

Kelly lifted the tray. "I'm fulfilling his mythical request for coffee," she said.

"Where at?"

"Ah, well that's more tricky. He's supposed to be either in his office or he's got a private box on the top floor. I struck out on the office so I'm giving the box a whirl."

"And when you find him?"

"I'll pour his coffee and ask him if he killed his wife."

"What if he doesn't want to answer?"

"Well then he won't get any mints."

McCarron gave a harrumph that almost made it to laughter. The lift reached its designated floor and stopped. The doors opened at a leisurely pace. Kelly was through them almost before the gap was wide enough and would have hurried along the corridor to the boxes had she not realised McCarron was still unable to move quickly. She paused, masking her impatience as she waited for him to catch up.

But as her gaze swept almost idly across the area surrounding her she froze.

"Stop," she said in a low urgent voice. McCarron had worked enough crime scenes to respond instantly to the tone as much as anything else.

"What is it?"

Kelly shifted her grip on the tray and pointed, eyes fixed on the floor. "Cast-off," she said.

There was a small side table with an arrangement of flowers on it against the wall a little further along. She carefully stretched across to deposit the tray. Unencumbered, she checked the area around her feet before crouching to inspect the blood drop as closely as she could.

"Still liquid," she said over her shoulder, keeping her voice hushed. Kelly knew as well as anyone that blood clotted in minutes. For it not to have done so meant whoever left this trail was close by.

She glanced both ways, wary, then widened her gaze, found a second droplet and a third stretching away along the polished floor. They were elongated ovals with a distinct tail at one end like a comet. The tail was at the front. It would have dropped from the wound and hit the ground at an angle, breaking the surface tension that had held it spherical in freefall.

"Which way are they headed?" McCarron asked from above her.

Kelly just pointed, back towards the lifts. From her vantage point she could see the trail stopped neatly by the doors to the second lift. She remembered pressing buttons for both. If the wrong one had stopped, the chances were she could have been faced with the unknown victim—or assailant.

She rose, stepped back carefully and summoned the lift again. It arrived quickly but was empty when it arrived except for more blood. Stationary cast-off this time, the drops circular, almost 20mm in diameter but with a crown pattern around the edges that told Kelly they'd fallen from a height.

"Whoever it was, they were either still walking or being carried, and they were leaking steadily," she murmured.

"Could just be a nosebleed," McCarron said quietly behind her. "You know how they can gush." But he kept still so as not to contaminate possible evidence, she noticed, and his words lacked a certain conviction.

Kelly frowned, remembering the layout from Lytton's guided tour. "The private boxes each have their own bathroom," she said. "If somebody had a sudden nosebleed surely they'd head for one of those rather than drip all over the building?"

"Not if it was staff rather than guests." McCarron gave a one-shoulder shrug and offered her a worn out smile. "Just playing devil's advocate, Kelly love."

She didn't respond to that, backtracking to follow the blood trail upstream towards its source. She found it in the doorway to one of the boxes. It did not altogether surprise her to realise it was the one that had been assigned to Lytton and Warwick.

They hugged the wall outside the box. There were several drops of blood clustered on the smooth floor surface near the handle side where someone might have paused to shut or lock the door before moving off along the corridor. Kelly unbuttoned the waistcoat that formed part of her borrowed uniform and wrapped her hand in the material before reaching for the doorknob.

Just before she got there, McCarron stayed her arm.

"Are you sure you want to do this?" he whispered.

"No, but if I hand it over to the cops at this stage who knows what the hell will happen," she whispered back.

"It's not the cops I'm worried about."

Kelly hesitated a moment then turned away. She retrieved her tray from the side table and came back with it.

"Camouflage," she mouthed when he looked bewildered. She did not think he needed to know that the stainless steel tray itself, not to mention most of its contents, would also make very handy improvised weaponry.

McCarron let out a long breath then used the corner of his own jacket to turn the handle. Surprise would only offer a momentary window of opportunity, so Kelly stepped through quickly, moving to the side. McCarron followed more out of loyalty than eagerness, she felt sure.

Inside they both stopped dead. On the floor in front of them was a lump shrouded partially by a man's morning suit jacket and partially by what looked like a fur rug. One lifeless hand stretched out from underneath it as if in supplication. The smell of violence was dark and sickly in the air.

Outside the glass the crowd was roaring home the first winner of the day. Against the scene that suddenly presented itself Kelly had a sharp vision of Romans at the Coliseum baying for slaughter.

It was McCarron who went forward, picked up a corner of the rug with his finger and thumb and peeled it heavily away from the body.

"Well, I reckon we don't need to search any further for your blood," he said at last, his voice husky. "Any idea who he is?"

Kelly realised she couldn't avoid looking at the body any longer and it had nothing to do with general squeamishness. She swallowed as she let her eyes skim over the lifeless features.

Recognition hit her in a cold wash.

—132—

"WHO IS HE?" McCarron asked. "Or should I ask who *was* he?"

Kelly Jacks had leaned down to examine cast-off blood spatter across the far wall of the box. "Steve Warwick," she said without looking round. "He was Matthew Lytton's business partner."

"That's odd."

"Not really. You'd expect him to be here on their big day."

"I didn't mean that," McCarron said, and there must have been something in his voice because she rose and turned towards him, graceful where McCarron felt lumbering. And achingly tired. He was, he recognised in no fit state to go wading in trying to make sense of a crime scene—and certainly not one like this. Never mind that they'd no right to be here in the first place.

In fact between his conscience and his cast elbow it was a toss-up which was troubling him the most and he'd gone in search of water to swallow a handful of painkillers.

"The bathroom door's locked—from the inside," he said now, stepping away and lowering his voice.

Kelly came to him around the edges of the room, careful where she put her feet. She gave the door a cursory glance then fetched the teaspoon from her discarded tray of coffee. She shoved the flat end of the spoon into the centre part of the lock, using it as a makeshift screwdriver and twisting it until the indicator tab went from red to green.

McCarron watched her deft movements with a little stirring of unease in the back of his mind.

"Kelly love—"

She silenced him with a look. "You might want to stand back for this," she murmured. "Just in case."

He would have argued but she already had her shoulder against the door, holding the tension off the lock while she nudged it open.

The bathroom was small, lined with tiles and had no external window. The light was on, the extractor humming quietly in the background. The first thing they saw was the white pedestal sink, covered in a pink wash and dotted with clogged lumps of sodden tissue paper. A ruined towel sat in a soggy heap on the floor beneath it.

Kelly pushed the door wider and they both heard a strangled gasp from inside.

It was, McCarron judged, a sound more likely to be made by a victim rather than an attacker. He moved to the doorway.

"It's all right, you can come out," he said gruffly. "They've gone whoever they are and we're not going to hurt you."

Kelly flicked him a brief glance that made him hope he hadn't been optimistic about the last part but inside the bathroom a figure uncurled itself from a poor hiding place squashed down alongside the toilet bowl and tottered out to meet them.

It was a dark-haired woman, stooped in fear, her makeup streaked from tears and ineffectual scrubbing. She was wearing a dowdy black dress covered with ominous damp patches that gleamed in the lights. She looked terrified.

"*Yana?*" Kelly's voice was a mixture of surprise and exasperation. "What the—?"

"You know her?" McCarron asked.

"She's Steve Warwick's ... wife," Kelly said choosing her words with care.

At that moment the woman Yana seemed to catch sight of the partially covered corpse and dashed across the room to fling herself down on top of it in a storm of weeping.

McCarron could only watch while it took Kelly several attempts to prise her away, by which time the taller woman's hands and her wild-eyed face were sluiced with the dead man's blood.

"Leave him," Kelly said a mite sharply. "There's nothing you can do for him and you're contaminating the scene."

Yana Warwick slumped at the admonishment. Docile now, she allowed herself to be led to a chair and pressed into it. McCarron threw Kelly a reproachful glance. It was coolly returned.

She crouched so she could force Yana to meet her gaze then asked in a more gentle voice, "What happened here?"

"B–bad men," Yana said. "They come to our house—this morning. I getting ready." She bit her lip as she flapped a hand towards her ruined dress like a kid who'd had a new toy broken by the bullies.

McCarron claimed to be no expert but he didn't think the outfit would have been flattering even before it was liberally splashed with blood. And being a man of the old school, he kept such an opinion firmly to himself.

"And?" Kelly prompted.

Yana gave her a wounded look but said meekly, "They bring me here. I–I lock myself in bathroom but I *hear* what they do to him." She raised her head, eyes brimming. "I hear him screaming—"

"It's all right lovey," McCarron said hastily, trying to avert the inevitable shed of tears. "You don't need to go over it again."

"What about the coat Yana?" Kelly asked. "Where did that come from?"

Yana stared at her for a moment. "C–coat?"

Kelly jerked her head towards the makeshift shroud. McCarron had never understood the fascination for fur. In his opinion it invariably looked far better covering the animal that originally owned it. But, he conceded, maybe that had something to do with the price.

"There was woman with them," Yana said. She shivered. "I think ... I think maybe *she* do this. She is—how you say?—one cold bitch."

Kelly straightened, frowning. "Yeah I'll say she is."

McCarron had seen that narrowed-down gaze before. At complex crime scenes Kelly had possessed moments of complete motionless while she mentally teased out a tangled thread of evidence and it had begun to unknot itself for her.

And if he hadn't been still sluggish from his injuries and the after-effects of the medication they'd shovelled into him since his op, McCarron reckoned he might have put it together sooner himself.

He opened his mouth. Kelly shot him a warning glance that cut him off before he had a chance to speak.

"We'll make sure this woman doesn't get away with it," she promised. "Ray, you stay with Yana. I'll go find the cops."

"C–cops?" Yana said, voice rising. "No cops! I not trust them."

Kelly met McCarron's eyes with a gaze that was flat and implacable.

324

"Don't worry—it's clear what happened here," she said grimly. "The evidence speaks for itself."

—133—

LYTTON CAME ROUND and found his head in a vice being pounded by sledgehammers from the inside. At least, that was what it felt like.

To begin with it was all he could do to lie very still while he tried to find a way around the pain inside his skull. After a few moments he realised he didn't have much of a choice in the matter.

He was lying on his side with his hands bound at the wrists behind him. The ground underneath felt hard, cold and damp. He could feel no wind so he guessed he was inside but couldn't be sure. His eyes seemed to have been glued shut.

That was only one reason for the sense of panic that engulfed him.

Lytton could smell the blood, taste it thick and cloying in his nose and the back of his throat. An image of Veronica dead amid a splash of scarlet ruin, and then Steve Warwick's sprawled body, hit him with a jolt that took away what little breath he had left.

Try as he might he couldn't remember what happened next— only that it had been a shock. Even more of a shock than finding his partner beaten to death on their day of glory.

But what?

He bit down on his fear and bucked furiously, bulking the muscles in his shoulders and forearms. He thought he felt something give a little between his wrists, transferring a pressurised stab into his hands. If he didn't get loose soon he was going to lose all feeling in them.

The realisation gave him the impetus to try again, a thrashing effort that turned the pain vicious enough to be frightening. The kind of pain that came with serious injury. He lay still, gasping and began to wonder if his eyes were open after all but it was dark. Or if he'd gone blind.

And in the buzzing blackness he heard the sound of a door handle being rattled.

Lytton froze, straining to hear above the thunder of pulse beating in his ears. In the background he could hear the sounds of the racecourse—the commentator's voice, the crowds—but muffled and at a distance. So whatever had happened he hadn't been taken far.

The rattling stopped. Lytton was wracked by indecision. Did he call out and chance rescue—or would attracting attention mean they'd finish what they'd started?

He took a deep breath.

—134—

DI O'NEILL RATTLED the handle of yet another locked door and sighed in frustration. This was all taking far too long.

He heard footsteps, turned to see Dempsey approaching along the basement corridor.

"Anything?"

Dempsey shook his head, hunching his shoulders inside his jacket. "Not a very trusting lot are they?" he said. "Every door's locked up tight."

"Yeah," O'Neill muttered, "and if there are explosives here they could be behind any one of them."

He raked a hand through his hair, pursed his lips. Outside, the noise of the crowd swelled and broke as another stampede of winner and losers romped across the finish line. The headline race was rapidly approaching, he knew, and with it the perfect timing for a monstrous act of violence.

"We need to go back to Cheever," he said. "Get him to rustle up a dog team."

"Got to be the fastest way boss." Dempsey was already turning away. "I'll keep searching."

"No," O'Neill said quickly. "I'll grab someone from racecourse security with some keys and do that. Why don't you go and see if you have better luck with the charming Mr Cheever than I did?"

"But—"

O'Neill glared at him. "It might have been phrased as a question, detective constable but that doesn't mean it wasn't really an order deep down."

Dempsey must have known what O'Neill was doing. He hesitated for a moment as if to argue then nodded gravely. "Give me the shitty end of the stick why don't you?" he said but it was a half-hearted protest. He turned on his heel without waiting for a reply and hurried away.

O'Neill watched him go, aware of the inexorable ticking noise inside his head, his imagination painting a cartoon alarm clock surrounded by wires and sticks of ACME gelignite.

For a start, you can give over thinking like that.

He shook himself and reached for another handle.

—135—

WHEN THE DOOR of the storeroom rattled from the outside, Dmitry froze. He was halfway through unloading a linen hamper filled with wine- and sauce-stained tablecloths and napkins. The hamper was what he wanted. A plastic tub on castors, it was plenty large enough to conceal-carry a body if he cracked a couple of the long bones to fold it inside. He didn't think the body would object.

He waited utterly still, listening. And something in the quality of silence told him that whoever stood outside the locked door was listening too.

Dmitry relaxed slightly knowing they would tire first. He gave them nothing to sustain their interest, whoever they were.

After a moment or so he heard the grit of footsteps turning away, their muffled echo growing fainter. Another doorway, another rattle and pause. Check and move on.

Security guard maybe? Dmitry was unconcerned. He could handle the calibre of man who would work here. Especially one not high enough up the food chain to be trusted with his own set of keys. Either that or he was simply too lazy to use them.

Dmitry finished emptying the hamper, working quickly, leaving a few of the larger tablecloths in the bottom and adding some used towels from the washrooms. They would be more absorbent.

He grimaced. *Damn Myshka and her temper!*

In a pocket his iPhone began to sound. He dug for it, glanced at the display.

Speak of the devil ...

"What is it?" he greeted, brusque.

Myshka showed her displeasure at his tone by a brief offended pause. "Where are you?" she demanded, matching him.

"Basement."

"Well get back up here," she said. "Quickly."

He let his breath out through his nostrils. *What do you think I'm doing—stopping for a cigarette break?*

"I needed something to carry your—"

"Never mind that," she growled. "The girl has found him anyway. She is with her boss—the old man. I manage to get out of there just in time. But if you hurry ..."

Dmitry shoved the hamper away from him. "I'm on my way."

—136—

IT TOOK KELLY a while to work her way down the building. Despite her words to Yana about fetching the cops—and the inevitable arrest which would follow—she had no intention of giving herself up just yet. Even allowing for shock and the obvious language barrier there were holes in the woman's account that Kelly could have driven a bus through.

If Yana had locked herself in the bathroom as she'd claimed, where had the blood she'd tried to wash away come from? Indeed, why had she scrubbed herself clean in such an apparently methodical way if she was in shock and terrified? The woman herself appeared uninjured. And although she'd reacted to her husband's body with apparent horror, Kelly was unconvinced by that. In her experience people lied a lot more readily than the physical evidence ever could.

In her brief examination of the private box she'd seen cast-off blood spatter across the walls and furniture. The voids and overlaps told her the beating had been prolonged and vicious. Without a more scientific analysis she could only guesstimate the point of origin but everything pointed towards the central conference table. There were enough small gouge marks and scratches on the surface to show that Warwick had probably been restrained there while he'd been worked over. It had not, she noted grimly, been a quick nor easy death.

And whatever she might say, Kelly suspected that Yana had been in the room while it had been happening.

Maybe she'd wanted to?

Maybe, she wondered with a sickened realisation, *the beating had been* for *Yana.*

She shook her head. She was allowing supposition to creep in and that was what had helped convict *her* six years ago.

Allardice made sure of that.

"I think you're involved somehow, Yana," she said out loud to an empty room, "but if you're innocent I'll do my damnedest to prove it."

The question remained—who else had been in that room when Steve Warwick died? They had walked out dripping either Warwick's blood or their own and summoned the lift at the end of the corridor.

And despite her determination to keep an open scientific mind, she couldn't help the fear that unknown person might be Matthew Lytton. She told herself it didn't matter but knew she was lying.

Kelly pressed all the floor buttons and held the doors open at each stop, bending to check the floor for any signs her quarry had passed that way.

By the time she reached the basement she was beginning to wonder if she'd missed it. Maybe *they'd* noticed the blood while they were in the lift and taken steps to stem the flow. In which case, the cast-off trail might be much less noticeable or have stopped altogether.

But as the doors slid open at the final stop she saw at once that this was not the case. If anything, the blood drops were larger and more frequent.

Compared to the luxurious decor upstairs the basement was utilitarian with no frills, lined by what looked like storerooms. The floor was painted concrete and the blood had disintegrated into satellite spatters as it hit and dispersed. Among the general stains and scuff marks ignored by the cleaning crew, it would not be obvious to the untrained eye.

She stepped out of the lift feeling a slight pang as the doors closed behind her, cutting off her escape route. The patches of blood were larger, Kelly saw, which the analytical side of her brain knew was simply down to the way it reacted to the roughened surface on which it fell. Nevertheless, her purely emotional side could not suppress a shiver.

The evidence led her to a doorway on the right. Kelly reached for the handle.

And stopped.

In the past she had worked the most horrific crime scenes but always with the knowledge that some other brave soul had been there first, cleared and secured the area. That whatever she found and documented was safe, in a way.

Now her brain raced ahead. On the other side of this door could be either another victim or a murderer. She had already been tried and convicted once. Did she really want to go leaving traces at another scene? Would anyone believe she had nothing to do with it? Her imagination rioted.

"Would you please explain to the court Miss Jacks why you decided to investigate this yourself instead of doing what any normal, sane, law-abiding person would do—staying well clear and calling the professionals?"

Kelly let her hand drop and backed away from the door, her only instinct now to get out of there without discovery.

—137—

HARRY GROGAN YANKED open the door of the private box with more force than was strictly necessary. The doors up here were sturdy solid timber and it bounced loudly against its stop.

He halted, took a breath. It was futile, he recognised, to take out his anger on inanimate objects. He stepped through, closing the door more calmly behind him and straightened his camel coat.

It was time to go down and see the colt saddled, to listen to the trainer's brittle confidence and last minute instructions to a jockey who knew the horse better than anyone.

Grogan loved that part of ownership—watching the colt filled with the buzz of imminent action, seeing him stride round the parade ring with arrogant ease and burst from the starting gate like a grey rocket.

But part of the pleasure for Grogan had always been the sharing of it. And now Irene was not able to do that he'd thought his mistress might prove a worthy substitute.

Grogan reached the lifts and looked round automatically for Viktor then scowled. Staff, he realised, stabbing a finger on the call button, were starting to be a right royal pain in the arse. It was time for an organisational shake-up.

And he'd start with bloody Dmitry. Grogan knew he'd told him to make himself scarce but this was taking the piss. He'd expected to be photographed out there with a glamorous woman on his arm and muscle by his shoulder. Instead he'd be facing the cameras alone and that put out the wrong message for a man in his position. It was all about perception. He dealt with people who needed to be convinced he was still a force to be reckoned with or they'd start trying to elbow in and take what he'd fought so hard to acquire.

There would be hell to pay later.

The lift arrived. Grogan checked his watch as he stepped inside. He was cutting it fine but he knew he made the trainer nervous and that in turn communicated itself to the horse. Better for him to arrive at the last moment, stay only as long as necessary then return to his lofty aerie to watch the race itself.

And if he was compelled to spend this moment alone, that was just the price of his success.

Grogan fished in his pocket and dragged out his cellphone, hit the speed dial for Dmitry one last time. The number rang out half a dozen times then disconnected. Grogan blinked and tried again. This time it hardly rang before disappearing into silence.

"Ignore me would you, you ungrateful little bastard?" he murmured. "I'll cut you off at the knees—you and your—"

The lift doors opened at the ground floor. Standing outside them was a high-ranking member of the Jockey Club who stepped back when he saw the grim expression on Grogan's face.

"Good God Grogan, you look like you're off to the gallows. Something I should know about the form of that colt of yours?"

Grogan took a breath, squared his shoulders. "Not at all, my lord," he managed. "And just to prove it why don't you come and watch him saddled with me?"

"Eh, of course old chap," the man said. "Delighted."

But Grogan did not miss the hesitation and would not forget it either.

One day all these bastards are going to give me the respect I deserve ...

—138—

DMITRY WAS IN the stairwell climbing when his phone buzzed. He reached for it, saw Grogan's name come up on the screen and rejected the call without pausing. It rang again immediately. Dmitry almost threw the phone through the window, stabbing the button to ignore it again.

"*Svoloch!*" he growled, repeating Myshka's earlier curse. *Scum.*

Above him he heard a door slam, glanced upwards but saw nothing. He swore again, in several languages this time, as he took the stairs two at a time.

The lift doors were closing as Dmitry yanked open the door leading from the stairwell. The floor indicator light showed the lift was heading downwards.

He spun and ran back for the stairs.

AS SOON AS the lift began to slow, Kelly jammed her finger on the Doors Closed button and sent it back up again praying the software wouldn't have a nervous breakdown and leave her stranded and exposed.

Fortunately the machinery obeyed without protest, climbing steadily. Kelly had no idea what the word she'd caught actually meant but she'd reacted on inflection and accent. It sounded kind of Russian and filled with invective. Either would have been enough to spook her. Both together sent her fleeing.

The lift reached the top floor and she braced for attack but when the doors parted the corridor was empty. She dived out and ran to the private box where she'd left McCarron and his charge.

She burst in, slammed and locked the door behind her. Someone had pulled the fur coat back over Steve Warwick's body, she saw. Her imagination had the cover moving slightly as though the corpse under it still breathed.

McCarron rose shakily from a chair. She took one look at his face and knew.

"Where's Yana?"

"I'm sorry Kelly love," he said. "I went to use the bathroom. I told her not to open the door for anyone except you but—"

"And she did a runner," Kelly said flatly.

"No, I think they took her. I heard a scream—by the time I got back out here she'd gone. I'm sorry."

"Not your fault."

Kelly shook her head reluctantly. Yana wasn't telling her the truth about what happened but that didn't necessarily make her guilty of anything more than evasion.

McCarron nodded to the locked door. "I'm guessing you didn't find the cops, then?"

"No but I was almost found by the Russian guy—Grogan called him Dmitry."

"The one who jumped me?" From his face Kelly couldn't tell if McCarron was pleased or unnerved at the prospect of meeting his attacker again.

"The one who jumped both of us," she said.

He dropped back awkwardly into his chair as if exhausted or defeated. Or both. "Christ Kel, if he's got her ... we've got to do something."

"I know," she said. "And as soon as I work out what, I'll get back to you on that."

—140—

MATTHEW LYTTON HAD worked out in theory how to free himself, but the practice proved long-winded, frustrating and painful.

His wrists were bound behind him with plastic cable-ties, the kind he'd used hundreds of times on site to secure pipes or wiring. Once they were zipped tight the only way to release them should have been with cutters. He'd long ago discovered that jamming something like a nail-head between the locking tab and its ratchet track would loosen them off.

Of course, there was never anything like a protruding nail about when you needed it. He searched fruitlessly, writhing on the concrete floor and ruining his best suit in the process. Something tickled his nose and he twitched away but it was only a shed rose petal from the crushed buttonhole at his lapel.

He froze then squirmed until the miniature bouquet was right to his face. The roses had no scent but he guessed that some varieties were bred only for their colours. What the buttonhole did have, however, was a good sharp pin securing it.

Getting the pin loose with his teeth was the easy part. As was dropping it to the floor and manoeuvring to grasp it between fingers and thumb. But trying to contort his wrists far enough to reach the ties—when he couldn't see what he was doing and his head felt about to explode—almost defeated him.

Lytton struggled for what seemed like hours. And every time he moved it was as if his head was filled with liquid that sloshed backwards and forwards inside his skull creating an almost unbearable pressure. The effect was motion sickness that left him in constant danger of throwing up.

He gritted his teeth and kept working at it. He had only a hazy picture of what had happened to bring him here. His conversation with that smug copper O'Neill was reasonably in focus but after that it started to blur. He even thought he'd seen …

No!

With a final burst of adrenaline-fuelled anger his wrists came free. The wrench nearly made him pass out, the room spinning crazily so that he had to grab the floor and hold on until it stopped lurching under him.

Hesitantly, he sat up and reached to his face, half afraid of what he'd find. A sticky mess covered his eyes and he groped for the end of his tie to scrub at it until he managed to peel his eyes open.

The first thing he saw was the blood. His hands were coated with it, mostly dried and cracking and laced in deep under his nails. His wrists were raw.

Lytton reached up to his head gingerly but apart from a lump the size of half a tennis ball it felt reasonably intact. He'd seen enough pub brawls in his youth to know scalp wounds could bleed like a bastard.

Good job I have a thick skull.

He looked round then slowly and carefully and saw he was in a storeroom. He could hear the commentator starting the build-up to the big race and realised he should have been out there—both of them should.

Looking down at his hands, at his ruined tie and bloodstained clothing, Lytton couldn't suppress a twisted smile. Not quite the image of sophistication he'd wanted to present.

Still, getting out of *here* was a good plan before whoever had dumped him like this came back to finish the job.

He was sitting propped up against some kind of packing case covered with a sheet that slid sideways as he pulled himself to his feet. When the room stopped swaying around him Lytton glanced down at it automatically.

What he saw there had him stumbling back.

"Jesus Christ …"

—141—

WHEN DMITRY'S IPHONE rang again he was outside. He was standing on the lower walkway where Kelly Jacks had made her death-defying leap the last time they'd met here, scanning the crowd in vain for any sign of her.

He was reluctant to venture further out onto the racecourse. Something told him his prey was still in the building and being spotted out here by Grogan would be … awkward at this stage.

"*Da?*" he said, terse.

A female tut-tutting noise in his ear made him jerk the phone away as if burned. He checked the display and scowled.

"What do you want Myshka? I'm busy."

"Is that any way to speak to me when I call to help you?"

"Unless you have access to the racecourse CCTV system and can track one woman in thousands, you cannot help."

She sniffed. "No faith. You not need to find *her* if she find us, no?"

Dmitry simmered in silence for a moment. He didn't mind so much that Myshka was the bright one, if only she didn't have to *gloat*.

"Go on."

"Where are you?" And when he told her she commanded with supreme confidence, "Get back up here—quietly. I have perfect bait. She will come."

—142—

THE TRILL OF a cellphone caught Kelly by surprise. Not recognising the ringtone, she glanced across at McCarron but he shrugged.

"I only have one cellphone Kelly love and I believe you may have, erm, borrowed it."

She stood, swung to try and get a bearing and then stilled.

"Oh you have to be kidding me …"

The morning suit jacket over the body of Steve Warwick was moving she saw. It shivered gently with each vibrating ring of what must be his own phone, still in his pocket.

With great reluctance Kelly patted him down. Half of her was hoping that the damn thing would stop before she found it but luck was not on her side. The display screen showed a number she was not familiar with.

"Are you sure this is a good idea?" McCarron asked.

Kelly gave him a lopsided smile. "Hell no." But she pressed the button to receive the call anyway. "Hello?"

The tinny speaker emitted a burst of noise so loud and distorted that Kelly almost dropped the phone. It took her a moment to distinguish the voice and another to recognise it.

"Yana?" she said loudly. "For heaven's sake calm down. Where are you?"

"I–in another box, I think," Yana sobbed. "They bring me here—"

"Who?"

"Man who work for Harry Grogan. He grab me. They lock me in here. I frightened!" Her voice rose into a wail on the last word.

"Stay with me Yana! We'll come and find you. Don't worry."

"Hurry! She say she kill me—woman who kill Steve. Oh God, they here! I—"

Her voice chopped off into a harsh shriek followed by a background clatter and then silence.

"Yana? *Yana?*"

McCarron was at her shoulder, his battered face pale enough for the bruises to stand out lividly against the anger. "Where is she?"

"Grogan's box by the sound of it," Kelly said without thinking.

He wheeled, had nearly made it to the door before she caught his arm—the one without the cast.

"Ray for God's sake, what do you think we can do? And how on earth did Yana just so happen to get hold of a phone? This whole thing has 'trap' written all over it."

"And if it isn't—what then?" McCarron asked. "I've stood by in the past and let people get away with murder Kel. I'm damned if I'm going to do it again."

KELLY LED McCARRON out of Lytton and Warwick's private box and to the entrance to another that was only two doors down.

"Are you sure?" he asked.

Kelly nodded. "Shula gave me a rundown so I wouldn't get lost with orders."

"Shula?"

Kelly shrugged and indicated her borrowed uniform. "She's the one who gave me this."

But McCarron's attention had been diverted by the smear of blood on the door handle. "Why grab Yana and then stash her so close?" he wondered aloud. "It makes no sense."

"There's a lot about this that doesn't," Kelly said looking up and down the corridor before dragging out her makeshift picks. McCarron noticed that she avoided touching the blood as she delicately raked the pins inside the lock. "Ready?"

He took a breath, aware of a sudden tremble at the backs of his knees. "Would it make any difference if I said no?"

Something flickered at the corner of her mouth. "You were the one overcome with gallant bravado a few moments ago," she said and pushed the door open.

Yana was sitting slumped at the wide table, a mirror of the one where her husband had been beaten to death. She was cradling her head in her hands and jerked upright when they entered.

"Are you all right love?" McCarron would have hurried forwards but Kelly put out a warning hand.

"Of course she is," Kelly said in a dangerously soft voice. "It's all going just about according to plan, isn't it Yana?"

Yana raised her head slowly, her eyes reddened and her face swollen with tears. She gave a helpless shrug. "I–I not understand ..."

"Did you beat your husband to death yourself or just help tie him down while your pal Dmitry did it for you?"

Yana gaped. She wasn't the only one. She turned a beseeching gaze on McCarron but Kelly's voice snapped her attention back again.

"Don't look to him for help," she said. "He might be a soft touch but he can read the evidence just as well as I can. Probably better—when he's a mind to." She paused. "You weren't locked in the bathroom while Warwick was killed, Yana. You were out there with him, close by and unrestrained. Given time I could tell you exactly where you stood for each blow."

McCarron cleared his throat. "Kelly love—"

"You heard us coming and you tried to clean up as quickly as you could and when that didn't work you made sure the first thing you did was throw yourself weeping on the corpse, hoping the new blood would obscure the old."

"She crazy!" Yana's eyes skipped from one to the other in apparent bewilderment. "I no understand what she saying," she protested, voice rising with distress.

"What I'm saying," Kelly said helpfully, "is that there was a woman in that room all right and she definitely was 'one cold bitch' as you put it. But the evidence points to *you* and *she* being one and the same. And unlike people, the evidence doesn't lie."

Except when it's made to.

McCarron couldn't help the thought sliding through his mind. Yes he'd seen it all, the way it looked, but he vividly remembered working the scene of Kelly's supposed crime all those years ago when she had also looked *so* guilty that nobody harboured any doubts. Nobody except him.

"What I don't understand is why here and now?" Kelly went on. "Surely if you really wanted to get rid of your abusive spouse you could have dreamed up something less ... public?"

He looked at the frightened woman cowering in front of them, the picture of innocence but all the time he kept getting strobe-like images of Steve Warwick's body, of the blood sprayed around the walls of the room nearby and of the man who'd attacked him in the hallway at the office, beating home the message with each blow. McCarron stared harder and this time he thought he saw a desperate cunning under the show of emotion. He straightened his shoulders.

"Public's better than private," he said aware his voice sounded rusty in his throat. "More confusion, more foot traffic, more evidence to be interpreted. And there's always the chance to cover it up with some other crime." He forced himself to look at Yana with an impassionate eye. "Planning a nice fire are you love?"

Yana gave a gasp that became a howl and then turned to his amazement into laughter.

And as she laughed it was as though she threw off the timid personality like a cloak. Her shoulders lost their rounded outline, her neck lengthened, her chin lifted.

"Public is perfect," she agreed. Even her voice had changed, become strong but with an underlying husky note, almost a purr. "He was *big man* in public who liked to play games and be spanked like *little boy* behind closed door. So—more public is better, yes?"

—144—

DMITRY FLATTENED AGAINST the wall next to the doorway just in time to hear the laughter. He recognised it and cursed inside his head.

It was not the laugh of the submissive Yana but of Myshka at her bad boldest best.

What the hell *does she think she's playing at?*

Dmitry reached inside his jacket and pulled out the Glock. It was the same gun Myshka had used to kill Viktor in the silent woods. He knew he should have buried it with the body but something had warned him to keep hold of it in case of trouble.

It was not *so* difficult to obtain guns in a country where nobody outside the police or military were supposed to have them but it would still have taken time. Time Dmitry suspected he would not have.

He checked there was a round in the chamber and slipped his trigger finger inside the guard, just taking up the pressure on the blade that formed the safety. Then he took a long deep breath.

He went into the room fast, hitting the door with his shoulder, kicking it shut behind him already bringing the gun up.

Myshka was sitting at the table like a *czaritsa* holding court. Not just the chattel of a Russian czar, but more like an empress in her own right. The other two whirled at his entrance but she just sat and smiled at him.

"You have met Dmitry, of course," she said as if she'd stage-managed the whole thing.

"Of course," the woman said, her voice low and bitter.

Kelly Jacks. It was hard looking at her now to balance her small stature with the trouble she had caused him. And despite the gun in his hand she was looking at him with more anger than fear. She was dressed as a waitress. *Clever*, he acknowledged. Who noticed waitresses?

The man, McCarron, seemed more shaken. It could have been the gun or simply the fact that they were face to face again for the first time since Dmitry beat him into unconsciousness. Either way the old man had almost shut down, curled in on himself. He would be no threat.

"Steve Warwick I can understand—almost," Kelly Jacks said. "But did you have to kick Elvis into a brain-damaged coma?"

For a second an image of a quiffed and sneering distant pop star gyrated into his mind. "Who?"

She shook her head. "You didn't even know his name did you? The kid in the flat in Brixton. He tried his best to give me to you. It wasn't his fault he didn't succeed."

Dmitry stared at her with a lack of emotion that was not an act. *Why do you care?*

"The race is about to start," he said to Myshka, not taking his eyes off Kelly Jacks. "Everything is ready. We need to finish this."

"Of course," Myshka said. She rose, graceful. "Any last requests?"

"Yes," Jacks said. "Why did you kill Veronica Lytton and make it look like it was connected to that old murder I investigated?"

Myshka pursed her lips. "Such an cgo," she murmured. "There *was* no connection except in your own mind. *Lady* Lytton, she see too much, hear too much and she begin to suspect poor little Yana is not what she seemed, so—" an elegant shrug "—she have to go."

She made it sound so easy Dmitry thought, when it was not Myshka who had to see it through. But he remembered the way she'd murdered her inconvenient husband. She had not taken the easy way then ...

"A coincidence?" Kelly Jacks's face was blank with shock.

"They happen," Myshka agreed, obviously enjoying her discomfort. "She did not believe in pills, but her husband he shoots and I knew she would *so* hate to have that lovely face ... spoiled."

"But ... then you killed Tyrone—the same as ..." Her voice petered out. She took a couple of tottering paces sideways, steadied herself with hands braced on the back of a chair.

"You were pain in ass by then." Myshka smiled at her again. "You can thank Matthew for that."

"What?"

"You did not know? He ask Steve to find out about you on Internet and *he* delegate to me. Perfect way to deal with you was with your own past."

"Myshka," Dmitry warned. "We do not have time for this."

"No," she agreed. She checked the time. "He will be back soon." Her eyes drifted over the two of them, the old man and the waitress, as if they were of no account. "Put them with the others."

Your word is my command. "Dead or alive?"

She raised a disinterested eyebrow. "Does it matter?"

Dmitry considered for a moment then brought the Glock up double-handed and lined up the sights on the centre of the old man's chest. McCarron caught the movement and his head jerked up, finally coming out of stasis.

"Wait—"

"What?" Dmitry asked over the gun. "You think you can persuade me to sit down and talk about it?" As he began to take up the pressure on the trigger a blur of light and dark hit his peripheral vision as Kelly Jacks heaved up the chair she'd been gripping.

"Take a seat," she growled and sent it spinning for his head.

Dmitry swung the gun blindly in her direction and pulled the trigger.

145

DI VINCE O'NEILL was outside on the lower walkway overlooking the parade ring when he heard the shot. He'd been waiting, not patiently, for the head of racecourse security to authorise someone to release him a set of keys for the storerooms when the sound cracked out overhead.

O'Neill had heard enough gunfire in his time to duck instinctively. He knew there was no mistake even before the glass began to fall around him like deadly shards of rain.

The panic was instant, blossoming outwards as people scattered. The fear transferred itself to the horses in the parade ring—highly strung at the best of times and already snapped tight with pre-race nerves. They shied and skittered as the people bellied outwards away from the building.

It was only when the building didn't follow the glass down—when the rain became a shower rather than a deluge and no bodies fell—that the crowd's rush ebbed and a morbid curiosity took over. They stopped, began to stare and point.

O'Neill shifted his gaze upwards too. He saw a blank emptiness at the window of one of the private boxes where he should have been able to see only reflection of sky.

"The whole pane's gone," said the man next to him. "Damn lucky nobody was killed, eh?"

But O'Neill didn't share his relief. He knew what he'd heard.

Nobody killed? That remains to be seen.

"Boss!"

O'Neill turned, saw Dempsey approaching at a run. "Did I hear—?"

"Yes." O'Neill grabbed his arm. "Keep your voice down and comc with me." They headed for the nearest entrance, pushing against the flow. "What did Cheever say?"

"He was a bit less combative this time round," Dempsey said hurrying to keep up. "No more helpful, mind you, but not as rude with it."

"Yeah, well maybe this will change his mind." O'Neill shouldered open the door and punched the call button for the lift. He glanced at the floor indicators, found them both stuck at the upper levels and headed for the stairs with a frustrated grunt.

When he saw the man half a flight above them—staggering and barely upright, clinging to the banister with blood coating his head and one shoulder—O'Neill's first thought was that he'd been shot. Putting it all together on the fly it was a logical assumption. He took the intervening steps three at a time and caught the man under the armpits just as he would have fallen.

It wasn't until he'd propped the injured man against the wall that he realised he knew the face under all that gore.

"Lytton? What the hell happened?" he demanded. "Where are you hit?"

"Over the head," Lytton said sounding blurry but remarkably calm. "That bitch ..."

"Jacks?"

"Hmm? What? No, not her—that bitch Steve's married to," he mumbled. "Who would have thought it?"

Dempsey leaned in. "Mr Lytton we just heard a shot—"

"No he wasn't shot."

O'Neill straightened, exchanged a worried look with his DC and asked carefully, "Who?"

"Steve," Lytton said. "I think she beat him to death, poor bastard."

"Where is she now—Yana Warwick?"

"Don't know." He tried to stand, swaying precariously. "Probably far away if she's any sense. Where we should be."

O'Neill jerked his head. "Get hold of Cheever again," he told Dempsey. "Tell him we need back-up. Never mind a possible bomb scare—this has just become a murder scene."

He started up again but Lytton's voice stopped him in his tracks. "You said 'possible' bomb scare?" he queried. "You might want to re-think that one just a little ..."

146

GROGAN WAS STILL in the parade ring with his trainer when he saw the window fall. Like O'Neill he had no problem identifying the gunshot for what it was.

His immediate concern was for his horse. The grey colt took any excuse to spook when he was race-fit. At the onset of the commotion he reared up, trying to yank away from his lad.

The prospect of such a valuable animal running amok on a crowded racecourse made Grogan abandon his dignity and grab hold. Eventually, between them—he, the lad, and the trainer—they managed to calm the colt down. As much as he'd allow himself to be calmed.

This could have cost us the race.

By the time he could step away, straightening his tie and wiping his hands, the panic was largely over. Grogan saw a couple of men hurrying for the entrance to the stands and clocked them as police even in civvies. He followed the gazes upwards and saw at once the shattered window in the private box at the top of the stand.

It only took another moment to realise whose box it was.

With a final nod to the trainer he walked briskly across the grass. The entrance to the building was being guarded by a member of racecourse security who stepped into his path.

"Sorry sir, there's been an incident upstairs. If you wouldn't mind—"

"Yes I would mind," Grogan said going toe to toe. "And bearing in mind the amount of money I've paid to enjoy watching my horse run from up there, unless you want to be hearing from my brief, you'll let me through."

The security man quailed under Grogan's stare and jerked his head without a word. As if not actually inviting him to pass would be an excuse later, Grogan thought savagely. *If you were one of mine sonny, I'd sack you on the spot.*

He was still simmering as he summoned the lift.

147

INSIDE THE PRIVATE box only two people were still on their feet.

Kelly Jacks was one of them.

She'd seen McCarron go down in response to Dmitry's gunshot but not as a direct result of it. He'd clearly thought the Russian was going to kill him, had risen clumsily, unbalanced in his panic, tripped over his own feet and fallen.

The shock and the pain of landing heavily, on top of his recent injuries, kept him down. Kelly was praying it was no more than that.

She'd hurled the heavy conference chair at Dmitry at the same moment he'd pulled the trigger. His automatic flinch had pulled the shot wide of its intended target. Instead it smashed the glass of the central window and kept on going to God knows where outside.

The chair had a metal frame and legs and a substantial seat. It caught Dmitry across the jaw and shoulders, jerking his head back with a grunt. He let go of the gun as his legs went from under him and he toppled onto his back.

Yana dropped her composed act and pounced for the gun, scrabbling on her hands and knees. Kelly leapt forwards and kicked it hard enough to send it spinning under the table and across the far side of the room out of reach. Yana gave a howl of rage.

Kelly's eyes flew back to Dmitry who'd managed to roll onto his side propped on his elbow. He was floundering and groggy and, from the way he held himself, she judged she'd either severely bruised his shoulder or possibly broken his collarbone.

Just to make sure he was out of the game she bounced on her toes and kicked him under the side of his jaw. She heard his teeth clack together as he flailed backwards again. This time he lay still enough to convince her he would not be a problem in the short term.

Yana let out another feral cry and bent to cradle the fallen man's head tenderly. "Dmitry!" Her shakes and pats had no effect.

"Let him sit this one out Yana."

"*Bitch!*" Yana hissed, rounding on her. She held up a hand, finger and thumb squeezed together almost touching. "We are *this* close. Why couldn't you keep stupid long nose to self?"

"I did keep my 'stupid long nose' to myself," Kelly shot back. "I queried the Veronica Lytton scene, was told to go ahead and we cleaned it. All that evidence gone without a trace. You should be bloody thanking me, not murdering my friend and setting me up."

"You interfere just by who you are," Yana said. She rose, began to circle. "Lytton, he doubt because of you. He want to keep looking—want *you* to keep looking." She shrugged. "So we had to get rid of you."

"And you thought it would stick—setting me up for Tyrone— even though they can test for ketamine in my hair for months afterwards?" she said, injecting scorn into her voice in place of bravado. "You must have known they'd tumble to it eventually."

Yana shrugged again. "It not matter," she said. "After today, nothing matter."

Kelly felt a cold shiver that was not just because of the cool breeze gusting in through the broken window. She was aware of the noise outside—first screams and shouts and now some kind of reassuring drone from the public address system, trying to refocus everyone's attention on the big race. People would remember today she thought, but not for the reasons Lytton had hoped for.

Lytton!

"What did you do with Matthew?"

"Don't worry, he is all taken care of," Yana said with a smile that did nothing to reassure.

Kelly flicked her eyes towards McCarron. He was sitting with his back against the table leg, clutching his cast arm with a look of intense concentration on his pinched face as if trying to will his way around the pain.

"What the hell is worth all this suffering?" She shook her head slowly. "What do you hope to gain?"

"That is easy question—everything," Yana said. "Soon, it *ours.*"

Uncomprehending Kelly gestured towards the unconscious man on the floor. "You and Dmitry?" she queried. "You think you can trust a thug like him? What makes you think he won't turn on you too as soon as you've got what you both want?"

"Oh, Dmitry would never turn on her," said a voice from the doorway. "Would he sweetheart?"

Both women spun to find Harry Grogan had quietly opened the door and was standing in the frame taking in the room at large. Kelly found her voice first.

"What makes you so sure?"

Grogan was staring at Yana as though it was the first time he'd set eyes on her and he didn't like what he saw. He spoke without shifting his gaze.

"Because she's Dmitry's sister."

—148—

GROGAN TOOK IT all in before he stepped into the room. Dmitry was well out of it, limbs threshing weakly. There was an older man Grogan didn't know on the floor near the table. He looked as though he'd been through the wars and was not out of them yet.

That left the two women.

They couldn't be more different in looks but there was the same streak of steel running through both of them, he realised. Only, with Kelly Jacks it was forged in fire, clean and bright. He wondered why he'd never seen the sheer contaminated greed in his mistress before.

"Hello Myshka," he said. "Having fun sweetheart?"

Kelly Jacks raised an eyebrow. "'Myshka'?"

"Means 'mousy' in Russian, I believe," he noted. "Not exactly an apt description of Yana when you see her like this is it? Bit like calling a short-arse Lofty."

A smile twitched at the corner of Kelly's mouth. Yana didn't quite get the reference but if the stiffening of her spine was anything to go by she knew enough to be insulted by it.

"You know her," Kelly said. Not a question.

"In the biblical sense," Grogan agreed. "And for one of the hardest coldest bitches I've ever come across, I must say she was ... passionately inventive between the sheets."

Yana glared. "If I am a man, cold and hard would be prized."

"But the shame of it is you're not," Grogan said flatly. He glanced pointedly at Dmitry, beginning to struggle feebly to rise like a beetle on its back. "Still twice the man your brother ever was though."

"Dmitry is good man!" Yana said, hands bunching into fists as if ready to swing a blow. "You never give him chance to prove himself. You treat him like servant—like a dog."

"I treated him like he was fit to be treated," Grogan said. "A guard dog that's used to roughing it but is not allowed inside on the furniture. What—you thought I'd groom him to take over? Some kind of surrogate son?"

Grogan intended the comment to be flippant, but saw immediately from Yana's face that was exactly what she'd been hoping.

"You should have trust him more."

"If today's anything to go by, looks like I've been trusting him too much as it is."

For a moment nobody spoke. The wind blew in through the broken window, flapping around the table. Beyond, Grogan could hear the commentator revving up the crowd ready for the start. *If this turns nasty I might never find out if the colt wins.*

"So Yana—Myshka whatever her name is—is your girlfriend as well as Steve Warwick's wife?" Kelly asked. "Not too much trust to be had anywhere is there?"

"She got her claws into me when I was in Moscow a few years ago," Grogan said. "Saw me as a meal ticket but not a visa." He flicked his gaze to Kelly. "Never going to divorce my Irene, no matter what state she's in. "'Til death do us part and all that. So she set her sights on Warwick instead. What have you done with him by the way?"

"He's dead," Kelly said. "They beat him to death."

"Well at least he went out with a smile on his face then," Grogan said and at her grimace of surprise added, "He was into a bit of S&M on the quiet was young Stevie boy."

Kelly spread her hands. "I don't understand any of this," she said sounding abruptly annoyed by the fact. "What does setting me up for murder and killing her husband gain her for heaven's sake?"

"Freedom. Power," Yana said proudly. "And money—a *lot* of money."

"Not anymore sweetheart," Grogan said. "I saw enough coppers milling around outside to scupper any plans you might have had about getting away with it. Won't be long before they start finding the bodies."

Yana considered this for a moment, her gaze turning inwards. It *was* a shame Grogan thought. Yana would have made the ideal right-hand man—if only she had been a man. Intelligent, ruthless and inventive in more places than just the bedroom, she would have been a worthy heir.

Perhaps I should have looked beyond the backside and the boobs, he thought regretfully. *Ah well, too late now.*

"You'll have no freedom and no power in prison. Trust me, you won't enjoy the experience," Kelly Jacks said, her voice matter of fact without gloating. "And you'll be a little old lady by the time you get out."

Yana's head came up, her gaze glittering. "I not go to prison," she said through her teeth. "I rather die!"

Just for a second Grogan thought it was merely the woman's sense of high drama coming to the fore. Then she pulled something from her pocket and held it up. He recognised a BlackBerry, the casing a pale metallic blue.

The Myshka he knew had an iPhone but the device held no special significance for him. If her tense reaction was anything to go by the same could not be said of Kelly.

"That's Veronica Lytton's isn't it?"

Yana smiled, a deep, rich Myshka kind of smile. "Of course," she said. "I take it from her just before she die. And now I use it to finish this." She deftly keyed in a number. "Is ... poetic, no?"

And she hit send.

"HOLY SHIT," O'NEILL murmured.

They were down in the basement storeroom and he'd pulled away the cover that Matthew Lytton had pointed out.

Beneath it was a bomb.

At least, it was a pile of paper-wrapped blocks of what looked distinctly like explosives, attached to one of the support pillars. Through a couple of rips in the outer packaging O'Neill could see orange plasticine-like material, soft and malleable.

The blocks were linked together by a mass of different coloured wiring. Nestled in the middle was a cellphone with wires hot-glued into the casing. It didn't take a genius to work out that was the remote detonator.

O'Neill had been through the basic course for identifying suspicious packages and a frantic voice in the back of his head was yelling, "Semtex!" He even thought he could smell something like anti-freeze and recalled one of the instructors joking that by the time you could smell explosives strongly enough to identify them, you were usually far *too* close.

He acknowledged this wasn't his field of expertise but something told him the amount and the placing would be more than enough to bring the whole of the stands crashing down around or on top of him. He took an almost involuntary pace backwards and slapped Dempsey's hand down when he would have started dialling his own cellphone.

"Don't be an idiot! Get to a safe distance before you use one of those things. Tell Cheever to evacuate the whole place and call the bomb squad. Now!"

Dempsey didn't argue.

As he dashed out he almost collided with Lytton who was leaning in the doorway and holding onto the framework in order to stay upright.

"Inspector—"

"And you Mr Lytton. Get the hell out of here."

He'd half-turned away so it was only out of the corner of his eye that he caught the display of the cellphone detonator as it lit up like the proverbial Oxford Street Christmas lights.

"Holy shit," he said again.

—150—

KELLY HAD NEVER actually been inside a building while some mad Russian woman attempted to blow them all to kingdom come but she had a pretty good idea this wasn't how it was supposed to go.

Yana was staring at the BlackBerry with her face screwed up as if it had personally insulted her. She stabbed her thumb against the keypad again, redialling.

As if once wasn't enough.

Kelly suddenly realised that she was just standing there— they all were—and letting this bitch have another go at killing them all.

Anger sizzled like a starburst inside her head. She took two rapid strides and launched, hitting Yana in the chest and bowling her straight off her feet. The BlackBerry spun out of her hand and clattered under a low sofa against the wall, shedding half its casing and the battery en route.

If Kelly hoped the shock of the attack would keep Yana from fighting back she was soon disappointed. The Russian woman bucked and clawed like a beast under her, howling.

Kelly jerked her face away. She levered her upper body upright, keeping her knees wedged either side of Yana's waist and tried to pin the flailing arms. Inevitably, one got loose and caught Kelly a stinging blow to the cheek, drawing blood.

"OK," Kelly muttered. "You want to play dirty ...?"

She began to punch, hard and fast, pounding her fists into the other woman's face. It was the way she'd learned to survive in prison—never to start a fight but always to finish it. As fast and brutal as possible. Less time to get hurt herself and it never did her rep any harm to be known for outbursts of absolute violence.

By the end of her sentence nobody had wanted to take her on because they knew if they didn't put her down quickly there would be no respite until she was forcibly dragged away.

McCarron didn't have the strength in his current state to force her to do anything, but his shouts finally penetrated the toxic mist of rage.

"Kelly love." His hands were on her shoulders, his voice hoarse and desperate. "For God's sake, you'll kill her!"

"We'll be all square then," Kelly said gasping for breath. But she unclamped her hands from Yana's dress and let the woman's unresisting head drop back to the floor. It landed with a hollow clunk. Yana groaned through split lips. Her nose was busted, possibly a cheekbone too, Kelly noted with satisfaction—she was not going to look alluring to anyone without weeks of recuperation and probably a skilled cosmetic surgeon.

Kelly got to her feet, shaky from the adrenaline hangover. Her knuckles were already beginning to swell and tighten. She could hardly make a fist although most of the blood, she reflected, was not hers. She thought of Tyrone and her only immediate regret was that McCarron had pulled her away from Yana too soon.

It's not enough Ty. It will never be enough.

She heard another groan. Dmitry was showing signs of coming round. He rolled onto his hands and knees, spitting blood and what might have been a tooth onto the polished floor.

Kelly twisted out of McCarron's grasp and booted the Russian solidly under the chin and then again in the ribs as he started to drop. She only realised afterwards that she'd done it in the wrong order.

Should have gone for the ribs first—made the bastard feel it.

Then the world settled and her narrowed-down field of vision widened out. The breeze was cool against her sweating skin and the commentary on the race that blared in from outside was growing in pitch and tension.

"Saved me the trouble," Grogan said calmly moving past her.

"Yeah well," Kelly said. "You didn't have a shovel on you."

Grogan didn't reply. He stepped over Dmitry's outstretched legs and went to the window, just close enough to the gap to look down onto the course.

"Christ Almighty," he yelped. Kelly and McCarron hurried alongside him. "I've missed half the bloody race!"

Below them a close-grouped herd of thoroughbreds swept through the final turn and stretched for the finish, the combined thunder of their hooves rolled up from the turf like distant gunfire. Kelly could see the only grey in the race was two back from the leader and bunched in next to the rails. It was impossible not to watch the final stages of the battle unfold.

"Come on, come on," Grogan growled beneath his breath. "Put your bloody foot down ..."

As if hearing the command the crouching jockey began to wave his whip. The colt flattened, barging his way forwards. The finish line flashed nearer. The second horse fell away, drifting outwards, his burst of acceleration spent.

One remained. The colt went after him with furious pace, utterly focused. As they crossed the line Kelly could not have said which was in front.

"Bloody hell," Grogan said, his voice a growl. "If he's lost it on a photo I'll skin that jockey—"

"I skin you all first!"

They whirled. Yana, forgotten in her injury, was back on her feet and clutching the gun dropped by Dmitry. She held it with the competent grip of someone who has handled firearms before and knows how. Her face was a mess of blood and venom.

—151—

THE SHORT HARSH smack of the gunshot echoed high above the racecourse, audible even over the bellowed roars of the betting public, just as the last of twelve runners in the Lytton-Warwick Cup crossed the finish line.

A moment later the woman's body fell from the open box above the stands. With such a nail-biting climax to the day's big race, nobody saw the beginning of her fatal plunge but they heard her screaming all the way down.

There wasn't time for her to reach terminal velocity nor for the weight of her head to invert her in flight to the classic head-down dive. So she was in an almost supine position, back arched and limbs trailing, when she hit the rail of the walkway above the parade ring in a clean line at the waist.

The nearest witnesses later claimed they heard her spine shatter like dry kindling in a fire.

The impact cut off her cries like a guillotine. Spectators who'd ventured back onto the walkway for a better view of the course, despite the crunch of glass fragments under foot, fled in renewed panic.

From there the woman cartwheeled limp and broken down into the parade ring itself. She landed not neat and together, the way such deaths are usually portrayed, but face down in a buckled nightmare of dislocation and distortion.

There was a brief pause then the screaming started again. And this time it came from many voices.

—152—

O'NEILL ARRIVED AT the doorway to the private box out of breath, having just run up six flights of stairs from the basement level. Dempsey was at his elbow and the DI was vaguely irritated to note his skinny sidekick had not even broken a sweat.

O'Neill muscled through the doorway knowing that if he didn't get in there fast after shots fired Cheever was liable to turn the whole thing into a long drawn-out negotiation.

Inside the room were three men, two of whom he recognised, and one who was lying face-down on the floor and not easy to place. O'Neill glanced at the inert form and decided there'd be time to get to him later.

The other two men were near the conference table in the centre of the box. Former CSI Ray McCarron was sitting down, his skin waxy and grey, as Harry Grogan tightened a belt that was doubling as a makeshift tourniquet around his upper arm.

As unlikely scenarios went, O'Neill considered this had to be right up there.

"About bloody time," Grogan said glancing up. "Any chance one of you little Dutch boys could stick his finger in this particular dyke? I've got a horse to unsaddle."

"Dempsey—you passed First-Aid a lot more recently than I did," O'Neill said. "See what you can do."

Dempsey threw his boss a dark look but hurried across. As soon as he loosened the tourniquet blood welled out of what looked suspiciously like a gunshot wound.

"Bugger it," McCarron said through thinned lips. "I'd only got the one good arm left."

Grogan straightened his cuffs and began to move past O'Neill.

"The horse can wait—this is a crime scene. I can't let you leave until we have a statement."

Grogan showed his teeth briefly. "Take more than you and the boy to stop me seeing if that bloody colt of mine is worth the money I've put into him," he said. "Either arrest me right now or get out of my way."

O'Neill knew clout when it was being brandished in front of him but he didn't have to like it. "I'm sorry sir but I can't let you leave."

"Name a station and I'll be there first thing tomorrow morning with my team of lawyers. Try to delay me now and I'll have 'em running rings round you for months."

O'Neill hesitated a moment then stepped back with a curt nod.

Grogan had sense enough not to crow in victory. But in the doorway he paused, turned back and gave the room a final visual sweep. "Bloody shame she had to go like that," he said, no emotion showing in his face, and went out.

O'Neill turned on McCarron. "'She'?" he demanded. "And a shame she had to go like what?"

By way of answer McCarron flicked his eyes in the direction of the shattered window. It was only when O'Neill leaned out carefully over the long drop that he saw the corpse below. It was too far away and too badly mangled to identify. He wouldn't even like to confirm the gender with any degree of certainty.

"Shit!" he said. "You were with the force long enough McCarron. Why didn't you say something before I let Grogan waltz out of here?"

"He had nothing to do with it," McCarron said quietly. "I—"

"Ray," said a new voice, low with warning. "Shut up."

356

O'Neill looked up and there was Kelly Jacks, dressed as a waitress, emerging from the bathroom with a towel torn into strips as an emergency dressing. Her face was scratched, hands beat up like a boxer after a tough bout but her eyes were clear and her gait was steady. O'Neill felt his shoulders come down without realising he'd tensed them.

A bloody survivor, that's what she is.

Dempsey, on the other hand, jolted upright like he'd been cattle-prodded. "Kelly Jacks, I am arresting you for—"

"Oh can it Dempsey," O'Neill snapped.

Kelly Jacks grinned at Dempsey's hurt incomprehension. "A bit eager to get down to business isn't he?" she said.

"These youngsters tend to get over-excited and go off at half-cock," he agreed. Out of the corner of his eye he saw Dempsey blush to the roots of his hair. "No foreplay."

"When my fingers have turned blue it means you need to slacken that thing off," McCarron told him helpfully, nodding to the tourniquet.

"Don't worry," Kelly said, eyes still on O'Neill. "I'll come quietly. It's all over."

"Not quite." O'Neill nudged the man on the floor, rolling him onto his back to get a clear look at his face. "Ah. Dmitry Lyzchko I presume."

"If you're looking for his loopy sister, she's down there," Kelly said.

O'Neill took a long breath. It was a mess, no doubt about that. "Want to tell me what happened?"

"Dmitry had a gun. We fought. He dropped it. Yana got hold of it, took a pot shot at Ray and went out the window."

"Just like that, hmm?"

Kelly's gaze was level. "I'm summarising."

"It was my fault," Ray McCarron said suddenly.

"Ray—"

"Now it's your turn to shut up Kel," McCarron said with a weary smile. "Like you said, Yana got hold of Dmitry's gun and I tried to rush her."

O'Neill raised an eyebrow at the cast arm. "In your condition?"

McCarron gave a tiny shrug, the most he could manage. "I was nearest," he said. "She got a shot off, winged me, but we struggled and ... she tripped and fell." He took a deep breath, glared at Kelly when she would have spoken again. "It was *my* fault," he repeated speaking slowly and distinctly so there would be no mistakes. "I was trying to stop her killing us all and I didn't mean for it to happen but it was entirely down to me that she fell, OK?"

—153—

LYING PROPPED UP on the bed in the room of his small hotel near Earls Court, Frank Allardice watched events at the racecourse unfold on the TV news.

The cameras had lingered on the tall screens they'd erected around the woman's body in the parade ring. They were usually brought out to protect the public from seeing fallen horses being put to the bolt but they were just as useful for this kind of eventuality. They'd needed a lot of them though. She'd managed to spread herself over a pretty wide area, poor cow.

When Allardice had seen Lytton's name connected with the event he'd wondered, just briefly, if Kelly Jacks might show up there. And ever since the news had broken that a woman had fallen—jumped or been pushed, take your pick—from a private box high above the stands, he'd wondered about that too.

Well, hoped, more than wondered.

Having Kelly Jacks as the one splattered all over the parade ring would certainly tie up a few annoying loose ends.

Allardice reached into the ice bucket on the bedside table and dragged out a can of lager he'd bought from the open-all-hours place down the road. He wiped the outside of the can on the duvet, cracked open the ring pull and took a swig.

The news cameraman had finally realised that a set of dark green screens were not exactly photogenic and was panning across the mass of police and emergency services and bomb-disposal personnel. If they'd all paid to get in, Allardice reflected, the racecourse would have doubled their gate.

And then he caught a glimpse of a face he knew.

DI Vincent O'Neill, looking grim-faced and like a right hard bastard.

O'Neill was walking away from the stands, his hand on the shoulder of one of the waitresses. It was only when the girl turned slightly towards him, looked up, that Allardice realised he knew her too.

He reared upright, slopping lager onto his shirt, and stared narrow-eyed at the TV. "Well, well, Kelly bloody Jacks." He toasted the image on screen. "You got her Vince old son."

In that case he had no idea who the dead woman was, but if Jacks had been found at the scene of another violent death that wasn't going to look good for her in court was it? No, the body count was high enough on this one for Kelly Jacks to be locked away until she was a very old lady.

All in all, not a bad outcome.

But as the camera stayed with the detective and his charge a niggle of doubt crept in. If Jacks had been arrested why wasn't she cuffed? O'Neill wasn't a soft touch as far as female prisoners were concerned—unless she wasn't actually a prisoner. Because, now he looked closer, that hand on the shoulder seemed more solicitous than custodial.

Oh shit ...

Allardice shoved the lager aside and rolled off the bed. Within half an hour he had packed, checked out and was on the Piccadilly line heading for Heathrow.

—154—

DMITRY CAME ROUND not in the public First-Aid post but in the Jockeys' Medical Room reserved for more serious injury, with two uniformed cops standing over him.

"Where is Myshka?" was all he wanted to know. He said the words over and over through clenched teeth.

Eventually, in his best soothing bedside manner, the duty Racecourse Medical Officer broke the bad news.

Despite his injuries, which included a fractured jaw, broken collarbone and cracked ribs, Dmitry went berserk.

One of the constables was later treated for concussion, the other for dislocated fingers. The reinforcements, who quickly arrived, piled in with gusto.

Even so, they had to taser him twice before they could get him under control.

—155—

KELLY SAT IN the back of an unmarked police Mondeo, alone and apparently forgotten.

O'Neill had put her into the car with a not unkind command to, 'Stay there.' She did not have the energy to do much else.

She knew what came next—a succession of interview rooms and holding cells, having her clothing taken away and replaced with prison garb that always smelled the same and felt the same. Duty solicitors who were overtired and overstressed and didn't care one way or another if you were guilty or innocent, providing the case was put away neatly.

Prison gates, bars, locks, keys and the smell of sweat and fear and desperation. Years of it.

I don't know if I can go through all that again.

She thought of Ray McCarron who was on his way back to hospital complaining bitterly but still adamant that he was responsible for Yana Warwick's death. And if he was feeling guilty enough to take the fall, a part of her *so* wanted to let him.

It was a bad choice of words, she acknowledged. Or maybe it was apt. She shook her head—such distinctions were currently beyond her.

In all likelihood he wouldn't go down for it. He would plead self-defence and—regardless of who'd been the last person to touch Yana before she went over—that's exactly what it was.

Kelly knew her word as a witness would not carry much weight but as far as a jury knew, Harry Grogan was the proverbial pillar of society. He'd already made it clear that he was prepared to look anyone in the eye and swear it had all happened the way McCarron claimed.

She just didn't know why. Was he hoping such an act would give him a hold over her, or make her grateful enough to stop being such a nuisance?

And if Ray *was* found guilty—what then? *Do I say nothing and let him serve his time? Owning up when it's all over will create a far bigger mess. They'll probably send him down for perjury on top of everything else—and me alongside him.*

It was a situation not without parallels to the one McCarron had found himself in six years ago. Ironic, in its way.

She tilted her head back and closed her eyes. She was tired, she admitted. More tired than she'd ever been in her life.

She thought of Tina and wondered if Elvis had come out of his coma and whether she would ever again be able to speak to the woman who had probably saved her life in prison.

And sitting there amid the noise and confusion, Kelly felt suddenly very alone.

—156—

MATTHEW LYTTON WATCHED Kelly through the side window for a moment. She looked lost and vulnerable, like a child left in the back seat by a parent who might never return.

He took a breath and opened the car door. Her eyes shot wide, twisting instinctively to meet the threat as he slid in alongside her and shut the door behind him.

There was a second of silence between them.

"The child locks are on," Kelly said dryly. "So I hope you brought a flask and sandwiches because you're stuck in here with me now."

I can live with that.

He smiled. They'd taped a dressing over his scalp wound that felt like a comedy hat perched on top of his head. Whenever he moved his face the tape pulled at his skin.

"I wanted to thank you," he said. "Without you chasing all this down I would never have known what really happened to Veronica."

"I can't say with complete honesty that I did it willingly—or for your benefit."

"I know," he said. "Result's the same though."

She nodded gravely, paused. "Do you think we ever will really know what happened?"

"Yana had Vee's BlackBerry—O'Neill showed it to me," he added when she looked surprised. "I can't think of a legitimate reason for Yana to have kept it all this time and not given it back to me unless ..." He shrugged. "I never guessed, all this time, that Steve was having an affair with his own wife. How bizarre is that?"

"It's perfect when you think about it," Kelly said. "After all she was never going to divorce him over it was she?"

"She was a vampire," Lytton said. He thought of his charming, flawed partner. O'Neill had shown him the body too. He'd concentrated on the details to make a formal ID, a small scar on the back of Warwick's left hand, his watch and wedding ring. Anything so he didn't have to look at the dead man's face. What was left of it.

"I thought she was Russian rather than Transylvanian."

He managed a half smile. "Russian, Ukranian—something like that. But she sucked the life out of everybody she came into contact with," he said. "Steve, Vee, even that brother of hers Dmitry, and Grogan of course."

She sat up suddenly. "I never asked. Did his colt win the race?"

"By a nose."

"Oh thank God for that," she said. "He'd never have forgiven me otherwise."

Lytton didn't quite get how it would have been Kelly's fault but he let that one go. Instead he sighed, rubbed a weary hand across his eyes. "Christ, I need a holiday."

"You and me both," she agreed. "But I have a feeling mine might be spent at Her Majesty's pleasure."

FRANK ALLARDICE WAS having a late supper at Heathrow when his cellphone rang. He'd spent an agonising afternoon and evening waiting for a standby seat that never materialised before finally succumbing to airport food.

He fished the phone out of his pocket and flipped it open, still shovelling overpriced shepherd's pie into his mouth.

"Yeah?"

"Frank? Where are you?"

As soon as he recognised Vince O'Neill's voice Allardice thought about lying. Then the public address started squawking about passengers not leaving baggage unattended and that idea was well and truly buggered.

He chewed and swallowed. "At Heathrow, sampling their culinary delights—although 'delights' is perhaps putting it a bit strong," he said easily. "What can I do for you Vince?"

"We picked up Kelly Jacks this afternoon," he said. "Thought you'd like to know, seeing as you had such a special interest."

Shit! What do you know?

"Good job," Allardice said. "Knew you'd get her in the end. Any ... trouble?"

"You haven't been watching the news have you?" O'Neill said, amusement in his voice. "Guy got beaten to death at a racecourse, a woman fell from the stands and we found enough explosives to blow the place sky high."

Allardice whistled, hoped it sounded convincing as surprise. "And Jacks was involved in all that? She's gone up in the world."

"Nearly did—she was in the stands at the time," O'Neill said.

He paused and Allardice had to force himself not to jump into the silence like a guilty man. At the next table a fractious family were scarfing down chips with everything, surrounded by enough carry-on luggage to outfit a small town. Allardice hoped they were not on his flight—when he eventually got one.

"So pat-on-the-back time from old man Quinlan," he said at last. "Feather in his cap to have Jacks safely under lock and key before he hangs up his spurs eh?" He was suddenly aware that he was using one cliché after another but O'Neill didn't seem to notice.

"Yeah ... listen Frank, I was hoping to be able to deal with Jacks quietly but with everything that's happened, well, it's all going to have to go by the book. We've been giving her the third degree and I have to tell you that your name keeps coming up."

Allardice felt his heart suddenly start to punch against the inside of his ribs. "Stands to reason," he said gruffly. "I put her away last time. You'd expect her to hold a grudge."

"Hmm, but it's getting harder to keep a lid on things and I'm sure the last thing you want is to end up helping us with our enquiries." O'Neill sighed. "I would have thought there's sod all we can prove after all this time but I just wanted to give you a heads up. It's opening a bit of a can of worms to be honest."

Allardice put his fork down slowly. "Thanks Vince," he said. "I mean, obviously there's nothing in what she says but I appreciate the warning."

"No sweat," O'Neill said. "I'll do my best to minimise the damage, shall we say?"

"Yeah," Allardice said. "Thanks again. I owe you."

O'Neill's laugh was jarring. "And I'll collect—you can be sure of that. You can show me the sights next time I grab a cheap last-minute package to Spain."

Allardice tried to put the uneasy feeling in the pit of his stomach down to the shepherd's pie but he forced a cheerful note into his voice.

"The beer's on me, old son," he said. "Definitely."

—158—

"HE'S ON THE move!"

DC Dempsey followed former DCI Allardice's progress through the airport on a series of CCTV monitors. He was in the security control room at Heathrow surrounded by more surveillance equipment than he'd ever seen in his life.

The camera operators were slick he had to admit. They kept track of Allardice as he moved from one zone to another, always overlapping. Dempsey was amazed anybody managed to get away with anything.

Half of him was a little freaked out by it all and the other half was bubbling with suppressed excitement. The kind of thrill you only get when you're closing in on a target and he has no idea whatsoever that he's been rumbled.

"He's heading for the payphones," his liaison officer said. A youngish guy, thickset and purposeful.

"Can you move your people in close enough to hear anything?"

The liaison grinned at him. It would have been smug had he not been young enough to be buzzed by the job. "Better than that," he said. "Bill, give me audio and filter out whatever background chatter you can."

The camera zoomed in unobtrusively to show Allardice looking around, all casual, before he picked up the receiver and dialled.

"Hello? You know who this is ... I'm on my way back to sunny Spain mate. Job's done. Looks like we can rely on young Vince to put it to bed all neat and tidy... Yeah well, you owe me—big time—and I'm like a bloody elephant. I never forget to collect on my debts ... Yeah, cash is always 'acceptable' mate. You know where to find me."

He put the phone down, looked around again and wiped his hand on the leg of his trousers before striding away.

"Sweating about it, weren't you Frank?" Dempsey murmured.

"They're calling his flight," the liaison said. "Do you want an intercept?"

Dempsey shook his head. "Watching brief only—them's my orders."

The liaison grinned again. "Well the Spanish authorities are a lot more amenable about extradition these days aren't they?"

"Too right."

One of the techs—the guy called Bill—broke off from his computer keyboard long enough to scrawl something on a pad and rip off the sheet, handing it across. "That's the number your man called. You should be able to trace it easily enough."

Dempsey read the digits and hoped his eyes hadn't bulged as much as it felt they had.

"Oh yeah," he said. "We'll trace that one. No problem."

—159—

MATTHEW LYTTON STOOD by the open window of the room that had once been his study and stared down into the rear courtyard where a large white van stood parked.

This time there was no crime-scene cleaning logo on the side of it, no Tyvek-clad figures reclining in the front seat. And no Steve Warwick about to stroll breezily through the door behind him.

Instead, the van belonged to a local catering company. He could see the serving staff in their uniforms unloading trays, stacks of tablecloths and crates of glasses from the rear. Just for a second his imagination painted one of them into a slight figure with choppy black hair and a loose-limbed stride. The illusion ballooned and then burst as soon as the girl turned in his direction.

It wasn't Kelly Jacks.

Lytton sighed. "No," he muttered under his breath, "I guess you have no reason to be coming back here."

Considering he hardly wished to be *here* himself, he couldn't blame Kelly for that.

In his hand was a cup of coffee and he lifted it to take a sip, checking his watch as he did so.

By this time tomorrow, it will all be over.

It was a month after the Lytton-Warwick Cup. A month since the death of Steve Warwick and Yana—or Myshka, or whatever the hell she was called.

And a month since he had last seen Kelly.

Tomorrow morning was the memorial service for Vee. Her parents had pushed for the service in the church of the local village, on the spurious grounds that it dated back to Saxon times and therefore had some kind of worthy pedigree. Lytton failed to see quite what that had to do with anything, except perhaps to subtly remind him of his own lack of breeding.

Having a memorial service at all was at his in-laws' request, although 'insistence' might have been a better word. But Lytton had not argued against it. Perhaps now it had emerged that Veronica did not, after all, take her own life they felt the need for some kind of public vindication.

Nor had he objected to footing the cost, which they had automatically expected of him. And when he glanced over the sizeable guest list and found he recognised very few names, he hadn't raised objections about that either.

Some of those travelling from further afield would begin arriving that afternoon, ahead of tomorrow's *performance*— there was hardly another word to describe it. His mother-in-law had pointed out it was silly for them to cram themselves into local B&Bs—there were no suitable large hotels close by—when the house itself had a surplus of rooms standing empty. Lytton had agreed on the basis that *she* organised it. It was only habit that made him oversee the details before he paid the bills.

The result was that he felt somewhat detached from the whole exercise as if he was the manager of the venue rather than an active participant.

After all, Vee's body had already been laid to rest. He'd said his goodbyes, made his peace, and played a small but not insignificant role in uncovering her killer.

What else was there?

A gust of wind chicaned through the open window and nipped at the fabric of Lytton's shirt. It was getting colder, he realised. Autumn had crept up when he wasn't looking and soon it would be winter. Before long the stores would be putting up Christmas lights and advertising late-night shopping, and then the winter sun getaway advertising would start.

"Maybe it *is* time for that holiday," he wondered aloud.

There was nothing to stop him going, except a lingering sense of *waiting*.

Waiting for Kelly.

As for the rest of it, that was getting sorted, slowly enough. The insurance company was stalling paying out on the key-man policy on Steve Warwick until the criminal investigations were complete. They had been clearly suspicious of Lytton's own possible involvement too. But considering Yana had also had a bloody good go at adding him to the body count, his legal team were confident they would settle. It was only a matter of time.

The inaugural Lytton-Warwick Cup had not exactly gone according to plan, but it had certainly gained so much publicity—good and bad—that next year was a done deal. The TV people had already signed up, although Lytton had told them in a dry tone that he couldn't promise peripheral events would be quite so ... exciting in future.

And he'd changed the name slightly. Calling it the Lytton-Warwick *Memorial* Cup now seemed doubly appropriate.

The police had finished questioning him weeks ago, the business had been put into a holding pattern and the country house was already half packed up and on the market. He had an exclusive and very private resort in the Bahamas all picked out for his own personal getaway.

All he hadn't been able to bring himself to do was get on a plane.

Lytton stepped back from the window and swallowed the last of his coffee, placing the empty cup down on the desktop. His broadsheet daily was still spread across the surface and his eyes slid again to the news item on Kelly Jacks.

In the days immediately following events at the racecourse Kelly's face had been plastered all over the front pages. They'd vilified her unchecked as some kind of psychotic rampage killer. Over the weeks that followed she had been tried, convicted and practically crucified in the press all over again.

Lytton had learned that Kelly was being held on remand at Holloway prison but so far she had refused all his requests to see her. Lytton had tried to arrange to pay whatever bail amount was necessary to get out, only to learn she hadn't asked for bail to be granted in the first place.

And now, today, when he should be giving all his thoughts to the memory of his dead wife and to his imminent guests, Lytton found himself distracted by the image of a small slim woman with wary eyes the colour of good aged brandy. He remembered watching with his heart in his open mouth while she effortlessly scaled the outside wall of the house near Battersea Park, then transformed herself in the lavender dress and jacket for lunch at the racecourse.

He thought of her fierce determination throughout to prove her own innocence. And he wondered exactly when, where and *why* that fire had gone out of her.

—160—

KELLY JACKS WALKED along an all but deserted beach of pale yellow sand, watching as a stately Mediterranean sun winched itself out of the sea to the east, ready for another day.

She wore a skinny top and shorts and carried her sandals so she could walk up to her ankles in the surf where the water felt warm as a Jacuzzi. After only a couple of days her skin had lost its prison pallor and taken on a healthier glow.

Since her arrival here she had eaten seafood so fresh it practically still wriggled, swum, snorkelled and slept like the dead. *All the esses*, she thought idly.

And if certain faces still haunted her, at least they'd stopped crying through her dreams.

She felt rested, yes, but not yet relaxed.

Not yet.

Further offshore the swell was languid, the water therapeutic as it came and went on the beach, dragging the sand oozing from beneath her heels and between her toes. It would be so easy to stay here, where nobody knew her, to burrow in and hope the rest of the world would forget about her too.

Kelly gave a snort of self-derision. "Yeah, like *that's* going to happen."

She veered away from the water's edge, trudging through the softer sand and bypassing the serried rows of empty sun loungers with their folded parasols. She headed towards the pretty little promenade with its cafés and bars. Some were already preparing to open for breakfast and the smell of cooking drifted evocatively on the morning air.

She climbed the half-dozen concrete steps and padded still barefoot towards the table of the nearest, where a man sat reading an English newspaper. He was wearing sunglasses and a pale shirt with the sleeves rolled up to reveal a pink explosion of freckles.

"I hope you've put sunblock on today," Kelly observed as she took the seat opposite. "Otherwise they'll be able to fry eggs on you."

Detective Constable Ian Dempsey lowered the paper and inspected his scorched arms with a slightly sheepish expression.

"Factor fifty." He lifted the sunglasses, wincing as the true extent of his sunburn became apparent to him.

Kelly glanced at the headline on the newspaper he'd put aside. Finally, some other disaster had relegated her to the inside pages.

"Maybe the furore *has* actually begun to die down," she said without much conviction.

"At least until you get home," Dempsey reminded her with a cheerful lack of tact. He reached for his cellphone, which lay face up on the table and waggled it at her. "Just had the call, by the way. You ready?"

She slid her feet into her sandals and rose. "I've been ready for six years."

He flushed a little at that. "Um, look Kelly, you *are* going to let the locals handle things, aren't you?" he said. He fumbled through the unfamiliar coinage to pay for his coffee, not quite meeting her eye. "I mean, if *I'm* here as a courtesy then *you're* here 'cos somebody much higher up the food chain than me did some serious arm twisting. I don't want to have to explain, through an interpreter, how justified you were in kicking this bloke's bollocks into his throat."

"I'll be good," she promised meekly.

He shot her a quick look as if suspecting derision. Then he shook his head and smiled.

"To be quite honest, I wouldn't blame you if you *did* let him have it," he admitted. "But I didn't say that, of course."

"Of course."

Together they strolled along the street, stopping occasionally to read the menu boards. Kelly tried to behave casually, as if their eventual choice was entirely random. The rapid thunder of her heart made it hard to swallow.

They loitered a moment longer, then Dempsey murmured, "Shall we?" and they walked into the dim interior.

Inside, the bar was a mix of old English polished wood and splashes of local decoration, terracotta and brass. A surprisingly successful blend of two cultures that really should not have worked but somehow blended smoothly. Ceiling fans turned lazily to keep the temperature cool and pleasant as a temptation to wander in out of the pre-noon heat and stay late into the evening.

This early, though, the place was empty except for three men sitting at a table in the back. As soon as he saw them enter, one of the men got to his feet and came forward to greet them.

"We're not quite ready to serve breakfast yet, folks," the man said, "but can I get you coffees or a ..." As soon as he got his first good look at the pair of them his voice shrivelled into silence.

"Hello Mr Allardice," Kelly said in a deadly soft tone. "Remember me?"

Former Detective Chief Inspector Frank Allardice was not a stupid man. He had recognised her instantly and, having done so, it only took another moment for him to size up Ian Dempsey and make him for a copper, even burnt Brit red and in his civvies.

He had too much bottle to actually run, but Allardice shoved past the pair of them and made for the street at a brisk walk. The snarl on his face as he went dared them not to get in his way. Dempsey stepped aside and let him go.

The two men at the back of the bar were on their feet by then. The first watched Allardice make his exit and then he *did* run, tearing out through the rear kitchen in a flash. The last man hesitated only for a second. His eyes made fleeting contact with Kelly's before he was sprinting too.

And if the first man was only vaguely familiar she would have known the other anywhere.

Detective Inspector Vincent O'Neill.

"Fleeing at the first sign of customers, eh?" Dempsey shook his head in mock dismay. "Now that's no way to run a business."

Outside there was a burst of noise—harsh shouts in Spanish and swearing in English, followed by scuffling feet and the solid thuds of subduing blows. Kelly listened, hoping for more, but it seemed the fugitives submitted with disappointing speed.

Members of the *Cuerpo Nacional de Policía* poured in through both front and rear entrances, hustling their three handcuffed prisoners before them like they were running bulls.

The tall slim officer who seemed to be in charge shook hands with Dempsey and the two began a brief conversation that was largely conducted in gestures and pidgin.

Kelly edged quietly around the group of cops until she was only a metre or two away from the prisoners. Allardice glared at her with all the arrogance she remembered so well from interrogation. But she saw the sweat on his forehead begin to dribble at his temples, and knew he was seriously afraid. It was only the presence of his fellow detainees that gave him any remaining spine. Like he could take it, just so long as he wasn't taking it alone.

Her eyes passed to Vince O'Neill. He returned the stare impassively for a moment before offering a wry smile.

"Nice to see you off remand, Kelly," he said. "Although if you hadn't been so stubborn Matthew Lytton would have stood bail for you weeks ago."

Kelly shrugged to hide her pleasure and surprise. "It gave me time to think," she said, "about the massive civil action I'm going to bring for wrongful arrest, conviction, and imprisonment."

At that the third man's head snapped up. His gaze swivelled between Allardice and O'Neill as if trying to work out which of them had sold him out fastest.

"Look," he began, trying in vain to catch the eye of any Spanish officer who might possess half a dozen words of English. "I don't know what's going on here, but I've just retired from a very high-ranking job with the British police, and I'm merely visiting two old friends ..."

But then the lead Spanish officer finally understood what Dempsey had been trying explain, mostly via the medium of mime.

"Ah, *si*!" the man cried, a huge grin appearing from beneath his generous moustache. He pointed at Vince O'Neill and said, "*Clandestino,* eh?" and then rattled off orders to his men.

They broke into wide answering smiles. The one standing nearest to O'Neill quickly undid the cuffs, offered him an apologetic shrug.

Kelly watched the realisation grow in the third man's eyes, that this was no random event but more of a carefully orchestrated operation. That his reputation, his pension and his marriage were about to go to hell and all his dirty little secrets were going to be spread across the tabloids like intestines across a butcher's slab.

After a few moments she turned away without speaking. There was nothing she wished to say to the man who had engineered her ruin and now would be the instrument of her redemption.

O'Neill nodded his thanks to the Spanish cop, then jerked his head to Dempsey. "Nice work, Ian," he said. "Your collar, I think."

Kelly thought Dempsey flushed with pride, but it could have been the sunburn. He stepped forward.

"*Ex*-Chief Superintendent John Quinlan," he said in a calm and steady voice. "I am arresting you for conspiracy to pervert the course of justice ..."

—161—

THANK GOD IT'S nearly over.

Sitting in the front pew of the ancient church, the words ran through Matthew Lytton's head.

The vicar was into his Benediction. Vee had been an occasional churchgoer—more for its social implications than out of any true belief—so at least the man was able to speak from slight personal acquaintance.

Then there was only one more hymn to go before Lytton could get out of this suffocating place and this suffocating suit. And, above all, away from these utterly suffocating people.

The vicar was meandering his way towards a solemn close. Lytton shifted on the old wooden pew and was suddenly aware of the feeling he was being watched.

As casually as he could he glanced back over his shoulder—straight into the eyes of Kelly Jacks.

He felt the jolt of her unexpected presence like a physical blow to his gut. He tensed in visceral response and forced himself not to turn and stare.

Even so, there was no mistake.

In that brief glimpse he registered her bare head among the sober hats, her shoulders draped with an overlarge black topcoat that drowned her small frame.

His mind began to race. What the hell was she doing here? There had been no official announcements and he'd been following the whole travesty with a close eye. Christ ... had she escaped?

He realised the vicar had stopped speaking, the organist was flexing his fingers and the rest of the congregation was rising around him with a chorus of coughs and shuffles. His mother-in-law glared at him from across the aisle, as if not being first up was a sign of disrespect.

He had put his foot down about the final piece of music. Vee had always loved the intricacies of Bach, and in particular the chorale movement *Jesu Joy of Man's Desiring*.

His mother-in-law had been vaguely horrified at the suggestion. "But, it's so ... unsuitable, Matthew. You had that played at your wedding."

"All the more reason to play it again at her memorial service then, don't you think?"

In the end the woman had given in with some attempt at grace, although he noted from the Order of Service that she had disguised his choice by using its lesser-known German title—*Herz und Mund und Tat und Leben, Bach-Werke-Verzeichnis 147*.

He stood silent while the vastness of the Bach cantata washed over him, but felt only impatience for it all to be over.

Kelly ... here ...

Even then he couldn't make an immediate escape. He was expected to stand in a receiving line with Vee's parents, accepting clammy handshakes and the awkwardly mumbled conventional expressions of regret.

And all the time he was searching for another sign of Kelly. But she didn't present herself to him or his in-laws and when the church had emptied out he could not see her hiding in the shadows.

He thanked the vicar and handed over the promised donation cheque for a job well done. Outside on the bowed stone steps he shook his father-in-law's reluctantly offered hand and air-kissed his mother-in-law's powdered cheek. He was amazed the caked layer of makeup hadn't cracked from the sheer effort of holding her disdain in check.

"You'll ride with us back to the house?" his father-in-law suggested stiffly when they reached the lane where people were climbing into their cars. Lytton had approved the hire of the Bentley they'd wanted, even though the distance from house to church barely allowed it to warm up.

"I have my car here," Lytton said, gesturing to the Aston Martin.

They sniffed at that, said they'd see him at the catered lunch in half an hour, and left.

Lytton headed off into the surrounding graveyard, pulling his wool overcoat a little tighter around him to ward off the sharp and sneaky wind. He found her by the wall right in the far corner, still with the ridiculous topcoat wrapped around her and a small rucksack tucked at her feet.

"Kelly!" He hurried the last few strides finding he was suddenly breathless. "What arc you doing here?"

"I came to see you," she said. "I asked at the house and the caterers assumed I was a late guest of some sort. They gave me directions." She fingered the lapel of the coat. Beneath it he could see a bright shirt and khaki cargo pants. "I didn't know, until I got here ... I borrowed this from one of the chauffeurs so I wouldn't look so obviously out of place inside. I didn't realise ... I'm sorry."

"I'm not—sorry you're here, that is," he said, feeling a genuine smile start to form. "But what I actually meant was … The last I heard you were in Holloway. How did you …?" He groaned. "Oh please, tell me you didn't scale the bloody walls?"

She laughed and he realised he'd never heard her laugh and he liked the sound of it, husky with just an edge of badness to it.

"What, you think at this very moment some deputy US Marshal is organising a hard-target search of every henhouse, outhouse and doghouse between here and Islington?"

He knew she was trying to make light of it by paraphrasing *The Fugitive* but somehow that only made the situation seem more desperate.

Heedless of what happened the last time he grabbed her, Lytton closed in and gripped her upper arms, forced her to focus on his face.

"Kelly, please, this is serious. If you're on the run I can help. I know a guy with a fast cruiser moored at Lymington. We can have you out of the country by tonight."

She went very still. "You'd do that?" she said. "For me?"

"I won't see you go back to prison for something you didn't damn well do."

She stepped in, looked up into his eyes. "They didn't let me go, Matthew," she said with gentle deliberation, "because they didn't need to. I was never really on remand. Not this time."

He tried for incisive. Instead all he managed was a stuttered, "W–what?"

"O'Neill asked for my help to catch the guys who set me up— just sit tight in solitary for a few weeks and let him get on with it," she said. "Allardice did the dirty work, but it was Chief Superintendent Quinlan who Callum Perry was trying to blackmail. He was the one who decided to get rid of Perry and use me to take the blame."

"And O'Neill can prove all this?" Lytton demanded.

"That's what he's been doing," she said. "They've had forensic accountants tracing the money, including the funds Allardice transferred out to Spain to start his bar. O'Neill had to play along and wait until Quinlan took his retirement package and went out with a new payoff before he could arrange to have the pair of them grabbed."

"Which he's now done," Lytton guessed, and heard the utter relief in his own voice.

"Which he's now done," Kelly echoed, satisfaction in hers. "I've been in Spain seeing this thing through. Got back this morning and came straight up here." She nodded to the rucksack at her feet.

"Well I'm glad you did," he said. "Am I supposed to ask why?"

She gave him a smile that was almost shy. "O'Neill told me you offered to post my bail. I wanted to … thank you. In person."

He realised he was still grasping her upper arms and he loosened his grip, slipping his hands round onto her back and tracing the outline of her shoulder blades, the indentations of her spine, with his fingertips. He watched her face all the while, saw what he hoped to see and began to draw her closer.

At the last moment Kelly brought her hands up and wedged them against his chest.

"No," she said, but when he would have released her with a muttered apology she added, "not here, that's all. I mean, I want to, don't get me wrong. I wasn't sure if *you* did, but … I meant not right outside the church where you've just held your wife's memorial service."

"Where, then?" The question came out more starkly than he intended.

Another gust of wind whipped between the gravestones and she shivered. "Anywhere that isn't so damned cold would be a good start."

Matthew Lytton smiled.

"I hear the Bahamas is very nice this time of year …"

—Acknowledgements—

GETTING THIS BOOK to fruition seems to have been a long and tortuous path, and I'm eternally grateful to the various people who test-read it, either in small chunks or the whole thing, some of them several times: JT Ellison, Sarah Harrison, Kate Kinchen, Kirsty Long, Michelle Wilbye, Tim Winfield, and all the members of the Warehouse Writers Group in Kendal. You have the patience of a whole congregation of saints.

Further editorial input came initially from Stephanie Glencross, and latterly from Rhian Davies. Thank you both so much for your efforts.

Specific information on certain aspects of climbing was provided by Jo Roberts, and on forensics by Home Office Pathologist Bill Lawler. I am aware that the Government-run Forensic Science Service, based at Lambeth, was closed in March 2012, but you'll just have to suspend your disbelief long enough to understand that the events of this book took place before that date, if you'd be so kind.

And finally, a big thank you to my talented designer, Jane Hudson at NuDesign, who came up with the stunning cover for this novel.

ZOË SHARP opted out of mainstream education at the age of twelve and wrote her first novel at fifteen. She became a freelance photojournalist in 1988 and wrote the first of her highly acclaimed Charlie Fox crime thrillers after receiving death-threat letters in the course of her work. She has been nominated (sometimes more than once) for Edgar, Anthony, Barry, Benjamin Franklin, and Macavity Awards in the United States, as well as the CWA Short Story Dagger. The Charlie Fox series was optioned for TV by Twentieth Century Fox. Zoë blogs regularly on her own website, www.ZoeSharp.com, as well as wittering on Twitter (@AuthorZoeSharp) and fooling about on www.Facebook.com.

DIE EASY
Charlie Fox book ten
by Zoë Sharp

The tenth in Zoë Sharp's highly acclaimed Charlotte 'Charlie' Fox crime thriller series.

'In the sweating heat of Louisiana, former Special Forces soldier turned bodyguard, Charlie Fox, faces her toughest challenge yet.'

Professionally, Charlie's at the top of her game, but her personal life is in ruins. Her lover, bodyguard Sean Meyer, has woken from a gunshot-induced coma with his memory in tatters.

Working with Sean again was never going to be easy, but a celebrity fundraising event in post-Katrina New Orleans should have been the ideal opportunity for them both to take things nice and slow. Until, that is, they find themselves thrust into the middle of a war zone.

When an ambitious robbery explodes into a deadly hostage situation, the motive may be far more complex than simple greed. Somebody has a major score to settle and Sean is part of the reason.

Only trouble is, he doesn't remember why.

And when Charlie finds herself facing a nightmare from her own past, she realises she can't rely on Sean to watch her back.

This time, she's got to fight it out on her own …

"Zoë Sharp is one of the sharpest, coolest, and most intriguing writers I know. She deliver dramatic, action-packed novels about characters we really care about. And once again, in DIE EASY, Zoë Sharp is at the top of her game." **Harlan Coben**

Lightning Source UK Ltd.
Milton Keynes UK
UKHW04f1048250818
327759UK00008B/251/P

9 781909 344327